KU-640-181

Praise for *A Thief's Justice*

'This is great fun. A soldier turned spy toting two pistols named Tact & Diplomacy; a seething, grubby 18th-century London; crooked politicians, whores & thief-takers; a young male prostitute accused of a crime he didn't commit. The language is colourful and the action never stops'

Laura Shepherd-Robinson, *Sunday Times* bestselling author

'With an eye for period detail and an ear for the language of the streets of 18th-century London, Douglas Skelton serves up a witty, suspenseful tale of historical espionage in *A Thief's Justice*. Swashbuckling spy Jonas Flynt is a complex rogue who will have readers clamouring for more'

Candace Robb, *Sunday Times* bestselling author

'It is rare for me to find a new writer with a unique voice, historically accurate, writing a well-plotted and -crafted crime story, as well as creating believable characters, and giving great insight into how people used to live. *A Thief's Justice* achieves all of those in bucketloads. The plot rattles along at a great speed, introducing fascinating characters, using a lot of terms and language from the period. This book is not just "highly recommended", it is essential reading!'

Michael Jecks, author of the Medieval West Country Mystery series

'Jonas Flynt is a deliciously real and complex character who plies his covert trade in the streets of a Georgian London that is so well realised you look for the mud on your shoes when you put it down. The plot builds in an organic and believable way and the reader is drawn into its intricacies just as Flynt is, not knowing the outcome but knowing that there must be justice. With a developing cast of characters who, it is to be hoped, will continue to feature in subsequent books, Skelton is building an absolute cracker of a series here'

Alis Hawkins, author of *A Bitter Remedy*

Praise for *An Honourable Thief*

'Fast, furious and with a glint of gallows humour, this is high-octane historical fiction'

Daily Mail

'A pacy and thoroughly engrossing thriller packed with intrigue, action and character'

The Herald

'I loved this book. Swashbuckling action against a vivid historical backdrop. Heroic heroes and venomous villains'

Ian Rankin, *New York Times* & *Sunday Times* bestselling author

'An absolute triumph ... Five stars from me, and I look forward to reading more of Jonas's adventures'

James Oswald, *Sunday Times* bestselling author

'Uniquely combines a page-turning thriller with a perfectly evoked sense of time and place. Powerful stuff from a master of his craft'

Craig Russell, *Sunday Times* bestselling author

'High adventure meets espionage thriller as Jonas Flynt battles the tide of history and the deadly secrets of his own past'

D. V. Bishop, author of *City of Vengeance*

'Reads like a genuine eighteenth-century spy novel. I see a long future for Jonas Flynt'

Ambrose Parry, author of *The Way of All Flesh*

'Anyone who enjoys a good historical mystery and likes an edgy, charismatic protagonist is going to love the adventures of Douglas Skelton's new hero, Jonas Flynt'

S.G. MacLean, author of *The Seeker*

'Pitch-perfect stuff. Like all great historical novels you'll feel you're there! This is a departure for Skelton, who seems born to write high-end historical fiction'

Denzil Meyrick, *Sunday Times* bestselling author

'Skelton's mastery of time and place inhabited with richly drawn characters is a delight. It held me to the last tantalising page'

David Gilman, author of *The Englishman*

A Thief's Justice

Douglas Skelton has published twelve non fiction books and ten crime thrillers. He has been a bank clerk, tax officer, shelf stacker, meat porter, taxi driver (for two days), wine waiter (for two hours), reporter, investigator and local newspaper editor. He has been longlisted three times for the McIlvanney Prize, most recently in 2022. Douglas contributes to true crime shows on TV and radio and is a regular on the crime writing festival circuit.

Also by Douglas Skelton

A Company of Rogues

An Honourable Thief
A Thief's Justice

DOUGLAS SKELTON

A Thief's Justice

CANELO

First published in the United Kingdom in 2023 by

Canelo
Unit 9, 5th Floor
Cargo Works, 1-2 Hatfields
London SE1 9PG
United Kingdom

Copyright © Douglas Skelton 2023

The moral right of Douglas Skelton to be identified as the creator of this work has been asserted in accordance with the Copyright, Designs and Patents Act, 1988.

All rights reserved. No part of this publication may be reproduced or transmitted in any form or by any means, electronic or mechanical, including photocopy, recording, or any information storage and retrieval system, without permission in writing from the publisher.

A CIP catalogue record for this book is available from the British Library.

Print ISBN 978 1 80436 089 7
Ebook ISBN 978 1 80436 088 0

This book is a work of fiction. Names, characters, businesses, organizations, places and events are either the product of the author's imagination or are used fictitiously. Any resemblance to actual persons, living or dead, events or locales is entirely coincidental.

Look for more great books at www.canelo.co

Printed and bound in Great Britain by Clays Ltd, Elcograf S.p.A.

I

1

London, 17 February 1716

The air was heavy with candle smoke, and though the temperature beyond the foggy windows was plunging, this upstairs room was warm thanks to a fire blazing in the grate and the proximity of gamblers standing at, or wandering between, the gaming tables. There were cries of delight and groans of exasperation as bets were laid, cards dealt and money won and lost. Those women present either perched themselves beside the man of their choice or wafted around the room along with the tallow fumes, flirting here, enticing there, settling on a cull with the bunce to pay for a tupping. Servants weaved around the patrons, delivering drinks and food or stopping to trim the wicks of candles editing excessive smoke.

Jonas Flynt had left the piquet table, his winnings safely within the pocket of his long dress coat, and wandered the room, his gaze seldom far from the game of hazard at a long table against the far wall. He had kept an eye on it all evening, for he was not in this room atop the Shakespear's Head Tavern for sport alone. He stopped just short of the long table to observe a squat fellow in a long powdered wig replete with ringlets, his blue velvet jacket grasping his frame as if it did not wish to let go, his pale brown waistcoat unbuttoned. He swirled the dice cup in his right hand as though he were an apothecary concocting a salve, while his left rested protectively on the pile of coins before him. Men with money riding on his throw waited with bated breath, hope, even dread, etched upon their faces, which flickered in the yellow candlelight.

A man who Flynt vaguely recognised gave him a brief nod.

'He's declared six as his main,' he informed Flynt in a low murmur, though he had not asked. Flynt nodded his thanks nonetheless and watched the dice tumble down the table.

'A four and two,' declared a man on the opposite side of the table, already taking money from those around him. Clearly he had wagered on the little man making his mark. Throwing a six or a twelve were winners. If the dice had revealed any total other than those, then the gambler would have been paying out rather than raking in.

'The beak has been throwing lucky bones for an age,' the man told Flynt. 'I ain't never seen a run like it, Captain Flynt.'

So the man knew his name, but Flynt could not dredge up his in return. He prided himself on a memory for faces but this man's features were only faintly familiar. His use of 'captain' placed him as one of the fancy, or at the very least one who lurked around the fringes. But then, there were many who knew him in this world, if by reputation only. He searched his memory and finally came up with the name Ned Turner, a crimp with whom he'd transacted business back in his high toby days on the heaths around the city. A good fence was necessary to those who made their living on the roads and Turner had been an honest dealer.

The dice were returned to the gentleman, who fondled them like a lover for a moment before popping them in the box while further bets were laid and accepted. A lanky, mournful gent Flynt guessed to be the banker of the game looked on unhappily, no doubt feeling the pain of the thrower's luck in his purse. Beside him stood another individual, well-built, well-dressed, his wig powdered to perfection but his face pinched as he absently jingled coins in his hand while watching the caster with suspicious eyes. Flynt knew this fellow; he had kept him in view throughout the evening. Lord Augustus Fairgreave and his two friends were completely unaware of his surveillance as Flynt had taken care to hood his interest. Luckily the other gentlemen at the piquet table he had recently vacated had limited skills in turning the flats and so the diversion did not impede Flynt from relieving them of their purses.

'Seven is my main,' the rotund man rattling the dice declared in a voice that was clear and commanding. He was a beak, Ned had said, and as a judge he would need to speak decisively and make himself heard. The banker nodded his assent before closing his eyes, no doubt praying that God would have the grace to intercede in his favour.

Flynt asked Turner if he wished to try his luck betting against the judge.

'I'll take your wager, Captain, for his good fortune can't last.'

Flynt was not so certain. He sensed something in the atmosphere that he had not felt in many a year, and that was providence smiling upon a man as it had never smiled upon him before. The gaming tables witnessed such moments all too briefly and they were to be savoured... and profited from. He staked a tidy sum on the little judge's luck holding and Turner matched him.

'Throw the damned bones, sir,' Fairgreave ordered, his tone clipped, suggesting he had been betting the wrong way. The caster seemed not to notice the imperious tone and continued his agitation of the dice. Gamblers have their traditions, their touchstones, and Flynt wondered if it was this man's habit to caress them with something akin to affection before depositing them in the box and applying a particular number of shakes before letting fly. When he finally did, the gamesters and onlookers alike seemed to hold their breath, every pair of eyes watching the cubes bounce on the table and then roll to a halt against the raised edge. Flynt craned over their heads to see what the telltale dots revealed. The judge had called seven as his main so he needed to throw that or an eleven to win.

The dice revealed a three and a two.

The player had hit crabs, a losing throw. A collective groan rippled around the table but Fairgreave's mouth tightened into a satisfied grin. Flynt handed his wager to Turner.

'I told you it couldn't last,' Turner said, beaming. 'Luck is a lady of fickle affections.'

Flynt studied the judge who now had the dice returned to him. 'But sometimes she likes to toy with us men, as all ladies do,' he said. 'She knows she has the upper hand at all times. I believe she is merely teasing the caster to remind him that he is nothing without her guiding his hand.'

A sly look flickered in Turner's eyes. 'Would you care to back your belief with your purse?'

A further sum was agreed and all eyes returned to the little man in the velvet coat, once again rattling the bones in the cup. His failure to hit the main or an eleven to win the previous throw had considerably increased the odds against him. He must now throw a five to win. The odds of him hitting that mark were long but Flynt tended to favour such outside chances.

The shaking stopped. The dice flew. Bounced. Tumbled to a rest. The chatter at the other tables died as all attention was drawn to the judge's table.

There was silence as the numbers were revealed.

Then...

'A five!'

The cheers outweighed the jeers and Flynt palmed his winnings from the now sour-faced crimp. 'Damn the man's luck.'

Flynt grinned as he slipped the coins into his pocket. 'You will understand if I do not echo your sentiment, Ned.'

A smile puckered Turner's lips. 'We win, we lose – ain't that the way of it?'

'In life and in gaming, Ned. The living is in the playing of it.'

The man's gaze eased past him to the other side of the table. 'I'd hazard that Lord Fairgreave don't share your philosophy.'

Flynt watched the tall nobleman shoulder his way towards the judge, by now holding the dice once more and rolling them around in his palm as he had before.

Ned Turner leaned closer in to Flynt. 'I believe Justice Dumont has annoyed that gent, Captain.'

Flynt could tell by the aggressive swagger that Fairgreave was indeed intent on confrontation but, as a judge, the little man would surely not be susceptible to such bullying. Indeed, Dumont was clearly aware of the tall noble's approach and appeared unconcerned. However, his lordship had two companions who, although red-faced with wine and heat, carried with them the air of men who would do anything to ingratiate themselves with those they saw as their betters, in this case, Lord Fairgreave. If there were to be any trouble, it would be from one of them.

'I would see those dice, sir,' his lordship demanded, using his height and steady gaze in an attempt to intimidate.

The little judge stared back at him, apparently far from daunted. 'And why would you wish to do that, my lord?'

'You are uncommon lucky with them.'

The discourse around the table hushed. Even the buzz of conversation elsewhere in the cramped room was cut short as faces turned their way. Lord Fairgreave had all but accused a man of cheating and this exchange could end in an unfortunate way if the judge decided that his honour had been besmirched. Flynt had researched Lord Fairgreave and he was reputed to be most proficient with a sword and, if rumour were true, had never been bested in a duel. The judge did not strike Flynt as a man who was adept with weapons, his domain being books and words. Nonetheless, the little man smiled sweetly.

'You think these bones be cogged?'

Flynt suppressed a smile as Fairgreave seemed confused by the judge's use of street slang, 'cogged' being the criminal world's term for the loading of dice. Comprehension dawned only when one of Fairgreave's companions whispered an explanation in his ear. 'I know not, sir, hence my desire to inspect them.'

'Sometimes desire is best kept private, my lord, and unspoken.' Justice Dumont allowed the articles in question to roll easily around his palm as if daring the man to snatch them. 'If they be cogged would I have lost that earlier throw?'

Fairgreave looked around him, suddenly aware that he had allowed his anger over his losses to overcome his common sense, but he had embarked on this course of action and could not back down, so adopted the tactic of the privileged by ignoring the facts and pushing his original premise. 'You may have means of enhancing your luck by the way you palm them before shaking the box. By sleight of hand you may switch honest dice for loaded ones. Or somehow you manipulate them to achieve your main.'

The judge seemed more amused by this than insulted. 'By God, sir, I am damnable dextrous with my fingers, am I not? Perhaps I should be earning my crust by joining the tumblers and jugglers at the fairs.'

Fairgreave's face darkened at the mocking laughter around him. 'Will you allow me to inspect those dice or not?'

The judge made a show of considering this request, then shook his head. 'I think not. It is enough you have impugned my good name without playing into your phantasmagorical belief that I am somehow possessed of conjuring skills to rival Merlin. If you have lost money, sir, then it is because you backed the wrong play and not because I am in some manner supernaturally gifted.'

'If I have impugned your good name, sir, then perhaps you should demand some satisfaction.'

The echoes of the laughter stilled as the audience realised that this little drama was reaching its climax. The judge looked around him, then down at the dice in his hand. 'You mean a duel, I believe, and as an officer of His Majesty's courts I could not possibly employ myself in such an undertaking. However, as you be particular adamant that you must examine these inoffensive little cubes, then have at it, sir.'

He threw the dice towards Fairgreave, who attempted to catch both missiles but failed miserably. They bounced from his chest and tumbled to the floor. This display of his own lack of dexterity evoked further laughter from all around and Fairgreave's face turned ever darker. He did not stoop to retrieve them, which would not be seemly for a peer of the realm, but waited until one of his acolytes scrambled below the table to fetch them and placed them in his hand. He rolled them around on his palm with the forefinger of his other hand, then picked each up to shake them against his ear to listen for any liquid within before holding them closer to his eye to inspect them for shaved edgings or hairs attached to one face in order to give it the advantage. His lips thinned when he found nothing.

'Well, sir?' Dumont asked. 'Do you acknowledge that it is not through any illicit means that your luck has been so poor this night?'

Lord Fairgreave was in no mood to acknowledge any error on his part, for in Flynt's experience such was the way with gentry. The man slammed the dice down on the table and with no further word, though his final glare towards Justice Dumont spoke volumes, spun on his heel and strode towards the door, his shoes clicking on the bare floorboards like a drumbeat. He snatched a coat and hat from the girl guarding such apparel and stormed out, his two friends flapping like coat-tails behind him. The silence following their departure was broken by Judge Dumont coughing then laughing, the sound of the dice as he dropped them into the box unfeasibly loud.

'Well,' he said, 'shall we play, gentlemen? I warn you all, despite his lordship's display of petulant intervention, I believe my luck holds.' He began to shake the dice. 'The mark is nine...'

Flynt would have been happy to remain and perhaps add to his funds, but for him the night's gaming had another purpose and such conviviality was merely a bonus. He tarried a few moments to allow his quarry sufficient time to descend the stairs, slipped the serving girl a few pennies for her trouble, then followed. The stairs were narrow and dark but he had trod them many times before so knew them well. He reached the tavern below in time to see Fairgreave and his companions exiting onto Russell Street. Flynt eased his way through the mix of swell and fancy, rich and poor, for the pursuit of pleasure in London was most democratic.

They waited on the street, but Flynt knew not for him. Fairgreave would not have taken the shame heaped upon him in the gaming room well and would be intent on resuming his remonstrations of the little judge away from witnesses. He and his friends barely glanced at Flynt as he left the tavern, thrusting his hands deep into his thick gloves, pulling his coat tighter to his throat and adjusting his scarf around his lower jaw to ward off the frightful cold which threatened to freeze the very lungs. It would not do for his face to be recognised as one that had dogged them all night, even though they had paid little attention to their surroundings, aside from accosting a doxy or two or exchanging words with acquaintances. Nevertheless, he kept his face down as he walked beyond them, glancing back only briefly to ensure they had not subsequently taken an interest in him. He stepped nimbly into the mouth of an alley, positioning himself in the dense shadows in order to observe without himself being observed. If any had witnessed his manoeuvre he was confident they would assume he was answering a call of nature, even though he was not liable to expose his tackle to these elements, for his piss would surely solidify as it left his body. Winter had bit hard, and even the Thames had fallen victim to its cold embrace, the waters freezing to such an extent that Londoners had taken to walking upon it. A winter fair had even been erected upon the ice, with stalls selling foods and entertainment. Flynt understood that it was not a phenomenon completely unknown but it had not occurred for over thirty years, and he found it curious to stand upon the bank below London Bridge and stare at what had once been in motion, sluggishly to be sure until it was forced between the parapets of the bridge, but was now still, as though some primeval winter deity had laid its hand upon it.

He flattened against the wall and fixed his attention on the trio of swells who had taken up position on the opposite side of Russell Street. By their manner of lurk, it seemed obvious to him that they were intent on some form of low toby, but their victim would not be random, even though they were not the usual type of footpad in their fine clothes and wigs. His lordship had clearly been irked by his losses at the hazard table and it seemed he intended to have his funds returned by means of robbery. That a peer of the realm would resort to such action did not surprise Flynt: the sense of entitlement of those in high places often led to low behaviour. Fairgreave believed he had been cheated and so felt within his rights to take back his coin by any means necessary. If there was a profit in it, all the better.

When tasking him with this mission, Colonel Nathaniel Charters had not outlined his reasons as to why Fairgreave needed to be watched. Charters sat at the centre of a web of informers and operatives – the Company of Rogues – like a black spider hungry for information, and so it was possible that he had been given intimation that his lordship was prone to such acts as this whenever he felt the need. Flynt had been ordered to observe and report only, so if this were the case then he had no doubt that Charters would store the information away for later use, perhaps to blackmail Fairgreave into some covert work in defence of the realm. Flynt knew a little too well how adept the colonel was at such extortion.

The cold nipped at his fingers even through the leather of his gloves, so he thrust his hands into the deep pockets of his greatcoat, his silver cane tucked in the crook of his elbow, the wide brim of his hat further shading his features though not impeding his view of the street or the door to the tavern. He shifted his feet to keep the blood from icing, being careful not to make any noise.

Russell Street was uncharacteristically quiet, the denizens and visitors preferring to remain indoors as close to a heat source as possible. There were a few hardy souls abroad, however: link boys carrying lanterns guided their customers through the darkened streets; some flash coves on their way to or from debauchery; Covent Garden Nuns and their lower market drabs sauntering by, one or two spotting Flynt as he waited and tarrying long enough to size him up as a possible cull, but moving on when they realised he had no interest in generating heat by dancing the goat's jig. They exchanged a few words with Fairgreave's hangers-on, who showed willingness for a tumble, causing Flynt to worry that they might use his alley for a bit of against-the-wall rutting, but a terse word from his lordship put all notion of sexual gratification from their mind. The rebuffed whores moved on in search of men more eager to part with their coin.

Flynt was on the verge of giving up – despite his careful movements his feet were growing numb within his long boots – when he saw the little judge emerge from the tavern, his portly frame well insulated from the cold by a thick coat. He had pulled his hat tightly upon his head and was wrapping a warm muffler around his throat, but stopped when he saw Lord Fairgreave and his friends waiting for him. He glanced up and down the street and, seeing it deserted, as if some cataclysm had occurred to remove all human life but the three men before him, took a half step back towards the tavern. The action seemed involuntary for he made no move to re-enter the establishment. He stood his ground as Fairgreave crossed the street towards him.

'I would have words, little man,' Fairgreave said. Flynt was close enough, hidden in the shadows, to hear the words, but distant enough to prevent him from discerning if the judge was shocked by being thus addressed or distressed at being confronted in such a way.

Dumont's response was calm, however, with any trepidation he felt at being bearded by these men not evident. 'I would have thought you had said sufficient at the gaming tables, Lord Fairgreave.'

Flynt pushed himself from the wall, his silver cane now gripped comfortably in his right hand, while with his left he unbuttoned his coat. Attending the tables while armed was a shocking display of poor manners but that did not mean he had left his rooms in Charing Cross without his pistols. They were secreted within two special pockets sewn into the lining of his greatcoat, for Flynt never knew when it might be necessary to apply Tact and Diplomacy to a situation. He had little intention of using them this night, but life had taught him that it was always advisable to be prepared.

'I think not,' Fairgreave said. 'I think perhaps too much was said and too little done to my satisfaction.'

The judge looked from Fairgreave to his two friends. Flynt thought he could see a slight smile on his lips, as if he found this entire scene worthy of a comedy in the Drury Lane Theatre. 'You attempted to inveigle me into a duel earlier, sir, and I did not bite. I take it this is the point in our discourse where you formally challenge me, then? Where there are no witnesses?'

Fairgreave stepped ahead of his colleagues. 'I have no need to take the field of honour with a man who has so little that he would cheat at games of chance.'

Again the judge did not rise to the insult. 'You inspected the dice, you know them to be fair.'

'I know that you had more luck than any man has a right to.'

Dumont shrugged. 'That is true, I did have a decent run, and you, sir, were on the wrong end of it. But you did not tarry to see the epilogue to our little drama, for after you left I lost... and heavily.' Now Flynt was certain the judge smiled. 'Perhaps you were my lucky charm, my lord.'

Those final words angered Fairgreave even further. 'You are a cheat, sir, and, I believe, a liar. I will have your purse so that I may take back what I lost.'

Dumont held his hands out in apology. 'I regret my purse is as empty as your conscience would appear to be.'

His lordship bristled at this and drew himself to his full, not inconsiderable height. 'My conscience is untroubled by punishing a cheat and a thief, sir. Your purse, sir, that I may see for myself whether you are indeed also a liar.'

Dumont tilted his head as he considered what he knew was not a request before he signified acceptance by hitching his shoulder slightly and slipping his hand from his glove to reach into his pocket. 'I do have something here that may interest you, my lord.'

The hand reappeared with a small Queen Anne pistol. The weapon was useless at any great distance but in this instance it was a matter of inches away from Fairgreave's face. Alarmed, he took a step back.

'Before you ask, my lord,' Dumont said, 'this is indeed primed.' With one swift movement he cocked the weapon with his thumb. 'Now it is also cocked and I will not hesitate to perforate you or any of your friends if you continue in this attempt at highway robbery.'

Fairgreave tried to bluster, his eyes on the barrel of the pistol. 'Highway robbery? I am no common thief, sir, I am Lord Augustus Fairgreave and I—'

'A fine name but you remain a bully and a scoundrel. You are also a poor gamester and, what is worse, a poor loser.'

One of Fairgreave's companions leaned towards him and whispered something. Flynt strained to hear but caught nothing, although the judge evidently heard every word. 'It is true that you are three and I have but one ball in this pistol. But the question you gentlemen must consider is which of you will be in receipt of that ball?'

'You would risk the noose for a few coins?' Fairgreave said, his initial shock overcome by his natural arrogance.

'You would risk a hole in the head for the same? As for the noose, what I do would be in defence of self. What you do would be in furtherance of larceny.'

'And how would you prove that?'

The judge's pistol flicked away from Fairgreave for an instant. 'What transpires here is witnessed.'

Flynt realised with a sinking heart that the man's eyes were as sharp as his wits and he had spotted him in the shadows. Fairgreave and his friends twisted round, squinting into the dark.

'Step forward, stranger,' the judge shouted. 'Let us see you.'

Flynt sighed, for he had no option but to do as he was asked.

'Who are you, sir?' the judge asked.

'A pedestrian, like you,' Flynt replied.

Fairgreave peered at him. 'Why would a pedestrian hide in the gloom of an alleyway?'

'I was taken short,' Flynt explained, 'and had to relieve myself.'

The judge's lips twitched a little. 'I would know your name for any investigation into this matter.'

Flynt knew he could not reveal his identity. 'I think this situation can be resolved without recourse to the authorities.'

'I am the authorities, my friend.'

'Even a judge can keep some matters out of the public eye.'

The man who had whispered to Fairgreave strode towards Flynt and pushed him hard on the shoulder. 'Be off, whoever you be. This is no business of yours.'

Flynt did not like to be pushed by anyone. Ordinarily he would have pushed back but he was very much aware that his work here was intended to be covert. His orders were that he should not have direct contact with Fairgreave, and this inadvertent involvement was too direct for his liking. 'I am merely making my way home.'

The eyes of the man who had pushed him narrowed. 'You are Scotch?'

'Scottish,' corrected Flynt.

The man thought he had the upper hand and he played it. In fact he used both hands to propel Flynt backwards with a double thrust to the chest. 'Then take another route to whatever pisshouse you infest and leave us to our business, Scotchman.'

Covert be damned, Flynt thought and rapped the handle of his cane on the man's forehead. The move was swift and sharp and the man was unaware it had happened until silver made contact with flesh and bone. He blinked frequently, his mouth gaping as he stumbled back, one hand rising to the red welt already forming on his skin. Flynt had intended only to warn, not to incapacitate, but the individual was obviously not one to heed such a message. He roared in fury and lunged with arms outstretched, his hands tightened into claws as if he meant to scratch the skin from Flynt's bones. He didn't get far. Flynt sidestepped neatly and delivered a heftier blow to the back of his head. The man grunted once and pitched forward onto the road, his knees hitting the ice-hardened ground with force, his palms squelching in some particularly liquid horse droppings that had not yet frozen. At least, Flynt presumed the ordure to be horse for it was not unknown for some drunken sot to drop breeches if the street was deserted and squat where he stood. The man began to push himself upright again, curses flowing as easily as the manure had done from whatever creature left it, but Flynt had learned that once a man was down it was better he remain that way. He swung the cane a third time, feeling it crack against skull. He knew the hat and wig the man wore would soak up much of the force, protecting him from lasting damage, but the blow was of sufficient strength to lay him flat out, his face now landing in the remains of the putrid dung. Flynt inserted the toe of his boot beneath the man's chest and flipped him onto his back, for it was ignominious enough to have been bested without drowning in diarrhoea, be it equine or otherwise. He then whirled to face any further assault from Fairgreave or his remaining companion. Neither of them had moved during the encounter but were staring at their erstwhile champion now recumbent amid the filth of the street with a mix of surprise and revulsion. Judge Dumont also watched, the hand holding the pistol now crossed over the other in front of him, his wide smile showing he had been hugely entertained by the display.

Fairgreave's attention finally shifted from his friend, who was now groaning and moving his leg as if trying to rise but lacking the strength to do so. 'Who are you, sir, that you would treat your betters in such a foul fashion?'

'Who I am is of no consequence. As to this fellow being my better, I would take issue.'

Fairgreave sneered and looked about to argue the point when Judge Dumont spoke. 'I would suggest you take your friend away from here, Lord Fairgreave. There is a sufficiency of detritus in these streets as it is.'

'Our business is not yet concluded, little man. I would have my funds returned.'

'Then you must take that up with the gentlemen to whom I subsequently lost it, for I am devoid of coin.'

'I would have proof of that,' Fairgreave said, reaching out towards the judge's pockets with intent to rifle them but stopping when the Queen Anne pistol was once more levelled in his direction.

'You forget my little friend here. And I would point out that the odds have now evened.'

Fairgreave's focus swayed between the judge and Flynt. He was a man who was unused to being denied his wishes and struggled to understand why it had occurred this night. As he deliberated, the tavern door swung open and Flynt heard a voice call out. 'Is all well, Captain?'

Flynt glanced back and saw Ned Turner with his arm around an amply proportioned Covent Garden Nun known as Drury Lane Tess. She was a buxom, good-natured woman who had clearly imbibed a surfeit of liquor, for she swayed like a thick oak in a storm as she did her best to focus upon the scene in the dark street.

'All is well, Ned, my thanks to you.'

Ned's gait hitched a little as he took in the scene, eyes moving from Fairgreave and his friend to the weapon in the judge's hand and finally to the man still sprawled on the ground. He came to a halt, Tess with her hands on his shoulder for support, her tongue already searching for an ear to probe. 'Be you certain of that?'

'A slight accident. The gentleman lost his footing and hit his head. His friends here were about to take him to seek a barber-surgeon, were you not, gentlemen?'

Fairgreave had sufficient wit left to realise that his particular game had run its course so he reluctantly gestured to his remaining friend that they should assist their wounded comrade. They hauled him to his feet, supporting him when his legs seemed unable to do so, simultaneously but unsuccessfully endeavouring to avoid the excrement smeared on his face, hands and clothes.

Fairgreave grimaced as he realised his hand had come into contact with something foul and treated the judge to a final glare. 'This does not end here. You may have the word of a gentleman on that.'

The judge slipped the pistol back into his pocket. 'Your word it may be. Whether it is that of a gentleman is debatable.'

Fairgreave's mouth opened and closed like a trout's as he sought a retort. Finding nothing, he instead helped cart his still groaning burden away. Ned Turner watched them go as he idly fondled the plumper parts of his paramour for the night, and when satisfied they had no intention of returning, gave Flynt a nod. Flynt returned the gesture with an appreciative bow, and watched as the crimp led Tess in the direction of Drury Lane.

'I thank you for your intervention,' said Dumont. 'I have no idea what would have occurred had you not been present.'

Flynt continued to regret that intervention even though it had been unavoidable, for the man's eyes were sharp as they studied him.

'That fellow called you Captain – you are a military man?'

'I was, but the rank is honorary.'

Dumont took a half step back as he considered this. 'Honorary, you say? May I ask your name? After all, I think it is only fair that I know the identity of my deliverer.'

Flynt was unwilling to part with that even now. 'I believe you had the matter well in hand without my intervention.'

He was sure the judge had detected the obfuscation but the man did not pursue. 'I remain unconvinced. I was playing a part, you must realise, for I suspect I would not have hit anything had I discharged my weapon. My marksmanship is far from adequate and my deliberate mien was merely a mask for abject terror.' He once more took Flynt's measure. 'Although I would hazard such incidents are not beyond your ken, friend.'

'I have encountered such men in the past, your honour.'

'You know I am a judge?'

Flynt jerked his thumb over his shoulder towards the Shakespear's Head. 'I was witness to at least part of your run of luck at the hazard table and heard it whispered among the gamesters you were on the bench.'

'They did, did they? It is heartening that my fame is so widespread. Was the person who informed you of my name a lawyer? A court officer?'

Flynt smiled as he thought of Ned Turner's profession. 'No, but he is acquainted with many guardians of the law.'

Dumont smiled back, understanding immediately. 'And those with whom they deal, I have no doubt.' He paused for a moment, then looked back towards the tavern. 'I feel some warmth is needed and also something to calm my vapours. What say, as a thank you for your service, that I buy us a brandy to fire our blood against this damnable cold?'

Flynt looked to where Fairgreave had vanished into the night, knowing well that he was unlikely to find him again. 'I would be delighted, your honour. But I thought you had lost heavily at the table?'

Dumont grinned and reached into his pocket, producing a purse fat with coin. 'Never trust a lawyer, my good captain.'

2

In the tavern, a fiddler with a crooked back accompanied by a drummer and a blind man on a flute were playing 'The Bay of Biscay, Oh', a group of sailors bellowing the lyrics while swilling ale and fondling the breasts and buttocks of the bawds who attended them. A small dog lay at the feet of the sightless flautist, its head between its paws, as pot-boys, serving girls and drunkards busied back and forth.

They found a table against the far wall and Flynt, out of habit, took the chair from which he had full view of the room as well as the various doorways: the exit to Russell Street, another beside the bar that opened to a storeroom and the owner's private apartments, and the one leading to the upstairs room. He hung his hat over the back of the chair but kept his silver cane on the table, his right hand resting upon it, seemingly in a relaxed manner but ready to snatch it up if required by circumstance. Dumont waved towards a young woman who bore the distant expression of someone who was so used to revelry that it no longer filled her with joy, but when she saw who beckoned something like life kindled in her eyes.

'Melody, my dear,' said the judge, his own grin warm and welcoming as he greeted her like an old friend. Clearly the judge was a regular imbiber in this tavern. Flynt had seen the girl before but had not known her name. She was little more than fourteen years but there was a pallor to her complexion and a weariness in her demeanour that told him she had lived more in her young life than some had at twice her age.

'What will be your pleasure tonight, your honour?' Her accent was of the north and spoke of hills and dales rather than the streets and alleyways of the city.

'My friend and I will each have a brandy, my dear.' Dumont then held up a single finger. 'No, bring a bottle. Expense be damned.' He winked towards Flynt. 'It is not every day that a man faces death and yet survives to tell of it.'

Flynt remained silent. He doubted if the judge had been in danger of anything more serious than a beating from Fairgreave and his men, although such an attack could easily become lethal.

Melody smiled, something Flynt suspected did not often grace her features, then left them to fulfil the order.

'You are on first-name terms with other serving girls or that one only?'

The judge sat back. 'I know many people. Be good to those who serve you and they will be good to you, that's my motto.'

'There are not many in your position who share such a philosophy.'

'There are a few, but in general you are correct.' He glanced around the tavern, taking in the throng. 'We are an unfair society, are we not? A great divide between rich and poor, those who have everything and those who have nothing, a corrupt society from top to bottom, and yet all classes and castes come to places such as this and rub shoulders – and other parts of the anatomy in upstairs rooms, to be sure, although I have not myself enjoyed such pleasures, I must hasten to add.'

Had any other man said that, Flynt would have raised a sceptical eyebrow, but there was a probity that walked with the judge that told him he spoke the truth.

'I am a married man, sir,' Dumont amplified. 'My Matilda was a fine catch and I still fail to comprehend what she saw in me, for even in my younger days I was neither fair of countenance nor Adonis in frame.' He studied Flynt's features. 'Be you wed, sir?'

'I regret that such an arrangement is not something I will see in my life.'

'Why not?'

Flynt took time to consider. He liked this man but he had to remind himself that they were, effectively, divided by the law. In addition, his heart lay in a place from whence he knew it could never be recovered.

'My lifestyle does not lend itself to marital bliss.' He could see that Dumont was intrigued. 'I am a gambler, your honour, and as such I keep long hours. Also my temperament precludes being tied to a single person.'

Dumont understood. 'Ah, you are a ladies' man, sir?'

'When I get the chance,' Flynt said with a smile.

'And such chances come your way often, on that I would stake my fortune.'

Flynt bowed his head both in thanks and in acknowledgement, his mind suddenly turning to Belle St Clair whose room was but a short walk from Russell Street. Their relationship had been more commercial than romantic but she remained particular about who she allowed in her bed, no matter how much bunce they offered. The owner of the house, Mother Grady, kept her for special culls and Flynt had been lucky enough to be numbered among them... as long as he paid. He preferred such an arrangement, for he knew that allowing anyone into his heart caused only pain, both to himself and them. He had not visited her for many weeks now so it was always possible he was no longer welcome.

Justice Dumont dug around in his pockets and produced a pipe into which he tapped some tobacco. He fired it from the candle flame on the table between them before settling back in a comfortable manner to scrutinise Flynt through the cloud of smoke that billowed from bowl and lips.

'So, your name, sir, if you please.'

Flynt took a breath, knowing he could scarce avoid now parting with his identity. He considered a lie but sensed this man's wits were as sharp as his eyes and he would recognise fakery if he saw it. 'Flynt. Jonas Flynt.'

'And there are those who call you Captain?'

'Aye.'

Dumont's lips worked at this. 'I have heard talk of a Flynt, late of the high toby trade on the heaths.'

'I have also heard of him,' said Flynt carefully.

Dumont took his pipe from between his teeth and studied the smouldering tobacco. 'They called him captain, as I recall, as so many land pirates are addressed. A right royal scamp, he was, but no bully ruffian. Rich pickings only, never the lowly. Gallant to the ladies, stern to the men but little violence, unless necessary.'

'That is what I heard too.'

Colonel Charters, his former military commander and the man for whom he now toiled, had another story to tell, which he dangled over Flynt's head like a noose, of a rich woman robbed of jewels and her young male companion brutally beaten, but that tale was false. The robbery had taken place, but it was another highwayman who committed it, not Flynt. He knew not who that was but someday he would find out.

The pipe was now wedged in Dumont's mouth and they were silent as Melody returned with the bottle of brandy and two cups. Dumont removed some coins from his purse and handed them to her. 'A little extra there for you, my dear,' he said.

She looked at the money and her eyes warmed as she saw that his little extra was in actuality quite a sum. 'I thank you kindly, your honour,' she said, giving him a little curtsey and a smile.

'Not at all, my dear, it is but a mere bagatelle. But you be sure you keep that money for yourself, don't be handing it to yonder rat-faced rascal behind the bar there.' He jerked his head towards the owner of the establishment, who surveyed his domain from behind sharp little eyes in a verminous visage.

'I won't, your honour,' the girl said, thrusting the coins into the pocket of her smock as she turned to answer the call of another customer but then came back and kissed the judge on the cheek. It was very swift and she was gone in an instant but the judge flushed and his hand darted to where her lips had been.

Flynt asked, 'You were generous with her, I take it?'

Dumont waved the comment away. 'To me it was a trifle, as I said, but to her it was a tidy sum. If we cannot help those around us when we are able, Flynt, then why did God place us on this earth? You helped me this eve, I take that gift and pass it along to that young wench.'

'If her employer finds out, he will take it from her and beat her for keeping it from him.'

Dumont nodded. 'I am aware but I will return and check on her and if she is in any way molested it will be my pleasure to make that odious little brute suffer.'

Flynt suppressed a smile, having no doubt the judge would do as he said, not by inflicting physical violence but by more subtle, legal means. Dumont poured them each a hefty measure of spirits and then lifted his cup. 'To Captain Jonas Flynt, a true knight of the road.'

Flynt raised his own, knowing well that the judge was deliberately using a term for highwayman while also acknowledging his acts in the street. 'A tarnished knight, I regret.'

They each took a sip. It was not a fine brandy but he welcomed its heat in his belly.

'We live in a world that is tarnished,' said the judge, seemingly not noticing the poor vintage. 'All we can do is seek that part of it that yet gleams and cleave to it.'

Flynt agreed. He had seen how corrupt and venal life could be and harboured few doubts that Dumont's profession had also introduced him to more than a little hardship. Flynt tried to focus on the things of life that were unsullied by the ugliness of humanity – a perfect turn of a card or throw of a dice, the fresh, clean air of the heaths as he rode across them, those moments when he forgot his own sins. But such moments were short-lived.

'I wonder what happened to him?' Dumont's voice was almost dreamy in its inquiry.

Flynt was momentarily confused. 'Who?'

'The other Captain Flynt. The highwayman.'

'It is my understanding he gave up the trade,' replied Flynt. 'It became too much like hard work, I understand.'

'I wonder what he does now, this namesake of yours?'

'I heard he died.'

''Tis a pity, I would like to have met this man.'

'In your courtroom?'

'I would hope not. I think he may be a fine fellow, despite his larcenous tendencies, and I would make his acquaintance and be proud to have it. Though if I did see him on the wrong side of the bench then I would not hesitate to heap the full weight of the law upon him.'

'If he were guilty.'

Judge Dumont laughed. 'Sometimes even if he were not. Between you and I, friend Flynt, guilt or innocence does not concern me when sitting upon judgement. Only what is proved.'

'Do you believe you have convicted the innocent?'

'Without a doubt, without even a shadow of a doubt. But the law is the law and evidence is evidence, and even though I may suspect lack of guilt I cannot act upon it.'

'Even if it means a trip to Tyburn for the poor wretch falsely accused?'

'Even then. In my personal life I may question the severity of our laws for certain offences, but in my public duty I am unwavering. And yet there are sins in this great city of ours that go unpunished, are there not? I am sure you have witnessed this for yourself.'

'All of life is steeped in sin.'

'Ah! You are a cynic, friend Flynt, a student of Antisthenes. And do you also sleep in a tub, like his pupil Diogenes of old?'

Flynt laughed. 'No, I sleep in a room in Charing Cross. And there are no stray hounds around, unlike Diogenes' apartments.'

The judge seemed slightly surprised. 'You understand my allusion?'

Flynt understood he was expected to display his knowledge. 'Antisthenes was a philosopher in Ancient Greece who studied under Socrates. He taught in an old gymnasium called the Kynosarge. From that came Kynikos, the collective term for his students – including Diogenes. Our word "cynic" stems from the Latin version of the Greek.'

Dumont erupted in a delighted laugh. 'Bravo, friend Flynt, bravo. You are a man of action and yet you know your classics.'

'I was raised by an aunt in Edinburgh who ensured that I read widely.'

'She must have been a fine, wise woman.'

'She was, though I did not appreciate that at the time.'

'She is gone now?'

'Aye.'

Dumont's face was solemn. 'It is often the way – we do not appreciate what we have until they are beneath the clay. And your people?'

'My father still lives, my mother died when I was but a babe in arms.'

'I am right sorry to hear that. Your father is a good man?'

Flynt had some questions regarding Gideon Flynt's past but did not hesitate to reply. 'He is. He owns a tavern in Edinburgh. He was a seafarer for much of my childhood but aye, he is a good man.'

'You have been away from home for many years, I take it?'

'Aye.' Flynt left it at that. He liked this little man, sensed there was a decency in him that was absent from many of his contemporaries, but Flynt did not like to look back too often. He tended to live for the day, for yesterday was gone and tomorrow was promised to no one. He had returned to Edinburgh only once in fifteen years and that had proved to be heartbreaking.

Dumont must have sensed that he did not wish to delve any further into his past, so he filled their cups again and raised his own. 'To life, to love, and to hopes of a better world.'

Flynt raised his cup and drank, but knew that such hopes were like the tobacco in the judge's pipe: they burned bright for a time but soon died.

–

They emptied the bottle of brandy, Flynt having only two, albeit large, measures, but the judge bested him at a rate of two to one. The man was as drunk as David's sow but still able to steer a course, as Flynt's father would say. That course may not have been steady but he was unlikely to collapse in the street before he reached his home. Flynt himself was merely chirping merry as he watched the judge weave away from him towards Button's Coffee House then disappear into the darkness. In their brief acquaintance he had come to like the fellow but was aware that should he ever find himself in the dock and under his gaze he could expect no preferential treatment. Dumont had revealed himself to be a man who believed in justice without favour, which made him somewhat unique in Flynt's experience, as judges tended to see their function as upholding the state no matter what.

After they parted, with the brandy warming his blood and helping stave off winter's bite, Flynt made his way to Covent Garden, where he stood in the shadow of the piazza and gazed across at Mother Grady's house on the corner. A candle guttered in the window he knew to be Belle's, meaning she had company, which was no surprise, for she was much in demand. He had stood on this spot many times, always at night under cloak of darkness, a motionless figure amid the twilight commerce of the Garden. The pickpockets, the pimps and the prostitutes of all classes passed him by as he stared at the house but never ventured across the street. He had not seen Belle since his return from Edinburgh a little over two months before, for his trip to the place of his birth had rekindled old memories he had thought long burned to ash. Belle had made no effort to contact him either, which did not surprise him as she was not a woman to pursue close relationships. Yet he had to deny himself her pleasures for he knew that when he lay with Belle it was someone else's face he saw, someone else's skin he caressed, someone else's scent he breathed, someone else's name he whispered. Cassie was in Edinburgh, a widow now, bringing up her son. Their son, Flynt believed, although she had never confirmed it. He sent money periodically, had even penned a letter or two, but she had never written back. He deserved that, for he had vanished from Cassie's life for fifteen years and allowed her, and his family, to believe him dead.

He wondered if Belle missed him. More likely she missed his coin. Even so, he felt something like loss as he forced himself to turn away and make his way back to his own lodgings.

3

18 February 1716

The day was another bitterly cold one but Flynt knew he would have felt a chill even if it had been high summer. This place always affected him in that manner and he knew no amount of thick clothing would ward it off. Over a seething sea of bobbing heads numbering in the thousands he watched the preparations around the triangular construction that formed the focus of attention of this multitude of Londoners. This was all theatre, a show for their delectation, but one where all artifice was removed. The stage consisted of three sturdy cross beams rested on triple uprights to form a towering triangle, but the players in this grim drama would not magically revive at show's end to take their bows. There would be no facsimile of death here.

The gallows stood where the Oxford Road met the Edgware and Bayswater roads, amid green land with few buildings. That was changing, though, for cities grow like stains and Flynt knew it was but a matter of time before the fields beyond the triple tree would become brick and wood and smoke, corrupted by filth and stench.

They called the site Tyburn Tree, among other names, even though felons had long since ceased meeting their end below the branches. It could handle eight necks per beam but this day only four would be turned off the carts. Despite his solitary position on the edge of the crowd, he could see the eighteen-foot-high gallows clearly enough, though he did not particularly wish to. Distance made the features of the condemned indistinct, nooses already looped around their necks though the other ends had yet to be fastened to the beams. They stood with heads bowed on the edge of the carts on which they had been conveyed from prison, the three-hour journey to Tyburn broken for exhortations to repent their sins while filling their bellies with wine and ale. One had drunk so much that he swayed and had to be supported by the Newgate Prison chaplain, the Ordinary, who continued to mouth words of piety.

For some here, however, the entertainment might prove costly. Circulating among the pie sellers, sweetmeat vendors and purveyors of gin were light-fingered young men on the foist and Flynt knew there would be many a pocket picked or fabric slit this day. One such nimble-fingered dipper caught his eye, and he recognised Jack Sheppard's cocky swagger. He watched as a gentleman was purposely jostled by a young accomplice, allowing Jack's adroit fingers to pluck a silk kerchief from the man's pocket before the lad casually sauntered away to smoothly transfer the stolen wipe into the hands of an older lad whom Flynt knew to be his brother, Tom. This was how he had first met the boy, not at Tyburn but in the piazza at Covent Garden one evening. It must have been one of Jack's few failures for he had not been so light of touch on that occasion. Flynt had felt the dive and had fastened his grip on the boy's slim wrist before silk was fully free from pocket.

He diverted his attention to the group of men standing somewhat closer to the gallows tree. They were further from him than he would have liked but following the previous night's encounter he felt it wise. He should have known that they would have been here, for there were few of their caste who would miss the sight of the lower classes dangling at the end of a rope. Spotting Fairgreave and his friends was a bonus, however, for it was not Flynt's choice to stand in the freezing cold and watch these poor wretches meet their maker. He had been summoned.

'Who is Ketch today?'

The familiar voice came from Flynt's right. He had not seen or heard Colonel Nathaniel Charters approach but that was the man's way. He liked to be surreptitious in his movements. In his business, it paid to go unnoticed, although at six foot, slim to the point of skeletal, his wig powdered white, his face weathered but still handsome and wearing a fine coat of green shot silk with its right arm hanging empty, going unnoticed was a quite a feat. If Flynt hadn't known the truth of it, he might have believed that Charters had the limb purposely amputated in order to keep a world of secrets up his sleeve.

'Marvell,' Flynt replied, even though he had not caught sight of the hangman's face. 'I think.'

The colonel grunted. 'The former blacksmith? Not that rascal John Price then, a man for whom a station at the gallows is most fitting, but perhaps not as the executioner. The man was a thief as soon as he popped from the shell.'

Each hangman was known familiarly as Jack Ketch, after the official executioner from fifty years before. John Price held the office now and was no better or worse than other men who had fulfilled the duty, but he was not highly thought of in general. He had been a thief and became hangman straight from a period in Newgate himself, his time in the navy proving useful in the tying of knots.

'And what felons do we have meeting their maker this day?' the colonel asked, as he observed the final rope being thrown and fastened.

Flynt knew the names of the accused. He believed that if he was to witness the final gasping breath of a man then he should know at least that much. 'Arthur Driver, Jem Horner, Ralph Spicer and Edward Cash.'

'And their crimes?'

'Horner and Spicer were peter flickers.'

Charters winced. 'Please, Serjeant Flynt, you are not speaking with one of your denizens of the streets. The King's English, if you please.'

The colonel always referred to Flynt using the rank he had gained, if not for long, while serving the old queen. His reaction to his use of thieves' cant was feigned, for Flynt knew he could speak it as fluently as any rogue. Nevertheless, Flynt obliged him.

'They robbed coaches by cutting bags from the rear and making off with them. Cash stole five silk handkerchiefs. And for that he will die.'

'Property is property, Serjeant, and the law is there to protect it.'

'It was always my belief that the law was there to protect the people.'

'Certain people. The remainder are little more than property.'

Flynt could never tell if Charters was toying with him when they had these conversations. 'Cash has seen but fifteen summers.'

Charters was silent for a moment as he considered this. 'Then he should have been more careful where his young fingers strayed, should he not? A rogue is a rogue, no matter his age. Anyway, he does not hang for the stealing of a kerchief or two, but that the populace here gathered come to understand that kerchiefs are not to be stolen.'

Flynt said softly, 'There are those who say I'm a rogue.'

Charters maintained his gaze on the gallows while straining to hear one of the condemned as he addressed the crowd. 'There are indeed, and I would be one of them. However, some rogues have their uses, I find.' Realising that they were too far away to catch the words, he shrugged, gave up. 'And the fourth scoundrel? What was his crime?'

'Murder.'

Charters waited for further words but when none came he smiled. 'What's this, Serjeant? No condemnation of justice for a man killer?'

Flynt felt his own hypocrisy stab at him, for he had taken many lives yet felt no sympathy for the man Driver at all, and that amused Charters immensely. 'He deserves to die,' Flynt said, 'as long as it is certain that he committed the crime.'

'He was tried and found guilty; the facts speak for themselves.'

'Sometimes the facts do not reflect the truth.' He recalled the words of the little judge from the evening previous. 'True guilt or innocence matters little in the courts. Only what can be proved. And sometimes a lie can be proved far more easily than a truth.'

'So you think this fellow Driver be innocent?'

Flynt knew only what he had read or heard but it was sufficient to know the elusive truth of it. 'No. From what I understand the man is as guilty as Judas, but his death will not prevent future crimes of that nature. It is merely judicial vengeance.'

'Punishment, Serjeant. It is punishment for transgression. Driver, like those other miscreants, knew well the penalty for his crimes if caught and gambled on that basis. Now the wager is lost and they will pay their due.'

Flynt fell silent as he scanned the crowd. Jack was still threading his way through the bodies, keen eyes on the hunt for likely marks, his brother shadowing him. He spotted the burly figure of Jonathan Wild, the thieftaker, among a knot of dignitaries near the gallows, two of his men by his side. He recognised the solid bulk of Blueskin Blake, his watchful eyes ever alert for signs of attack on his master, but knew not the equally powerful second man on the other side, who followed the proceedings with rapt attention. Flynt thought, but could not be certain from this remove, that he also saw the well-padded frame of Justice Dumont himself among those to whom Wild, ever mindful of his upward mobility, paid court.

'So to your report, Serjeant,' Charters said. 'What of my Lord Fairgreave?'

Instinctively Flynt's gaze turned to where the man himself stood, sipping from a glass of wine poured by a liveried servant and laughing at the men awaiting their end. 'There is little of note to relate. He is like any other of his station. Feckless, useless and hardly worth attention.'

Charters' lips thinned in disapproval. 'Yes, yes, I am well aware of your antipathy towards our noble lords and ladies, but as to whether he is worthy of your attention, that is not your decision to make. Tell me of his movements.'

'He is here today,' said Flynt, nodding towards the man and his companions, their eyes fixed upon the gallows. Charters' own eyes roamed over the crowd, finally picking them out.

'He rises late, he parades around town in the latest fashion, he games until cockcrow, he wenches when he feels like it,' Flynt said. 'And at present he seems to feel like it with considerable regularity.'

Charters scrutinised the man they were discussing. 'His wife is away in the country, so he feels footloose and fancy free, I'll wager. Any wench in particular?'

'He seems to favour expertise over virtue, although he has visited a house in Golden Square.'

'Inhabited by whom?'

'I have no clue, but he has called there twice and remained within for over an hour on both occasions. I saw no other person leave or arrive but I had to desert my post regularly. Someone such as I loitering tends to stand out.'

Charters surveyed Flynt's black greatcoat, black breeches and black boots as if seeing them for the first time, even though it was his customary garb, then pursed his lips in agreement. 'A house not his own in Golden Square,' he said thoughtfully as he processed the information. 'Think you Lord Fairgreave has some tasty piece in high keeping?'

'I have no clue. I remain uncertain he would wish to part with coin sufficient to keep a lady in such comfort. His tastes run more to Covent Garden Nuns and the cheaper the better.'

'You have seen this?'

'On two nights recent I've seen he and his two friends visit a bawdy house in Holborn and on one occasion they shared a wench in an alleyway.'

'In this weather? That was most intrepid of them.'

'I declined to observe the actual event; I draw the line at being witness to rutting for you, but can vouchsafe that they were not there for long.'

Charters snorted. 'I am surprised this infernal cold did not freeze their members. As for his gaming, I already knew he enjoyed a wager. At Mrs White's Chocolate House I once saw him bet a thousand guineas on which of two raindrops would trickle to the bottom frame first.'

'And did he win?'

'He did, much to the chagrin of the gentleman who lost.'

Flynt let a moment pass before he said, 'Lord Fairgreave also does not like to lose.'

'Does anyone?'

'His lordship takes it too far.'

Flynt quickly outlined the events of the night before, admitting he had lost sight of Fairgreave after the encounter in the street. Charters' eyes flashed with sudden anger. 'Damn it all, man, you attract trouble like flies to horse shit. You were meant to see without yourself being seen.'

'It was not my intention to interfere but His Honour Dumont's eyes were sharp and he picked me out in the darkness.'

Charters' jaw tightened. 'Aye, Sir Geoffrey Dumont misses little. Does he know of what business you were about?'

'No, he thinks me rogue and gambler.'

'And he is not wrong. But Fairgreave had discourse with you, correct?'

'It was unavoidable.'

Charters sighed and again studied Fairgreave as if estimating the distance between them. 'You will have to be even more invisible now, won't you?'

'It would help if I knew what I was looking for. So far the man does nothing that is out of the ordinary for a wealthy wastrel. Why is he of such interest?'

The colonel did not respond, for his attention was distracted by a mixture of groan and cheer from the crowd as one of the men jerked and twisted in the noose. Hanging was not a quick death and it would take some time for him to die. Portions of the crowd fell silent as they watched the final convulsions of a fellow human being, as if there were a sudden kinship between he and they. Others laughed and cheered.

The cart on which the second man stood was pulled away and his body swung, his legs jerking as if the movement would relieve the bite of the rope on his neck. Again there were pockets of silence in the onlookers but cheers greeted the end of the third man, so Flynt presumed him to be Driver. There were those who were here for entertainment and those who were here to see the finishing of the law, but there were others who came to support and somehow bring succour to the condemned, as if to show that even though they died an undignified death straining and strangling on the rope with their bodily functions opening for all to see, there was some sympathy there. For Driver, however, there was no such compassion, and as he swung, his pinioned legs kicking, his arms struggling to free themselves from their bonds, there was a swell of noise from the crowd.

'Who did Driver kill?' Charters inquired.

'A stable boy, I believe.'

'He seems an unpopular fellow. Were you acquainted?'

Flynt shook his head. 'His was a pleasure that escaped me. I feel sure I am all the better for it.'

Then came time for the boy, who seemed to have shrunk in stature the closer he came to his moment. The horse was led away and young Richard Cash was hauled from his feet, which kicked and lashed in tandem with the other victims as he too spun on the rope. A collective groan escaped from those watching at the front.

'Justice must be seen to be done,' said Charters.

'A boy's life for a few pieces of silk? Is that justice?'

Charters' gaze was cool as he looked from the Tyburn Tree back to Flynt. 'Without justice, without law, we have anarchy. That boy stole some kerchiefs one day, but what of the next? What would he take then? Your purse? My purse? A life? Yon hellhound Driver was no doubt once a lad such as he, yet by your own lips you condemn him. A heart filled with larceny will never change and can only grow darker.'

'But a larcenous heart can be used by you,' he observed.

Charters smiled and returned his attention to the final struggles of the condemned. He might just have witnessed an entertainment by Mr Colley Ciber at the Theatre Royal for all the impact the death of those wretches had on him. 'I believe I give you focus on matters greater than larceny.'

Flynt stared over the heads of the crowd towards the bodies still writhing against the rope and pulled his coat tighter against the chill.

Charters saw the movement and smiled. Flynt had already suspected that this meeting place had been chosen specially, to remind him of the threat he held over Flynt's head. 'Walk with me, Serjeant.' He saw Flynt glance towards Fairgreave. 'Leave him for now. I have another appointment to attend and I wish to speak further with you. At any rate, this damnable cold is settling in my bones.'

Flynt did as he was told, searching among the crowd for the men whose job it was to protect Charters while abroad, for though his duties for the government were known by few, there were enemies both foreign and domestic who suspected the retired soldier was more than he seemed. As they walked, Flynt picked out two men dressed in the livery of coachmen ploughing a parallel course through the milling throng, their demeanour outwardly relaxed but he knew they were ever-vigilant for any sign of attack. It was a skill Flynt himself shared. As Charters had once told him, there was no reason why two old comrades in arms should not meet on occasion, and it was no secret that one had saved the other's life, but even so, Flynt retained a wary eye for anyone paying them overmuch attention, in particular Fairgreave and his friends, who he could also see making their way towards the city. It struck him that this was a curious procession they made, him still keeping one eye on the three men while walking with Charters, who was in turn being watched over by others.

'We suspect his lordship may have Jacobite sympathies,' Charters said at last, keeping his voice low. 'His father, the late Lord Fairgreave, was friend to King James, though he renounced him, at least publicly, following the Glorious Revolution. The young Lord Fairgreave's mother was Roman Catholic, though she also renounced her faith and embraced the Church of England. There was talk, however, that she still celebrated the Mass in secret in their country home on occasion. Your Lord Fairgreave may have been influenced by their views.'

Charters calling the man his Lord Fairgreave was unwelcome but Flynt had little inclination to argue the point. 'And what of it? There are many, no doubt, who perhaps saw the return of the Stuarts as a way of bolstering their own fortunes. The Earl of Mar's rising in Scotland has come to nothing.'

'Aye, 'tis true, that was little but comedy in the end.'

'Tell that to those who died at Sheriffmuir and Preston. And to those awaiting execution for their part in the rising.'

Charters said nothing for a few paces and when he did speak, his voice was soft. 'You are right, Serjeant, I misspoke. You and I know that such matters are not to be made light of. Those who died were brave and honourable, on both sides, and there are decent men who lie in the Tower awaiting their date with Mr Marvell's axe. His experience of wielding hammer at anvil will stand him in good stead to separate heads from necks.'

Eight peers had been imprisoned in the Tower of London for their part in the attempt to foment a full-scale rebellion in order to place James Edward Stuart on the throne his father had lost over a quarter-century before. They had been captured at Preston, which was as far south as the rebellion had reached. They had lost their estates and were now due for beheading on Tower Hill. As Charters had stated, Flynt had little sympathy for nobles on either side of the border but he still thought that a barbaric and unjust end.

'There remains danger, however,' Charters continued. 'The claim to the throne by the Pretender, James Edward Stuart, remains a dagger aimed at the heart of the monarchy. Had Mar's ambitions not outstripped his abilities then things may have been very different. Are you aware the Pretender has fled Scotland again?'

Charters' intelligence system was extensive and Flynt was not surprised that he would know this before the rest of the world. 'I did not.'

'Aye, departed from Peterhead a few days since. The clans have melted into their glens once more, as is their wont, but there remains intrigue aplenty.'

'And you think Fairgreave forms part of such intrigue?'

'I have heard little more than a whisper but these can very soon become a shout,' said Charters.

Flynt thought about this and dismissed it. 'He is a bully and a fop. He is brave at a table and they say adept with a duelling blade but I do not see him as being a man of action.'

'He is well connected and impetuous, as you witnessed for yourself last night, it seems. There is talk that he may have run with the Mohocks.'

Flynt had experienced the Mohocks only once, quite soon after he returned from fighting in Flanders. They were young aristocrats and sons of the wealthy who thought themselves above the law and, naming themselves after the North American natives, had run riot in the streets, their brains stimulated by indulgence in opium. He had come upon a group of them as they outraged an elderly lady, throwing her to the ground, and he challenged them as they were ripping at her clothes with their swords. He cut two with his own sword before the others deserted. The wounds he had administered were not mortal, for the two he had tangled with were able to limp off, but he wished he had not exercised such self-control for when he went to the woman's aid he found they had cut off one ear and had almost sawn off her nose. If Fairgreave had been one of their number, he now wished he had not been so lenient the night before.

'He was prosecuted for being with the Mohocks?'

Charters gave him a reproving look. 'You *know* there was no punishment meted out, Flynt. By God, the gentleman said to be the ringleader was voted to Parliament two years ago. Indeed, Dean Swift even opined that the escapade entire was a Whig plot to undermine the Tory government and by establishing such mayhem in the streets perhaps make it easy to engineer assassination of the queen's ministers. I do not adhere to Swift's assertion; I merely repeat it. My point is that your Lord Fairgreave may be enraptured by the romance of such intrigue and so be tempted to act rashly. If the Jacobites mean to extract the prisoners, then with his connections, he could be invaluable.'

'Has he shown overt sympathy to the Stuart cause before?'

'Nought that is known and though he professes to be Whig he has no love for the King or his ministers, who refused him a seat at the table, not that he has any particular aptitude for government.'

'That has never been a stumbling block as far as I can see,' said Flynt, provoking a sharp look from his commander.

'That tongue of yours could one day talk you into the Tower yourself, Serjeant.'

Flynt laughed. 'The Tower is not for the likes of me. It would be the lice of Newgate that would feed on my flesh.'

'Nonetheless, you would do well to curb that seditious streak of yours.'

'I will do my very best, Colonel, but make no promises.'

Charters suppressed a smile. 'Ah, Flynt, I do enjoy our little exchanges.'

'I am glad to be of service. And that said, now that I am known to Fairgreave, I take it my usefulness in this operation is at an end?'

'Not at all. You will continue to keep watch on him but this time ensure that you remain in the background. He may not recognise you in daylight – I take it he was the worse for excess of wine?'

'He'd had a few, certainly.'

'Good. Given his Mohock association then perhaps he had imbibed on something other than wine. That, coupled with the darkness of the street, could yet shield your identity from him. And even if he does recognise you, by the sounds of it you both frequent the same low places and favour ladies of ill repute so he may think nothing of your paths crossing again.'

Flynt almost laughed out loud as Charters was known to favour those ladies with considerable frequency himself, and was often to be seen in gaming houses and rooms across the city.

A coach waited just ahead of them, the driver already climbing down in order to open the door for his master. Flynt saw the two sentinels close in, their hands never far from sword and pistol. Charters came to a halt near to his carriage. 'I would know more of this house in Soho that he visits and suggest you use your considerable skills and that famous charm to gather such intelligence. If there is a fancy piece there, and she is fair of face, then I feel sure that will not be a hardship for you.'

Flynt had hoped the events of the previous evening would have precluded him from further involvement but such dreams often were spoiled by Charters. 'While I am investigating the house I cannot keep my eyes upon Fairgreave. I have skills, to be sure, but I have not yet mastered the art of being in two places simultaneous. That will necessitate my recruiting some assistance, and perhaps the greasing of a palm or two. I have already had considerable expense these past few days in your service, and some funds would be useful.'

Charters seemed amused. But then Charters always seemed amused by Flynt. 'And who would you be thinking to recruit?'

'I think you can leave that to me, as I am certain you will not delegate any other of your Company of Rogues to aid me.'

Charters kept the other members of his clandestine society a secret and Flynt had never known him to allow any to work together, leading him to muse on occasion as to whether someone with whom he was dealing was essentially a colleague.

Charters regarded Flynt through narrowed eyes. 'Are you telling me that fortune did not smile upon you at the tables?'

'I regret that my attention was more on my duties than on the cards and I find myself somewhat out of pocket.'

Charters chuckled, making it obvious he believed not a single word. 'If you would be so good as to inspect the pocket to your right, you will find that such a deposit has already been made.'

As the colonel climbed into his carriage and the driver fastened the door, while the two watchers took their place up front and at the rear, Flynt patted the side of his coat and felt the welcome bulk of coin. Charters was as skilled at inserting items with his one hand as Jack was at removing them with both. Had he not been a professional soldier and now spymaster for the Crown, the colonel would have made an expert pickpocket, and that thought had him examining the crowd as the coach pulled away, searching for young Jack. He spotted him surreptitiously slipping what seemed to be a swollen purse to his brother. The boy smiled as Flynt neared him, his walk cocky, his eyes and ears always alert for an opportunity of thievery. Flynt saw him eye a carelessly replaced silk wipe protruding from a gentleman's coat pocket but then decide against lifting it.

'Nice day for a hanging, ain't it, Mr Flynt?'

'You should pay greater attention to this day's work, Jack lad,' he said, nodding to the gallows. 'One of those poor souls was little older than you. Take it as a solemn warning, for if you continue with the diving trade you will surely end up as a blossom on yonder tree.'

Jack looked over his shoulder at the four corpses still swinging on the beam. Soon they would be cut down and their remains handed over to the anatomists, if their families did not get to them first. Marvell the hangman would claim their clothes as a perk of the job.

'Don't you worry about me, Mr Flynt. The Tyburn jig may be what lies ahead but I'll lead the bastards a spirited dance till then.'

Flynt was not surprised by the response, for the lad had expressed similar sentiments previously and he had little doubt that the boy would do as he intended. Like many other young men, Jack had learned his quick-fingered trade in the charity schools established during the reign of the old queen. He had been taken under the wing of a draper in the Strand but was now apprenticed to a carpenter in Drury Lane; even as an honest man, his life would be short so the rope held few terrors. The lad's mind was as nimble as his fingers and no matter what words of caution or warning he was given, Jack would go his own way.

When Jack faced him once more, his smile had broadened. 'But you're a pot calling a kettle black, ain't you? You ain't no angel.'

Flynt kept his smile in place but Jack's point was well made.

Jack stepped even closer. 'What you doing here anyway, Mr Flynt? I didn't reckon you as a cove what likes to witness collar days.'

'I had an appointment with an old friend.'

Jack adopted an exaggerated leer. 'A friend, eh? A lady friend, perhaps.'

'Far from it, Jack. A gentleman I knew in my army days. An officer.'

'An officer? That makes him a swell. He don't mind being seen with a rogue like you?'

'It's complicated, Jack.'

The boy shrugged and looked again to his brother Tom who held out both arms impatiently. There were culls to be fleeced and the day was not getting younger. Jack waved him away. 'That's life, though, ain't it, Mr Flynt? But that's why I will lead a merry life. It may be short but it won't have no complications.'

Life was seldom simple but Flynt had no time for such a lesson. 'I have a job for you.'

Jack's face became businesslike. 'A paying one?'

'Is there any other kind?'

Jack's smile returned. 'Not in my book, Mr Flynt. What does you need from me? You want something lifted, a crib to be cracked?'

'A watching lay, no more.'

Jack was not surprised as he had carried out such surveillance tasks for Flynt before. 'What is I watching?'

'Not a what, a who.' Flynt jerked his head in the general direction of Lord Fairgreave, who had stopped to exchange words with some acquaintances. 'There's a cove over there – take an easy look, don't be obvious – tall gentleman with two others. He's wearing a blue coat, white stockings, carrying a long cane.'

Jack was an old hand at studying something without being conspicuous, so his glance in the direction Flynt directed was casual but pointed. His sharp young eyes fell on Fairgreave immediately. 'He's a swell, right? Dresses in the pink of the fashion, don't he? Him and his hangers-on.'

Trust the lad to spot Fairgreave's modish dress right off, thought Flynt. 'He does that, lad. I need you to stay on his tail, and don't let him out of your sight for a second. You need to piss, you make sure you know where he is before you unbutton, is that clear?'

Jack nodded. 'So who is he and why you got an interest in him?'

'His name is Lord Fairgreave and my interest need not concern you.'

Jack's customary grin grew. 'You want me to stand budge? You sizing him up for some sort of toby lay, Mr Flynt? 'Cos I know some coves who could help you with that...'

'I'm certain you do, Jack, but though I wish you to spy upon him, I'm not planning highway robbery. I have an interest in his movements but I have business elsewhere today. There's bunce in it for you but you have to do as I say, right?'

The boy looked offended. 'Has I ever let you down yet, Mr Flynt?'

Flynt was forced to admit that the boy spoke the truth. He held out a sixpence. 'Here's a simon for you, on account. You'll get more when the job's done.'

The coin was taken and slipped into the boy's pocket so quickly Flynt was barely aware it had been removed from his fingers. 'You knows I'll do the job, Mr Flynt.'

Flynt saw that Tom Sheppard continued to watch them. His eyes were sharp too, and he would have seen the exchange of coin and be wondering what the transaction was for. Flynt pulled another sixpence from the pocket of his greatcoat. 'This is for Tom, take him with you. Two pairs of eyes are better than one.'

Again the coin was out of his grasp with amazing speed. 'And make sure you give it to him, Jack. Don't pocket it yourself.'

Jack was already moving away but he turned and gave Flynt that grin again, holding his arms out from his side like Jesus on the cross as he continued to walk backwards. 'What you takes me for, Mr Flynt, some sort of thief?'

4

Charters knew well who Flynt had in mind to recruit in his work. He had been aware young Sheppard was working the crowd at Tyburn and knew him to be a sparky, smart lad with a propensity for thievery. Charters had considered folding him into his Company but decided against it. Flynt made use of the boy's skills and could be trusted to ensure that the real reasons for any tasks appeared nefarious and not in protection of the nation's security. As the carriage pulled away from the execution ground, he watched from his window as Flynt made his way back towards the triple tree, no doubt in search of his young assistant.

His coach pulled up on Chesterfield Street and he instructed his men to wait for him, then disembarked outside Mrs White's Chocolate House. He had been a patron since it was first established in the dying years of the old century by a gentleman whose given name was Francesco Bianco but was known to all and sundry by the anglicised Francis White, this being more to an Englishman's taste than the surfeit of vowels that formed the Italian nomenclature. Charters enjoyed coffee, but the sweetness of hot chocolate mixed with cinnamon was more pleasurable to his palate. There were additional attractions in this establishment, for Mr White began to sell tickets for theatrical performances and then instituted a gaming room, where those who enjoyed a wager, the turn of a card or throw of dice, could satisfy their vices. When Francis passed on, the establishment fell into the keeping of his wife Elizabeth, a tough-minded woman whose eye for profit was exceeded only by her ability to ensure that all bets were met on time. Under her stewardship the reputation of the Chocolate House grew and behind the elegant Mayfair facade clustered the great, the good and the grandiose of the day. It was here that the ever alert Charters picked up items of gossip that often proved useful in his work. Few knew that the one-armed retired colonel, a hero of Flanders and a gentleman of leisure thanks to a pension and a private fortune, who sat in his customary chair by the fire sipping chocolate or wine while reading a newspaper or a book, was actually the man responsible for the domestic security of the nation. Only a handful of men at the highest level knew of the existence of the Company of Rogues, and even they were unsure as to its full extent, while none but he knew the names of those in his employ.

As he stepped from the carriage, he perceived a man lying motionless on the pavement, while a burly porter in the establishment's employ ushered pedestrians along with a stern look and a gruff word. That look and tone became more respectful when he recognised Charters and doffed his cap. Charters peered at the prostrate man, assessing by his clothes that he was a tradesman, but without further investigation could not say in which line of work.

'What is occurring here, DeVere?'

The porter's name always seemed too aristocratic for its bearer. Charters knew he hailed from Smithfield and was the son of a butcher so suspected the surname had been adopted to make him more pleasing to the house's clientele.

'Colonel,' DeVere replied. 'This fellow here don't seem to be in plump currant.' He amended his speech. 'Begging your pardon, sir, I meant he has been taken out of sorts, it seems.'

Charters ignored the use of street jargon. 'Have you sent someone for help?'

DeVere looked decidedly uncomfortable. 'I haven't as yet, sir. I've been sent here by those two gentlemen...'

He almost imperceptibly directed his head backwards to the door of the Chocolate House, where two men watched the proceedings on the street with interest. One, whom Charters recognised as Sir Richard Lomax, was not dressed sufficiently to protect him from the bitter elements and he hopped from one foot to the other as if desperate to make water. The other appeared well insulated against the cold in his brown coat of top quality wool, for he stood uncannily still, his hands folded atop a cane adorned with a silver wolf's head. Charters was not surprised to see the tall, powerful figure of Lord James Moncrieff, for he had expected him to accompany the gentleman he knew would be waiting inside. He did feel distaste rising at the sight of him, however. Sir Richard was a fool but there was much about this individual, newly ennobled on the death of his father in Scotland, that stirred up his bile.

Charters leaned in closer to DeVere, who now knelt beside the stricken individual. 'For what purpose?'

When DeVere looked up at him, it was with a mixture of pain and distaste. 'Begging your pardon, sir, but it seems the two gentlemen has a wager.'

'What kind of wager?'

'Charters, old man.' Sir Richard had moved halfway down the steps. 'Be so good as to leave old DeVere be. He is doing us a service.'

While DeVere laid the back of his fingers on the cheek of the man lying before them, Charters straightened. 'What service does he perform?'

'Moncrieff and I have some sport riding on that fellow and we would know who has won. I entreat you, sir, let DeVere be about his task.'

Charters regarded Moncrieff, watching them from the top of the steps as if he were an Olympian god gazing upon Greece, then repeated his earlier query. 'What sport can you have on this poor soul?'

When the man refused to reply, Charters looked back to DeVere as he raised his head from the man's chest. 'I'm afraid this cove is dead, sir.'

Sir Richard cackled and clapped his hands, either through delight or to bring some circulation back to his fingers, as he turned his attention to his friend. 'Ha! There, Moncrieff – as I told you. He was dead before he even hit the ground.'

Moncrieff seemed bored as he held out a quantity of coins. Sir Richard took the money and had the decency not to count it before he thrust it into his own pocket.

DeVere's voice was thick with sadness and pity as he said, almost in a whisper, 'They saw this poor man drop right here, sir, right in front of the steps. One minute he were walking along quite the thing, the next he was as you see him now. It appears they laid bets as to whether he was alive or dead, sir, then instructed me to come out and find out the lay of the land, as it were.'

Charters felt his gorge rise. He had been born to good fortune, had known comfort all his life, apart from on the battlefield. He had watched friends and comrades die. He had shed the blood of others and lost an arm for queen and country. He had ordered men to be killed for the same cause. For him death was not something to be taken lightly and he sincerely regretted his recent flippancy regarding the impending executions of some good men. But now, here were these two civilians, who had never seen action and whose dedication to country began and ended with raising a glass to the monarch's health, laying money on whether a man lived or died on the city street.

'DeVere, have this poor man's body removed from the public gaze immediately and arrange for a wright to collect it. My staff will assist you,' he ordered as he gestured to his men on the carriage. 'But first check his pockets for some form of identification so that his family might be informed. If there is none then make inquiries as to his business in the vicinity and work from there.'

'But sir...'

'I will discuss the matter with Mrs White, fear not, and any expense I will meet. Do all this and do it all now.'

He produced two shillings from his pocket and handed them to the porter, who accepted with profuse thanks, his face continuing to betray his distaste for what had occurred, a distaste Charters shared as he lingered on the steps below the two noblemen. 'Do you think it fitting that two gentlemen of your station be seen wagering over a man's mortality?'

Sir Richard's laugh was slightly nervous and his voice trembled slightly. 'What of it, old man? He was only a tradesman and he was dead – he knew nothing of it. We saw a chance for sport and we took it.'

'I enjoy a wager myself but there has to be limits, man. Do you gentlemen have no decency? No respect for a human being?'

Moncrieff regarded Charters with a coldness that had nothing to do with the temperature. 'As Sir Richard said, he was but a common man and there was no harm done.' His voice carried the tone of a man who saw himself as above the law. Charters had met those of his kidney before – politicians, noblemen, churchmen – and he despised them, even though he had to transact business with them. 'The man was dead and no physician could change that.'

Charters knew well that further discourse was nought more than a waste of time and breath, so he contented himself with a disapproving shake of the head as he brushed past them. He tolerated Flynt's disdain for the upper classes partly because he knew how dissolute they could be. He lived his public life as that of a man of means enjoying his middle age, such enjoyment being mainly the pleasures of the flesh and games of chance. He did not comment on politics or criticise those in power, even though he had his views, for to fulfil his office he must by necessity deal with those who walked those corridors. However, situations such as this tended to loosen his tongue and he knew that any further conversation might prove intemperate.

'Your appointment awaits you within,' said Moncrieff, following Charters into the foyer and gesturing to a doorway to the left before making his erstwhile gambling partner fully aware that he was not invited by delivering a dismissive nod. Sir Richard mumbled an apology and shrank away. Charters entered the main salon and found a small, round man seated in a comfortable chair by a blazing fire, one leg crossed over the other and his foot tapping as though he had been hitherto waiting patiently but said patience was now stretched thin.

'I have been awaiting you, Colonel,' said the man, his tongue still having a flavour of the flat Norfolk lands of his birth. Charters had little time for Sir Robert Walpole, though by dint of political necessity he now had to work with him. After all, he was Paymaster of the Forces and as such was one of the few in government who knew even a little of Charters' true occupation in service to country. His presence in the salon explained its emptiness, for usually by this time of day it was filled with gentlemen seeking leisure, pleasure and transacting business. Moncrieff had made it his business to attach himself to Walpole's hide like a tick to a dog. Walpole was bad enough to deal with, but being with that one was like consorting with the devil.

'James, close the door, if you would be so kind,' Walpole ordered. 'Then stand you by it to ensure we are not disturbed.'

Moncrieff did as he was bid and Walpole waved his hand towards the tall, mahogany wingback chair opposite as if giving Charters permission to sit, his eye casting towards the mantelpiece where one of Mr Daniel Delander of Fleet Street's fine walnut and oak bracket clocks kept time. 'You are normally here by mid-morning, are you not? It is near midday.'

His voice carried an accusatory tone which Charters did not appreciate, but he bit back a response as he settled himself onto the thick cushion. He had been outspoken enough for one day. 'I regret, Sir Robert, that I had an appointment elsewhere.' He lowered his voice, although there was nobody around to hear. He suspected Sir Robert had arranged it that way and Moncrieff standing sentinel was mere show. 'Matters of security, you understand.'

'It is a matter of security that brings us here, Colonel Charters,' Moncrieff said, his accent barely holding a trace of his native Scots.

Walpole waved a hand holding a crumpled piece of newsprint as if dismissing Charters' explanation of his tardiness as having no import. 'Have you seen this scurrilous libel?'

He held the paper out so Charters took it from him and unfolded the wrinkles caused by Walpole's grip. It was an edition of the *London Tribune*, a comparatively new publication that had emerged on the closure of the *London Guardian* in 1713 and specialised in gossip and attacks on the Whig government.

'I have not, Sir Robert,' Charters said, scanning the text which outlined Walpole's career to date and debated his fitness to hold office. At this first hurried reading Charters saw no libel, scurrilous or otherwise.

'We want that infamous publication stamped out of existence, Charters.'

'*We*, sir?'

'The government, the cabinet. Lord Townshend and I,' he then added as an afterthought, 'and others, of course. We have all been targeted by this vicious little publication and we want it stopped. Even Lord Moncrieff here.'

The cabinet was led by Lord Halifax, at least on paper. In reality it was Lord Charles Townshend and James, Earl of Stanhope, who were the dominant forces in government, both aided by Townshend's brother-in-law, the portly man before him quietly fuming over the contents of the pamphlet. His lordship was a decent man and the earl was a cunning political operator, as was Sir Robert Walpole, who was known for his loyalty to his party. However, Charters found him perhaps too cunning, too self-serving. Walpole was a country squire and had his good points but his eye was fixed on garnering power and that alone made him suspect, for Charters believed he would be none too picky as to how to attain it. He had the makings of a great man but Charters knew that the greater the man, the greater their compromises. The Scotsman was a darker force moving below the surface. He expressed no desire for office; he had inherited a fortune from his father who died the year before at Sheriffmuir, having come out for the Pretender in support of John Erskine, the Earl of Mar.

'And how do you propose to stop it, Sir Robert?' said Charters, already sensing what was coming. 'The pamphlet is published anonymously, probably written by some penniless scrivener in Grub Street and printed by one of the many presses there.'

'That will be your problem, Charters.'

Charters had expected that this issue would become his, but even so, he felt his heart sink. He had more important things to deal with than the vanity of politicians.

'It undermines the integrity of the government and it must be stopped,' Moncrieff continued.

Charters read the text once again, combatting the need to point out that Walpole had indeed been found guilty of corruption just three years before and had spent some time in the Tower, having been impeached and ejected from his seat in the Commons. Charters knew that once free he had embarked on writing a series of pamphlets attacking the then Tory government – and anonymously too. The irony of the situation was not lost on Charters, but on that too he kept his own counsel.

Walpole grew impatient in waiting for a response. 'Need I remind you that your livelihood depends on funding from my department. And that the very existence of your – what is it called? – Company of Rogues is also made possible through our largesse?'

Charters was aware that Walpole had already headed a secret committee investigating the previous Tory government, looking for ways in which it had mismanaged the nation's affairs, and that it had led to the impeachment of senior ministers. Indeed, the Earl of Oxford was already languishing in custody alongside the Jacobite lords in the Tower, while Viscount Bolingbroke had fled to France. It would be very easy in retrospect to find – or rather fabricate – evidence which suggested Charters' organisation acted against the needs of the British people. However, he could not give in without speaking plainly.

'With respect, sir, I cannot see any legal reason why we could shut this down, even if we could find the source.' He raised the pamphlet. 'There is nothing here that is false.'

Walpole's initial glare over his orders being challenged softened as he took another tack. Trust a politician to try to handle him, Charters thought.

'This is a Tory rag, Charters, and it is trying to undermine the probity of this government. As you know I have experienced their vicious propaganda first-hand when they accused me of corruption. They were lies and yet I was punished.'

It was true that no evidence was found that money had been diverted by Walpole from government funds, but that didn't stop him from being found guilty by the House of Lords, losing his King's Lynn seat in the House and spending time in the Tower. He might have been the victim of Tory party machinations, and the stories in the *Tribune* might well be another example, but he was more than capable of such underhand dealings himself. Walpole could manipulate, dissemble and disinform with the best of them; better, in fact, for he was a second-generation nobleman and had something to prove.

Walpole leaned forward, all the better to utilise the charm that had allowed him to ease his way through government. 'This country needs stability, my dear Colonel, you above all should understand that. We have had a tumultuous experience of late. War, trouble in the north, papist intrigues, the death of our dear queen and the installation of a new monarch. We have had ten elections in twenty years and we need to take time to catch our breath, to prepare for the great and glorious future our nation deserves.'

Charters wondered idly if the man was seeking his assistance or his vote. It was Walpole who had contended that in order to achieve political stability the tenure of an MP should be extended from three years to seven. From there it would be an easy stretch to ensure that they stay in office for life and be untroubled by the need to seek approval at the ballot box.

Walpole gestured to the publication in Charters' grip. 'That sort of filth does not help us. And to top it all, we have the damned Germans to deal with, whose counsel His Majesty trusts above all others, however misguided that may sometimes be, for what can these Teutons know of our good English way of life, eh?'

'What do you propose I do, Sir Robert?' Charters asked, steering the conversation away from criticism of His Majesty King George's reliance on his own people. 'It may be possible that we could find the press and smash it to pieces but a new one could be operational in days.'

'My dear Charters,' Walpole said, his smile seemingly sincere, but Charters knew he was being handled, 'if there were one man in all of England who can find out where this blasted press is, then it is the one now sitting before me. You are an honourable fellow and your love of your country is well known. Not by many, to be sure, because the nature of your work for the state must be kept secret, but by those of us who can best appreciate your skills. Your Company of Rogues is a vital part of our defence against our enemies, both abroad and at home. In this case, as a beginning, I would suggest that the lion's head be removed once and for all.'

The lion's head was a marble letterbox, said to have been designed by the artist William Hogarth, attached to Button's Coffee House in Russell Street. It had been used by readers of the defunct *London*

Guardian, which was based within the premises, to alert the editor to news and gossip, and even anonymous articles were posted through its mouth. Charters had heard that latter function had been inherited by the mysterious publishers of the *Tribune*. Although he found the design overly elaborate, it had become a much-loved object in the Covent Garden area.

'That would prove to be unpopular among the people, sir,' Charters said, pointing out the political dangers of such a move. 'They would take it badly and hold it against he who ordered it.'

'The people be damned,' said Moncrieff. 'Let them take it as they will.'

Walpole breathed heavily through his nose but held up a hand to silence Moncrieff. He was not known for his understanding of the mood of the people but he recognised its importance when it was presented to him. 'Colonel Charters has a point, James. We are here for the people, are we not?'

Moncrieff had the grace to leave that unanswered and Charters knew why, for Flynt was not alone in his belief that men like Walpole put person and party before people. Moncrieff would utilise that to further his own fortunes.

'Such direct action is not advisable, I understand that,' Walpole said. 'But, sir, I would entreat you to mobilise those considerable resources maintained by the public purse to silence the author of these lies.'

'I regret, Sir Robert, that even with those *considerable resources*, uncovering the man behind these words may prove not only difficult but impossible.'

A gleam shone in the politician's eyes and Charters knew what he was going to say even before the words were uttered. 'Oh, my dear Charters, I already know who penned these words. He was seen by friends, two nights ago, using the lion's head, and it is known that he does not favour His Majesty's government overmuch, being an arch Tory.'

'Then that makes the task much easier to perform. Who is this individual?'

Walpole smiled for the first time since the conversation began and Charters knew then that all else had been feint, that delivery of this name was the true aim of the conversation. When the politician spoke it, Charters wondered at the nature of the world, for it was the second time he had heard it that day.

5

The mistake may have been in talking to the maidservant, but Flynt reasoned that it was not an obvious one, for the girl could just as easily have not mentioned the conversation to her employer. After all, experience had taught him that if he needed to know anything about a house then simply walking up to the front door and asking questions was liable to avail him nought and perhaps even have him arrested. No, his time committing crack lays, breaking into the houses of the rich, proved that the best way to garner intelligence was to talk to the servants. A coin or two slipped from his palm into theirs generally ensured their silence regarding his inquiry, most servants in the city not being well paid and often flitting from one house to another.

The square itself was slightly irregular and he had walked the perimeter and through the ornamental garden that formed the centre, all the time keeping his attention focused on the door to the house he had observed Fairgreave visit. This perambulation also helped keep him warm. The sun shone as bright as summer but the cold hung in the air, attacking the flesh with its chill sting. The snow that still lay frozen in less salubrious addresses had been cleared from these streets, no doubt by an army of servants despatched with shovel and brush, but here and there a stray patch remained. It was a slow day in Golden Square with very little activity, and he was aware that even though he remained in constant motion he was somewhat conspicuous, but he was experienced enough at casing cribs to ensure that his interest was not overt, giving the impression that he was merely a gentleman braving the extreme chill for a constitutional. As he walked, ensuring to bow his head courteously to the very few ladies and gentlemen he met, both out of politeness but also to conceal his features without making it too obvious, he pondered the notion of the city as a living creature, constantly growing and reaching outwards. He had once worked with a cracksman, Old Tom Schofield by name, who specialised in robbing the cribs of the gentry and could pick a lock in a matter of moments. Old Tom had begun life in the bleating rig trade, stealing sheep from the fields around the city, but had given that up for the more gentlemanly art of going upon the dub. He had told Flynt how much London had grown even in his lifetime and this piece of ground in particular, the land south of Holborn that had been called Soho, had once been a plague pit and then arable lands. Old Tom had been a veritable fount of knowledge concerning the city and once Flynt had even assisted in cracking a crib in this very square, then owned by an admiral of the fleet. They had made off with a pretty haul in plate and jewellery, made even more sweet by the knowledge that the man was responsible for sending his men into a storm in a vessel that was unfit for service but managed to escape punishment for its subsequent loss by blaming a junior member of staff, who later took his own life. As they had kept watch for the opportunity to sneak in and plunder the bastard, Old Tom had recalled his own father telling him that the land on which these handsome buildings now stood was once known as Gelding Close, for it was where such animals were kept, but as development proceeded 'gelding' became 'golden' and the beasts were replaced by people. The square had been built over time in order to house the gentry and Flynt was aware that the disgraced Viscount Bolingbroke had lived here in a house that was often a scene of great conviviality, but following his flight to the Continent on the ascension of the King and the collapse of his Tory government, it fell forfeit to the Crown. The remainder of the houses were occupied by peers, politicians and the privileged. The terraced rows of brick townhouses showed some conformity of style, most three storeys in height, a few four, each a width of three windows, the roofing steeply pitched and broken by dormers, and the very air carried the heady aroma of prosperity.

He had been there for an hour when he saw the young girl leave from the front door, which he found unusual. Someone of her station would be expected to use a rear entrance and, judging by the way she ducked down the slight of steps to the street and moved swiftly in the direction of Lower John Street, one of four ways out of the square, Flynt suspected she knew she had broken rules. He walked swiftly after her, catching up before she hit Brewster Street. He did not fret over leaving the house unwatched, for he was confident that if Fairgreave should pay the house another visit then Jack would not be far in his wake. Positioning himself so that he could still see the square, although not the front door of the house, he gave the servant his best smile and what he hoped was a courtly bow as he doffed his wide-brimmed hat, there being something less threatening in a man who approaches a lady bare-headed. She was taken aback but he hoped his polite manner would reassure her, though her eyes remained cautious. He estimated that she was of about fourteen years, her features pleasant but sharpened by her position in life and no doubt already years of hard work.

He apologised for detaining her in such a fashion but told her that he was interested in renting rooms in the house from which she had recently exited, then inquired, most politely, if there were any available.

'The owner be a countess of the West Country, sir,' she said, her accent proving she was London born, 'but she come to town only seldom. She do rent rooms as furnished apartments but there ain't none available.'

He affected dismay at this. 'Ah, 'tis a shame for I do find the appearance of that particular house most pleasing. Who would it be occupying the rooms, perhaps they may vacant presently?'

She readily volunteered that there was an artist living off an allowance from his doting mother in Suffolk, a silk merchant, and a retired army officer who spent his evenings carousing with old comrades and weaving home in a state of considerable intoxication.

'And then there is my mistress,' she added.

'Ah,' Flynt said, throwing the dice and hoping to hit his mark, 'a most beautiful lady?'

What may have been a smile flirted with her lips. 'My mistress is most fair indeed, sir.'

He adopted a more conspiratorial tone. 'I confess I caught me the merest glimpse of your mistress and that first and only sight finds me stricken with a desire to make her further acquaintance, hence my inquiry regarding accommodation.'

When the maid hesitated to speak further, he threw the dice again, hoping that her life of service and drudgery had not stifled any romantic yearnings she may have had. 'You are young, my dear, and I feel sure you must have experienced such emotions and you will understand the depth of my feelings.'

She did seem to soften at this, her gaze casting to the ground, but her words seemed to be delivered by rote, as though it were a catechism beaten into her. 'I has little time for such fripperies, sir, for romance is for those who can afford such leisure time.' She took a deep breath and glanced around her as if fearful of being overheard. 'But there was a footman at a previous position and him and I, well, we was right friendly. But I lost my place in that house when my employer found us together. I was gutted, I was, but I'm working here at Golden Square now and I hope you understand that I cannot lose another position.'

Flynt said he totally understood while also taking some silver from his pocket and letting it jingle in his hand. 'All I need is a word or two about the lady in question, for if I was somehow able to inveigle myself into her affections it would be useful to learn what I can. I can assure you I would never break our confidence and your position will not be at risk.'

Eyes fixed on the coins, she said she could not tell him much. 'She is foreign, at least her accent be strange. She speaks the King's English but I hears traces of the Frenchies and something else, too, what sounds occasional like your own accent, begging your pardon.'

A thought as to the woman's identity made Flynt smile a little.

'How long has she been resident here?'

'She is only recent like established herself here. She has travelled abroad for some years, I thinks, but now she rents the second floor, though it be merely a parlour, a bedchamber and an antechamber for her personals and such like. There's a kitchen below in which she has her meals prepared and a small room where I sleeps. It's a good room and I has it to myself for none of the other tenants has servants engaged. I ain't never had a room to myself before.'

Flynt took this in, mulling over his suspicion as to the lady's identity, then inquired as to whether she was a good employer.

'Right kind and considerate she is, and has even promised to take me with her when she returns to her travels.'

'And when will that be?'

'Soon, she says, a few days hence.'

He thought of Fairgreave. 'As a great beauty and a woman of some means, she must have many gentlemen callers.'

The girl shook her head. 'She has very few callers, two ladies but also one gentleman, a swell by his clothes and manner.' Her face hardened further. 'When he speaks to me personal it's like I'm dirt, not that he speaks direct to me often. Some swells is nice but he looks right past me like I am just a piece of furniture that is useful when needed but invisible when not.'

He thanked the girl, gave her the money, and stared after her for a moment as she scuttled along the street on whatever errand she had been sent, his mind working on what she had told him. So there was a lady after all, and the odds were very much in favour of the unpleasant gentleman who called upon that lady, and who treated the girl with such disdain, being Fairgreave. The maid's description of her mistress had popped a name into his mind, followed by that image of a pert smile and a coquettish lift of an eyebrow. She would not have returned to London so soon, would she? Unless she had business on behalf of her masters in Paris.

He walked with some speed back to Golden Square and took up his position in the gardens, once again adopting the air of a man in pursuit of leisure. It was very pleasant in this wide open space where the smells and ordure of the city streets did not impinge. After speaking to the girl he knew he had to be sure that his suspicions concerning the beautiful short-term tenant were well-founded.

His mistake in speaking to that maidservant became evident a further hour into his surveillance, when he saw the first man enter the square to take up a position at the corner of Lower James Street, followed by another at the parallel Lower John Street. They did not have the look of tradesmen, nor did they have the appearance of residents of this well-to-do locality. Their attention was fixed firmly upon him and he surmised that the errand the girl had been beetling away to perform was to alert whoever these men were of his presence. He glanced the length of the square to the corresponding upper parts of James and John Streets that led to Beak and Silver Streets where, as he suspected, another two men had stationed themselves. He unbuttoned his coat to enable easier access to the twin pistols thrust into his belt, transferred the grip of his silver cane to his left hand, all the better to grasp the handle with his right if necessary, and watched as a fifth individual headed towards him, his body broad and powerful, his head devoid of periwig, his hair scraped tight to skull. His face was taut with belligerence and betraying the look of one who was no stranger to violence. A deep scar hacked a wide clearing through his beard, the result, Flynt guessed, of finding himself on the wrong side of a sabre slash. His coat was open to reveal a brace of pistols. He did not know the man's name but he had seen him before, that very morning, standing by Jonathan Wild's side at Tyburn.

The man came to a halt a few paces from Flynt, noting the butts of Flynt's own pistols showing beneath the coat. He seemed unperturbed by the firepower, no doubt satisfied that he could match it. He seemed relaxed, his demeanour that of a man used to situations such as this. Flynt was also relaxed but primed to react to any attack, while also keeping part of his attention on the doorway of the house.

'What's your business here, mate?' The voice was coarse, carrying the weight of a man who expected people to tell him what he wanted to know or pay the price.

Flynt cared little for what the man expected. 'Who wishes to know?'

'I am here…' He paused to indicate his men stationed at the corners of the square like the Four Horsemen of the Apocalypse. 'We are here on the orders of the thieftaker.'

Flynt made a show of studying the sentinels. 'Which thieftaker despatched you?'

The man frowned. 'There is only one, mate.'

'There are two who are paramount, Mr Wild and Mr Hitchin. I would know which of them is your superior.'

The man's upper lip twitched in what might have been a sneer if the tightening of skin around his scar did not inhibit the movement. 'There is only one what matters and that would be Mr Jonathan Wild.'

Flynt already knew this was Wild's man but enjoyed forcing him to explain himself. 'I would hazard that Mr Hitchin would disagree with your judgement.'

The man's grin was lopsided, revealing some missing teeth. 'Well, mate, I shan't be losing no sleep over what that molly disagrees with. Now, I asks you again, what's your business here?'

Flynt's mind flitted over why Wild would be alerted to his presence or why he would even care, unless he believed there was a crack lay being planned. If that were the case, the self-appointed Thieftaker General would be interested only in his cut. Mr Jonathan Wild was the biggest thief in the city, even though he ostensibly worked on behalf of the victims of crime eager to have their purloined goods returned in exchange for a reward. Wild had often planned robberies in the first place and employed a small army of men such as the one now before Flynt to carry them out, but also used that same workforce to track down freelance operators who had indulged themselves in thievery without his sanction. The jails of the city were filled with those who had refused to grant this petty Caesar what he believed was his tribute by right.

'My business is my business and not that of anyone else, including Jonathan Wild,' Flynt replied, his hand easing to the handle of his cane. One twist and there would be a surprise in store for this fellow.

The right side of the man's face creased further, while his left resolutely refused to match it, giving him an off-kilter mien that was distinctly unfriendly. 'He said you would say something like that, Jonas Flynt. And that when you did we was to bring you in to have a discussion.'

Flynt shot another look beyond him to the house. That he had been observed from one of those windows was of no doubt. But this fellow had called him by name and yet they had never had former acquaintance. That meant whoever had sent for them knew his identity.

It also meant he was now convinced as to who it was who had sent for them.

'Mr Wild and I have had business before and I feel sure he would also have told you that I would not readily agree to such a request.'

The man opened his coat wider. 'We all carry barkers such as these, mate, and not a one of us is unaccustomed to their use, don't you worry, so why not just come with us nice and polite like. There's no need to spoil such pretty surroundings with blood, eh?'

Flynt flicked his coat back too. 'I am not alone either, friend, and I can assure you that it would not be my blood alone that stains these streets.'

The man was unperturbed by the sight of the pistols. 'We are five to your one, or can't you count?'

Flynt allowed himself a leisurely look at the man's companions, who remained in position to block off any means of escape should Flynt choose to run. He had no intention of doing so. He was confident he could take this fellow down with a single sword strike, then despatch two of the men with his pistols as they rushed towards him, using his blade to drop a fourth. If all went to plan, the fifth was likely to turn tail but if not, and he did not make the error of coming into sword strike range, then Flynt would think of something.

The click of hooves on the roadway made Scarface turn slightly, so Flynt decided it was time to show him that talk was one thing but action was better. He sprang forward, slid the blade from his silver cane and had it resting on the man's throat before he even knew what had happened. 'What occurs in the next few minutes will be of no concern to you, sir, for your blood will already decorate these stones.'

The man's speed at overcoming his shock was admirable. He showed no fear as his right hand twitched towards one of his pistols. Behind him, the carriage they had heard emerged from Lower John Street and came to a halt outside the house.

'I wouldn't touch those barkers,' Flynt warned, cursing the fact that this encounter had reached a tricky stage, because it meant he could not give the waiting carriage the scrutiny it deserved. The driver had climbed down and disappeared on the opposite side of the vehicle, no doubt to open the door. The hand of the thieftaker's man had frozen but movement at the edge of Flynt's vision signified the outliers moving in, their fingers already reaching for their own weapons. 'Unless you wish to provide work for the barber-surgeons, or more likely a meal for worms, I would instruct your companions to stay where they are.'

The man waved a hand towards the men and they came to a halt but remained ready to act. 'You is making a fierce mistake, mate.'

From where he stood, Flynt could see only the top of the front door beyond the carriage but it had opened, instinct telling him that the thieftaker's men had been summoned to allow her the opportunity to exit without being seen. 'I have made mistakes before.'

'You may not live to make another.'

Flynt's smile was like a death's head grin as he heard the carriage door slam. 'Perhaps, but rest assured you'll be waiting for me in hell. Now, sir, I would know your name.'

'Does it matter? Although you has me under your blade, we still holds the upper hand so our acquaintance will be brief, I'm thinking.'

Flynt pressed the point of the blade further into the man's throat as the driver climbed back into his seat and cracked the whip over the pair of horses. 'You already know mine and I feel it socially awkward not to know what name I would have the mason etch on your tombstone.'

The curious grin appeared again. The man had faced eternity before, of that Flynt was certain, and like him he had won the day, so was confident history would repeat itself. 'Not that it matters but it's Warwick, Richard Warwick.'

'Well, Dick,' Flynt said, watching the carriage pull away but unable to see who was within, 'suppose you tell me what connection Mr Wild has with the lady who has just left that house yonder?'

Warwick half turned to look at the house. 'I know of no lady in that crib nor any other in this place. Mr Wild received word you was here and he sent us to fetch you, that's all. He seemed unconcerned whether you was alive, dead or just bleeding.'

This had the ring of truth, for Wild was unlikely to share his machinations with his bully ruffians. He would simply issue an order and expect it to be obeyed. The thieftaker had sent such as Mr Warwick to him before and why he thought it would be successful this time was beyond him.

'Go back to your master then and tell him I decline his invitation,' Flynt said, 'and that next time he wishes my society he should send a messenger and not a gang of footpads with notions above their station.'

That offended Warwick. 'I ain't no footpad.'

'You are no choirboy, either.' Flynt pressed the point a little deeper, drawing a trickle of blood. Warwick didn't even flinch. 'You're also no stranger to pain, Dick, or meting it out, I'll wager. But listen and listen well, if you come at me again in such a fashion then you will be introduced to such pain as you could never imagine.'

Warwick's glare was filled with defiance as he backed away three paces and only then did he raise a hand to the blood oozing from the prick at his throat. He stared at the stain on his fingers. 'You will not get the better of me again, Jonas Flynt. I don't take kindly to being shamed.'

'Better shamed than dead, Dick,' said Flynt, his left hand resting on the butt of a pistol.

Warwick maintained his heated gaze upon Flynt as he walked backwards from the park. Flynt was ready for him should he decide to come back for more while also remaining ever watchful that the man's companions did not cast themselves in the role of hero of this little drama, but none had changed position. He himself didn't move until all five had melted from the square, when he retrieved his cane from where he had dropped it and sheathed his blade. The carriage had come to a halt in Upper John Street and he was certain he saw the curtain of the rear window flip back a little as the passenger observed the scene. He didn't see her face but he still tipped his hat and bowed.

Well played, he thought, well played.

6

Sir Geoffrey Dumont and Flynt dined that evening at the Black Lion in Drury Lane. When the judge suggested the venue, it crossed Flynt's mind that he knew of his association with Colonel Charters, for this was a favourite meeting place of his, in the very upstairs room that had been reserved for their meal. Such suspicion ensured that Flynt merely sipped at his wine, pleading that the previous evening's imbibing had upset his stomach. Dumont insisted that a drop of wine does wonder for a digestion that was out of sorts then proceeded to attack the bottle himself as if his vitals were in an uproar.

They dined on white soup, venison with artichokes and French beans, followed by raisin pudding. Flynt had never taken to the dried fruit, feeling them to be nothing more than grapes with a lack of commitment. During the meal they discussed the affairs of the day, Dumont dominating the conversation with entertaining gossip from the Session House. Flynt remained careful as to his own utterances in case this was some kind of test. As far as he knew, the judge could be part of Charters' Company and this was all an elaborate ruse to see if he could keep his own counsel.

Dumont temporarily set the wine aside to order coffee. He winked at Flynt and lowered his voice, perhaps out of consideration for the young girl who served them; not that it mattered for she had no doubt heard far coarser talk, the tavern not being the most delicate of environments.

'Does wonders for the old Thomas, does coffee, puts some fierce ardour into dancing the blanket hornpipe, don't you know,' he said. 'My dear wife and I still enjoy vigorous matrimonials, even after near twenty-five years of being wed. Like young lovers, we are, on a tryst. A fine woman, a most fine woman. Three sons she has borne me, none has survived beyond infancy, but that was no fault of hers. That's life, eh, Flynt? Or death. But coffee, my boy, that's the secret. Puts a punch in the man's jizz. And chocolate, for the lady of course, not the gentleman. Makes her exceeding fertile, did you know that?'

Flynt confessed he had not heard of this.

Dumont nodded sagely. 'Aye, chocolate makes her innards more receptive to the seed, helps it grow. I once met a fellow, medical man he was, swore by it. Said his wife had brought forth twins three times through the eating of chocolate. Three sets of twins, Flynt, what are the odds of that, eh? I know not if they survived but still, three doubles. Now there's a throw.'

Flynt doubted whether coffee and chocolate did assist in matters of a reproductive nature but he did not argue. He smiled politely and let the judge ramble on, his speech becoming increasingly loud as the alcohol took hold. Finally, the girl cleared the table of the plates, set a bottle of brandy before them and left them alone. Dumont excused himself and retired behind the screen in the corner to relieve himself in the pots provided, and Flynt heard him humming softly as his water rattled in the porcelain. He emerged again, wiping his hands on his breeches having dipped them in the bowl of clean water provided. His pace was steady and true, so he had not yet reached the depths of inebriation of the previous night. He sat down heavily in his chair and stared at the bottle of brandy.

'They baptise their spirits here, did you know that, Flynt?'

Flynt did know that the owner Joseph Hines watered down the liquor, all the better to increase profits.

Dumont picked up the bottle and stared at it. 'Disgraceful way to treat good French brandy. Rum Katz you fellows of the streets call it, correct?' Flynt nodded and Dumont set the bottle down again. 'Although I do believe our fine host, Mr Hines, takes delivery of moonshine, smuggled into the Romney Marsh by a gang of owlers led by the local vicar, if you can believe it. Or so the Excise believe, but they cannot catch the rascal. Too slippery for them, it seems.'

He uncorked the bottle and poured himself a measure, holding it towards Flynt, who declined. Dumont replaced the cork and sat back, holding his cup in one hand but not drinking. Flynt had heard of the owlers of Romney Marsh, so called because they worked by night using the hoot of the bird as a signal to their colleagues. He had also heard tell of the good reverend but had never encountered him. Perhaps one day he might meet this man who led the revenue men a merry dance across the Kent coastline.

'There are many slippery characters in life, are there not, Flynt?' Dumont continued. 'I expect you have encountered more than a few in your day?'

'I have met more than a few, 'tis true.'

'But not all out-and-out rogues, eh, Flynt? I have often said that you can trust a dishonest man more than an honest one, for you know where you are with one you know to be a rogue. It's the honest ones, or those who purport to be honest, you have to be wary of, for they can knife you and preach that it is for your own good while doing it.' Dumont fixed him with a sudden, steady gaze. 'You have been slippery yourself, I'll be bound. No, don't deny it. We are friends here; you have taken no oath and I am not a judge this night.'

Flynt chose his words carefully. 'I have had my moments, to be sure.'

He wondered where this was leading, for he sensed that there was something Dumont wished to say. He let the man reach his point in his own time.

'You are a Scot, are you not?'

'Aye,' said Flynt.

'Are you Jacobite? Or do you favour Whig or Tory?'

'I favour nought but myself.'

The judge accepted this without further inquiry. 'We are governed by rogues and charlatans; are you aware of this?'

Flynt took a deep breath. 'It is my opinion that no matter who governs, they are all the same. Whig, Tory, Scot, English, Hanoverian, Jacobite. All have their nose deep in the trough.'

'Aye, but some have their snouts in deeper than others and they be the ones who preach patriotism like it is holy writ. It be my experience that the man who embraces the flag most ardently is only looking for the means to pick its pocket. I accept what you say, for in truth it be most accurate, but the men who now have the ear of the King are the worst I have ever seen. Any party that would give position and favour to such as Sir Robert Walpole is beyond the pale. Have you met him, Captain Flynt?'

'I have not had the honour.'

Dumont grunted. 'There is no honour in that one, only self-interest. And he is not alone in this cabinet.'

Flynt smiled. 'I take it you are Tory.'

Dumont looked up and gave a small laugh. 'You think me partisan in my views? You think me somehow bitter that my party has been excluded from government by a king who believes us to favour James Edward Stuart? No, I do not advocate a return of the Stuarts, although I do admit Bolingbroke was less than circumspect in his dealings and he be in exile because of it, but 'tis fact that though this king has little interest in England and has all the arrogance of his station, he is at least Protestant. The Stuarts were little more than tyrants. Their hubris exceeds even George of Hanover and there is always the danger that they would heed Rome before their own ministers, for history has taught us that they have insufficient regard for those ministers. This belief of the divine right of kings that runs through their line is troubling, while their disdain for the rule of Parliament is unacceptable.'

'But you said that it is your belief that Parliament is riddled with corruption.'

'Aye, this nation has become increasing corrupt. There are govern-ments within government – committees, star chambers, cadres of men who plot and plan. But there is another, a government behind the government, if you will. Faceless men who remain in the shadows but whose pernicious influence is most potent, for they control either directly or indirectly the men who rule. And their influence extends to both parties, I am most distressed to admit.'

'So it is your contention that Parliament is hopelessly undermined by these groups?'

'Not hopelessly, there are good men remaining, while even bad men can do good sometimes.' He gave Flynt a pointed look. 'Is that not so, Flynt?'

Flynt, still on his guard, felt it politic to remain silent. That Sir Geoffrey Dumont knew something of his past, or at least had sensed it, was clear. He liked the man but he was not going to say anything that might implicate himself. And yet the judge was giving voice to sentiments that were unbecoming to one in his position. He had not openly criticised the King but he had said enough to have him removed from the bench were he to repeat it to the wrong ears. This talk of a secret government was new to him, though he had some limited experience of dealing with a group who styled themselves the Fellowship.

With no reply to his query forthcoming, Dumont said, 'No matter, I do not expect you to reveal your past to me, but suffice to say that I have heard rumours in the Bailey of a man of the streets who, like the Lord, works in mysterious ways. They are little more than whispers in corners and echoes from roof beams, but they say he is a rogue and a thief that carries with him justice in the form of twin pistols and a walking stick with lethal properties.' The judge's focus shifted momentarily to where Flynt's silver cane rested on the table. 'They say this man is vengeance, and where he walks, death walks with him. A good man walking in a bad man's flesh, so to speak. In your travels, Flynt, have you heard tell of this?'

Flynt dismissed the notion with a grimace. 'A street myth is all it is.'

'Perhaps. Perhaps not. But if there were such an individual, then I would have him know that he has a friend in the Bailey. And that friend would be obliged to know that, should anything untoward occur to him, that this individual would take up the standard and punish those who caused it.'

Flynt saw the earnest gleam in the man's eye and realised that this man he had come to like was troubled. 'Is there something you wish to share, Sir Geoffrey?'

Dumont had leaned across the table and appeared to be considering expanding further, his body tense as if he were bracing himself, but then he relaxed a little and eased back in his chair. 'No, my friend, I was merely expressing hope that such an angel of vengeance exists. Perhaps if he did we could all sleep easier in our beds.'

Flynt studied him for a moment. 'One man's angel is another man's demon, however.'

Dumont gave him a pointed look. 'Sometimes it takes a demon to do an angel's work...'

At meal's end, Dumont bade his farewell, saying he had an appointment that he must attend. He gripped Flynt's hand tightly before leaving the room, his voice still but his eyes filled with a plea, though for what Flynt did not know.

'It is right good to make your acquaintance, friend Jonas,' he said. 'We are fast friends, you and I, are we not?'

Flynt hesitated for a brief moment, for he was unaccustomed to such a bond being formed so quickly. 'Aye, that we be, Sir Geoffrey.'

'Geoffrey is sufficient, my friend.' The judge had not yet released Flynt's hand. In fact, he clasped his other hand over their knot of fingers. 'There be no need for formality between friends.'

Flynt did not attempt to retrieve his hand. 'Do you require company to attend this appointment? The hour grows late and there are many dangers out there.'

'I am well acquainted with the streets, Jonas, and have my pistol with me. And this rendezvous is not for you, I'm afraid.' He stared down at their still enmeshed hands. 'Promise me this, my friend, should anything befall me, if I be suddenly disgraced, for instance, that you will not believe whatever official explanation is forthcoming.'

'Do you expect such a thing to befall you?'

Dumont's gaze was fixed upon their clasped fingers and seemed unwilling to break the connection. Flynt frowned, again sensing a troubled mind.

'What business are you about, Geoffrey?'

'This night I know not what I am about but there are other matters of which I have been made aware that speak of chicanery at the highest levels. Should these men learn that I know of their tricks, then my liberty at the very least would be forfeit. They will stop at nought to ruin my reputation, to bring me low, in order to hide their own deeds. I believe one good man has already died for their secrets.' His eyes dropped to the floor and he shook his head sadly. 'Poor William, God rest him.' Before Flynt could inquire further, the judge returned his earnest gaze to him, his fingers tightening on Flynt's own. 'I may depend upon you to defend my honour should such a thing occur? If I be disgraced or if harm befall me, you will take up the banner on my behalf?'

Flynt was nonplussed over what it was that he was expected to do, given he had no notion as to what the judge referred to, but nonetheless he did not hesitate. 'You have my word of honour.'

Dumont smiled, pumped their hands once, then released them. 'And that, my good friend, is sufficient for me. My heart is lighter with the knowledge.'

He exited first and Flynt tarried a while to give him the opportunity to descend the narrow staircase to the tavern below. There was no reason why they should not be seen together again but he felt it was advisable for both their sakes. Flynt was thoughtful as he waited a few minutes, his hat and coat held in his hand. That the judge was trying to tell him something was evident and he wished he had simply come right out and said it plain. That he knew of his past was clear, it would have been a simple matter of asking a question or two in the right ear and there would be many such ears in the Session House on the Old Bailey and its environs. He remained unsure if Dumont knew of his association with Colonel Charters. He did not know how many people were aware of Charters and his work, though he would wager not many beyond the upper echelons and the back rooms of government. Was it possible that a justice would know? As to the talk of an angel of vengeance, that really was myth making. At Charters' behest, and occasionally on his own initiative, he had come into conflict with evildoers but he was no instrument of justice, at least not in his own mind.

Then there was the wrongdoing at which he had hinted: *chicanery at the highest levels*. Was it in the legal profession? Government? Or was it at Kensington Palace, the King's seat of power? And who was this fellow William who had died? Flynt was not a man for riddles and he detested a mystery but Dumont had presented him with both.

As he entered the busy tavern, he saw Sir Geoffrey's back vanishing through the doorway and into the frosty night air. Flynt recalled his words regarding the men who wished him ill and considered following him, but Dumont had made it clear he intended to keep his rendezvous alone. All the same, Flynt was in two minds about allowing the judge to walk the streets without protection until he became aware of another instrument of justice sitting at a table set apart from the crowd of revellers. Jonathan Wild had his back to the wall, his head encased in a long dark wig, his face lightly powdered, his clothes that of a gentleman, as was the sword he had taken to sporting that lay before him on the table. On his right sat Blueskin Blake, his nickname down to the dark beard that constantly bristled his chin and jaw. Blake was well known to Flynt through dealings the previous year and he suspected there was little love lost there. To Wild's left was the scarred face of Richard Warwick. It was not the presence of these two bully ruffians that disturbed Flynt, however, but the sight of young Jack standing before Wild, apparently in deep conversation. Flynt trusted the boy as much as he trusted anyone, but he prayed that the lad was not allowing his gums to flap unduly. Wild had an intelligence network to rival that of Charters but the less he knew of Flynt's business, the better. He remained conflicted over following the judge's wishes or providing him with security, and had little desire for an encounter with the Thieftaker General of London but he had to interrupt his exchange with Jack. With a final glance at the doorway, he sauntered towards the table through air thick with candle and pipe smoke, weaving between the drinkers, the bawds and the pot-boys. Warwick saw him approach and nudged his master, but Flynt was aware that Wild would have spotted him as soon as he had appeared in the doorway.

'Ah, it's my old friend Jonas Flynt,' Wild said. Despite his attempts at appearing to be a London gentleman, his accent betrayed his Wolverhampton roots. Jack turned, no evidence of shock or guilt on his face, which pleased Flynt for it suggested that whatever the boy and Wild had been discussing, it did not involve him.

'Mr Wild,' Flynt said, believing it always best to be courteous until the time came not to be. He nodded a greeting to the two men flanking him. 'Blueskin. Dick.'

Blake remained impassive as he regarded Flynt but it was clear that Warwick remained hot following their encounter in Golden Square, for his visage was as creased with belligerence as the tight scar tissue allowed. Flynt gave him a wide smile, which seemed to amuse Blake, but only deepened Warwick's scowl.

Wild returned his attention to Jack. 'That'll be all, lad. Off you go now, for I would have a moment with this gentleman. You do know each other, yes?'

'We've met, ain't we, Mr Flynt?'

'We have,' said Flynt, there being no reason to say otherwise. He had no doubt been seen in the boy's company and Jack had the wit to understand that to deny acquaintanceship would only arouse suspicion.

'I've had my eye on young Master Sheppard here for some time. I've been very impressed by him,' Wild said, looking directly at Flynt, his smile very much how a spider might look as it gazed upon the fly trapped in its web.

'Onwards and upwards, eh, Mr Flynt,' Jack said as he moved away, a surreptitious wink forcing Flynt to battle a smile.

'Smart lad,' said Wild after Jack had left them. 'You have utilised his particular talents, I understand.'

Once again, Flynt saw no reason to deny what the man already knew. 'He is a nimble boy and as you say he is bright. He also knows his way around the city.'

'Aye, he is a light-fingered little wretch but I have uses for such as he. If he cleaves to my service then he has a bright future before him.'

'Or a noose,' said Flynt.

Wild smiled. 'His world is in a perpetual twilight cast by the shadow of Tyburn, is it not?'

Flynt acknowledged that with a tilt of the head. 'We are all but a hangman's fart away from the triple tree.'

'Some of us, perhaps.' Wild's smile remained easy and familiar. 'I sent my man for you today and you declined my invitation.'

'I believe we discussed previously the fact that I will not be sent for.'

Blueskin shifted his position. Wild had once despatched him to fetch Flynt but he had been shamed and sent back without his weapons. Blake was not one to forget such a slight, despite the work they had done together in Scotland. It had been an uneasy alliance and this was the first time Flynt had been in the man's company since. By his look and posture, it was clear that friction remained. Flynt knew he had an enemy in Blueskin that was held at bay only by the strong grip Wild held on his subordinates, for they knew that if they did not follow his orders then they could end up enjoying the dubious hospitality of one of the city's many prisons, or dangling in that Tyburn twilight. Warwick's name must also now be added to the list of the thieftaker's acolytes who viewed him with contempt.

As if he knew what Flynt was thinking, Wild cast a sidelong glance towards Warwick on his left, who was staring at Flynt as if he could set him aflame with his thoughts. 'Richard was in Golden Square on official duties.'

'He is not a member of the watch.'

'My men are above the watch.'

'Not officially.'

Wild had to agree with that. 'We perform duties by custom and practice, certainly, but we provide a service to this great city which is appreciated by the high and the mighty. And we had been alerted to the actions of a fellow lurking in a suspicious manner in a residential square. That was you, by the way.'

'I had worked that out, thank you.'

Wild steepled his fingers in front of his chin, his elbows resting on the arms of the chair which Flynt noted had an ornately carved high back and a well-padded seat. It resembled a throne. A cut-price one, but a throne nonetheless. Flynt had frequented the Black Lion many times and had never seen this particular chair, so he presumed the proprietor brought it out only for special patrons, such as Wild.

'May I ask why you were lingering in Golden Square, Flynt?'

'You may ask but I wouldn't expect to be enlightened if I were you,' Flynt said. 'Just as I would not expect you to tell me who alerted you to my presence.'

Wild unlaced his fingers to tip his hands back at the wrist in an open gesture. 'A concerned resident it was.'

'A concerned resident who thought to contact you and not the watch?'

'The good works of my office are known by all classes. Sometimes the old men of the watch are not sufficiently' – he searched for the correct word – '*forceful* enough in dealing with potential miscreants.'

Flynt knew that Wild had been contacted for a particular reason. Whoever was lodged in that apartment wanted him moved on and, not wishing to do so herself, and not trusting the men of the watch to be a match for him, had called on the thieftaker to send his bullies. An ordinary thief would either have gone with them quietly or bolted, but Flynt was no ordinary thief. If the woman in that house was who he suspected, she should have known that, so it was just as likely that she used the thieftaker's men merely as a diversion to allow herself to leave unobserved.

'Do you know the lady?' Flynt asked.

Wild's expression was innocence in the extreme. 'What makes you think it was a lady?'

Flynt laughed. 'Come, Wild, let's put the verbal fencing to one side. There is a lady in a particular house on the square in which I have an interest; what that interest is need not concern you at this juncture. She is the one served by the girl who alerted you. Now, do you know her?'

'I do not. Her maidservant came to my offices in the Little Old Bailey, told me that the notorious villain Jonas Flynt had been seen casing her mistress's crib. Naturally, I acted immediately.'

Flynt watched the man's eyes carefully as he spoke and for once saw no sign of dissemination. It had taken some time for Warwick and his companions to arrive, so he assumed that the servant had been making her way to alert Wild when he had intercepted her but saw no reason to miss the opportunity to turn a coin when he began to interrogate her concerning her employer. A sedan or even a hackney carriage would have completed her journey to the upstairs room of the Blue Boar Tavern where Wild held court. He suppressed a smile as he pulled a vacant chair from the table behind him and sat down. He hadn't been invited to do so but he had no intention of standing on ceremony with the likes of Jonathan Wild. He glanced around as if to ensure that nobody was listening before he leaned forward, placing one elbow on the table, and lowered his voice. Wild also edged forward in order to catch his words.

'As we are being so forthright with one another, I will tell you that I have a crack lay in mind. I believe there are jewels in that house worth a king's ransom and I mean to have them. You, of course, will receive a taste of the proceeds, as befits your office.'

An avaricious look that he could not conceal gleamed in Wild's eye. He knew of Flynt's reputation so would be aware that if he was planning a housebreaking, it would be well worth it.

'When do you plan to pull the job?'

Flynt sat back. 'You know me, it will be when I know the time is right. So I would appreciate it if you gave me the space to operate. Also, it wouldn't do the reputations of you or your thieftakers any good if it was bruited abroad that you knew a thief had been casing the crib and you failed to apprehend him.'

Wild considered this. If there was one thing he valued above money, it was his reputation. As he mulled, he took the conversation in another direction. 'You were in the company of Sir Geoffrey Dumont, both this night and last. You grow uncommon friendly with the judiciary, do you not?'

Did this man miss nothing? Flynt kept his manner loose. 'It never does harm to have a beak on your side.'

'He is not known for his corruptibility, that one.'

'Then he is a rarity among men. But I assisted him last night and tonight's dinner was by way of thanks. A refusal might have offended.'

Wild seemed to accept this. 'As to Golden Square, the lady in question already knows we were sent for.'

'She will not take it further, I assure you.'

'How can you be sure?'

Flynt chuckled. 'You know my reputation. I do not leave anything to chance. Just let me do my work unhindered by the attention of your associates.' At this he cast an eyebrow towards Warwick. 'Dick here is not someone you can easily miss. He arrived in the square today with all the subtlety of a brigade of dragoons.'

Blueskin's laugh barked out loud, confirming that there was no love lost between him and the other man. Warwick glared at him. His mood seemed to have darkened even further during the conversation.

'Fuck subtlety,' he snarled. 'We was there to detain you. We don't need no subtlety to roast a scurvy cracksman.'

'And how did said roasting work out for you?'

Warwick didn't reply but his look spoke volumes as he rose from his chair and reached for his hat and coat. 'I ain't sitting here bandying words with no scumsucking son of a bitch what thinks he is above us all. Sorry, Mr Wild, but that's the way of it.'

Wild casually swept an imperious hand in Warwick's direction. 'You have my leave to go, Richard, and be about our business.'

Warwick acknowledged this with a nod and treated Flynt to a final glare before he walked to the door and left without looking back.

'I fear you have upset Richard, Jonas,' observed Wild, his lips sporting a thin smile, then jerked his head towards Blueskin, who had sat back with his arms folded while Warwick stormed away. 'You do seem to make a habit of irritating my associates.'

'Blueskin and I have reached an understanding, I believe,' said Flynt.

'I wouldn't be banking on that, Flynt,' Blake growled.

Blueskin had little affection for him but if he ever came at him, it would be from the front. With Warwick, on the other hand, he would have to watch his back.

7

Having reached at least a tacit agreement with Wild that he would leave him be for now, but also knowing that it was not worth the paper on which it was not written, Flynt wrapped himself in his greatcoat and hat, pulled on his gloves, adjusted his scarf around his jaw to keep as much of the bitter cold at bay as he could and prepared to step out into the night. He was under no illusions that all he had bought from the thieftaker was time but he was satisfied that for now he could continue his investigations without interference.

Before he left the doorway of the tavern, Flynt took Tact and Diplomacy from the special pockets of his coat and thrust them into his belt, the butts protruding over the front of his thick velvet waistcoat. He then buttoned his greatcoat and moved into the street. As he walked down Drury Lane, he heard a voice calling to him from the shadows of a passageway between two buildings and perceived Jack's slight figure beckoning him to follow. The boy moved almost the complete length of the gap before he stopped near a wooden fence. The ground was strewn with rubble and detritus and Flynt kept an eye out for rats. He had little time for the creatures: they made his skin crawl and there had been a recent glut of them in the city as the cold made them ever more assertive in search of food. However, he saw none, although the gloom was so dense they could be hiding within it, waiting to lunge. He steeled himself for the sound of scrabbling claws.

'Sorry about that inside, Mr Flynt, but that bastard Wild nabbed me as I walked past. I was in there looking for Edgeworth Bess, fancied myself a bit of a tumble.'

Bess was a beautiful girl to be sure, if she cleaned herself up a bit, but her eye for profit and fondness for gin were liable to get her into serious trouble one day. Flynt had often noticed Jack's wandering eyes rest on her plump pleasures. He was a growing boy, after all.

'You have the bunce for her?'

Jack winked. 'A kind and generous fellow gave me a down payment just today.'

He was referring to the money Flynt had given him at Tyburn. 'I would have preferred you spent that money on food or clothing. Even a gift for your old mum.'

'Why pay for something what you can steal, eh, Mr Flynt?'

Flynt couldn't help but smile. Wild had mentioned Jack's light fingers and for once he had to agree. However, he also knew the boy was loyal and had a joy for life that was infectious. 'What did Wild want?'

'He wants to use me on the streets. He knows I know my way around the manor and I hears things. You know that too, Mr Flynt.'

'And are *involved* in things too, remember that.'

Even in the dark, Flynt could see the boy's wide grin. 'He knows that too.'

'So he wants you to turn snitch, is that the way of it?'

The grin died. 'That is the way of it, right enough. It don't sit well with me, Mr Flynt, honest it don't. Wild has got wind of a gang of lumpers down the docks and wants me to sniff around and find out what I can. He also knows about the low toby I've been on, acting as carrier for some natty lads in the Garden, spotting likely marks in the taverns. Says if I do what he says, and peach on the rogues working the Pool, I won't see the inside of no cell in Whittington's College.'

Flynt knew Jack had been luring well-oiled victims out of the drinking dens of Covent Garden and into the arms of a gang of footpads. Wild could easily have him thrown into the care of Newgate Prison, known as Whittington's College thanks to the former lord mayor's bequest to have it rebuilt three centuries before, but had reasoned the lad was better in the streets working for him.

'That's dangerous work, Jack,' said Flynt, concerned for the boy's safety, for the dockside thieves who Wild wished Jack to find out about were not men who looked kindly upon spies and informants.

Jack was customarily matter-of-fact about his predicament. 'It is what it is, Mr Flynt, and ain't no use in me kicking about it. If I don't do what he says, he'll dub me in for the low toby jobs and it's the hangman's jig for me and no mistake. At least if I nose around the docks for these coves what is stealing off the ships then I've got a dog's arsehair chance of keeping my neck the length it is.'

'It will mean Wild has you in his clutches, Jack, and he will never let go.' Flynt realised that he was in a similar predicament, but in his case it was Colonel Charters who held the power of life and death over his head.

Jack seemed downhearted at that, something Flynt thought he would never see. 'Ain't nothing can be done, Mr Flynt. And don't you be having no word with him, neither. This is my mess and I'll find a way out, you just see if I don't. It's all part of the flash life, ain't it, Mr Flynt? Either rough or smooth and no in between.'

Flynt understood. Had this been caused by anything Jack had done for him then the boy would have been happy to have Flynt come to his assistance, but it was not. This was something he had to deal with himself. The boy was becoming a man and Flynt was proud of him for it.

'What of your task for me?'

Jack seemed relieved to talk about something else. 'That cove don't do much. He don't leave his house till midday, then goes to the Shakespear's Head for a snifter and then to a coffee house with a sign of the star outside, a right cunny warren that place, and stays there for the rest of the afternoon. He must be a proper goat, your man, and none too choosy. I've seen some of the nuns what use the back rooms in that place and I wouldn't be surprised if he didn't end up with a proper dose of the flap dragon. I followed him back to his crib and he didn't come out for a while. I was about to leg it, 'cos it was only a matter of time before I was approached by someone – after all, I doesn't exactly fit in society, does I? – when he comes back out and he hops a chair.'

'Did you catch where he was headed?'

'Golden Square is what I heard.'

Damn it, Flynt thought, he must have missed him, but the more he considered it, it was of no consequence now. His focus had to be on the lady in Golden Square. Whatever it was that was going on, he suspected that Fairgreave was a mere pawn. She was the one moving the pieces, of that he was certain.

A soft scuff of a foot drew his attention to the street end of the passageway where he saw dark shapes moving towards them in the gloom. This was no shortcut and no thoroughfare so whoever approached was not about to discuss the weather.

'Go, Jack, and be speedy,' he said with some urgency. The boy needed no further encouragement. He scaled the wooden fence with ease, one foot launching himself from a horizontal spar, both hands gripping the top and hauling himself over as though it was second nature to him. Flynt turned to face the men as they broke into a run towards him, his blade already free from the sheath, one hand pulling back the folds of his coat to ease the reach for his pistols. He did not wish to use them – the streets were lawless but pistol shots would still excite attention, even on such a cold night – but he would if he had to. He did not know how many they were but readied himself for two at least, possibly more.

He balanced himself in a loose crouch, legs apart, one slightly in front of the other, sword held steady. In such a situation deliberation was everything, a second's hesitation would be fatal, so he was fully prepared to wound, maim, even kill whoever it was threatening him.

There were three of them in the end, and had they been able to come at him together he might have fallen victim, but the narrow confines of the passageway prevented such an attack. Two had knives, the one in the lead levelled a cocked pistol, so he was the one who had to be dealt with first. Flynt threw the silver sheath of his sword at him, the movement distracting him for only a brief moment but sufficient for Flynt to leap forward, sweep the pistol muzzle upwards, ignoring the explosion of its discharge into the air, and then thrust his sword deep into the man's belly. Knowing he could waste no further time on him, he threw him back towards the nearest of his companions, slamming them both against the wall. The third man skirted round them and launched himself, the knife in his right hand raised. Flynt ducked under it while simultaneously lunging upwards to send his sword under the man's chin. The man came to a sudden halt, his blade clattering to the ground, blood gushing from the wound, a grating sound emanating from his throat. Flynt slid the sword free, left him to stagger backwards, and turned once again to the other two. The man still holding the empty pistol leaned against the wall, gasping through his pain as he clasped his free hand to his abdomen, but Flynt suspected the wound was not imminently mortal. He kept him in view while focusing on the third man, who had recovered his balance and was now circling towards him slowly, his weapon held blade downwards so he could protect himself and slash both forward and back when needed. His other arm was crooked before him in such a position that he could ward off Flynt's blade if he had to. Here then was someone who knew his business. The fellow might suffer a slash to the arm from Flynt's sword but his thick clothing would offer some protection. When his erstwhile companion with the neck wound finally crumpled to the ground, he merely stepped over the body as if it were a minor impediment. His attention did not waver from Flynt, his movements economical and alert. By his stance Flynt could tell this man was a seasoned street fighter so would make a more worthy adversary than the first two, who were no neophytes but had each made basic errors. To best this one, he would need to exercise some Tact.

He took out that pistol and put a ball into the man's chest, bringing his advance to a sudden halt. The man straightened slightly to stare at the blood bursting forth from the hole in his coat as if wondering how it had got there. Then he looked towards Flynt in disbelief that such a calamity had occurred. Flynt gave him a little shrug, a mute apology for being so unsporting, then watched as the man's legs gave way and he crumpled to the ground.

Dark blood streamed between the fingers of the fellow still propped against the wall. His knees looked ready to buckle but he raised his head slightly when Flynt stepped to his side. There had been two pistol shots and querying voices rose in the street. He didn't have much time. He withdrew his second pistol and placed it against the man's temple.

'Who sent you?'

The man prised his hand away from his wound and showed Flynt the blood. 'I am dying.'

'Perhaps,' said Flynt as he jammed the muzzle of his pistol tighter against his skull. 'But if you do not answer my question then you most certainly will. Now, who sent you?'

The man breathed heavily, his hand back at his wound. 'I need help.'

Flynt sighed and placed the barrel of his spent pistol against the sword wound and dug it in. The man screamed and writhed, tried to escape the agony, but Flynt pressed harder. 'Who...'

Another thrust of the weapon.

'...sent...'

He burrowed the pistol in deeper, causing blood to cascade.

'...you?'

The man howled. 'I don't know and that's the Gawd's honest! Ben there told us you had coin for the taking.' He raised a trembling finger in the direction of the man Flynt had shot. 'That's all he said. That you was a swell with a fat purse.'

Flynt knew the truth when he heard it, at least truth as far as this soul understood it, so withdrew the instrument of torture and allowed the wounded man to slide to the ground with his back to the wall. He was weeping. This may have been nothing more than a low toby lay, a street robbery, but there may also have been something deeper behind it. The little judge was not the only one with enemies and Flynt's mind jumped to Warwick. He could have had time sufficient on leaving the tavern to gather these men, for the streets were awash with coves who would spill blood for coin.

The voices in the street grew closer and the faint glow of torches began to bleed across the mouth of the alley as their bearers sought the source of the gunshots. He placed his weapons back under his coat, found his silver cane on the ground and sheathed the sword. With a final glance at the would-be assassin, still sobbing but his breath growing shallow, he stepped quickly down the passageway towards the street, fighting the bitter bile rising in his throat at what he had done. But that was his way: do what was necessary with speed, regret it at leisure. Those three men would not have hesitated to kill him and probably young Jack too. Even so, he knew what he had done this night would haunt him on other nights to come.

8

Flynt was dreaming of soft skin and softer lips when his landlady gently tapped on his door. Over the years he had developed the skill of sleeping lightly, for in his line of work a sound sleep could be lethal, and he was awake instantly, although the image of the woman in his dreams remained with him. He knew well the beautiful face and thick black hair curling down over her bare shoulders but it had been months since he had gazed upon her. He would never see her again, he feared. Given what had occurred the previous year he *should* never see her again, for he had brought her nothing but pain and heartbreak.

He rose from his bed, pulled on his breeches and wrapped himself in his coat against the fierce cold in his room to open the door on Mrs Wilkes with her hands clasped before her apron in her customary stance. She was a tall woman, severe of face and sharp of tongue but she protected him like a mother wolf did her cub. Her husband owned the Golden Cross, the inn in which Flynt kept his rooms, and two years before he had assisted them with some bully ruffians who had demanded money to protect the premises. Flynt knew the crew in question and explained to them that such extortion brought considerable danger to their health, pointing out that the establishment already had sufficient protection, and emphasising both points with flesh wounds, bruising and one opened face that left an ugly scar. He still saw that particular individual in the streets now and then but the man tended to find a pressing need to cross the road. Following that service Flynt had been allowed to live in these two rooms rent-free, in return for which he sometimes assisted in the tavern below, dealing with rowdy customers.

The inn was close to the private stable where Flynt kept his horse, which he visited regularly even though he knew the retired army colonel who owned the stables ensured the animal had the best of care.

'You have visitors, Jonas,' said Mrs Wilkes, her voice crisp and businesslike as ever but shielding a kind nature. 'A man and a lady.'

The way she said that gave him pause. He saw the sparkle of amusement in her eyes. 'Did they give their names?'

'No, but I know who the lady is. Never thought I'd see her in the Cross, to be sure.'

Flynt was intrigued. Mrs Wilkes seemed impressed and that did not occur often. 'Did they intimate what business they had with me?'

'Only that it was of a personal nature. The lady's tone suggested it was not my place to pursue the matter any further.' Mrs Wilkes's own tone did not betray whether she was offended. 'I've situated them in the small private room below and served them with coffee and eggs while they wait for you to make yourself presentable.'

Although wide awake he still felt the fog of sleep slightly mist his brain. 'What is the clock?'

'It's gone eight. There will also be coffee and scrambled eggs waiting for you when you come down.'

He was certain he detected a trace of a smile as he thanked her and she turned away while he closed the door. Few people knew where he lived, although it would be an easy matter for anyone to trace him should they feel the need, but even fewer felt themselves welcome enough to call upon him. As he washed, brushed his teeth with ground cuttlefish bone and salt mixed with orange flower water, then dressed in his white shirt, black waistcoat, black breeches and black coat, he wondered who it would be. Not Colonel Charters, for though he was a notorious rake he was not likely to attend him with one of his conquests in tow. He pondered the mystery as he stamped his feet into his boots and headed downstairs.

The private room was situated at the end of a long corridor leading from the tavern's bar to the rear entrance and it was used for similar functions as those in the Black Lion and the Shakespear's Head. The

Charing Cross area was replete with places of entertainment and diversion and so Mr and Mrs Wilkes made this room available for activities between gentlemen who enjoyed a wager or those who found amusement in pleasures of a more sensual and private nature. Voices drifted into the corridor from the bar, for this was a coaching inn and catered to customers throughout the day and night. He was able to avoid the large tavern room by turning right at the bottom of the stairs to reach the private chamber.

He had not expected to see Belle St Clair sitting at a table sipping coffee accompanied by the hulking figure of Jerome Laverick. Belle was dressed in finery which only heightened her striking beauty. Mrs Wilkes had laid out her best porcelain, he saw. She may have known Belle by reputation, as she said, but that didn't mean she would not treat her as a lady. Even in the world of sexual commerce, in which the Wilkeses played their part, there was a pecking order and Belle was at the very top.

He hid his initial surprise well, he thought. He nodded a greeting to Jerome, who said in his heavy Yorkshire accent, 'It be good to see thee, Mr Flynt. It's been some time.'

Flynt felt guilt stab at him but he didn't know why. 'I have been otherwise engaged, Jerome, but it is good to see you too. I hope you and your aunt are well?'

Jerome had been employed by his aunt as house bully to protect the women, a task he performed with some skill, for he was a big strapping lad made strong by the fresh air and wide skies of Yorkshire. When his mother passed away, Mother Grady had agreed to take him in, and as soon as she set eyes upon his powerful frame knew he would prove a match for her drunken, and occasionally lovestruck, clients. Annabelle St Clair was one of the girls he protected and Jerome was extremely fond of her. Flynt could not blame him, for she was the type of woman that could steal a heart with a glance. She had arrived as a child on board ship from the Indies, where she had been purchased and shipped back to London with others to be inducted into the mysteries of the seraglio. She learned her lessons well and was now Mother Grady's prize attraction.

'Belle, it's good to see you.'

Belle, as was her way, got straight to the point. 'I need your help, Jonas.'

Her voice still carried a pleasant Caribbean lilt, but this day it was tinged with urgency. He shot a glance at Jerome but saw nothing in that broad, open face that betrayed what was amiss. He pulled a chair out from the table and sat down.

'Has something happened?' he said, genuinely concerned. 'Is all well with you?'

Belle took a breath. 'I am well; Mother Grady is well.'

Flynt cared little for Mother Grady's health but did not give voice to his thoughts.

'It is on a friend's behalf that I am here,' Belle continued. 'I apologise for disturbing you so early.'

He waved that away, for he should have arisen long before this. He had an appointment with Charters at eleven of the clock and the colonel was not one to tolerate tardiness. 'Tell me,' he said.

'There is a young friend of mine, by name of Sam Yates.'

A young friend and a man, Flynt thought, a customer perhaps? But Belle seemed to read his thoughts.

'He is… not a young man who likes women, if you understand. And he pursues my own profession, working out of Mother Clap's house in Field Lane.'

Flynt understood. This Sam Yates was a male prostitute, a molly, and Mother Clap's off Holborn was a renowned private residence, coffee house and bawdy house for men who preferred the company of their own gender. 'And he finds himself in trouble?'

She paused, but looked deep into his eyes. 'He has been accused of murder, Jonas. The thieftaker's men caught him in the grounds of St Paul's, standing over the body with the victim's blood still fresh on his hands.'

The environs of the cathedral was a notorious meeting place for men such as Belle's friend so it sounded to Flynt that perhaps an assignation had been arranged and gone awry, or that the wrong person had been approached and it had turned violent. 'Who was the victim?'

'A judge called Sir Geoffrey Dumont.'

Shock numbed Flynt for a few moments and he could not find any words. Belle saw this momentary inability and her eyebrows raised in an unexpressed query.

'I knew Sir Geoffrey Dumont,' Flynt explained, his voice barely a croak. He did not fully understand why he felt such distress, for he barely knew the man.

Belle displayed some surprise. 'You knew Dumont? And how did you become acquainted with a beak?'

'It's a long story.'

Belle considered that for a moment then accepted it with no further questions. For now. 'And did you know of his inclinations?'

A shake of the head. 'He was married, had children, though none survived.'

Belle's smile was grim. 'That means nothing. Married men have tastes of which their wives know nothing. It is the likes of Sam and I, those of us who lie beyond the matrimonial bed and the pious vows of devotion, who understand and cater for these secret vices. And often pay dearly for them. I have known men such as your Judge Dumont. They hide their true selves with skill.'

Flynt did not reply. He cared not how people found their sexual release, as long as they did not prey on children or animals. They could go with women or men, or multiples of both, as far as he was concerned. He was startled by this revelation regarding Sir Geoffrey's murder. Flynt had lived a life surrounded by such bloody acts but this one had his fingers tingling.

Belle leaned forward over the table. 'Jonas, I'm here because I don't believe Sam would do such a thing. He is a sweet, gentle soul. From what little I know it would appear this was an act of considerable violence and he does not have it in him to mete out any form of brutality.'

'We all have violence in us that can rise to the surface when the proper stimulus is applied.'

And some have more violence within than most, he thought, his mind flashing to the three men in the passageway the night before.

Belle's shake of the head was emphatic. 'Not Sam, you can take my oath on that, Jonas. I have learned to judge character well. You know that all who work in Mother Grady's must develop this skill, and I can tell you that Sam Yates did not kill your judge. Somebody else did this deed and poor Sam is made scapegoat.'

Flynt was finally over his initial surprise but still took a moment to consider what she was telling him, the judge's words returning to him.

Promise me this, my friend, should anything befall me, if I be suddenly disgraced, for instance, that you will not believe whatever official explanation is forthcoming.

This was not disgrace. This was murder. Was it possible that those at the highest level intimated by the judge to be involved in something nefarious had bypassed attacking his reputation and arranged to attack his person?

'What would you have me do, Belle?'

'I know Sam and I know you too, Jonas Flynt. I know what kind of man you are. I know the flesh of you and I know the taste of you, but most of all I know the make of you. You are a man who can navigate the twilight world of this city. You are cognisant of the alleyways and dives and taverns and docks. You know the thieves, the rogues, the fly men, the flash men, the upright men and the gentlemen. You are of them and yet you are a man apart, for you have a sense of honour and justice that they do not possess. You can ask questions where a woman of my profession cannot, even if accompanied by the good Jerome here. But most of all, you will believe me when I tell you that Sam Yates is innocent of this but he will surely hang if we do not come to his assistance. That is what I would have you do, Jonas Flynt, come to his assistance, to my assistance, and in return for your labours I will pay you a fair price.'

He began to dismiss any suggestion of accepting money from her, but she silenced him with a raised hand and a look that would brook no objection.

'But know this, Jonas Flynt, if you tell me you cannot do this for me, then I believe you know me almost as well as I know you and you know that I will do it on my own.'

–

The streets already teemed with carriages and chairmen and hawkers going this way and that at the confluence of Charing Cross when Flynt ventured forth. The sky was a dazzling blue and the air was again cold enough to freeze whale oil. At least that's the way it felt to Flynt even though he was snug under his various layers. Belle and Jerome had left him to his breakfast and his thoughts. Flynt understood that she knew him well and he her. But there were many things here that he did not know. He did not know the truth of what had occurred the previous night at St Paul's. He did not know if Sir Geoffrey was the type of man who would arrange an illicit assignation with another man. He did not know this Sam Yates and what manner of fellow he was. He did know one thing, though, and that was that Belle meant what she said. If he did not assist her, she would investigate the matter herself. Given the fondness he had for her, a fondness that extended beyond the carnal, he could not in all conscience allow her to do that.

The distinctive figure of Blueskin Blake lingered by the statue of the first King Charles heroically astride a fine horse opposite the coaching inn. It was plain that he was there for the express purpose of communicating with him, for the man made no attempt to mask his presence. Indeed he stared directly at him, so Flynt weaved between the traffic, stepping over the fresh residue of the passing horses steaming in the cold, to stand before him in the old king's shadow.

'Don't tell me I am summoned again to see Mr Wild. I thought we had an agreement.'

'Mr Wild don't know I'm here.' As he spoke, Blueskin's mouth twisted slightly and he looked somewhat uncomfortable. He was many things – a rogue, a violent man, often a liar – but he seemed to show Wild an unaccountable loyalty and for that Flynt afforded him grudging respect. It suggested that the man still possessed some semblance of honour, misplaced though it was.

'Then why are you here?'

Blueskin hawked up some phlegm and sent it flying towards the base of the statue. 'We don't like each other, Flynt,' he said.

'You wound me, Blueskin, for I thought us brothers.' In truth he was at best indifferent to the man, though he did take an inordinate amount of pleasure in making sport of his ilk.

Blueskin studied the words for a moment as if he thought they might not be sarcastic, decided that indeed they were and took his hat off to rub his fingers across his scalp. 'I think there's something rum about you, Flynt. I can't quite put my finger on the why of it, but I know there's something decided rum. And it ain't just because you is a rogue, even with your fancy manner and the disdain you show for honest rogues like me. There's something more, something...'

When the man broke off to search for the right word, Flynt suggested with an arched brow, 'Rum?'

Blueskin breathed heavily through gritted teeth, his breath frosting like smoke from the fire in a dragon's belly. Flynt regretted his jest for the fact of it was that he could find nothing erroneous in Blake's summation. He knew himself a rogue and there was indeed something rum about him, thanks to the work he performed, but he had limited time to converse.

'As much as I would enjoy bandying words with you, Blueskin, I have an appointment most urgent, so perhaps we could—'

Blueskin interrupted him. 'One day you and I will have a strong disagreement and it will lead to blood, of that there is no doubt.'

'I hold you no particular ill will, Blueskin.' That much was true, but Flynt could not help but agree with him. One day they would go head-to-head. There were some events in life that were unavoidable.

'Yeah, I'll be bound. But you has nettled Richard Warwick and he ain't the cove to be so abused.'

The memory of men left dead or dying in the alleyway the night before rose in Flynt's mind but he felt it politic to profess ignorance. 'Dick? What does he have to be angry about?'

'He is in a high passion because of the way you shamed him yesterday in front of his crew. He is very proud, is Richard. And he don't like to be called Dick.'

'A Dick he is to me and a Dick he will remain.'

Blueskin almost smiled. 'Then you will continue to nettle him and one day he will have his satisfaction, so that is why I am here, to warn you.'

Knowing that the man may already have attempted such, but having no desire to allow Blueskin satisfaction by exhibiting any concern, Flynt took an exaggerated step backwards. 'Why, Joseph Blake, you do care, despite your admonition!'

Blake once again examined Flynt's words and tone briefly to ensure that they remained sarcastic. He seemed relieved that they were. 'Take my advice, Flynt, you stay away from him. He is not an easy man to like and he is not a good man to cross. And he has took you into a fierce disfavour.'

'As you say, you and I are far from bosom friends, so why are you so concerned?'

Blueskin chose his next words carefully. 'Because as I said, sooner or later you and me will have a brush with one another, you can bank on that, and I wants to be the cove what spills your blood. I will not give the likes of Richard Warwick that honour. It is mine and mine alone.'

There was more to it than that, Flynt was certain. He had sensed there was animosity between Blueskin and Warwick the night before. He suspected that Warwick had begun to replace him in Wild's trust and Blueskin had taken that badly.

'That is fair warning then, Blueskin,' said Flynt. 'But please, allow me to ask you this: do you know of the murder up by St Paul's last night?'

Blueskin seemed to puff himself up. 'I am a thieftaker's man, of course I knows of it.'

'Were you present at the detention of the suspect?'

'No.' He smiled. 'As it happens, it was Richard Warwick's crew what lifted that molly. But from what I hears, that creature Yates ain't no suspect, he has been caught red-hand, and you can take that literal for the blood was still wet and the blade lay at his feet. He's for the dangle, that's for damn sure.'

Warwick again. First in Golden Square, then with Wild in the tavern, and now it was his men who had been on hand to take Sam Yates into custody following Dumont's death. Then, of course, there was the question as to whether he had sent the three men the night before. All the augurs did point to them crossing paths, and swords, in the future.

'He was friend to you, this judge, am I right?'

'A recent acquaintance, nothing more,' Flynt said, it being the truth but not the whole truth.

'Did you know he liked to navigate the windward passage?'

Flynt kept his irritation from showing. 'I'm not sure he was.'

Blueskin sneered. 'All evidence to the contrary, I'd say. Else why was he up St Paul's that time of night and meeting with a Mother Clap molly?' He paused to study Flynt afresh. 'You want some more advice, free gratis an' all? Don't be sticking your nose in this. It's as plain a case for the Tyburn Tree as ever I heard. Your friend the judge fancied a bit of backgammon and he arranges to meet this molly up there but it all goes horrible wrong when the boy tries to rob him. He fights back and the boy kills him. Good riddance is what I say. Never did like mollies, makes me want to flash the hash when I think what they does to each other.'

The image of Blueskin puking was not something Flynt wished to dwell upon. 'Each to his own, Blueskin, each to his own.'

'Well, as long as they keeps themselves to their own then that's fine by me. But if one ever tried to touch my Thomas I'd lace him up good and proper.'

Flynt played what he had told him over in his mind. Why would Dumont be at a known meeting place for such men? And if he was that way inclined, why meet Sam Yates there, when he could easily visit Mother Clap's and use one of her rooms? Belle was convinced that her friend was innocent but Flynt did not know him, although they had agreed to visit him in Newgate Prison later that afternoon.

Blueskin decided he had said all he had come to say, so he placed his hat back upon his head. 'Mark what I says, Flynt. Keep your eye on Warwick. He's a bad bastard.' He dropped his voice conspiratorially. 'I'm a rogue and I have killed; that is something you and I share, but Warwick? He takes pleasure in it. It's in his blood. His father was a murderer and his brother too, and both ended up as gallow blossom. He's a bad 'un, Flynt, and there ain't no mistake about that.'

'Aren't we all?'

Blueskin didn't argue that point. He gave Flynt a curt nod and began to walk away.

'Blueskin,' Flynt called after him and the man stopped to turn again. Flynt gave it a moment's pause before he said, with sincerity, 'Thank you. You had no need to warn me of this.'

Blueskin seemed on the verge of saying something further but then thought better of it. Flynt knew that the man wished to retain any future revenge for past slights for himself but he still decided that one good turn deserved another. He glanced up at the effigy of King Charles towering above them. 'Do you know your Scripture? In particular Psalms?' By Blueskin's puzzled frown he did not, so Flynt pressed on. 'There is an admonishment in Psalm 146 that urges men to put not their trust in princes. People trusted this man and went to their death and for what? The right of a man to rule through divine will. They died for it and he died for it and, indeed, many of the men who took his life, who had their trust in another prince called Cromwell, albeit of more common stock, had theirs taken on this very spot.'

'So what point do you make, Flynt, for I has business elsewhere?'

'Just this: Jonathan Wild sees himself as a prince and I would urge you not to put your faith in him. I sense you have loyalty to him but it is misplaced, for men like him have loyalty to themselves only. When it is advantageous to him or his pocket, he will betray you and, if luck is with you, it will be jail or a ship for the colonies or there,' Flynt gestured towards the pillory standing near to the statue. It was empty that morning but many a lawbreaker was regularly abused by the populace for minor and even some major offences. 'If luck is not with you, then you will find the road to Tyburn is not so long after all.'

Blueskin's sneer dismissed the idea. 'It will never happen. Mr Wild knows I am loyal to him and he trusts me.'

'It will happen, my friend. He will sacrifice anyone if it fills his purse or protects his own skin. Heed my advice; do not trust him.'

Blueskin shook his head as he stepped closer once more to stare directly into Flynt's face, his eyes hard, his teeth clenched. 'Here's more advice for you then. Never say a bad word about Mr Wild to me again or in my hearing, understand? He's given me work and a purpose. More than that, he's my friend.' He paused to let his words hang between them. 'Don't mistake what we has here between you and me as being between friends or even equals, 'cos we ain't neither. I knows what I am and I know what you is. You, Jonas Flynt, ain't nothing more than a sharper and a rogue and even if I doesn't spill your claret my own self I knows that the hemp is growing for you and I'll raise me a tankard of ale while I watches you dance the Tyburn jig.'

9

The ice on the river rose and fell as though the waves themselves had reared in surprise when the temperature dropped. Dogs raced across the surface and dodged between legs, making some already unsteady gaits even more perilous. Young boys slid upon the glaze, creating shiny patches that became additional hazards to perambulation. Boatmen who had found themselves put out of work by the phenomenon had become guides to the now solid thoroughfare, taking people to see the various attractions of the Frost Fair that had sprung up in the shadow of London Bridge, its nineteen parapets and various piers. One enterprising individual had turned his vessel into a sledge, which was dragged across the ice by a team of young boys. A carriage had deserted the streets to convey passengers on this new roadway. Frost rose from the surface like mist but, intemperate though the weather was, smallholders and vendors had seized the opportunity to turn a profit, so the cold air was sweetened by the aroma of roasting mutton and the tang of gingerbread as Flynt and Charters walked.

Flynt had asked what he knew of the death of Sir Geoffrey Dumont but the colonel had remained silent for a full minute while he stopped and listened to a recitation by the poet Mr William Ellis with the help of his wife, Bess. He had to compete not only with music from a trio of players in a stall behind them but also a tent that housed a makeshift tavern where a huddle of gentlemen had apparently been made deaf by the ale and gin they swilled and felt it necessary to converse in shouts. With Flynt's query still unanswered, the colonel seemed to tire of listening to poetry and moved towards another tent housing a printing press, where visitors to the fair could have printed a commemorative ticket of the event with their name upon it. They stepped over a small boy who had fallen headlong onto the ice but was laughing along with his friends.

'Stay away from that incident, Flynt,' Colonel Charters said finally. 'Let justice be done.'

'And what if justice is not done and an innocent man dies on the gallows?'

He saw Charters' jaw clenching and unclenching. 'You have other matters in hand and cannot waste time on some accursed crusade.'

'Sir Geoffrey was a good man.'

'Good men die every day. In any case, he was in the vicinity of St Paul's in the dead of night not for the benefit of his spirit but of his flesh.'

'I cannot believe that.'

'The lad who stands accused has stated that the judge invited him to meet him there,' Charters pointed out.

New friend though he was, Flynt recognised that he did not know the judge well enough to state without a shadow of a doubt that he was not attracted to his own sex. Still, that was no reason for murder.

'Keep your nose out of this matter, Flynt,' Charters ordered, his voice harsh.

'Colonel, I do your bidding in relation to the tasks you set me because you hold a capital crime over my head, bogus though it is. But in all other things I am my own man.'

Charters halted outside the tent bearing the sign of a rat in a cage, where mutton roasted on a string. He was about to answer when his eye was drawn away and Flynt glanced over his shoulder to see a group of well-dressed gentlemen making progress through the fair, pausing at the circle around a game of ninepins being played on the ice. They laughed as one of the players seemed to miss his throw before continuing their progress towards them. At the group's head he recognised the rotund figure of the Prince of Wales and the handsome face of John Churchill, the Duke of Marlborough, who gave Charters an unspoken greeting as they passed, barely noting Flynt at his side. 'Corporal John' the men in the ranks had called him, and many revered him but Flynt revered no man. In that spirit, when the fat prince passed he did not doff his hat and bow as Charters had, resulting in stiff glares from the royal entourage, even though George himself had not even noticed, being too busy chattering with Marlborough. One of the courtiers paused ever so slightly as he passed and gave Charters a hard look, his eyes flicking over and dismissing Flynt before he moved on. Flynt studied the silver walking stick with which he tapped at the ice as he walked. He had seen that wolf's-head handle before and knew the bearer to be the new Lord Moncrieff. By his demeanour and the confident way with which he tackled the treacherous surface – as if it would not dare cause him to lose his footing – he was most certainly chipped from the original block that had been Moncrieff the elder, whom Flynt had encountered in Edinburgh the year before.

Charters' voice snatched him from his thoughts. 'Damn it, man, would it have hurt you to show respect?'

The words were coated with amusement and he knew Charters was having sport with him. To an extent at least. His old commander was aware of his feelings regarding royalty and those who set themselves above their fellow men, but he would have preferred that Flynt at least occasionally played the obsequious game.

'Respect is earned,' Flynt replied, 'not something rewarded because you were born on the right side of a blanket.'

'He's the future king.'

'Yours, perhaps.'

'Yours too, whether you like it or not, and your open contempt does nothing but attract attention, of which our work desires very little. And, may I say, you are damnable bold for the son of an Edinburgh tavern keeper.'

Flynt allowed his eyes to linger again on the figure of Lord Moncrieff. He had never told Charters what he had discovered on his return to his homeland the year before, that he was not the son of a tavern keeper but of the late but unlamented Lord Moncrieff, the result of an outrage committed upon his mother. 'It will be a cold day in hell when I bend a knee to lord or liege, prince or politician, you know that.'

Charters waved his hand around him. 'Is this not such a day?'

'You think London hell?'

Charters' amusement seemed to solidify like the ice beneath their feet as he glanced towards the departing prince and his retinue. 'Sometimes, yes.'

With a noise emanating from his throat that was part cough but mostly growl, Charters swept beyond Flynt towards a goldsmith's where he paused to examine the goods on offer. Flynt felt that something about seeing the royal party, or perhaps the look that had passed between Charters and Moncrieff, had pierced the colonel's customary casual manner. Nothing further was said between them until Charters had completed his study and purchase of a golden locket. A gift, perhaps, for one of his lady friends.

'There was further death in town last night,' Charters said as they set off once more across the treacherous surface.

'There is much death these nights. People are hungry and they starve, for they cannot heat their homes sufficient.'

'Violent death, as you well know, is what I meant. Three men off Drury Lane. Two by sword strike, one with a pistol ball in the chest.'

So the third man had died after all. Despite the fact that the men had meant him harm, Flynt felt sadness at the news. He had taken those lives easily but not lightly. There was seldom any pleasure in the act, just the occasional necessity.

'London is a violent city,' he said.

'Hmm,' Charters said, the amused sparkle now returned to his eyes. 'You were in the Black Lion, I believe.'

Charters had informants in every corner of London, and even beyond. That was how he gathered the intelligence with which he performed his duties. That was how he survived political intrigue, for Flynt suspected he had scurrilous information on all who were either in government or who had ambitions to be. Knowledge was power and Charters used it as armour and sword, depending on his aims. For that reason, Flynt saw no reason to lie.

'I met with Sir Geoffrey for dinner, then exchanged a few words with Jonathan Wild on the matter on which I am retained by your good self.'

Charters grew more interested at the mention of the thieftaker's name. 'What business has that damnable rogue Wild with your mission?'

Flynt told him about the attempt to detain him in Golden Square and then of his conversation in the tavern. He had just ended his brief summation when a button seller walked by calling his wares and Charters stopped him to idly examine the variety of stock. While he waited, Flynt considered the attack the night before, his mind straying to Moncrieff. He had been targeted, and it could simply have been for a fat purse as the dying thief had stated. It was also possible it was Warwick's doing, but alternatively it could have its roots in Flynt's own past, either distant or more recent.

Spying nothing that took his fancy, Charters politely thanked the man and walked on before he asked, 'Think you that Wild is in league with Fairgreave and this mysterious lady in Golden Square?'

Flynt shook his head, filing thought of who had perhaps sent Ben and his crew for later scrutiny. 'No, I fancy his involvement was diversion only. The lady managed to leave while I dealt with his men but I was unable to identify her.'

'You think she is the key to this?'

'If she is who I think she is, then most definitely.'

Charters came to a halt and turned to face him. 'You believe you know the identity of this mysterious wench?'

'A suspicion only. I intend to confirm it this evening.'

'Will you share this suspicion?'

Flynt grinned, knowing how Charters would react. 'I think our mutual friend Madame Christian de Fontaine is back in London.'

'Hell and damnation!' The colonel's words were hot enough to melt the ice. 'The way that woman comes and goes unnoticed between France and these islands makes a mockery of our intelligence services. You would think a closer watch would be kept upon her.'

'Are you – *we* – not part of those intelligence services?'

Charters dismissed that easily. 'I have no remit to operate beyond these shores, you know that, but now that we know she is here...'

'We do not know that for certain.'

'Then find out for certain, man, for if she is then you can be damned sure there is mischief afoot...'

–

After he and Flynt parted, Charters returned to the carriage which awaited him at the Old Swan Stairs near to the bridge, fully intending to have it convey him to the home of a lady of his acquaintance for some much-needed warmth and comfort, and to allow him to present her with the locket he had purchased. Upon seeing Lord Moncrieff waiting for him he felt this ardour wilt. Charters could not stand the man but knew he could not avoid him. It was at times like this that he wished he possessed Flynt's boldness, but he must play the political game and he was as skilled at that as the intrepid serjeant was at turning a card or taking a life. As Moncrieff moved forward to meet him, Charters motioned for his men to climb aboard. What was to be said here was not for their ears.

Moncrieff leaned with both hands on his silver walking stick as he waited until the men were well out of earshot. Charters thought the wolf's head too ornate, but such men did so relish showing off their wealth.

'We have business, Lord Moncrieff?'

'I bring congratulations and gratitude.'

'From whom?'

'Sir Robert Walpole. He had confidence that you would deal with his... *issue* regarding the Justice, Sir Geoffrey Dumont, but did not expect you to do so with quite so much alacrity. I confess, we meant only for you to give the fellow a stern warning, not to bring his meddling to an end with such finality.'

Charters blinked. 'I had nothing to do with that tragedy.'

Moncrieff's smile was sceptical. 'Of course not, my dear Colonel, it is mere coincidence that on the very day the issue was brought to your attention Sir Geoffrey met his maker. Still, it was smart work, and the use of a sexual deviant was inspired.'

Charters hid his growing anger at the disparaging way Moncrieff spoke. 'As I said, Lord Moncrieff, I had no hand in the events of last night.'

Moncrieff even winked. 'Of course not, dear fellow. However, be assured that Sir Robert is most grateful and such patronage is a valuable thing to have tucked away.'

Moncrieff would know all about that, Charters thought, but did not insist on his innocence any further lest it be construed that he doth protest too much. He could not help himself from throwing something fresh into the conversation. 'The matter is far from over, though.'

'How so? The deviant will be tried, hanged and that will be the end of it.'

'One of my men has taken it upon himself to investigate further. He suspects that the young man may stand falsely accused of the crime.'

'One of your Company?'

'Yes.'

'Then order him to stop. Good God, man, do you not have control over your own people?'

'He is not an easy man to stop. That is why he has proved so useful in my work for the Crown.'

Moncrieff's smile was replaced by a scowl. 'Who is this fellow that makes so bold in matters that are not his in which to interfere?'

Charters was enjoying the man's irritation. He did not want Flynt to involve himself in any investigation, but if even the mere mention of it discommoded this pompous pup then it had achieved something satisfactory. 'Ah, my lord, as you know I never identify any of my people, for it is best that their names, as well as the work they do for this great nation of ours, remain hidden.'

Moncrieff breathed heavily through his nose and rattled the tip of his walking stick on the ground. 'Sir Robert will be unhappy to hear of this. He was delighted with the swift way the matter was resolved but any further probing into this affair would be unwelcome. It is best that the law be allowed to run its course without it being complicated in any way.'

'And are there complications to be uncovered?'

Moncrieff's gaze was steady. 'There are always complications, my dear Charters. I am sure you above all know that, particularly in this case, eh? My advice is to use every means at your disposal to halt this man's investigation.'

Charters recognised the accusation draped heavily over Moncrieff's words. 'I will endeavour to do so, for I have other work for him, but he is a most stubborn and wilful man.'

'It would be in your interests, and that of your Company in general, that you find a way.' Moncrieff paused slightly before continuing. 'After all, I feel sure that this man is not indispensable. He is a mere scoundrel, after all, otherwise he would not be in your employ. If he will not heed the instructions of his betters then perhaps he should be dealt with in a more permanent fashion.'

Charters resented the suggestion that he have one of his own men killed, especially from a man like Moncrieff, whose own father's loyalty to the Crown had been decidedly opaque. 'I have uses for this man and I will not lose him unless it is absolutely necessary. I will deal with him.'

'See that you do, Charters, see that you do. Bear in mind that we have other options open to us, other agencies that we could utilise should you find yourself unable to carry out my orders.'

It was on the tip of Charters' tongue to point out that his orders meant nothing to him, for he reported directly only to those at the top of the government. However, he reminded himself that Sir Robert Walpole was very close to the tip of that government, and Moncrieff was very close to him.

'While we are on the subject of thieves and vagabonds, I would ask you a question,' Moncrieff said.

'If I can be of service.' Charters hoped his tone did not betray his growing irritation.

'Would you know of a particular gallows bait rogue by the name of Flynt, Jonas Flynt?'

Charters quickly scrutinised the man in search of any indication that he was testing him in some way, but either he was not or he was a damn fine card player and used to hiding his expression. His quandary was that he was trapped between his impulse to deny knowledge of his former serjeant and the fact that some people knew of their shared past. A lie here was not advisable, he decided. 'I do, my lord. He was the infantryman who rescued me from the field at Malplaquet.' He jerked his empty sleeve. 'Saved my life, if not my arm.'

Charters had judged correctly, for he could discern by Moncrieff's reaction that he had already heard this. 'I seek him.'

'May I ask why?'

It was Moncrieff's turn to pause before answering. Charters realised that they were each playing a game here, both hiding their hand and letting the other see only what they needed to. 'I believe he murdered my father, may God rest his soul.'

From what Charters knew of the man, it was unlikely that God would allow his soul to rest. However, the suggestion Flynt was responsible for his death was a surprise. 'Murdered, you say? It was my understanding that your father died on the field of battle, at Sheriffmuir.'

'Aye, 'tis true that he was there but he was not a combatant. My father was on that accursed moor in a bid to dissuade the Earl of Mar from engaging with the forces of the true king. When he was unsuccessful in his task he sought to leave, and I believe encountered this man Flynt who took his life in a most brutal fashion.'

'Why? Was it in the furtherance of theft?'

'There was property taken but that was not the only reason for this vile deed, for it was a personal matter, and this detestable creature set out that day with murder in mind. He is a damned rogue and a killer and I will have my justice.'

Charters sensed in the heat of the man's words that said justice would not trouble the Session House court. 'The King's justice or God's?'

Moncrieff's gaze was cold. 'The King's justice *is* God's justice. I would have thought you would know that, given your occupation and the recent service you have performed for Sir Robert and the government.'

Charters allowed that to go unremarked upon, but he found this information most interesting. Flynt had told him that the old Lord Moncrieff had been killed in the furtherance of a mission and that it could not have been avoided. Charters had not cared to investigate further because he knew the dead man was either a profiteer or a traitor and he could not decide which was the worse. Flynt, though, had not mentioned a possible personal connection to him.

'So I ask you this, sir, do you know where he is? I have had men make inquiries in the gambling hells and drinking dens of Covent Garden but he has so far avoided them.'

Moncrieff waited while Charters' mind worked at speed. He had been unable to deny knowledge of Flynt because of their past, while the fact that they had been seen together meant that he could not lie about his continued association. Moncrieff may already know anyway, and this was an elaborate ruse to test his loyalty.

'You saw him only this day,' Charters said, silently cursing for allowing himself to be caught in this fashion. Flynt himself had often urged more circumspection in their dealings but Charters in his arrogance had dismissed them, believing that nobody would question an old commander spending time with a former subordinate who had saved his life. 'He was standing at my side as his Royal Highness the Prince and his party passed.'

He waited as Moncrieff cast his mind back to visualise the moment. 'So you have regular society with this wretch?'

'Not regular but we do occasionally run into each other, as we did this very day.'

'So you know not where he lodges?'

'It is my impression that he does not stay in one place terribly long,' he lied. 'He is a restless soul.'

Moncrieff kept his gaze level and piercing. 'And he is not one of your Company?'

'He is not,' said Charters, returning Moncrieff's gaze with equal firmness. *Damn it, Flynt, you can be a liability sometimes.*

10

They were used to the stench of the city streets but the noxious atmo-sphere in Newgate was almost overpowering. Belle placed a perfumed handkerchief to her mouth and nose while Flynt pressed the back of his hand to the lower part of his face to blot out the mix of aromas that assailed their nostrils. Body odour, sweat, the stink of the open cesspit, foul feet and even fouler breath mingled with the reek of cheap tobacco and even cheaper candles to stalk the corridors and halls along with the turnkey, who seemed not to notice it. Perhaps his years within one of the city's most notorious prisons had inured him. His rake-thin frame was wrapped in a thick coat and scarf, his arms seemed too long for his body, and his curious loose-limbed gait was part walk and part lope, so he widened the gap between them without even trying. He was a good few feet away, a lantern held high to light the way, for even though it was broad daylight outside, inside it was perpetual night.

Ahead of them was another turnkey, similarly clothed, escorting a well-dressed man and his lady, each with scented fabrics clasped to their faces as they stepped carefully over the grime. Their guide pointed in the glow of his lantern to various prisoners, while shoving away those who approached to beg. Gentlefolk on a paid tour of the horrors of Newgate, Flynt surmised, come to gawp at those more unfortunate than themselves, perhaps even to gaze upon one or two destined to travel the Tyburn trail. There would be little more thrilling to them than looking down upon a man, woman or child who knew the precise day and date of their death and to congratulate themselves on a comfortable, safe life that they themselves had not worked to attain.

Sam Yates had been imprisoned in the lowest ward on the common side of the prison, which housed those inmates who could not afford to pay the bribes sufficient to obtain accommodation in the slightly more luxurious master's side or a more superior ward above. Here some of the prisoners awaiting trial, transfer or transportation appeared well-fed and were clad in reasonably warm clothing to guard against the bitter chill that seemed heightened between these walls, but others, those who could not afford to purchase even the smallest luxury, lay in their filthy rags, their beards growing long and unkempt, their bodies strangers to soap or water. In the dim light afforded by the lantern held by the jailer, lice could be seen crawling on flesh and burrowing into matted hair while, much to Flynt's revulsion, rats scratched at the filthy straw on the floor in search of food. As the glow passed an emaciated individual suddenly snatched at one creature that had strayed too close but it darted away and the man sank back into the gloom, the prospect of meat lost to him. Some wretches clustered around Belle and Flynt, threadbare blankets wrapped around them that were obviously insufficient to ward off the cold, begging for pennies with which they could buy some basic amenity. Others were too weak or apathetic to even walk so merely raised a limp hand in supplication. Belle's eyes filled with tears as she handed out a few shillings, but finally Flynt had to take her arm and steer her while pushing the growing number of pleading souls from them. The turnkey did not come to their aid but instead watched and grinned, for he had already received his bribe – his garnish, as he called it – to allow them access.

'I told you this was not a good idea,' Flynt breathed into Belle's ear as they pulled themselves clear. 'I should have come alone.'

She shook her head in defiance as she addressed the turnkey. 'Why is Mr Yates being held here? He should be on the master's side as he awaits trial.'

'Don't know nothing about that,' said the turnkey over his shoulder. 'Put him here, Josiah Sprigwood, they says, so that's what I does and asks no questions, I don't.'

He came to a halt just behind the touring party, who were being shown one particular inmate who sat in the corner shadows, his back against the wall.

'So that's the wretch who took Sir Geoffrey from us, is it?' the man said, his words slightly muffled behind his kerchief.

'A neck ripe for the hanging,' said the woman.

'That's your man, over there,' Sprigwood said, then barked out a little laugh. '*Man*, I says, but he ain't a real man, is he? He's a filthy molly. We gets all kinds of coves in here, sooner or later: bully cocks, freebooters, nappers, prigs, fingersmiths, shavers, diddlers, sharps. But these Madge coves and backdoor ushers, they's the worst, I says. Why you wants to spend time with this creature is beyond me.'

The gentleman and his lady moved on, but on hearing Sprigwood's words, gave first Flynt, then Belle, a curious glance, no doubt wondering why they were interested in such a creature. Their pace quickened when they saw the dangerous glare in Flynt's eyes.

Belle made to move closer to her friend but Sprigwood barred her way with his hand out. Unlike the poor creatures further back it was a demand rather than a request.

'You've already had your garnish,' said Flynt.

'That were to bring you to this spot right 'ere, it were,' the turnkey said. 'That were guiding garnish, now you must pay for your ten minutes, that's visitation garnish, that is.'

Flynt's jaw tightened as he dropped coins in the man's outstretched palm. 'You should be locked up here along with these other souls.'

The turnkey looked at the coins, seemed to approve of what he saw and thrust them into the pocket of his shabby coat. 'I is locked up with 'em in a manner of speaking, but the difference is I goes home to my wife and little ones and they don't. And if I can make a little extra out of giving them some comforts, what harm is there in that, says I?'

Belle had walked around him as they spoke to kneel beside the figure sitting upright against the wall. 'These are not the clothes in which he entered this place, surely?'

Sprigwood did not even glance in her direction. 'I don't know nothing about that, I don't.'

Flynt glared at the man as he joined Belle, inspecting the floor for filth before himself taking a knee to see the young man more clearly.

Sam Yates was larger than he had expected him to be, his frame under the rags that covered him well muscled. His hair was blonde and worn long but already matted, his face wide and handsome and smeared with muck, while his skin was further discoloured by what looked in the dim light like bruises. As Flynt knelt, the young man tugged at his filthy shirt to cover his broad chest, the manacles around his wrists and chain leading off to link him with another prisoner sleeping to his right.

'They took my clothes,' the young man said, his voice, though cracked with tension and trembling from the cold, was deep and cultured, but still of the street. 'As soon as I came into this place. I was stripped and abused, what coin I had taken from me, and these garments thrown at me.'

Belle asked, 'By whom?'

'This place is full of thieves, it is,' Sprigwood interjected. 'They'll take anything, they will, and new meat like this one is fair game.'

'I sent funds for him when he was here incarcerated, to allow him to purchase comforts, where is it?'

Amusement flickered on the turnkey's face. 'Don't know nothing about that, I don't. No money has been lodged for him. Looks like somebody stole it, says I.'

Belle took a deep breath. Flynt knew what she was thinking. The coin she sent had indeed been stolen but by none other than this fellow himself.

Belle stood to face him. 'We will have privacy.'

The man rubbed a hand over the bristles of his chin. 'Stay with them, Josiah Sprigwood, they says; I will, says I. Orders they are, and I must follow them. Of course, if you was to pay the privacy garnish then I would be willing to forget those orders, I would.'

Flynt lost his patience with the man. He stood and crossed the filthy ground to stand before him. 'There will be no further garnish. You will give the lady and I privacy or by God I will clean this floor with your blood.'

The turnkey pulled himself to his not inconsiderable height. 'You think I am easily bullied, sir? You think I have not met many such as you, says I? Well, sir, I am not and I have. Stay with them, Josiah Sprigwood, they says, and stay with you I shall, no matter what threats you utters.'

Flynt leaned into the man's face and spoke quietly. 'Friend, I do not threaten. I make a statement of intent. You will leave us until called for or you will not return home this night to that wife and family.'

Sprigwood seemed set on defying Flynt but even in the dim light of the lantern he could tell that he meant what he said. He swallowed, his spine losing a little of its stiffness as his pomposity shrivelled, and he began to move away, muttering under his breath. He halted when Flynt added, 'And I would be obliged if you would unshackle our friend and take this other prisoner away, for we would speak without another pair of ears to listen.'

Newgate ran on two commodities, money and favour, and information could easily buy the latter. If this prisoner heard that of which they spoke he might be able to parlay it into extra food, better clothing, perhaps even a move to a more salubrious ward.

A sardonic smile stretched Sprigwood's lips as he looked towards the sleeping figure. 'Don't worry about old Simon, says I, for you would have to shout very loud for him to hear. He's been dead these two nights since.'

Flynt bent over the body, saw the face bleached of colour, the unmoving eyes devoid of life, the features frozen in a grimace. 'Then why in God's name is his body still lying here?'

'Don't know nothing about that, I don't. Ain't had no orders to move him, has I? So there he stays until I am told, keeping your molly company, says I.'

He walked away, his back a little straighter again with the satisfaction of having the last word. He did not go far, a few paces only, but Flynt judged it sufficient to allow them to converse without his hearing and returned to Belle and Sam, checking again before squatting that he did not kneel in anything foul.

'I think that poor old fellow must have died of the cold,' Sam said. 'It is devilish freezing here unless you can get close to a fire, but as you can see, I am unable.' He raised his manacled wrists and moved his legs to clank the chains around his ankles. 'It was that fellow Sprigwood who ordered me chained to that poor wretch, as punishment.'

'Punishment for what?' Belle asked.

Sam seemed uncomfortable and looked to Flynt, as if trying to place him. 'I don't know you, sir.'

'Jonas is friend to me, Sam, you may speak freely,' explained Belle. 'Why has that scrub Sprigwood punished you thus?'

Sam seemed unwilling to reply and darted a look once again towards Flynt.

'Speak freely, Sam, I told you, Jonas is my dear friend and is here to help.'

Sam swallowed hard. 'He desired me to take his manhood in my mouth. He said that as I did such for money then I would do it for comfort. When I refused, he allowed the prisoners to abuse me and take my clothing and coin. Whatever funds you sent for me, dear Belle, will have ended up in his pocket and that of the keeper.'

Flynt's growing anger rasped at his breath. He would have further words with Sprigwood before they left, he resolved, and perhaps also the keeper. He knew the position of overseer of the prison was auctioned off to the lowest bidder and employees like Sprigwood made at least part of their living off what they could gather in garnish, but that did not excuse the kind of treatment meted out to those poor wretches under their charge.

Belle laid a hand on Sam's arm, rubbing his skin gently with her fingers. 'Jonas and I will work together to have you freed, Sam.'

Sadness weighed down Sam's head. 'I fear it's all over with me, Belle. They have dubbed me up good and proper, there's no denying it. I shall appear across the way in the Session House presently and from there it will be Tyburn.'

The city court was contained in the Session House across the yard from the prison, all the easier to transport the accused for trial. The actual courtroom lay open to the elements for clear movement of air to avoid transmission of disease, but it was still a place Flynt tended to avoid. He had last attended it the year before to watch the trial of a fellow of his acquaintance named John Smith, better known as Half-hanged Smith for he had once dangled on the end of the rope at Tyburn for fifteen minutes without death taking him. He was reprieved but the experience did not force him to mend his ways. His trial in May was for breaking into a warehouse; however, his luck once again held and he was acquitted. John's history with the judiciary had enticed Flynt beyond the courtroom doors but he had felt something akin to panic for every minute he spent within those walls.

'I will defy them,' Sam said, his voice hardening, his head held high but his voice shaking. 'They will not have me.'

'How will you defy them?'

'They cannot try me if I do not plead. I will refuse.'

Belle looked to Flynt to speak. He cleared his throat. 'They will force you to plead, Sam. They will take you from the court and into the press yard and there they will lay you down on your back, your arms and legs tethered, and then they will set a board upon your chest and pile weights upon it. They will deny food and water and keep adding the weights until you agree to plead or you die.'

Sam's head slumped. 'Then I am a dead man no matter what, sir, for even should I proclaim my innocence, they will hang me, as certain as sunrise. And I am innocent, may God strike me down this instant if I am not.'

'Why have they done this, Sam?' Belle asked, her own voice beginning to waver at seeing her young friend in such a place and in such a condition.

He shook his head. 'I don't know, and that's the truth, Belle.'

'Did you know Sir Geoffrey Dumont?' Flynt asked.

'Never met the gentleman, not personal, but I knew of him.'

'So why were you meeting him at St Paul's?'

'Word was sent to Mother Clap's that I was to meet him there, that there would be coin in it for me.' He hesitated, as though unwilling to recall the events, then closed his eyes and continued. 'I found him already lying wounded from many blows, the knife still in his breast.'

He looked at Flynt. 'You'll think ill of me, sir, of my type, attending an assignation.'

'No, Sam,' said Flynt, resting a hand on the young man's shoulder but feeling no warmth in his flesh. 'I do not think ill of you, so put that thought from your head. I am here to help if I can. Tell me, who relayed the message?'

'I know not the name of who brung it, it was a street lad I was told.'

'And how came you to have blood on your hands?'

'I knelt beside the poor gentleman, touched him to see if he still lived, tried to withdraw the knife but it was fast stuck. There was still breath in him for he said something as he slipped away.'

'What did he say?'

'It was difficult to make out for there was blood issuing from his mouth and choking him but it sounded to me like he uttered the word "faint".'

Flynt sat back on his heels, knowing that the young man had misheard. With his dying breath the judge had murmured his name.

Ten minutes precisely passed before Sprigwood approached them again and said it was time to go. Flynt straightened and watched Belle wrap her arms around Sam as best she could and embrace him, whispering words of encouragement as she did so. Sam was already weeping and Flynt felt something stab at his heart and sting his own eyes. He did not know if this young man was responsible for Sir Geoffrey's death but he was still moved by the anguish Sam experienced in this accursed place, where the noisome air tainted the blood and men died of the cold only for their corpses to lie still in chains for days. His words earlier to Charters about a cold day in hell seemed apt here. Nowhere else could be so devoid of compassion, of decency. Flynt shuddered, and not because of the chill. This jail, like Tyburn and the Session House, filled him with dread, for the fear nestled somewhere in the recesses of his mind that here lay his future.

'Come then,' Sprigwood said impatiently. 'Ten minutes, I says, and ten minutes you have had. I have business to attend to.'

Sam's tears still fell and Flynt had to prise Belle away from him. She was also weeping and this surprised him. She was a highly prized courtesan, could command a top rate for her favours, lived in considerable comfort in Mother Grady's house and was free to come and go more or less as she pleased. But her life had not been easy. She had witnessed many hardships and privations and, importantly, remained someone else's property. He had never seen her so moved and resolved to inquire of her connection to the young man.

Belle, however, halted in front of Sprigwood and, despite the tears leaving tracks down her cheeks, glared at him. 'I will have you return Mr Yates' clothes as well as the funds I supplied for his comforts.'

Sprigwood smirked. 'The clothes is long gone, and as for those funds I knows nothing of them. They must have been taken by your messenger.'

'He would not do that, for he is an honest man, so the fault lies here and at your door.'

Flynt suspected the messenger in question was Jerome and, if so, there was no suggestion of him stealing it.

Sprigwood sneered. 'There ain't nothing I can do, and even if it were possible, I will not be ordered about by the likes of you. I knows your kind, I sees them in here all the time, with your airs and your graces and your fine clothing, but you ain't nothing but scum, says I, and proud I am to say it to your face. Your bully here can threaten me all he cares to but I will not take it back, no, says I, I will not. The day that Josiah Sprigwood is ordered around by a black whore is the day that the Lord God can take my soul to heaven.'

Belle's tears had halted now and Flynt saw a look on her face that he well knew. Her features had hardened, though a tiny smile graced her lips and her eyes shone in the lantern light. He had no intention of taking up her cause, for she was more than capable of handling herself.

Sprigwood took a step back when the Queen Anne pistol was drawn from Belle's hand muff and pointed directly at his face. Flynt knew this particular weapon was never far from her grasp.

'That soul may make its final journey sooner than you think, and I can assure you that it will not be to heaven,' Belle said. 'Now, your opinion of my race and my profession are immaterial to me so please do not think that I take offence. I have been called such before and no doubt will again, and usually by men who could neither afford me nor generate sufficient ardour to in any way satisfy me. Your children at home, I suspect, do not carry your blood in their veins, for I doubt you have it in you to spawn enough seed to do the job.'

Sprigwood was about to protest but she shook her head to silence him. 'I am talking, sir, and you will listen. Here is what will happen. My friend will be treated with kindness and respect for he has not yet been found guilty of any crime. He will have his clothes returned to him and some warm blankets. If his clothing cannot be found then you will provide new ones, warm garments, clean garments. Be assured I will return to see this is done. You will find the money I sent and it will be used for the purpose intended. You may keep a small portion of it, for you are due your *garnish*. If none of these things are done then, as your Lord God is my witness, your brains will garnish that wall. Do I make myself clear, you mackerel backed bag of pus?'

The man's Adam's apple bobbed during Belle's speech as though it were in a barrel trying to avoid the teeth of young lovers. He looked to those other inmates who had witnessed the scene, now gathered at a respectful distance, as if appealing for aid. Their faces were dull and expressionless and there was no encouragement of Belle's defiance, perhaps fearful of future repercussions, but equally there was no sign of any protest. Sprigwood understood that to all intents and purposes he was on his own.

'You can't make such threats to a man in my position…'

'I can and I have, and believe me when I say that I will not only carry it out, but it will be both pleasure to me and service to humanity. My companion and I will be gone from here as quickly as it takes for your heart to still. It is dark and who will be able to identify us? Certainly not you.'

'You would not get out of this precinct,' Sprigwood said, but his tone lacked certainty.

Belle smiled. It was a beautiful smile but here it was cold and deadly. 'Shall we put that to the test, sir? Or will you do as I say and live to garnish again?'

He swallowed hard again, then nodded. 'I will do as you say.'

As quickly as it appeared, the little pistol was returned to the confines of Belle's hand muff. She said nothing as she marched past the man, head held high, to return the way they had come.

Sprigwood looked at Flynt as though he were an ally, which he found puzzling for he had done nothing and said nothing to make him think that. 'Would she have carried out that threat?'

Flynt let him wonder in silence for a moment. Then, with a soft chuckle, followed Belle.

11

Belle awaited him in the Press Yard, staring at the wall of the Session House on the other side, and breathing deeply of the comparatively fresher air. Outwardly she appeared to have recovered her self-control but in her eyes he still detected the shadow of anguish at seeing her friend reduced to such a condition.

'Let us leave this foul place,' she said, already moving towards the gate.

He followed her. 'So how came you to be friend to young Sam?'

She gathered her thoughts, and he wondered if she was considering how much to tell him. 'His mother was one of Mother Grady's girls when I first arrived and she was very kind to me. I was a young girl just new arrived from the Indies. As you know I'd been sold at the block in Kingston, taken from all I had known, my mother, my brother, and transported across the ocean. London was' – she sought the most apt word – 'confusing.'

They were allowed through the gate with barely a glance from the guard to emerge onto the street where the bustle of the city underlined Belle's words. Carriages and wagons rumbled over cobbles, chairmen hefting sedans cursed pedestrians as they weaved their way through them, the ever-present street vendors enticed passers-by to examine their wares. Flynt recalled his first exposure to the city on his return from the wars on the Continent. In his youth he had been used to the hubbub of Edinburgh but the extent of it in London seemed even more chaotic. He could only imagine what it must have been like for a girl who had been used only to the relative peace of the tropics, albeit as a slave with its attendant iniquities, being plucked from one life and then finding herself lodged in a brothel thousands of miles away, to be trained in the art of pleasuring men, to boot. A friend like Sam Yates' mother would have been a great comfort.

'Miriam took me under her wing,' Belle continued as they walked. 'It was she who taught me how to survive among all this.' She waved her arm around her. 'Mother Grady may have ensured I had my letters and my numbers and initiated me in the desires of men but it was Miriam who was my true teacher. She told me to always retain a part of me inside, never to be revealed, to lock it away and keep it safe. Men would have their pleasure with me but they would never have me, not the real me.'

Flynt felt discomfort, for he had until recently been one of those men. 'What happened to her?'

'She died five years ago. She cut herself accidentally and the wound became infected and poisoned her blood. Sam was perhaps twelve years old.'

The boy was only seventeen, Flynt mused. He looked much older, but then even one night in Newgate could age a person, especially in the knowledge that a noose awaited come next hanging day.

'How did he become involved in the flesh trade?'

'There were few options open to a boy whose only experience was in a bawdy house. He saw things and learned things that a lad of such tender years should not.' Belle dwelt on this for a moment then, with a slight shake of the head, dismissed it. That was the life Sam had been born into, the life she had been forced into. There was no room for regret. 'After Miriam's death we all looked after him, even Mother Grady, but two years ago he ventured out on his own and gravitated to the molly houses along Holborn.'

'And now he is in Newgate.'

'Yes,' she said. 'Will that vile creature Sprigwood do as I instructed, do you think?'

Flynt thought about the man's face as he stared down the muzzle of the gun in Belle's hand. There was fear, certainly, but greed can often overcome that. 'If he doesn't then we will know and I will deal with him.'

'I will deal with him,' Belle said forcefully.

'No, Belle,' he said, unusually firm. 'You will not, for it would go hard on you. Dealing with scum such as Sprigwood is what I do and you must allow me to.'

'And it will not go hard on *you*?'

His thin smile was grim. 'It will be done in such a way that I will not be suspected. The city is a dangerous place, especially at night, and that is where I am most comfortable.'

She walked on without speaking further for a few paces. 'Why have you not been to see me, Jonas? I have not heard from you since your return from Edinburgh.'

Belle deserved an explanation, for even though what was between them had always been business, he was fond of her and had more than once tried to purchase her freedom from Mother Grady. Shortly before he travelled north the year before, the madame had bluntly told him that she was not for sale, for Belle had plans of her own and needed no man to act as saviour.

'My trip to my homeland brought back memories,' he said carefully. Like her, he kept parts of himself locked away.

'Of that woman Cassie?'

He was momentarily puzzled as to how she knew of Cassie, then recalled he had breathed her name the last time he and Belle had made love. 'Aye,' was all he said.

'You still have feelings for her?'

'It's complicated,' he said, hoping it would satisfy her. He did not wish to explain that he had been in love with his stepsister, had unknowingly left her pregnant when he ran off as a young man in search of adventure, and that the child now believed another man to be his father. Cassie wished to keep it that way.

'The question of life is complicated, Jonas, but generally the solution to it is simple,' Belle said. 'We wish to be happy, that is all. Safe and happy.'

'Is that what you wish?'

'It's what we all wish, whether we admit it or not.'

'And are you safe and happy, Belle?'

Belle stepped around a woman selling flowers to give herself time to consider the question. This was an awkward conversation for them both as they were not accustomed to laying bare their innermost feelings.

'I am safe, Mother Grady and Jerome see to that. I now have regular callers and none of them are troublesome – it was not always so.' She paused again, a slight smile finally playing on her lips. 'Although the one I favour most does not come calling.' She gave him a sideways glance and he felt himself flush as though he were a young lover on his first tryst. She looked ahead again and continued. 'I have my comfort. Despite my profession and my race I have respect among those of my station. Happiness, though, is elusive, is it not? I am content and at present that is all I can wish for. Perhaps, somewhere ahead of me, happiness waits. But you, Jonas, by your profession you can never be truly safe. And happiness is not something with which you are acquainted.'

He forced a smile. 'You know me so well, you believe?'

'Jonas, I know men and you are not so inscrutable as you think yourself. You are also my friend and I make it my business to understand my friends.'

He thought of friends from the past, none of whom lived. He thought of Cassie's face, her smile, her voice and the sadness in her eyes the last time he saw her.

When he did not reply, Belle said, 'You keep yourself apart, Jonas, and that cannot be advisable for anyone. I am a whore and yet I have many friends, and not just those gentlemen who seek out my services. I do not live in isolation.'

He thought about young Jack and Colonel Charters, considered whether they were friends but found he could not answer it. 'Many men live a life of solitude.'

'Yes, some have it thrust upon them by circumstance, some deserve to be alone, but you, Jonas, use such solitude as a fortress to keep the world at bay.'

He walked on without comment. Cassie's words came to him, spoken when she saw him again after many years. *There's a darkness that follows you. I see it in you, even if you don't know it exists. Leave us soon and never come back, Jonny, for I fear you carry the stench of death.*

He had not left them soon enough.

Belle must have realised that she was not going to glean anything further from him so reverted to the matter in hand. 'I take it our next step will be to visit Mother Clap's?'

'Aye,' Flynt said, relieved at the change in focus. He endeavoured to avoid self-contemplation, fearful of what monster he might find, but of late he had been unsuccessful. 'I would know who sent the message that summoned the lad to St Paul's.'

Belle glanced at the clock on the tower of St Sepulchre's Church and caught her bottom lip with her teeth. 'I cannot do so now, for I have business at Mother Grady's that cannot wait.'

Flynt took this to mean that one of those regular gentlemen callers of which she spoke had booked her bed and her body. For reasons that he did not quite understand he felt jealousy strike at his vitals, but he forced it away. He had no right to feel envious of this unnamed cull, for he had once been a regular too.

'Mother Clap's house is in Field Lane and that's not far from here. I can do this without your supervision, Belle.'

'I do not supervise you. I told you I would assist and assist I will.'

'Why call on my services if you are so set on investigating yourself?'

'Because, my dear Jonas, as you have stated, this is what you do. If you wish to know the correct way to pleasure a man then you would ask me, but even though I am part of the demi-monde I do not know how to navigate that world. If I wish to make my way through the shadowy areas of London then I must come to you, for you have the necessary knowledge, not to mention the skills, to guide me.'

He could see the sense of that but was determined not to let her know, for she was already too smug in regard to her insights into his character. Belle was too close to the truth and he did not like to be so scrutinised, not even by her.

–

After conveying Belle to Covent Garden, Flynt considered taking a chair to Golden Square, but decided against it. A further walk through the streets to Soho would continue to generate heat throughout his body, while being carried in a sedan by chairmen would not. If Belle's occupation temporarily prevented further inquiries into who had killed Sir Geoffrey, then he could make attempts to confirm the identity of the lady Lord Fairgreave had been calling upon. Belle had mentioned his skills and he needed to utilise them to do what needed to be done and that meant his fingers and mind must be alert. He feared neither would be possible after travelling in a draughty sedan chair and allowing the cold to numb his blood.

While he walked, he turned over the conversation with Sam Yates in his mind. He did not know the boy but he had to accept Belle's word that he was not capable of such a deed. The lad certainly looked powerful enough, though that went for little. The gentlest man he had ever met was a farm boy from Lancashire who had fled a charge of sheep stealing by taking the queen's shilling. Edward was his name, Big Ned they called him, which made up in accuracy what it lacked in wit. He was as large and as broad as the barn in which he told them he had been born. Despite his burly frame and bulging muscles, Big Ned was no fighter. He was more at home with the creatures they encountered during the Flanders campaign: the horses, the dogs that followed the camps, the cats. He once found an injured rabbit which he was nursing back to health until someone decided it was better in the pot. Flynt's heart was already being hardened by the tragedies of war but Ned's tears over the loss of the animal pierced it like an arrow. The fellow once cowered in fear as some soldiers, their brains addled by French liquor looted from a farmhouse, began to fight among themselves over God only knew what. Tensions and tempers often frayed when close to battle and that night something had snapped, and even though Ned had wanted none of it he found himself at the centre of the melee, where he curled up into a ball as fists and feet flew around him, jerking whenever a blow struck him. Flynt and his childhood friend Charles Temple managed to pull him clear and usher him to safety. As they watched him lumber through the camp, Charlie had observed that the lad was in for a shock when battle commenced. His foresight was uncanny, for Ned was cut down by a cavalry sabre as he fled his first engagement with the French. Flynt could not blame him for turning tail, for later both he and Charlie did the same during the bloodbath that was Malplaquet. Charlie had never been one to display great courage but, unlike Big Ned, he did find the strength to face the enemy on a number of occasions, perhaps bolstered by Flynt's presence, whom he thought fearless. Flynt was not fearless, though; he had merely learned how to hide his abject terror in order to complete the task in hand, which was staying alive. If, in order to achieve that aim, he had to kill or maim, then that was what he did, although he now was increasingly sickened by that of which he was capable. This skill to act without hesitation was something Colonel Charters recognised in him and utilised with frequency. The echoes of a conversation sounded in his memory.

'*Was it really necessary to kill them all, by the way?*'

'*It seemed like the thing to do at the time.*'

'*It so often seems to be thing to do at the time when you are involved, Serjeant.*'

But Malplaquet.

Ah, Malplaquet.

That had proved too much, even for Flynt. When he knew he'd had enough of slaughter, he didn't need to say a word, for Charlie could see it in his eyes. They turned and ran. If they had not, they might have fallen along with some twenty-two thousand of their comrades, their blood seeping into the foreign soil. And for what? To place the Spanish crown on the head of someone more palatable to politicians. Flynt didn't give a single damn whose royal buttocks graced the throne but he had grown tired of killing to take a worthless piece of ground or to give some bewigged peacock of a commanding officer a tale of glory to relate to his friends back in London. So he ran, and Charlie ran, but at some point they separated and Flynt found himself in a ditch, dragging a wounded officer from the teeth of rats feasting on the flesh of the fallen. That officer was Charters, who, while being carried back for medical attention, witnessed first-hand Flynt's ability to kill.

Once safe, his wounded arm sawn off, Charters saw to it that he was promoted to serjeant for his trouble, and he was obliged to remain with the campaign until hostilities ended, thanks to the colonel keeping a weather eye upon him, aided by his manservant Jacob Simmons.

The sights, sounds and smells of the battlefield accompanied Flynt as he made his way to Soho, though he never allowed the memories to mask his surroundings. It was his habit to be aware of everything around him, for he had learned to his cost that even a momentary slip of attention could prove painful, if not deadly. One such lapse had landed him on the wrong side of a severe beating in Edinburgh and he could yet feel the weight of his attacker's boot on his body.

Daylight had faded by the time he reached Golden Square and the air had turned ever more crisp. The weak winter sun brought a little warmth but with nightfall came the frost. Still, his perambulation had the desired effect and the blood coursing through his body warded off much of the cold. With luck he would soon be inside the house. He first sauntered around the square, studying the window for signs of occupation, confident that he would not be as visible in the gathering dark as he had been during daylight. Light flickered on the upper three floors but not the bottom. Good, he thought, the serving girl had told him that the lady in question occupied the rooms on the second floor. If whoever rented the ground floor was not at home then it made this evening's task that much easier.

He found a narrow lane leading from Brewer Street to the rear of the terraced row. An iron gate set into a wooden fence proved no barrier to his dub, a special lockpick given him by the same veteran cracksman with whom he had worked previously. Old Tom had been taken before his time, struck down by a carter carrying vegetables to market, the wheel crushing his skull. Even though Flynt had not been present when it happened, being at the time on yet another mission for Charters, he felt the man had been touched by the curse of his own friendship.

The gate opened into a back yard that required some attention. The ground was paved, certainly, but it was currently used as an outside storeroom, with crates and household ephemera stacked against the surrounding fence. A back door beckoned and he set to studying the lock before once again utilising his dub to open it with ease, thankful that he had no need to take more forceful action in order to gain access.

He found himself in the kitchen where all was dark and silent. Leaving the door ajar behind him – if he felt it necessary to make a swift exit he did not wish to waste precious seconds opening it – he eased around a large wooden table, pausing only to cut a chunk of cheese from a block sitting on a plate. On leaving the Frost Fair he had purchased a mutton pie from one of the vendors but had not eaten since and, though that was by no means an irregular occurrence, he found himself damnably sharp set. He nibbled at the sizeable slice of Cheddar as he moved towards another doorway, being careful not to bump into anything. He paused before trying the handle of the door, head cocked to catch sounds from above, hearing voices of at least one woman and one man. He tried to focus when the woman spoke to catch any inflection that might be familiar but it was impossible, for the voices were mere drones with no definition apart from the differing timbres.

He eased the door open a crack and peered beyond, finding a corridor with only a lamp on a side table lit to a low flame. He popped the last of the purloined cheese into his mouth, then pulled his neckerchief up over his chin and nose to disguise his features should he come face to face with any of the occupants. He stepped into the corridor, leaving the door open behind him once again, and crept along a narrow passageway cutting between the wall and the staircase, pausing at a closed doorway to ensure that there were no sounds from within and no sign of light bleeding at its foot. Satisfied that the ground-floor apartment was indeed unoccupied, he then moved silently to the front door and turned the key to unlock it, another preparation for any emergency escape that may become necessary. He turned to the stairway, his hand on a large polished brown finial that ornamented the newel post of the balustrade. Candlelight glowed at the top of the stairs and the voices were slightly more distinct though they remained resolutely unidentifiable. He sighed inwardly. Charters needed confirmation that it was indeed Christy de Fontaine who was in congress with Fairgreave and, for his part, Flynt was also curious. To progress any further was dangerous, but sometimes you had to chance all on a throw of the dice or turn of the boards.

He began to slowly ascend the stairway, hoping the wood underfoot would not creak overly much, each foot placed with care upon the risers. With a hand on the hilt of his sword stick, he reached the second-floor passageway, where a candle guttered from a silver holder on a side table halfway along the wall. At the far end, a long window overlooked the square. A door immediately to the left of the stairhead lay slightly ajar so he pushed it open further to allow some light in. He saw it was a bedchamber with an overly ornate Jacobean four-poster bed that seemed too large and ostentatious for the room. Another door on the far side would lead to an antechamber in which Christy, if indeed it was she, would perform her private functions.

He edged past the table carrying the candle to the foot of the next flight of stairs, glancing upwards briefly to ensure nobody was descending, then stepped to a second door, this one closed but not so tightly that light could not escape around the frame. More importantly, it was not a barrier to sound as he could now hear the voices more distinctly. He leaned in closer to concentrate. The man's he recognised as Fairgreave: he would recognise those lazy vowels and careless consonants anywhere now.

'I tell you again, milady, what you suggest is folly. It will never work.'

'It will work, my lord.'

It was a woman who replied. Though she spoke quietly, he could discern that she was cultured. She was, however, not Christy de Fontaine.

'I remain unconvinced of that,' Fairgreave said, 'and as I have explained many times over the past few days, I cannot risk my reputation, my very life, on such a risky venture.'

'And as we have explained, Lord Fairgreave, we do not wish you to take an active role in the endeavour, merely to facilitate the aftermath with your good friend, the envoy.'

'Signore Erizzo will also have nothing to do with this enterprise. It would cause a diplomatic incident should it ever get out that he—'

'He need never know. We have been over this, Lord Fairgreave. All we require from you is that you engage Signore Erizzo elsewhere for a day or two. An invitation, perhaps, to your country residence for some hunting and conviviality. While he is absent from London we will arrange for onward passage.'

'Onward passage to where?'

'That need not concern you. In fact the less you know, the better. Now, please tell us, for time is growing short – will you assist us or will we have to make other arrangements?'

We. Us. Did this mean they were part of a wider group or was there someone else in that room? If there was another person in there, and it was indeed who he believed it to be, then what in God's name was she doing? Too engrossed in embroidery to participate in the conversation? He smiled at the thought, for Christy de Fontaine was more likely to wield a stiletto than a needle.

He shifted his stance slightly, wincing as the boards creaked a little. He froze, fearing that they also would have heard, but the flow of conversation continued unbroken.

'I have given it considerable thought,' Fairgreave said, 'ever since the first request for my assistance came through your lady friend here...'

He was right, there was someone else in there.

'...but I regret, madame, I cannot be of service. Even though I do have sympathies for the cause – this Whig government be too damnable for any decent man to bear, and having a foreigner on the throne should be an affront to every true patriot – what you ask is too dangerous. I cannot risk my position, my estates...'

There was silence then, broken only by the voice he had expected to hear, saying, 'Augustus, darling, I would urge you to reconsider your decision.'

'Madame, I do not take it lightly, I assure you...'

Flynt smiled to himself, glad that his supposition had proved correct. Nonetheless, he drew one of his pistols, for the fact of it was that where Christy de Fontaine was, so also was her companion, bodyguard and, it was rumoured, consort, a large Russian brute named Gregor, who had once been part of the Russian Royal Guard but now served the Scots-born agent of France. Flynt had tangled with him once before and he was in no hurry to repeat the experience. He looked back along the passage again, suddenly nervous at the thought of the man perhaps already closing on him, but the corridor was empty save for the shadows cast by the capering candle flame.

'Then I very much regret your decision, Lord Fairgreave, I regret it very much indeed.' There was something in her tone that sent an alarm through Flynt's brain. Madame de Fontaine was beautiful, clever, witty and charming, but she was also deadly. Did he detect a threat? He thought it confirmed when she said, 'Gregor, if you would be so kind.'

So the big Russian was in there, that was a relief. At least Flynt knew where he was.

A large shadow passed at the foot of the door and Flynt involuntarily stepped back. In his mind's eye he envisioned Gregor, perhaps watching and listening as his mistress and the other lady had their conversation, now crossing the room towards Fairgreave. Flynt frowned. This did not bode well for his lordship, a judgement confirmed when he heard the man grunt in a mixture of pain and surprise.

Fairgreave's arrogance did not desert him. 'Take your hand from my arm, you hulking brute!'

Flynt considered his next move. He had discovered what he came here for and he should leave. But he knew Gregor and he knew his mistress, and he suspected that Fairgreave's refusal to assist in whatever enterprise they were planning was about to bring him a considerable amount of discomfort. He had no love for the fellow but could he in all conscience simply depart and leave him to his fate? Part of him proclaimed rousingly in the affirmative but another part, the secret part that Flynt tried to hide from others, knew that he could not abandon him. The man could be responsible for Sir Geoffrey's murder, but if that were the case and it could be proved then it would be a matter for the courts. And if they failed in their duty, then Fairgreave would fall foul of Flynt's own justice.

He sighed quietly and, after thrusting his stick back into his belt, withdrew his second pistol. With both Tact and Diplomacy thus deployed, he took a step back and, blocking Fairgreave's continued protests on the other side of the door, forced his concentration onto his breathing for a moment, ensuring it was even, that his grip was steady, that his thinking was clear. If this was to be done, it required shock value, and for that he needed to be in complete control of his body and his reactions. He inhaled deeply, let the air out slowly, quelling the scratching in his belly that he always experienced before situations such as this. When he knew he was ready, he raised his right leg and kicked the door open, stepping in with both pistols levelled, seeking Gregor first, for he knew he would be the biggest threat in the room. Or, indeed, any other room.

It was a large lounging chamber with two Queen Anne armchairs close to a raging fire, the heat from which he could feel on his face even in the doorway, a settee with arm flaps raised and upholstered in what looked like some form of tapestry. The dark floorboards were covered here and there by painted floor cloths. Christy was seated in one of the armchairs and appeared unsurprised by his appearance. The other lady he did not recognise, but her bearing and dress were of obvious quality, complementing the voice he had heard. She appeared taken aback at his entrance but did not move from her chair. Fairgreave stood by the settee, his face flushed presumably from his struggle to free himself from Gregor's grip on his shoulder. Despite that, he had frozen upon Flynt's abrupt entrance, his mouth agape. The gloved hand that held him, Flynt knew from painful experience, was hard and unyielding, for there was no flesh beneath the leather. He did not know of what that hand was made – wood, probably, possibly metal – but he still occasionally woke in the dark of night to the feel of its tightness upon his throat.

Gregor's expression was as impassive as ever but his stance suggested he was considering lunging towards him. The man was large but Flynt was also aware that he could move swiftly when he needed to.

'Please don't, Gregor,' he said, ensuring his pistol was aimed at the man's forehead, for he suspected a shot to the torso would barely inconvenience him. 'You are nimble, to be sure, but you cannot outrun a pistol ball.'

Gregor appeared to see the sense of this because he remained where he was, his false hand still grasping Fairgreave's shoulder. Flynt could see where the unforgiving fingers dug into the cloth of the man's coat. That would be painful, he thought, before turning his attention to the ladies.

Christy de Fontaine's smile was at once charming and mocking. 'Jonas, darling, I wondered when you would come calling.'

12

With one pistol trained on Gregor while the other hand plucked the kerchief from his face, Flynt bobbed his head in some semblance of courtly greeting. 'I apologise for this intrusion but I found it necessary,' he said, addressing his words to the other woman. 'I hope I do not alarm you overmuch. Madame de Fontaine, I trust you are well.'

'Oh, Jonas darling, I thought we had moved past such formality, please call me Christy. And you are welcome anytime, you know that.' She waved a finger towards his weapons. 'Although I regret your calling bristling with ordnance.'

'Circumstances dictate that I present myself with weapons cocked.'

Christy's smile was like a stolen kiss in a bedchamber. 'And are all your weapons cocked, Jonas?'

Madame de Fontaine's accent was a mixture of Scottish and French, the result of her northern birth and marriage to a French businessman who had the good grace to die and leave her with a fortune. That did not prevent her from supplementing her income by working for the French as spy and agent provocateur, and there were many men who found her most provocative indeed. She had once used her flirtatious wiles to try to manipulate Flynt but he had managed to keep her at bay. That said, there was a promise and a challenge in that smile that he felt deep in his breeches.

Nonetheless, he ignored the suggestive query. 'It is necessary because, as you are aware, I have danced with your man Gregor before and I am far from keen to repeat the experience.'

Gregor's bearded face remained blank but there was something in his eyes that Flynt did not relish.

'I would suggest that you instruct him to remain very still, for if he so much as breathes heavily I might see that as enemy action, and we wouldn't want any unpleasantness, would we? After all, blood would be so difficult to wash out of such fine floorboards.'

Lord Fairgreave finally found his voice. 'Do you know this ruffian, madame?'

Madame de Fontaine still sported that coy smile. An armed man bursting into her salon seemed not to have upset her equilibrium in the slightest. 'Oh, Jonas and I are old friends, are we not, darling?'

They had met only the year before but Flynt saw no reason to contradict her.

Fairgreave seemed to have forgotten the heavy weight of Gregor's hand on his shoulder. He pointed a trembling finger in Flynt's direction. 'That's the fellow who attacked my companions and myself in the street not two nights since!'

'Is this true, Jonas, darling?' Her brow furrowed with amusement. 'Did you really brawl in the street like a common criminal?'

'It wasn't much of a brawl, madame. A scuffle at best.'

'He disrespected my person in a most outrageous fashion,' Fairgreave insisted.

'There is much to disrespect, Lord Fairgreave,' said Flynt, and was rewarded with a look of indignation, pressing on before it could turn into bluster, 'but for now, I would request that you come with me.'

'I will go nowhere with you, unless it is to a field of honour where I would seek satisfaction.'

Flynt felt exasperation build within him. This bandycock had no idea the danger that surrounded him in this room and could think of nothing but preening before the ladies.

'Lord Fairgreave,' he said, struggling to keep his words even, 'I suggest you remain silent and allow me to remove you from this company for your own well-being.' Flynt looked to Christy de Fontaine. 'Madame, I would appreciate it if you would have your man unhand his lordship.'

Christy's lips puckered slightly as though she were pained by the suggestion. 'But Jonas, we were having such a lovely conversation before you interrupted in your customary dramatic fashion.'

He smiled. 'I suspect it was about to turn far from lovely for his lordship.'

Fairgreave seemed to at last comprehend the gravity of his situation. His attention moved from Flynt to Gregor's heavy hand, then to Madame de Fontaine. Understanding dawned and he attempted again to jerk free but Gregor's grip remained steadfast. Flynt straightened the pistol aimed at Gregor.

'Madame,' he said, the single word carrying a warning that he would not hesitate to fire.

Christy sighed and said, 'Gregor.'

The big Russian removed his hand immediately but the fire in his eyes that burned across the room towards Flynt suggested he would happily risk being shot for the chance to clasp his fingers round his throat.

'Step here to me, if you please, Lord Fairgreave,' Flynt said. The nobleman did as he was told without further protest. 'Now, we'll back out of the room slowly.' Flynt gave the unknown woman a slight bow. 'I regret, madame, that we were not properly introduced.'

'I do not regret that, sir,' she said, her tone bringing the temperature of the room down. 'I am not in the habit of being introduced to knaves who take what they wish at pistol point.'

He would wager that in her day she had met many well-spoken knaves in polite drawing rooms and at balls, but they would take what they wished with the scratch of a pen, a sense of entitlement and recourse to a law weighted in their favour. Nonetheless, he shrugged her comment away and began to follow Fairgreave from the room, his pistols remaining at the ready, every nerve tensed for an attack by Gregor, who watched his progress with a bland expression that seemed to convey so much violence without any real effort.

'We shall meet again, Jonas, I hope,' Madame de Fontaine said as he reached the doorway.

'Christy,' he said, slipping the key from the lock, 'something tells me that we will. Gregor, please don't pursue me. I hold you no ill will, although I feel you do not reciprocate. But be assured that if you come after us, I will take it badly and will not hesitate to put you down. I would hate to deprive your mistress of her companion.'

He gave Madame de Fontaine a wink, provoking a laugh, and then ducked into the passageway, closing and locking the door behind him. It was but a moment before he heard the handle being wrenched from the other side. He assessed the door with a professional eye. It looked sturdy but it would not take an individual as powerful as Gregor long to break it down. Fairgreave awaited at the top of the stairs, but Flynt took time first to snuff out the candle, then to lift the table from its place against the wall halfway along the passageway and set it carefully in front of the door. Then he motioned Fairgreave to keep moving and followed him to the ground floor.

'Where is your carriage?' he asked as he opened the front door and peered out. Gregor was formidable but he would not be surprised if Christy had other assistance, his mind jumping briefly to the three men who had attacked him. Had she sent them? He saw no men lurking in the shadows.

'It awaits in Brewster Street,' Fairgreave replied. 'I thought it prudent to leave it there and—'

The splintering of wood reverberated from upstairs as Gregor ripped the door free of its frame, followed by a clatter as the big man blundered into the table. Flynt was glad he had first extinguished the flame for he had no wish to set off a further Great Fire. The tactic had bought them a few moments only, but these precious seconds were often the difference between life and death.

'Then run, man, *run!*'

Even in these circumstances, Fairgreave could not shake off his upbringing. 'Running is most unseemly in a gentleman.'

Flynt heard Gregor's heavy footfalls above. 'Even if the gentleman's life depends upon it?'

He gave Fairgreave a shove, sending him careering down the short flight of steps to the street, then turned, waiting until he saw the

Russian's dark bulk at the top of the stairs bearing something long and heavy in his hand that he assumed was a poker from the fire, used no doubt to help prise the door open. He had warned him about following and now had to reinforce the message. Flynt fired quickly – there was no time for care in his marksmanship – and was rewarded with a grunt as the big man jerked to the side, lost his footing and let the poker tumble from his grip to bounce onto the risers. Flynt cursed his errant aim and levelled his second pistol, then thought better of wasting his final shot in the dark. He might need it later. Fairgreave, alarmed by the report of the pistol, was shooting frightened glances over his shoulder as he scampered in an uncoordinated fashion, his fashionable buckled shoes not conducive to such physicality. Flynt leaped down the steps and loped after him, drawing level with ease to grab him by the arm and propel him forward. Gregor erupted from the front door as if shot from a cannon. Whatever wound Flynt had inflicted was minor and clearly not troubling him in the slightest. He took the steps in a single jump and followed them at a brisk pace.

'Faster, in the name of God,' Flynt breathed, practically dragging Fairgreave and causing the man to almost lose his footing. The carriage waited at the corner of Brewster Street so he thrust his lordship ahead of him. 'Carry on but wait for me,' he ordered.

One terrified, wide-eyed glance at the Russian closing in on them was sufficient to galvanise his lordship and he did as he was ordered. Flynt turned sideways, pistol raised, and steadied his stance by placing his feet apart to soak up the recoil if – or perhaps when – he discharged the weapon.

'I won't miss this time, Gregor,' he shouted.

Gregor slowed, his breath frosting as he eyed the distance between them, no doubt calculating whether he could close that gap before Flynt could let loose. Gregor was a former soldier and well acquainted with violent situations, so he would be aware that the earlier shot was reactive, performed in haste, but this time Flynt's aim would be measured. Each man stared at the other in the dark Soho street, gauging what the other's next move would be. Flynt knew there was little time, for this was no side alley in the Garden but a residential street. Someone would have heard the first report and even now men of the Watch or the Sheriff's officers could be heading their way. He was in no mood to answer any questions and Charters would not thank him for becoming swept up in such an imbroglio.

Fairgreave called to him to hurry. He had reached the carriage and was holding it for him. The man was despicable in many ways but that single act did him credit.

'You've lost this hand, Gregor, my friend,' said Flynt, gradually easing backwards, never letting his eyes stray from the hulking Russian. 'We will no doubt play another soon.'

Flynt was unable to see the man's face clearly so could not discern any signs that he sought to deal those cards now. However, Gregor did not move as Flynt neared the open door to the carriage and backed in, the pistol still levelled. Fairgreave instructed his man to ride like the wind, his voice rising an octave or two with tension, and the driver duly complied, his whip cracking in the air above the heads of the pair of black horses.

Fairgreave slumped back in the seat, his breath rasping as Flynt craned backwards to ensure that Gregor did not follow. He saw no movement in the dark and began to relax, but kept his pistol cocked.

'I am grateful to you for waiting for me,' he said, finding it difficult to be civil to a man he had come to despise.

'I thought about leaving you to that brute, I sincerely did, for you would deserve it for your disrespect, but I realised you had performed a service for me back there so I owed you a debt.'

Flynt was aware that Fairgreave was not a man to carry a debt with good grace. 'Nevertheless, it was the honourable thing to do.'

'Honour, sir? Honour, by God! You have abused my friends, you have verbally abused me, you have laid hands upon my person this very eve. What does street dross like you know of honour?'

'Honour is not something that comes to a man simply because of his station, Lord Fairgreave. It's a virtue that comes from within, something that is developed and is the making of the man, not merely through an accident of birth.'

Fairgreave sat back in his seat and fell silent. Flynt knew his words would not make a dent in his armour of entitlement but he was glad he had said them. However, he had more important matters to which he must attend.

'What is it they wish you to do?'

Fairgreave's voice was coated with sulk. 'You expect me to break that confidence with the likes of you?'

'They were about to break more than your confidence.'

'How can you be so certain?' He faced Flynt again. 'Now that I reconsider, I do not believe they intended me any harm. You frighted me with your talk.'

'You felt the weight of that Russian bear's paw upon your person, Lord Fairgreave. Do you believe that was nothing but a friendly pat on the shoulder?'

The look in his eyes told Flynt he recalled the pain of the Russian's grip. 'I admit he was a touch heavy-handed – quite literally, as it happens – but they are ladies of quality and refinement. I cannot accept that there was malevolence afoot. I certainly cannot believe that Lady Nithsdale would be part of any such act.'

On hearing the name something clicked into place in Flynt's mind. Lady Winifred Nithsdale was the wife of William Maxwell, Earl of Nithsdale, one of the captured Jacobite lords awaiting execution in the Tower of London.

'Lord Fairgreave, I know Christy de Fontaine of old and I know of what she is capable. As for Lady Nithsdale, I cannot say, but you were being taken to a place where Gregor would convince you of the folly of your ways and the means he would have used would be decidedly uncomfortable. You must accept my word that I am here to help you.'

'Your word?' Fairgreave's eyes had widened as Flynt spoke but he still attempted some lofty disdain. 'I am a peer of the realm. I have lands, funds, respect, and you expect me to accept the word of a rogue? I do not know who you are, sir… Flynt, was that the name? Sounds frightful common to me. What gives you the right to question me? And to expect me to lay my affairs open to you?'

'Because at this moment I am all that stands between you and them.'

Fairgreave seemed determined not to understand the difficulty he faced. 'How can a rogue such as you protect me?'

'Sometimes it takes a rogue to combat a rogue,' Flynt said, almost adding *and to protect one* but now was not the time to antagonise the man.

'Nonetheless, my private affairs are none of your business, sir, and I will not discuss them further with you.'

Flynt sighed and decided to get straight to the nub of the matter. He prodded the pistol he still held into his lordship's ribs. 'I am making it my business.'

Fairgreave raised his arm to look down at the weapon. He blinked feverishly. 'You would murder me in my own carriage, in the public street?'

'I have done worse. Now, let us waste no further time. Do they mean to break Lord Nithsdale from the Tower?'

Fairgreave's head jerked away from staring at the pistol in shock. 'How do you—'

'It is a fair assumption.' Flynt cast his mind back to the overheard conversation. 'You mentioned a Signore Erizzo. Who is he?'

The man hesitated. Flynt pressed the muzzle tighter against his coat.

Fairgreave strove to inject a haughty tone into his voice, but his fear had stretched it until it was almost reed-like. 'Damn you for a son of a bitch, sir, I will not be so abused!'

Flynt rammed the pistol further. 'Who is Signore Erizzo?'

His lordship swallowed, his attempt at defiance evaporating. 'He is the Venetian envoy.'

'And he is friend to you?'

'Yes.'

'And what would be his contribution to this enterprise?'

'None, he would know nothing of it. It would be my task to take him from London for a few days, to my estates in the country. They would then use his home to house his lordship until they embark on safe passage from England.'

'Bound for where?'

'They would not share that with me.'

Flynt removed the weapon from Fairgreave's ribs, allowed it to rest on his lap once more, and sat back. 'And Madame de Fontaine? She is acting as agent for France?'

Fairgreave's attention had remained focused on the pistol but mention of his nation's traditional enemy made him look up in consternation. 'France, sir? I know not. She and Lady Winifred are friends. Apparently as a child Madame de Fontaine visited Terregles House in Nithsdale with her father regularly.'

So Christy was operating as a free agent in this matter on behalf of an old friend. He was secretly pleased because it meant she had some understanding of loyalty. They travelled in silence for a few moments, broken only by the rhythm of the horses' hooves and the scrape of the wheels. Fairgreave slumped further into the corner of the carriage as if all his years of privilege had suddenly been snatched from him.

'Do you really believe they meant me physical harm?'

'I do, or at the very least imprisonment until their plan was carried out, lest you report this to anyone.'

Fairgreave swallowed again, finally accepting Flynt's word. 'I must report this, mustn't I?' He began to argue with himself. 'But I cannot, for that would implicate me. And yet, does not duty demand that I alert the authorities? But then again, I do have sympathy with their cause...'

Flynt interrupted the monologue. 'Report nothing. Say nothing. In fact, send them a message informing them you have reconsidered and that you will do as they ask.'

Fairgreave regarded him with bewilderment. 'Have you taken leave of your senses, man? They will not believe me, especially after you spiriting me away under their noses.'

'Tell them that was what convinced you to agree to their enterprise. Tell them I continued to physically abuse you in order to discover what you knew, but you resisted and told me nothing.'

'Why would you be so interested in their plans?'

'Christy and I know one another of old, they will not question you regarding that.'

The nobleman thought upon this, then shook his head. 'They will never accept that I was physically abused by you. I have no bruises, no sign of duress.'

Flynt pulled his left arm back and delivered a punishing blow to Fairgreave's cheek, snapping his head backwards, his body seemingly turning liquid as he first slumped against the side of the carriage and then began to slip to the floor. Flynt caught him and propped him up again. The man's eyes rolled in their sockets and his neck appeared to have difficulty keeping his head in place, a dark bruise already shadowing his cheekbone.

'That should go some way to convince them,' Flynt said as he tapped his pistol against the roof to tell the driver to come to a halt. Flynt opened the door before the wheels had even stopped turning and addressed Fairgreave again, who was murmuring something indistinctly. 'Lord Fairgreave, can you hear me?'

The man laboured to form a response but finally he managed a nod and mumbled something that might have been an affirmative.

'You must convince them that you are with them, otherwise it will go ill for you. Do this, and do it well, for if they don't kill you, then I just might.'

He stepped from the carriage and waved the driver to proceed. As he watched it trundle into the darkness, he berated himself for being too impetuous, for he had acted without thinking. He should have left well enough alone; if they truly needed Fairgreave's assistance then they would not have killed him. He could only hope that the man could convince them otherwise.

13

Field Lane ran from Holborn Hill to Saffron Hill and many of the buildings had stood there even before the Great Fire of the previous century, Holborn being left practically untouched by the conflagration. The lane itself was narrow, even by London's standards, and Flynt thought by standing at its centre and stretching out his arms he might touch the ancient brick and wood buildings that rose on either side as if they were trying to intimidate. No carriage could traverse this cramped and filthy thoroughfare, nor would the drivers wish to, for even sturdy and muscular chairmen elected not to enter it after nightfall, for here cutthroats aplenty prowled in the dark. Such men watched Flynt and Belle as they passed, some in threadbare clothes, others in more presentable attire, but all sharing the same mean, hungry look as they calculated the odds of ramping them up and relieving them of their purses, before disappearing into the warren of even narrower alleys that cut through to the filthy back yards where pigs squealed and rutted. However, such coves had a preternatural gift when it came to sizing up the culls they victimised and they would sense that Flynt was not a man with whom they should cross swords. Nevertheless, lest one proved to be daring enough, or stupid enough, to try, Flynt kept his right hand on the handle of his sword and, despite the bitter cold, his coat open for ease of access to his pistols. Belle seemed oblivious to the men's presence, looking neither right nor left as she pressed a nosegay to her face, for the smell here was overpowering, but he surmised the other hand inside her fur muff gripped her little toby pistol. She concentrated on picking her way across the ice-hardened mud and grimy vestiges of snow mixed with the human outpourings that drained from the lodging houses and into the ditch that ran down the centre of the passage.

Access was further narrowed by stalls on either side from which hung all manner of handkerchiefs and garments, some very fine indeed, others not fit for use as a washrag. Flynt knew the bulk of these goods to be stolen, for here was where the likes of young Jack Sheppard would have brought the wipes he dipped from pockets at Tyburn to sell to the crimps who dealt in such goods.

Mother Clap's establishment was, on the face of it, a coffee house, but it was also a haven for those men who preferred the company of their own gender. Flynt had never been on the premises but he knew its reputation. Warm light shone through the grimy windows to illuminate the lane outside and stretch to the wall opposite. As they approached, a gentleman of obvious quality was in the process of leaving, accompanied by a young man, by his apparel a manual worker. They almost collided with Flynt and Belle in the confines of the lane and following the usual apologies, polite nods and bows there was a moment when the gent stared straight at Flynt and mutual recognition dawned. Flynt had seen him in the gaming rooms around the Garden, his hand usually on the fleshy rump of one of the women who worked such places. The man flushed, pulled his hat lower over his face and quickened his step, forcing his young companion to break into a run in order to catch up.

Belle had witnessed the exchange. 'A friend of yours?'

'An acquaintance.'

'He appeared discomfited.'

Flynt pushed open the door to the coffee house. 'He is the Tory member for a country constituency in the south. I believe he has a wife and children at home.'

'And here he is at Mother Clap's.'

'A man's true nature will always out,' Flynt observed as Belle stepped over the threshold.

'Of that, Jonas, I am well aware,' she said and looked around at the men at the tables, drinking coffee, wine and gin, some enjoying a meal. Among them floated what at first glance might have been ladies of the night but even in the brown light of the lanterns they were obviously men in women's make-up and clothing. These were the true mollys, the men who pretended to be women. Neither Flynt nor Belle were shocked or judgemental, for they were both accepting of other people's vices, she through professional necessity, he because he believed the world was made up of all kinds of people who deserved to live their life the way they felt necessary, as long as no creature was harmed.

A burly man with the face of someone well acquainted with the hard edge of a fist or two approached them, first regarding Flynt with curiosity, then Belle as she pulled down the hood of her red cape, for the sight of a beautiful woman in this place was unusual to say the least. He gave Belle a brief bow.

'How can I helps you, sir, ma'am,' said the man, his voice as rough and battered as his face.

'We would have words with the proprietor,' said Flynt.

'I is he,' the man said, raising in salute a hand large enough to blot out the light but with knuckles gnarled and mangled. 'John Clap, at your service. I owns this here place.'

Belle could not hide her surprise. 'You are Mother Clap?'

Good humour shone from the man's smile. 'That's my wife, Margaret. The gents what comes here, well, they calls her Mother, as a sign of respect and affection, for she takes care of them, if you will.'

Belle nodded, and Flynt was aware her understanding was not feigned. There was little to differentiate this house from the one in which she lived, apart from brighter lighting, a more aesthetic sense of decor and, of course, the coves who were its customers. Her own madame, Mother Mary Grady, was well respected by her customers too.

John Clap ran an appraising glance over Flynt. 'I would ask you what your business is for, begging your pardon, and you too, miss. Neither of you is the type of clientele we normally has. I'm sure you understands.'

'I am friend to Sam Yates,' Belle said and instantly John Clap's face became grim. 'I see you know of him.'

'Of course, Sam is a regular here, we even gives him room out back to lay his head. A decent lad, a good lad. Margaret treats him like the son we never had. It's right tragic what has befallen him and that is no lie.'

Flynt asked, 'Then you do not believe he is guilty?'

'Sam? Hush a cove? No way in hell – begging your pardon, ma'am, for my language.'

Belle assured him she had taken no offence with a smile and a wave of the hand. 'He tells us that the message was sent here to request his presence at St Paul's?'

'It were, that is true.'

'Who delivered the message?'

'You should speak to Mother concerning that, for I was elsewhere that night.'

'Is your wife here tonight?' Flynt asked.

'She is, she is here every night, for she takes this work most serious. You had best come through with me to the private apartments.'

He motioned them to follow and they made their way to a door at the rear, the curious scrutiny of the customers following them like an accusation. They did not belong here and everyone in the room knew it. The door led to a short corridor and then to a parlour furnished comfortably if inexpensively. The floorboards were bare and unadorned by any cloths. A wooden table with four chairs around it sat in the centre while a pair of high-winged chairs, their upholstery slightly tattered, faced the roaring fire, the sight – and sensation – of which was most welcome.

'Please, make yourselves at home while I fetch Mother,' John said, motioning towards the fireplace. 'She is upstairs in the marrying room, making it presentable for some gentlemen.'

The man left and Flynt took off his hat, dropped it on the table, then positioned himself in front of the flames to burn the cold from his fingers. Belle undid her thick cape, set her fur muff beside Flynt's hat and seated herself in one of the armchairs.

'The marrying room?' she mused.

Flynt shrugged, guessing that the room was where those gentlemen who required it could find a bed and privacy.

'Do you think this Mother Clap will cooperate?'

Flynt looked to the door. 'I don't know. Her husband certainly seemed amenable but she seems to be the driving force of this establishment and she may not be quite so open.'

'You have never met them before, I take it?'

He raised an eyebrow in her direction, a smile tickling his lips. 'My sexual tastes run in another direction, as well you know.'

She hitched a shoulder slightly. 'There are men who like to have a foot in both camps.'

'I am not one.'

'Does being here make you uncomfortable?'

'Not in the slightest. Do you find yourself uncomfortable here?'

'A bawdy house is a bawdy house, Jonas. The decor may change, the culls may change, but it remains what it is. At least here I will not be importuned.'

He felt himself smile. 'Unless it is I who does so.'

She returned his grin, but with a hint of shyness. 'With you it is never harassment, Jonas.'

'As long as I have the silver to pay.'

There was a pause that lasted a bit too long for Flynt's liking. He had thought they were engaging in banter, but the look she gave him in that moment suggested there was something more. Finally, her smile looking somewhat fixed, she said, 'You know the way of it with me. The silver, always the silver. Mother Grady would have it no other way.'

The door opened and a small woman wearing her grey hair long and untethered, but whose features were smooth and unblemished, entered carrying a mound of crumpled bed linen, which she dropped beside Belle's hat and muff on the table. She stood with one hand on the back of a chair as she took a moment to study them, first Flynt, her eyes flicking over his long black greatcoat, his black knee-length boots, then finally focusing on the silver cane still held in his hand. Flynt thought he saw something akin to recognition flicker before she turned her attention to Belle seated in the chair, and it was to her that she addressed her first words.

'I be Margaret Clap, and you, me duck, will be Belle St Clair, I take it?'

Belle's eyebrows twitched. 'You know of me.'

'Aye, me duck, I know of you and about you, so much that I feel I has known you all me life. Young Sam, he speaks of you right often and tells of your kindness to him when he lost his ma, God rest her.' Mother Clap returned her attention to Flynt. 'And who might you be, sir?'

'My name is Flynt, Jonas Flynt.' He affected a slight bow. 'At your service, madame.'

The woman's face crinkled into a smile as she remarked to Belle, 'Got good manners this one.' She addressed Flynt once again. 'Scotch, ain't you, me duck?'

'Scottish, aye. And you are from the middle lands between here and northern England, would I be correct? Although your accent mixes that land with these streets.'

'Aye, me duck, Nottingham born and bred but down here in this hellhole these twenty years or more, so have picked up the lingo. Me husband John – him you met – was with a travelling show, a fist-fighter he was, taking on all comers for t'sport of others. He was game, my John, never lost a fight, he did, and when I seen him work I fell for him instant. I was a Cousin Betty at the time, following the shows, the fairs, selling myself, but that all stopped when I met John. I took up with him, travelled with him, and when he had raised enough bunce we comes to London, his home, buys this place and sets down roots.' Having thus laid out her life story as though it were credentials, she pulled the chair out from the table and sat down. 'So, you want to ask about young Sam?'

'You are aware of his current situation?'

Margaret Clap sighed heavily. 'Aye, tragic, it is. I sent him some comforts to Newgate but not yet been able to visit. I will, though, right soon.'

Flynt doubted if those comforts ever reached the boy. 'Do you believe him guilty?'

The woman looked back to Flynt. 'Nay, that lad ain't capable of such a dreadful, wicked thing.' She addressed Belle once more. 'You know him, me duck, you know he's the sweetest, most gentle lad that ever drew breath.'

Flynt asked, 'He was here when the message came that sent him to St Paul's, correct?'

'Aye, that's correct. He lives here, I give him room upstairs to lay his head. He come here after Mother Grady decided he couldn't stay with you girls.' She held up her hand when she saw Belle felt honour-bound to defend her owner. 'Don't get me wrong, me duck, I know you in particular made sure that he had coin and clothes and I ain't condemning old Mary, she did what she had to do and she couldn't have a lad like him, one with his peccadilloes shall we say, in her house. Wouldn't look right, would it? She has a fine house up there in Covent Garden, never been in it meself but have admired it from t'outside, you understand. Mary Grady is not the one to cater to the molly trade, is she? So he came here and right glad I was too, for he is a decent lad.'

Belle tilted her head in agreement. 'Your husband said he became like the son you never had.'

'Aye, that he did. We had a boy but he was taken from us before he could even learn to spit. Stricken by fever and terrible spots, measles, they calls it. John and me, well, we had it when we was young 'uns and we survived, but little John? He was always more delicate. I always thought it were punishment for my past sins.' Flynt saw her eyes glisten with the memory, or perhaps it was misplaced guilt. 'Sam may have been growed when he come here, but I took to him straight off, I did, as did my John.'

'Forgive me, madame,' Flynt said, 'but if you loved him, why did you allow him to see company?'

Belle shot him a sharp look but he ignored her. He wished to know why a woman who treated the boy like a son would see him sell himself. Mother Clap was not offended, however.

'I understand why you ask that, Mr Flynt, but Sam is no ordinary molly for sale. He likes men, no doubt about that, but he don't sell hisself to just anyone and I don't let him, neither. He don't parade like some of those lads you saw next door, and I don't condemn them for it neither, for we all have to be true to our natures. When he gives himself, he does it for love, for affection, I sees to that. Yes, he turns a coin if the gentleman sees fit to show his appreciation but there are few other opportunities for such as he. We all has needs, and I don't condemn anyone for them, but he ain't no common whore.' She realised what she had said. 'Sorry, Miss Belle, no offence intended.'

Belle smiled. 'There is none taken. Like my owner, I do what I do and I see no shame in it. Mother Grady is a tolerable mistress and allows me to plan for my future. I am no common whore either, but I will not sell myself for much longer. I will have another life and will not end it as some cheap bunter, poxed and toothless, selling myself on the street for the price of a bottle of gin and a bed for the night.'

There was an understanding that passed between the two women of which Flynt was not a part and never could be. They lived at the beck and call of men in a world dominated by men but who had found a way to work within it while also using it for their own ends.

He cleared his throat, aware that as a man he was complicit in such a world. 'So Sir Geoffrey Dumont, then, was he a visitor to your establishment?'

'Nay, but we knew him. He passed judgement on Arthur Driver, as foul a villain as ever there was and that's saying something down here.' She gave Flynt a curious study. 'You would be knowing of him, I'll say.'

That the woman seemed to know something of him was plain. He cleared his throat. 'I was not acquainted with Driver personal, but I did see him drop.'

Her lips compressed. 'I saw that too, and a right good day it was.'

Belle asked, 'And why was Driver in particular such a foul villain?'

'He was a molly who could not accept his own lusts. He beat to death a young lad by name of Joshua Able, a working lad, like Sam, and in fact was friend to him. Sam provided information that helped bring Driver to justice.'

'Did he see the murder?' Flynt asked.

'No, there was plenty of folk there for the witnessing of it, for Driver was mad with the gin and he cared not what he did, and he knew it.

He claimed the lad had approached him with a foul suggestion and laid hands upon him uninvited. He thought he would never hang for the killing of a molly, but even so he still refused to plead, claiming that he did the world a favour removing such a creature from it, all the while not acknowledging his own true nature. There were those who agreed with him too, the pious bastards, but Driver was still taken to the press yard to force a plea from him. Damn near killed him, or so I heard.'

'What information did Sam provide then?'

'After he did for poor Joshua, the evil bastard hopped the twig, hid himself near here. An evil place this may be but it ain't no liberty zone, me duck. Sam saw him, recognised him for what he was and went straight to Mr Hitchin.'

Flynt frowned. 'Hitchin, not Wild?'

'Mr Hitchin is more amenable, privately at any rate, to the plight of men such as Sam and poor Joshua, him being of similar persuasion as it were. So when t'message comes for Sam to go see Justice Dumont, he thought it were perhaps something to do with that and off he went.'

'And you did not think it unusual that he request they meet at St Paul's in the middle of the night?'

She looked ashamed. 'I did not hear about it until after Sam had left. It were a busy night; many men had come in from the cold, but I saw the boy who delivered the message speak direct to Sam. He left word with one of the serving boys as to his destination.'

'Who was the boy who carried the message?'

'A young rascal by name of George Nicholson, Little Nick they calls him and right well named he is. He's a link boy and a messenger but a real natty lad. He looks innocent but is far from it, for he would take the teeth from your mouth if you gaped over long.'

Flynt noted the boy's name and resolved to have Jack track him down. If anyone would know where to find the young criminal, it was he.

Belle leaned forward. 'So tell me, why has this occurred? Why has Sam been swept up into this affair?'

Margaret Clap sat back in the chair and took a moment before she replied. 'There is a great deal of hatred against men such as Sam, Miss

Belle, I'm sure you know that. You too, Mr Flynt, for you are a man of the world. I feel that you have no ill will against them but you will know that there are many who is against them. Their passion is illicit and they must seek it in secret places and behind doors such as mine. I met many men such as they in my days on the road with John. Some were open about their needs, others were covert. Many were sad, ashamed of what is natural being deemed unnatural by those who hate.'

'It's true, the laws against sodomy are strict – whipping, pillory, even death,' Flynt observed. 'But there have been very few prosecutions in recent years.'

'Aye, it's been law since the days of old Henry, though little pay heed. But that is changing. What people does with their own bodies behind closed doors or in dark of night is becoming unacceptable, for even though it is unseen they believe that God can see, and therefore it is an abomination. You have heard of the Society for the Reformation of Manners?'

'Religious group, are they not?'

Mother Clap's mouth twisted as if she had tasted something bitter. 'Aye, good Christians all, who would see their fellow man beaten, whipped, abused and even hung for taking their pleasures. They supported that bastard Driver when he said he were performing a service for the community, and it mattered nothing that he was inclined that way himself. They has politicians who support them in public but in private they get up to all the sins imaginable. Mark my words, me ducks, there will come a day when we will see men lose their liberty and their lives because they dared love their own kind.'

'Men never do evil so completely and cheerfully as when they do it from religious conviction.'

Margaret Clap eyed Flynt curiously. 'I wouldn't take thee as philosopher, Mr Flynt.'

'Not I,' he admitted. 'A Frenchman by name of Blaise Pascal.'

The woman studied on this as if the thought were somehow alien. 'A Frenchie, you say?'

'Aye, but dead these fifty years or more.'

A slight smile ghosted her lips. 'Clever lad, though. Must have had Nottingham blood.'

Belle grew impatient with the diversion. 'You think this murder is in some way connected to this moral crusade? That they seek to condemn all by implicating Sam?'

'It has already begun. They have pamphlets saying that a good man has been lost to the lusts and perversions of the sons of Sodom. Men of the cloth will thunder come Sunday to their congregations about the threat such acts pose to the physical and spiritual well-being of the land. They mean to create a wave of hatred that will only be stemmed by blood. They will preach of heaven but will make a hell for some.'

There was a silence in the room broken only by laughter and voices from the coffee house out front and the crackle of the wood in the fireplace.

'Is it your intention to help Sam, then?'

Flynt realised Mother Clap's question was directed at him. 'We both will, if we can,' he replied.

Her gaze dropped to the silver cane. 'That be a nice walking stick, Mr Flynt.'

'Thank you. I like it.'

She sat back and studied him. 'I've heard tell of a man such as you, with such a stick. There's some call him good, others say something different.'

'The truth is, as ever, a mixture of both, Mrs Clap.'

'Like as not, ducks, but right pleased I am that Sam has you on his side. No offence, Miss Belle, but this here world is built for those with a dick between their legs, no matter how much influence we women may wield. I has no doubt you are a strong lass and you will fight for what is right but for this to be done, young Sam will need more than your good graces. It will need a man with enough good in his heart to see a great wrong has been done but a sufficience of the other to do what needs to be done.' She studied Flynt again, long and hard. 'It takes a man with darkness in his heart to stand sentry between heaven and hell.'

14

Flynt ensured that Belle was returned safely to Mother Grady's house and then visited the Black Lion in Drury Lane, where he suspected he would find young Jack in pursuit of Edgeworth Bess. She worked out of the tavern, sometimes taking a cull to the private room upstairs, more often than not tupping them in her own room in St Giles or even in a back alley. She wasn't much older than Jack, not in years, but the lad was much taken with her, and any spare coin he had was pressed into her hand, no doubt followed by his eager manhood. Now that he was in the employ of Jonathan Wild, Jack would have the wherewithal to finance his youthful houghmagandie, as they would have it back in Scotland. Whether or not his ardour was accelerated by genuine feeling for the lass, or merely the sap rising, Flynt could not tell.

The tavern was, as ever, a hubbub, with musicians striking a merry jig in the corner competing with voices raised in volume through liquor, while the air was filled with the customary candle smoke and pipe fumes mixed with the tang of ale and spirits together with vomit that had not been cleaned up. Flynt paused in the doorway, unwrapping his scarf from his neck and face as he scanned the room, easily picking out the lad at a corner table, with Bess stretched across his lap like a cat demanding a stroke. Her bodice was agape, displaying more of her charms than was currently fashionable, not that anyone in this place would care about fashion. Jack sipped from a tankard of ale while also seemingly transfixed by the sight of the twin orbs straining at the remaining buttons holding fast more by luck than tenacity. Bess herself nursed a bottle of gin with one hand while idly playing with the lad's hair. Jack's lustful look told him that they had either not yet satisfied his yearning, or he was ready for another session, but Bess seemed happy enough to stay where she was, her foot tapping the air in time to the music.

'Mr Flynt,' said Jack as he approached, his voice as lopsided as the grin on his face. 'How goes it, sir?'

Flynt pulled a free chair from another table, threw one leg over to sit astride it with his hat held in both hands before him, and nodded briefly at Bess, who regarded him with ill-concealed animosity. Once, while drunk, she had threatened to peach on him about an incident and he had been forced to outline the painful consequences of such a breach of trust. It would seem she had neither forgotten the encounter nor forgiven him for it. He couldn't blame her. He was not proud of himself but she had to understand that he was not a man she could play with.

Jack raised his tankard. 'This here Stitchback is powerful strong, Mr Flynt. You should try it.'

Flynt waved a refusal. 'I am weary, Jack, and ready for my bed.'

Jack leered. 'You will have some willing bobtail waiting for you, I'll be bound.' He leaned closer to Bess's ear. 'Mr Flynt has a lady of pleasure what he visits. A fine piece, she is, ain't that so, Mr Flynt?'

Flynt had no desire to discuss his love life in front of Bess. 'I will not stay long, Jack.'

'Don't let us keep you,' Bess said, her voice sharp.

Flynt ignored the hardness of her eye. 'I won't, but by your leave I would have a word with Jack here.'

'You go right ahead,' she said, her attention drifting back to the music. 'Don't you pay me no never mind.'

Flynt watched Jack while he calculated that the conversation was to be private. Eventually he pushed Bess from his lap. 'Go get yourself another bottle of rag water, Bess. Tell old Hines I'll stand the ben before we leave. He knows I'm good for it.'

Bess smoothed her dress down, made a show of buttoning herself up and then stood in front of him, her hand on her hip, her chin jutting defiantly. 'You want to see these goods, sir, you will cough up the bunce like all the rest.'

Flynt had no interest in the young woman in that way but he remained polite. 'I regret, Bess, that I would be trampled underfoot by the herd eager for such a sight. And anyway, this night you are being squired by young Jack here, and it would ill behove me to inject myself between you two. I feel sure Jack would have words for me, friend or no friend.'

Jack seemed somewhat bemused by the exchange and Flynt wondered how much ale had been drunk. Was he too beery to take in what Flynt had to say? However, when the lad spoke again, his words were clear and unsapped by ale.

'Leave Mr Flynt alone, Bess, you ain't his type anyway. Go do as I say, if you please. Him and me, we has business.'

'I promise I will not keep you from him for too long, Bess,' Flynt said. He didn't trust the girl but he did not dislike her. She was a survivor and he respected that because, in the end, weren't they all? They all did what they had to do, his work for Charters being a case in point. He was often called upon to commit questionable acts and if he refused then a noose awaited him at Tyburn. The colonel was grateful that Flynt had saved his life in battle, even at the cost of an arm, but in the end he used Flynt for his *own* ends.

Bess whirled on her heel then carried herself across the room to the bar as haughtily as she could, given the gin had adversely affected her equilibrium. Jack watched her go, his eyes taking in every part of her. 'By God, she has a fine arse on her. And it goes well with the rest, eh, Mr Flynt?'

Flynt was loath to discuss the girl in such a manner so he moved immediately on to the purpose of his visit. He leaned in closer and kept his voice low. 'I seek a lad named George Nicholson, Jack.'

Jack frowned. 'Little Nick? What you want with that rapscallion?'

Flynt smiled, for Jack himself was a champion rapscallion. 'I would speak with him about a certain matter. Can you find him for me, have him here tomorrow forenoon?'

Jack tutted. 'By Jesu, Mr Flynt, I could have him here in less time than it takes Bess there to sink a bottle of that rag water.'

Flynt glanced towards the girl, who was facing them with both elbows propped behind her on the bar. A man approached her, leering at her charms, and she glanced first at Jack then reached out to stroke the newcomer's arm.

'Tomorrow forenoon will be fine, Jack,' Flynt said. He looked back to the boy. 'How goes it in the docks?'

'Not heard nothing on the lumpers that would interest old Wild, but I'll keep the ear out.'

'I would advise you to tread carefully, Jack, both in the Pool and with Wild.'

'Treading carefully is what I does, Mr Flynt. Fleet of foot, quick of finger and nimble of brain, that's me, and you knows it.'

Flynt looked back to Bess who was now leading the man who had approached her towards the door. She shot a glance back at them and smiled.

'My apologies, Jack, for I may have lost you your paramour.'

Jack watched them exit the tavern, Bess giving him a tiny wave as she left. He smiled. 'No matter, a girl's got to make a living, eh, Mr Flynt? That is the way of it with us. I understands her and she understands me.' He picked up his tankard of ale again. 'But she'll be back, don't you worry none. She's sweet on me, that girl. She'll be back for her Jack, of that I is certain.'

Flynt had no doubt she would return and Jack would wait for her, but not because she was sweet on him. Edgeworth Bess could smell coin from a mile away and she knew there was silver in Jack's pocket.

–

Weariness had all but taken over his body by the time he reached the Golden Cross. It had been a long day and the sheer physicality of it had left him drained. All he wanted was to climb into bed and sleep for a few hours, hopefully devoid of any nocturnal wisps of memory featuring Cassie. Or Belle, for that matter. Her demeanour earlier when remarking upon his absence from her bed continued to puzzle him. Did she merely miss his custom or was it *him* she missed? He could not bring himself to fully believe that. Belle was hard-headed and, he had been told in no uncertain terms, focused on her goal, which was to win her freedom and set up a house of her own.

The Golden Cross inn was as raucous as the Drury Lane tavern in which he had left Jack, but he skirted the busy bar and made for the back stairs, climbing them as if his muscles had suddenly aged. He walked the corridor on leaden legs, finding his room key in the pocket of his greatcoat before he noticed that the door lay ajar and a candle guttered beyond. He was always careful to lock up behind him and he never left a wick burning, while his landlady would not enter his rooms without permission. He felt tension tingle his fingers as he silently slipped his cane into his belt and slid his pistols free. Again, he knew he had to make as showy an entrance as possible and was ready to kick it fully open when he heard the voice call out to him.

'Please don't make another scene, Jonas. I think one performance a night is more than enough, don't you?'

He eased the door open with the toe of his boot, pistols at the ready, to see Christy de Fontaine sitting on his bed. Pushing the door fully open he found Lady Nithsdale in the room's only chair. She did not greet him, but sat silently, prim and erect, as if in judgement. He peered behind the door, knowing to his cost and considerable pain that the big Russian was fond of lurking in such places.

'Gregor awaits us below,' Christy said, her eyes dancing with humour in the flame of the candle on the small table beside his bed. 'You really do have a habit of annoying him, Jonas. It's a very bad habit that I would urge you to break.'

Knowing Christy's word to often be as flighty as her nature, he took the precaution of checking the corridor to ensure Gregor was not stealing up on him, then stepped back into the room, his pistols remaining primed. This was becoming tedious. First Blueskin knew of his lodging place, now Christy. It was perhaps time to find new accommodation.

'You are surprised to see me here, don't deny it, darling.'

'How did you find this room?'

'Oh, I made it my business to know where you lay your head a long time since. I do like to know the men with whom I am involved. Please put those weapons down, darling, I would hate for anything unfortunate to occur. Lady Nithsdale and I do come in peace, I assure you.'

He uncocked the pistols and laid them on the dresser. 'And we are involved, you and I?'

Her lips corrugated in a tiny kiss. 'Oh, Jonas, we are inextricably entwined.' She rubbed one hand over the bed cover towards the pillow. 'At least in a metaphysical sense. The physical is yet to come.'

'I regret I may have to deny myself such pleasures, madame, for fear that you would kill that which you love, like some latter-day daughter of Danaus.'

She adopted an expression of pain. 'You wound me, darling, and after all we mean to each other. Anyway, there is but one of me and the Danaides who murdered their husbands on their wedding night numbered fifty. And I do not have a jealous father urging me to protect my kingdom as did they.'

Flynt recalled a comment made by Charters concerning Madame de Fontaine's late husband. *It is rumoured it may well have been of natural causes.* The fabled daughters of Danaus committed mariticide on their father's orders but he doubted if the bold Christy would need such an instruction if she felt it would further her cause.

He leaned against the wall so that he could keep a weather eye on the corridor through the open door, his pistols within easy reach. 'What do you want, madame? I am weary and wish to take to bed.'

'That is a lovely offer but we have business,' she said, and despite his misgivings concerning her character, her smile was like a lamp being lit. 'And anyway, Winnie here is easily embarrassed.'

He returned her smile. He couldn't help it. 'State your business, Christy.'

'Ah, you do remember my name after all. I was beginning to wonder.'

He sighed.

She continued to smile.

Lady Nithsdale cleared her throat. 'You are a Scot, Mr Flynt?'

'I am,' he replied.

'Do you have no love of your country?'

'Love of country often leads to bleeding for your country and I have done enough of that, thank you.'

'Not for Scotland, I will hazard. You have bled for this United Kingdom. You have bled for the English throne.'

Christy interrupted. 'As I told you, Winnie, Jonas is not a Jacobite.'

'Then he is for Hanover,' said Lady Nithsdale.

'I am for neither, my lady,' said Flynt. 'I care little for kings, whether they speak with German accent or whatever cadence James Edward Stuart has adopted.' He turned his gaze towards Madame de Fontaine. 'French, I might guess, but you would know more about that, am I correct?'

Christy shrugged it away with a jerk of the head and that enticing little smile of hers.

'Do you care for anything at all, Mr Flynt?' asked Lady Nithsdale.

Cassie came instantly to his mind, and a boy, her son, whom he saw only once. Then in a hurly burly of faces, his father Gideon and stepmother Mercy in Edinburgh, Belle and Jack in London. 'I do.'

Lady Nithsdale waited for him to amplify but when he did not, looked to her friend. 'We cannot trust this man, Christy. A man who cares nothing for his country is a man who cares nothing for others.'

He did not argue the point but waited silently to hear the reason for their invasion of his personal apartments, knowing it would come from Christy, and it was to her he directed his full attention.

'You trust me, my dear, and I am but the female equivalent of darling Jonas,' she said to her friend, the sincerity in her voice clear as she kept her gaze level on Flynt. 'And I trust him. To an extent, at least.'

'Then you must do whatever you feel you must, as you always do, Christy,' said Lady Nithsdale, still eyeing Flynt as though he might strike them at any moment.

'Jonas, darling, what did Lord Fairgreave tell you of our business with him?'

'Nothing,' he replied. 'As you perhaps have gathered from our exchange this evening, he and I are not on the best of terms.'

'And yet you felt it necessary to remove him from our company.'

'I may not like the man but I am not going to stand by and give you leave to do him harm.'

Lady Nithsdale gasped and Christy laughed. 'You think we meant him harm?'

'Why else would you place him in the care of your Russian behemoth?'

'Gregor would merely have taken him to his carriage and thence to a place of safety, I can assure you.'

Flynt smiled. 'In that case, Lord Fairgreave and I exercised ourselves for nought.'

'And you caused poor Gregor some upset too.'

'I think *poor* Gregor is easily upset.'

'When it comes to you, he becomes damnably close to hysterical.'

Flynt doubted very much if Gregor was capable of such an extreme emotion. 'No matter, in the end his lordship refused to tell me anything, despite my vigorous questioning.'

'Oh dear, I do hope you did not hurt the poor man!'

Madame de Fontaine's tone was of concern but Flynt did not believe it for one second. 'Not as much as I would have liked to, 'tis true.'

'And yet you protest concern for his well-being at our hands.'

Flynt recalled Blueskin's motivation for his warning regarding Warwick. 'If he is to be damaged, I would prefer it to be by my hands. Anyway, his coachman came to his aid and I was ejected from the vehicle very quickly, not to mention without ceremony, and he went on his way.'

It was clear Christy also believed not a single word but she allowed the lie to pass unremarked upon. 'Why did you access my home surreptitiously, Jonas?'

'I had heard whispers that you were back in London. I wished to have them confirmed.'

She tilted her head to one side. 'Oh, how sweet. Did you miss me?'

For some reason he felt his face flush. 'You might look at it that way. But another way is that wherever you go, madame, chaos does tend to follow. I would know what business you have here in London.'

'So you can somehow interfere with it, perhaps?'

He considered this carefully. 'That would depend very much on what it is.'

Her eyes narrowed as she weighed up whether she really did trust him. 'Do you act for the good Colonel Charters in this?'

Mention of the name caused his head to jerk instinctively towards Lady Nithsdale but Christy dismissed his concerns. 'I have known Winnie most of my life, Jonas. She knows all about me. She knows of my work, of my interests, all of my secrets. And I have many, have I not, Winnie?'

A suggestion of a smile from Lady Nithsdale briefly eased the severity of her expression. 'You have packed much into your young life, dear Christy. It's a wonder you have not been hanged, poxed or imprisoned.'

Christy accepted that judgement with a deft flick of her eyebrow. 'I have led a charmed life, to be sure, but one weighted with careful planning and friends in high – and indeed low – places. Dear Colonel Charters, for instance, being a case in point. Such a secretive man. Such an enigma. And yet so easily manipulated, do you not find, Jonas darling?'

'I do not have your charms,' said Flynt truthfully, before continuing with less candour, 'but in reply to your query, no, I do not act for him in this matter. This is purely private.'

Christy was as amused by this as she was by most things. 'Oh, Jonas, I do believe you are sweet on me!'

His cheeks burned again. He knew this was a performance, her way of controlling situations, but damn it, this woman had uncommon skill in making him feel like a young boy encountering his first flirtation. He hoped the blossoming of his flesh was not visible in the light of the candle. 'Madame, I cannot help what you believe.'

Christy leaned towards her friend. 'Always aloof, that's my Jonas, never admitting to his deepest thoughts,' she said as though he were not present, then looked back to him. 'But you had no need to enter by secret, a simple knock at the door would have sufficed.'

He smiled once more. Despite his exhaustion he found talking to her exhilarating. 'I like to make an entrance.'

'You do, yes – that you do.'

'Speaking of which' – he studied the door and the lock – 'how did you gain entry to my private apartments?'

Christy held up a metal spike. 'You are not the only one who is versed in the dark arts, my dear. And that door proved no barrier to my lock-picking skills, I can assure you. If I were you, I would raise the matter with the management of this establishment, for there are many thieves about this city.' She placed the dub in the small silk purse she carried on her wrist. 'But then, look at whom I tell.'

Lady Nithsdale lost her patience with the progress of the conversation. 'Christy, either say what you wish to this man or let us take our leave. The hour is late and I grow weary of your constant flirtation. If you wish I will return to your lodgings alone and leave you two to sate your lusts to your heart's content.'

If Madame de Fontaine was annoyed or pricked by the woman's words she did not reveal it. Her smile remained intact and her voice retained its lightness. 'Winnie can be such a serious person, but then, I suppose, if the man I loved were facing what he faces then I should wish to move matters along too. Darling Winnie, why don't you tell Jonas what we are about?'

Lady Nithsdale's expression clearly disputed the wisdom of the suggestion, but finally she took a deep breath and addressed Flynt directly. 'What do you know of my husband, Mr Flynt?'

'That he came out with Bobbing John—'

'The Earl of Mar,' she corrected.

Flynt continued as if she had not spoken. 'And that he was with the force sent south – perhaps an unwise move on Bobbing John's part.'

She barely held in her sigh at the continuing disrespect he had shown to the Scottish peer who raised the standard of the Stuarts at Braemar and set in motion the short-lived attempt to overturn the Hanoverian throne. The Earl of Mar was renowned for his tendency to flit back and forward on issues, and so had become known as Bobbing John. That indecision had proved incompatible with military success, for after initial gains he had dithered too long in Perth and in so doing gave the government time to muster force sufficient to keep him at bay on Sheriffmuir. Although neither army could claim victory, neither could they *proclaim* victory, which was an outcome well in keeping with the Earl of Mar's temperament.

'Your husband was captured at Preston,' he went on, 'and as we speak is rotting in the Tower of London.'

He stopped short of pointing out that he awaited execution at the hands of the headsman, dying slowly at the end of a rope being too common for those of quality. It was far more appropriate for a man of his station to have his head hacked off. It was at least less ignominious than the original sentence, which was to be hanged before being cut down alive and then his bowels wrenched from him and burned before his eyes. Then and only then would the head be struck from the body and the corpse hacked into four quarters and either burned or dispersed to be put on display in various parts of the country as a warning to others who might consider raising a hand against the monarch and his ministers.

'We intend to break him free,' Lady Nithsdale said.

Although it was what Flynt had expected to hear, the revealing of it so boldly to him was a surprise.

'I have done everything I can to have clemency granted,' her ladyship said. 'I petitioned that German who sits unlawfully upon the throne. I threw myself at his feet, and spoke in French, for his grasp of our tongue is vague at best. I explained I was the unfortunate Countess of Nithsdale and that he might not be ignorant of my person. I caught hold of his clothes and he endeavoured to escape from my hands. I was upon my knees before him but he turned and dragged me from the middle of the room to the very door of the chamber. I managed to thrust my petition into his pocket but it fell to the floor in his haste to escape me.'

She stared at Flynt, her eyes hard but glistening with tears as she recalled the scene.

'I had prostrated myself before him, grabbing at his thick little ankles, Mr Flynt. I demeaned myself. I pleaded with him to save my husband, to cancel the executions, to show some shred of humanity for a fellow nobleman, but it was all he could do to get out of the room without even looking me in the eye.'

Flynt had heard that King George was uncomfortable with such displays of emotion and may well have been trying to flee out of his own embarrassment. On the other hand, he may also have been unmoved by the plea, feeling that an example had to be made.

'He did at least have the sentence commuted from the original drawing and quartering,' he pointed out in the interests of fairness.

'And that makes it more palatable, does it?' Christy's voice was sharper than he had ever heard it and he realised in that simple statement she had revealed her true feeling in this matter. This was personal for her, and he reminded himself that if Winnie had been a friend since childhood, then no doubt so had Lord Nithsdale. In that moment, he knew for certain that she was not working here for any foreign power or even for the shadowy Fellowship.

He confessed it did not make it more palatable, then asked, 'Why do you tell me all this? Do you not fear I will inform the authorities?'

Christy's expression adopted her customary mix of mockery and coquetry. 'I told you, darling, I trust you. I know you have no love for kings, whether Hanover or Stuart. I also know that you would not support such barbarity as this.'

He considered reminding her that she often worked for the government of the boy King Louis XV of France and his regent, the Duke of Orleans, and the hands of few rulers were clean of blood. However, he decided against it as her earlier sincerity still echoed in his mind.

'As to why,' Christy continued, 'the answer is simple. We would have you assist us.'

Another surprise. This woman was forever maddening, bewildering, enticing and astonishing. 'What manner of assistance could I provide? I know nothing of the workings of the Tower.'

'You do not need to, for we have that well in hand,' said Christy.

'In what way?'

A warning look reached out from Lady Nithsdale to her young friend but she need not have worried, for Flynt could tell Christy was never one to speak without due consideration. She would tell him only what he needed to know and no more.

'Dear Jonas, please do not be offended when I say that it need not concern you. Where we do require your help is once we have William free of that pestilential prison.'

Flynt's mind leaped to Newgate and the conditions there. He suspected his lordship's apartments in the Tower would be somewhat superior.

'We shall hide him in a safe place but it will only remain that way for a limited time,' her ladyship continued. 'It is of great import that we transport him from this unhappy isle with some rapidity.'

'To France?'

A smile. 'Perhaps.'

He folded his arms and leaned against the wall once more. The safe place she mentioned would be the apartments of the unwitting Venetian envoy, if Fairgreave played his part, but he didn't wish them to be aware that he knew that. 'Your trust in me is not limitless, it seems.'

'Don't be offended, but you know as well as I that trust is far from an inexhaustible resource. It has its limits and so must be rationed.'

'What makes you think I can help with safe passage?'

'A man of your pursuits, shall we say, will have associates, I am certain, in the docklands or on the coast.'

'I would have thought you too had such contacts, given the way you come and go from these shores.'

'I regret that my usual channels are closed to me for the present. The affair of the document last year has lowered my stock with my Gallic employers.'

Flynt understood. He had met Christy de Fontaine when searching for a will writ in the hand of the late Queen Anne that was reputed to promise the throne to her half-brother, none other than James Edward

Stuart. Christy had sold the document to the highest bidder and that had not been the government of France, who obviously had an interest in its contents.

'In addition,' Christy said, 'there is a detente between Paris and London, for the moment. The king is but a boy of six summers who yet grieves the recent loss of his parents and brother. The country is weary of war with England and the Regent d'Orleans continues to show the hand of peace.'

'For now,' said Flynt. 'I feel sure his other hand still grasps a sword.'

'Peace is ever fleeting in this world and we must enjoy it while we can. I will regain the good graces of the French but for now it is best I do not use their network. As you will gather, this is a matter most personal to me, for I love William Maxwell as though he were of my own blood, and Winnie has long been a sister to me, but I confess that so far my attempts to arrange passage have been singularly unsuccessful.'

Lady Nithsdale was watching him with interest and she leaned forward. 'You will have gathered that I am not convinced of your faith, Mr Flynt.'

'Yes, I had developed that impression, your ladyship.'

'But Christy says she trusts you and I will abide by her judgement. Will you help us in our endeavour, sir? There will be hefty recompense for your services, of that you can be assured.'

The sound of singing floated up from the bar below and Flynt cast an eye along the corridor again as he considered the request. He did have a few contacts but, once again, he might use young Jack, whose knowledge of the city's underclass had proved useful to Flynt long before Jonathan Wild realised what an asset the lad could be. His recent work in the docklands would also be a boon. The question Flynt asked himself was, did he wish to aid them in this enterprise? Christy was correct, he found the notion of such punishment distasteful. There were others slated to die – indeed, junior officers had already been brutally executed in the north after a series of trials – but he supposed if even one could be saved then it appealed to that sense of adventure which, though somewhat jaded by cynicism, still burned within him.

However, though she professed to trust him, he could not say the same for Christy de Fontaine, who was at best mercurial in her loyalties, at worst downright treacherous. Then there was Charters to consider. That he was bound to his service, albeit unwillingly and by means underhand, could not be denied and the man would expect, by right or by duty, to be informed of such a security breach. Flynt, though, cared little for the security of the nation and on examination found little threat to it should one minor nobleman escape a dreadful death at the hands of a vengeful government. The man had already lost his lands and titles. He need not lose his head.

'My lady,' he said to Lady Nithsdale, 'do you give me your word of honour that you are motivated solely by a desire to save your husband?'

She seemed confused. 'What other reason would I have, sir?'

'A desire to strike at the throne, perhaps. That this enterprise is somehow funded by foreign powers unfriendly to England?'

Christy seemed surprised by his question, which for some reason pleased him, for she was not a woman who was caught unawares easily. 'Have you of a sudden become patriot, Jonas?'

'As you know, I have a duty. If this undertaking is purely personal, that is one thing, but if there is mischief hidden within your enterprise, then that is quite another and as such I would feel obliged to inform Colonel Charters of it.'

He assumed that Christy de Fontaine had told Lady Nithsdale of his work with the colonel, but he hoped not too much. Her ladyship compressed her lips in a tight line as she nodded her understanding. She did not like it but she accepted it. 'You have my word of honour, Mr Flynt. All I want is my husband free and away from this cursed land. There is no political motive behind what we do.'

Flynt well knew that even though there was no intent, there would be political effect, but her word was sufficient for him. 'Then I will help if I can.'

Lady Nithsdale had heard what she came to hear, so rose and smoothed down her dress. Christy leaned back on Flynt's bed, her hands behind her, and stared up at him, her smile now returned to her. 'Jonas, you did not ask me for my word of honour.'

He laughed. 'Madame,' he said, 'that would be like asking the rabid dog to give me his word he will not bite. In the end you will be true to your nature.'

He knew it was no simple matter to offend Madame de Fontaine and he had not done so now. She laughed; again it was like music. 'My goodness, Jonas darling, you really do know me well. But you have my word whether you want it or not. On this occasion I wish only to assist my dear friends.'

There was something in her words that he had never expected to hear, and that was sincerity. Christy de Fontaine was doing this purely out of friendship and that appealed to him.

'And what of Gregor and the enmity he holds me? I do not wish to spend time looking over my shoulder for him.'

She laughed once more. 'Jonas, I feel sure you do that as a matter of course, but you have my assurance that Gregor will cease any hostilities, at least temporarily until our venture is complete.'

'And when will that be?'

Christy looked inquiringly at Lady Nithsdale, who remained sceptical. 'If dear Jonas is to assist us, Winnie, he must know our timetable.'

Her ladyship continued to stare with obvious reservation at Flynt but her eyes betrayed that she understood the sense in her friend's words. 'Very well, if you trust this man, Christy, then I must also.'

Flynt inclined his head in thanks and she nodded back, then left the room. He waited for Christy to reply to his query. Finally, she stood from the bed, adjusted the folds of her dress and moved to stand before him, staring up at his eyes and searching there for he knew not what. She was remarkably close and the power of her beauty reached out to him like a caress. He knew this to be her way, he knew she used men's lusts as a weapon to get what she wanted, but he could not help but feel the excitement of her proximity. Her reaching out beneath his coat with a single finger to play with the buttons of his waistcoat was of little assistance to his weakening self-control.

Her voice was breathy, barely more than a whisper. 'Do I have your word, Jonas, that you will not betray our venture?'

'I believe I have already given it, in so many words at least.'

'Not in so many words; I wish to hear the actual words, for when I hear them I shall know you are ours.'

'I give you my word. Does that satisfy you?'

She laid her palm against his chest and slid her fingers between the buttons to caress his shirt. He could feel the coolness of her touch on his flesh. 'Not yet, but I live in hope.'

He still did not fully understand his own motive for agreeing but his word had been given and he would keep it. He gripped her wrist gently and pulled her hand away. 'When does the escape take place, Christy?'

As usual, she was amused by his ability to resist her advances. She stepped away. 'The twenty-third day of this very month. Thereafter we shall have safe haven for a day or two of grace but passage must be arranged for soon after.'

That was only a few days hence, he realised. There was not much time. 'And will you be travelling with the Nithsdales?'

'Yes, Gregor and I will travel as their attendants and I will have my own maid.' So she was keeping her word to the servant. Christy de Fontaine was a most complex individual.

'Is this a task you think you can undertake successfully, Jonas darling?'

Flynt had already formulated a way in which passage might be contrived. 'Leave it to me, Christy. I will not let you down.'

She tutted in a dramatic fashion as she slid past him to the door, her body closer than was necessary for such a move. 'Perhaps you already have...'

15

Flynt had not entered Ned Turner's haberdashery on London Bridge
for some time but the small space had changed little. Its shelves were
piled with bolts of Irish linens and French cambrics, Indian muslins,
calicoes and worsted shawls, while boxes and chests were stuffed with
needles, pins, ribbons, gloves, hats and mufflers. All of the items had
been legitimately traded so Ned could provide receipts, bills of sale and
proof of import on request. He was most meticulous in that regard and
he could without doubt make himself a tidy income if he walked the
way of the upright citizen. However, it was his less than honest pursuits,
his life as a crimp, that brought Flynt to this place.

When Flynt last had business with Ned, the man had owned a
warehouse near the Port of London where he stocked goods that he
had taken off the hands of thieves and would sell on after a period
of time, perhaps even in conjunction with Jonathan Wild who, for a
reward of course, returned stolen goods to their true owners. As such,
Ned had many contacts in the flash world and that made him a useful
partner for the thieftaker, who protected him from legal scrutiny, for a
time at least. As Flynt had warned Blueskin, Wild's loyalties were erratic
and he could turn on anyone – friend, partner, lover – with ease. Flynt
knew Ned to be a canny trader and he would have protected himself
somehow from any such betrayal.

'How's business, Ned?'

Ned was bent over his small counter scratching at paper with quill,
his hands in fingerless gloves, and there seemed genuine pleasure in his
voice when he looked up. 'Captain Flynt! Business is as cold as the ice

below, tell you the truth.' He dropped his voice, even though they were the only two in the room. 'Just as well this place ain't my real bread and butter. But I ain't seen you in here for too long.' His voice suddenly became darker. 'You gone back to the game, have you?'

'No, Ned,' Flynt assured him, 'I'm a gentleman of leisure now.'

'Then how can I assist you? You on the hunt for some new toggery?'

'My clothes are fine, thank you.'

'Then if it ain't trade and you ain't got something to do away, what can I do for you on this bright and early?'

'I need to tap into the keg of information you call a brain, Ned.'

'Tap away, if I can assist I will, you know me. As long as whatever I tells you remains under the rose.'

'Whatever you tell me is for my information only and nobody will know it came from you, on that you have my word.'

Ned closed his ledger. 'That's good enough for me, Captain.' He rubbed his gloved hands together. 'Come through the back here. I've got some brandy and we can keep the chill out.'

Flynt followed him through an open archway to a much smaller room, also near brimming over with stock. Ned shifted bolts of cloth to reveal an old wooden chair. He gestured to Flynt to take it but he declined.

'Then I'll sit, if you don't mind, standing in that cold gets into my bones, it do,' Ned said, reaching to a shelf for a bottle and two cups then dropping into the chair with a groan. 'That's better. My trotters feels like I've walked barefoot across the river. Suffer from this here cold something dreadful, I do. I ain't as young as I once was and that's a fact.'

Flynt accepted one of the proferred cups. 'None of us are. That's life, I suppose.'

Ned poured a liberal measure of the brandy into Flynt's cup. 'That's the cruelty of it, right enough.' He poured himself a stiff one, set the bottle on the floor beside him, then stretched his legs out before lifting the cup to his lips. 'Ah, that sets a flame to the blood, it does. So, what can I does you for?'

Flynt felt no need to mention confidentiality, for it was the man's stock in trade. 'I have to get something out of the country.'

Ned's tone became businesslike. 'Something as in goods?'

Ned was correct: welcome warmth spread through Flynt's body when he sipped the brandy. 'Not goods, no. Who can I talk to?'

'Under the rose, right?'

'Very much under the rose.'

'So this something that ain't goods is hot?'

'If found it could melt the river ice.'

Ned nodded his understanding, took another mouthful of spirits. 'You'll need to talk to the Admiral, then.'

Flynt had heard of this individual but he'd had little experience with the dockyard criminality so had never encountered him. 'Will he help?'

'For a fee, he will.'

'Can you get a message to him?'

Ned's exhalation through his teeth was sibilant. 'Not a good idea, Captain. Him and I don't have what you might call a cordial relationship, so much so that I don't have my warehouse anywhere near the Pool no more.'

This was news to Flynt. 'What happened?'

'Let's just say that he didn't take kindly to my arrangement with a certain thieftaker of our mutual acquaintance and it was made clear that I would be best advised to get myself shifted before someone dropped a heated coal on some whale oil.'

'Did the Admiral deliver this ultimatum in person?'

Ned laughed. 'He did not. There ain't many what has seen him. Keeps himself to the shadows, he do. The message was delivered by his man, Daniel Pickett.'

'So how can I contact him?'

'He's a canny upright man, he is. Moves his flash ken regular so nobody knows where he is. Best way is if you know a natty lad down the docks who can maybe steer a word in the right ear.'

Flynt knew just the natty lad, and as luck would have it he was seeing him shortly. He drained the rest of the brandy in his cup. 'Thanks, Ned, I'll give it some thought.'

Ned stood and stamped his feet a little to bring back some circulation. 'Word of advice, Captain, have a caution around the Admiral. He's like a proper wraith, he is, but he's deadly dangerous for all that.'

Flynt handed his cup back. 'I'm a cautious man, Ned.'

–

Little Nick truly was little. Flynt estimated his age as being no more than ten but he was so emaciated and diminutive that there was a possibility he could be older. His face was smeared with filth, his hair matted and his clothes reeked of sleeping rough. His eyes, though, betrayed a less youthful appearance. Jack's were filled with bright intelligence and sharp humour; Nick's resembled those of Edgeworth Bess – watchful, suspicious, ever alert for an opportunity or an attack. They were the eyes of an older rogue somehow transplanted into the grimy face of a child.

He devoured the broth that Flynt had brought him, tearing with his teeth huge chunks from the lump of cockle bread in his hand. Flynt himself would not eat such inferior fare but the lad had without doubt learned never to let a meal go by.

Jack and the boy were already in the tavern when Flynt arrived. There was a satisfaction in knowing that his young friend had proved dependable yet again. Belle had wished to be present but Flynt had managed to dissuade her, pointing out that street boys like Little Nick could often prove skittish around those dressed in finery. Flynt's customary garb of greatcoat, black breeches, black boots and wide-brimmed hat with a single feather were acceptable, but a beautiful lady in silk could scare him. Even so, the boy had eyed him edgily as he seated himself at the table.

'This here be Mr Flynt,' Jack said, laying a reassuring hand on the boy's arm. 'He wants to ask you a few questions, is all. Ain't nothing to be in a pucker about, trust me.'

Little Nick darted an uneasy glance towards the entrance, as if calculating whether he could reach it before either Flynt or Jack could bring him down. Flynt slowly removed his hat and laid it and his cane on the table. The boy watched his movements warily. This was a lad who knew only two things – that the city was large and he was small. The hand holding the wooden spoon was tense, the grip white-knuckle tight, the cockle bread in his other hand forgotten about for the time being. Flynt shot Jack a questioning glance but he merely wiggled his head ever so slightly, conveying that all was well.

His movements easy and unthreatening, Flynt reached into his pocket and produced a few coins, which he laid on the rough-hewn tabletop in a neat pile. 'This bunce is yours, George.'

The boy's attention had fixed on the money but he was startled by the use of his given name for he looked up quickly to stare at Flynt.

'And this is merely for being here. There will be more if you will allow me to speak with you on a matter.'

The boy's gaze dropped once more to the small tower of coins, studied them for a moment, then, like a creature darting out from a hole to snatch its prey, the bread was dropped, the coins were scooped up, and both payment and the hand that held it vanished under the table, no doubt to be deposited in some pocket or other. The hand then reappeared to snatch the bread, as if he was fearful either Jack or Flynt would grab it first, and convey it to the boy's mouth. A chunk was torn off by teeth that already appeared to be rotting.

'What you wants with me then?' Little Nick said while chewing. His voice was, like his eyes, old and wary. The words were croaked, as though someone had recently constricted his throat, but Flynt guessed it had been roughened by cheap gin. The world was large and he was small but drunkenness can make a boy feel ten feet tall.

'Two nights ago you conveyed a message to the house of Mother Clap in Field Lane, did you not?'

More chewing as the child considered whether to answer. He fell back on the technique of prevarication by posing his own question. 'What's it mean to you, begging your pardon, sir?'

'Just answer Mr Flynt's question, Nick,' said Jack. 'You ain't in no kind of suds, you has my oath on that, and you'll be in line for more bunce if you cooperates.'

Nick was not reassured by Jack's continued insistence that he was in no trouble but the prospect of further payment was enough, for he said with a hint of defiance that his continued tension contradicted, 'Yes, I tooks the message, I did, so what?'

Flynt had to be certain they were talking about the same message. 'It was a request for a certain gentleman to attend the vicinity of St Paul's, correct?'

A cheeky little smile began to form and he wiped his nose with the back of one grimy hand. 'Yes, a molly, it was. They's all mollies in that house.'

'Who hired you to deliver it?'

A slyness crept into his expression and Flynt knew the boy had realised he could turn this conversation to his advantage. Further funds had been pledged but perhaps he could bump up the amount. 'Now then, I ain't terrible certain I can pass on information like that, I ain't. I mean, the coves what gets me to run errands obvious don't want their business being spoke about, do they? Elsewise they would use a proper messenger, right, and not some natty lad likes me, eh?'

Such had already occurred to Flynt. 'I can assure you, lad, that nobody will know you have told me. But is this person some lusty rogue, then, who would do you harm if he were to learn you had peached?'

Little Nick was still working on that bite of cockle bread, for it could be difficult to soften, but his chewing slowed a little as he thought of this. 'No,' he said finally, 'he ain't no serious villain, he ain't. But he wouldn't be happy if he knows that I squeaked his name. And if you speaks to him, he will know it, as certain as Gawd's truth.'

Jack piped up again. 'Mr Flynt will protect you, Nick, you has my word on that. There ain't many who would cross him, and those who does end up striped or giving the crows a pudding.'

Flynt would rather that Jack had not stated so baldly that he was capable of wounding or killing but it had the desired effect. The boy studied him with renewed interest, Jack's words giving him confidence. 'You promise you will protect me, Mr Flynt?'

'You have my word.'

'And when Mr Flynt's word is given, it's likes it was uttered from the burning bush, Nick,' promised Jack.

Nick spooned another mouthful of broth, then looked at the cheap and coarse bread in his hand as if he had realised how foul it was, but in actuality he was reaching a decision. 'It was No Nose Kelly what sends me, it was. He calls me in from the street, says he has an errand for me and slips me a fadge then tells me to go to Mother Clap's house and find this here cove Sam whatsisname...'

'Yates,' said Flynt.

'That's the cove, yes. He says he was to meet a certain gentleman up by St Paul's at eight of the clock.'

'And was this gentleman's name mentioned?'

Nick chewed. 'Some legal cove, Dimmock, Derwent, or some such, I don't recall rightly now, but the message was that he wanted to meet this Yates cove over something uncommon urgent.'

'And no reason was given for this rendezvous?'

'Just that it was uncommon urgent, as I says.'

'Did you not wonder why the likes of No Nose Kelly would give you a farthing and have you perform this service, and not the legal gentleman himself, nor an official messenger?'

Nick was sufficiently comfortable to emit a short laugh. 'I ain'ts about to turn down no fadge, sir, not for just delivering a message, even if it were to a molly house. And does you know No Nose? He ain't the type to use official services, he ain't. I'm cheaper.'

Flynt thanked the boy and dropped on the table considerably more than the farthing the boy had been paid by No Nose Kelly. The coins were plucked away to join the others as Flynt, with a jerk of the head to Jack, rose and stepped a few paces away from the table, his hat and cane in hand. Jack muttered something to the boy about being back shortly and followed. Flynt made sure they were far enough away from Nick's alert ears, not to mention others in the tavern, before he spoke.

'Think you this is the truth?'

Jack scratched his head, his forehead wrinkled in thought. 'Little Nick do keep his fives a-going and is an old dog at the foist – he can make me look like a heavy-handed clodhopper – but I reckons he speaks straight. He ain't trying to gull you, Mr Flynt, he got no reason. And me telling him you ain't a fellow to brush with will have convinced him, don't you worry.'

Jack's appraisal of the boy's dexterity at relieving other people of their property was less reassuring than his judgement of his veracity. 'Does Kelly still live in St Giles?'

'He do, Mr Flynt. Got himself a pissy little room to himself in the Rookery.'

The Rookery was a collection of structures that formed the heart of St Giles dating back to the time of the last King Henry and his daughters, Mary and Elizabeth. It was a mess of wooden buildings so broken down that their destruction would have been a mercy had the Great Fire of 1666 reached them. It was populated by many Irish families, each often crammed into a single room. For Kelly to have a room to himself might be seen as a sign of his status in the community but Flynt knew differently. Constantine Kelly was a lowly rogue who would do anything for money, which was not uncommon, but his personal habits and physical appearance were so repulsive that even the meanest of mumpers in the streets avoided him when they could. Flynt had encountered him on numerous occasions and each time left feeling as if he needed to scrape his skin clean of some contagion. He decided he would see the man himself and not put Belle through such an ordeal.

Jack's usual cockiness deserted him and he seemed discomfited of a sudden. 'You ain't going to be wishing me to accompany you, will you, Mr Flynt? Only, I has to gets myself to the Pool for Mr Wild, see...'

He let the words trail away and Flynt almost smiled, knowing that the boy was unwilling to be in Kelly's society, and for that he could not blame him. He had little wish for it himself but he knew it was unavoidable.

'No, Jack, you be about your business. Make sure Nick there gets his fill of more food, and ask friend Hines if he has something warm in the back for the boy to wear. Tell him I will fully settle up later.' The tavern's owner kept a supply of clothing that had been left behind by various patrons, for inebriation caused not only deafness but also loss of memory. Joseph Hines would know that Flynt was good for whatever was owed, and would no doubt inflate the bill, for the politicians and the shadow men of whom the late Sir Geoffrey had spoken did not own the patent on roguery and thievery.

Jack's mention of his work for Wild reminded Flynt of his other function this day. 'Before you go, do you have any intelligence as to where I may find the Admiral?'

The guarded look on Jack's face told Flynt that he knew of the man's reputation but to his credit he didn't issue any kind of warning. 'I'll put the word out, Mr Flynt. If he can be got, I'll get him, you know that.' The boy moved even further away from the table and shot a furtive glance around him again. 'Those coves what came at us the other night, down the alley. I hears it was Ben Painter's crew.'

'One of his men mentioned a Ben, yes. You know of him, Jack?'

'Only that he's a claret spiller for hire, which means that weren't no ordinary low toby lay. Someone has it in for you, Mr Flynt.'

Flynt placed his hat on his head and adjusted the brim. 'Jack, whenever was it not so?'

–

St Giles was seen as the patron saint of outcasts, vagabonds and lepers so it was entirely fitting that the parish be named after him, not just because of the hospital that had been created hundreds of years before, but because the Rookery and wider environs had become home to a motley of bawds, coiners, dippers and assorted rogues. Flynt had been told it was not always so, that the area had once been the home of the affluent, but cities change and London was most progressive in that regard. The streets were narrow and cramped, the alleys and lanes that struck off them filled with debris and dirt, the open ground to the back, like Field Lane, populated by pigs. The affluent had given way to the effluent to transform the picturesque St Giles-in-the-Fields into a pestilential place, and Flynt had no trouble believing that the plague that had ravaged the city sixty years before had begun in this rat-infested hole.

Flynt's flesh began to creep over his bones as he entered the ancient four-storey building in which Kelly lived, for he could hear vermin squeaking and scrabbling somewhere in the gloom. He moved first to twist the handle of the rear door, but it was either frozen shut, somehow jammed or locked. There was one way in and out of this place. Always good to know.

Kelly had a room on the second floor and Flynt ascended the uneven stairs, his left hand gripping an unstable bannister of unfinished wood. Somewhere up above, children's laughter tinkled through the gloom, a cheerful sound that was quite at odds with the dour surroundings, but then this was probably the only life those waifs had known, and at their age they should seek light in such darkness. They would be poor and hungry, and though he hoped they had loving parents, being raised in the Rookery meant they would like as not gravitate to a life of crime and an early death. The road to Tyburn most often began in streets and hovels such as this.

The door to Kelly's room was flimsy and would not take much effort to kick open but Flynt decided that such a dramatic mode of entry was not required on this occasion. He was here to glean information, not to shock, although he was more than willing to use force if he had to. Kelly was a sly creature and would no doubt attempt to bargain. He loosened the handle of his sword stick before he rapped his knuckles on the wood, dislodging flakes of what was once paint that fell to the floor like dry skin, then listened for sound from within. He had no firm knowledge that Kelly would be at home but it was only just gone twelve and the likes of the Irishman would not emerge from his lair until at least mid-afternoon. Kelly, like so many of those in the Rookery and on its peripheries, was by nature a creature of the dark.

With no sign of life coming from within, he pounded the wood with the flat edge of his clenched fist, confident that he would not raise any undue attention. The Rookery was not a location for neighbourly displays. If someone heard his knocking, they would merely be grateful that it was not their door on the receiving end. Such forces of the law that existed seldom ventured into this maze of buildings, with only Wild's thieftakers courageous, or foolhardy, enough to risk it because many of them had been born and raised in these streets. Neither of the two other doors on the floor opened, nor did anyone from above venture to the stairhead to see the cause of such a cacophony.

A cough finally reached Flynt's ear, then shuffling footsteps.

'Who be there?'

The voice was thick and rheumy, as if the owner was in dire need of some epic expectoration, something Kelly was wont to do with sickening regularity, expelling thick gobbets of slime at his feet and sometimes managing to miss the floor and strike his own person.

'A friend, Con,' said Flynt, not wishing to have his own name bruited in this dim corridor. He used the man's given name, or a diminution of it, as the appellation 'No Nose' was not used to what was left of his face.

There was a grunt and another clearing of the throat, followed by the sound of something disgustingly viscous being hawked up and sent hurtling to the floor. Flynt resolved to ensure he took a wide step over the threshold, although the chances were Kelly would have left other lumps of slime throughout the room. He grinned at the sound of a heavy lock turning, for such security was of little consequence with such a door. Flynt reckoned even Little Nick could kick it in if properly motivated. It opened slightly and a single eye peered at him, looking him up and down as if appraising his apparel. Recognition dawned.

'It's yourself, Jonas Flynt,' Kelly said. Despite being away from Ireland for at least thirty years, the man's accent remained strong, but then, the house would be filled with Irish people, drawn to the Rookery by the need for cheap accommodation and a desire to be with their own folk, perhaps seeking to make their fortune in the big city but finding only poverty, venality and corruption.

Kelly still did not open the door wider in welcome. Instead there was suspicion and not a little alarm. 'What's your business with me?'

'A word or two, Con. In private, if you please.'

Kelly made no move to allow him to enter. 'A word or two, is it? And what would that word or two be about, if I may ask?'

'If you let me in, you'll find out.'

The solitary eye squinted along the corridor to the top of the stairs. 'Would you be alone now, Jonas Flynt?'

'I would be,' replied Jonas.

Kelly seemed unhappy, but he would have reasoned that he could not keep a man like Flynt out if he was set upon entering, so he eased the door further, then stepped away. 'Then bring yourself in and be welcome.'

The need to appear hospitable, Flynt thought, was something shared by Scot and Irish alike, even if they did not feel it. He removed his hat and stepped over the threshold. 'God bless all here,' he said, not because he was devout but because he thought it might make Kelly somewhat more relaxed.

'Ach, God has long forgotten the souls in this here Rookery,' said Kelly as he slouched across the room. He was dressed in a thick but threadbare robe over a grimy white shirt and grey breeches pocked with the residue of his errantly aimed phlegm. His hair was grey and usually tied back with a black ribbon but it was loose this day, draped lankly over his shoulders like a woman's shawl. He found a bottle with the dregs of what might have been brandy on a table beside the fireplace, where the final few embers of the fire glowed like eyes in hell. It was cold in the room and Flynt wondered why the fire had not been rekindled, then realised that, the robe apart, Kelly had been preparing to go out. The man turned, holding the bottle up and revealing for the first time his ravaged face. His nose was flattened, leaving his nostrils widened, his cheeks scarred by the residue of sores. The man had been stricken by the French pox following a session with a bunter in a backstreet whorehouse off Satan's Gullet, an alleyway of demonic reputation that made the rest of St Giles look like paradise. He had submitted to treatment, having a mercury salve rubbed over his flesh and being left to sweat it out, but not before the disease had eaten away at his nose and forced it to collapse inwards. The lesions on his cheeks were the memory of where the pox had blistered.

'There's just about another two swallows in this bottle, Jonas Flynt,' Kelly said. 'Would you be for joining me in a cup of the creature? A wee tightener to keep the cold of the day from the bones?'

Flynt judged that there was barely enough for one swallow, let alone two, so he politely declined. Kelly gave the contents a further appraisal and seemed grateful. 'Right you are, Jonas Flynt, but you won't be minding if I partake, am I correct? I'm right parched, so I am.'

Flynt gestured for him to proceed and Kelly uncorked. 'If you can't get to heaven, may you die in Ireland,' he said before tilting the neck to his lips, draining the contents in an instant. He gasped a little, then wiped his lips with the back of his hand. 'Ah, it kicks like an ill-natured donkey, so it does. I've tasted smoother and far better but you know what they say about beggars and choosers, am I right?' He laid the now empty bottle back down. 'So, Jonas Flynt, what business would you be having with the likes of me, then?'

'The evening before last you sent a boy with a message to the house of Margaret Clap in Field Lane.'

Kelly avoided Flynt's eyes by unfastening his robe. 'Did I now? I don't rightly recall myself.'

'Con, let us not play games. I would know on whose behalf that message was sent.'

The robe was stripped from his bony shoulders and he reached for a grey waistcoat draped over the back of a rocking chair by the fire. 'Somebody has been making sport of you, Jonas Flynt, for I have no knowledge of such a message and have never frequented the house of Margaret Clap.' He slipped the waistcoat on, began to fix what buttons remained. He still did not engage with Flynt's gaze. 'Would that not be a molly house?'

'It would.'

'And what is it that Jonas Flynt has to do with such an establishment?' Now he looked up and a leer crept across his lips. 'I wouldn't have taken you for a man who likes to navigate the windward passage.'

Flynt let that pass. 'I am making inquiries on behalf of a friend.'

'A friend, is it now?' Kelly smoothed his waistcoat down in what seemed an absurd show of vanity, then reached for a coat hanging on a nail hammered into the wall. 'And what sort of friend would that be, I wonder?'

'The sort of friend who would know why you sent a messenger to Mother Clap's to lure a young man up to St Paul's.'

Kelly turned away as he shrugged the coat over his shoulders, once again avoiding Flynt's watchful gaze. 'Lured? My, but that's a strong-sounding word, Jonas Flynt. Why would anyone wish to lure this Sam Yates anywhere?'

'I didn't mention his name, Con.'

Kelly's movements stiffened as he realised he had taken a false step and almost absently his hand slid into his pocket. He turned, the hand now back in view but aiming a small pistol, which he cocked with his other hand. He froze when he saw that Flynt already had one of his own pistols cocked and aimed directly at his head.

'Easy now,' Kelly said, his voice not heeding his own admonition for it had raised considerably. He managed a nervous smile. 'How can I be sure you do not simply point an unprimed pistol at me, eh?'

Flynt was calm. 'Carrying a pistol in London that is not primed and ready to fire is like entering a whorehouse without the time or the inclination. It can be done, but what's the point?'

Kelly's eyes narrowed as he examined Flynt for sign of a bluff. When he saw nothing, he coughed and swallowed hard but still did not lower his weapon. 'We're all friends here, are we not?'

'Friends don't pull toby pistols from their pocket.'

'And look at you now, with a cannon in your paw.'

Flynt's lips thinned. 'Then perhaps we're not friends.'

Kelly feigned being crestfallen. 'And me offering to share my last drop of the creature too. 'Tis a terrible breach of propriety, so it is.'

'Throw the weapon down and we can discuss the nature of propriety and friendship and why you would wish to send a young man you have never met to a rendezvous with a dead man.'

Kelly smiled and his tongue snaked out to wet his lips. He was nervous but Flynt knew that was when this man was most dangerous. A dog may lick your hand, but as soon as it feels threatened, it will bite.

'I don't think I'll be doing that, Jonas Flynt, for I know the kind of fellow you are.'

'Do tell.'

'You're a man killer, so you are. Oh, I know there are folk who say you are charming and very gallant to the ladies, and you can turn a card or throw the bones with coves of all types. But that doesn't change what you are and I knows it full well. You're a thief and a killer, and so I don't think I'll be dropping this here toby, thank you kindly, for I think it's the only thing standing between me and my maker.'

'I'm not here to kill you, Con.'

Kelly waved his free hand around the room. 'You're not here to rob me, for I have nothing worth the taking, so why else would a man such as you come see me?'

'As I said, information.'

'Aye, sure. And once you have that, then I'm a dead man, I'll be bound. There may not be much life left in this ravaged body but I'll be damned if I'll let you steal it.'

'Con, I assure you I mean you no harm.'

'Says the man with his pistol primed and cocked and ready to take my head off.'

Flynt sighed. 'I drew this for self-protection only, but if it will make you happier, I will put it away if you undertake to do the same.'

Kelly's eyes narrowed as he weighed up the offer. 'There is something else that they say about you, Jonas Flynt. That you're a man of your word. Do you give that word now?'

'I do, most freely,' Flynt promised, and as a show of good faith peeled back the folds of his greatcoat and replaced his pistol in his belt. For his part, Kelly thrust the hand holding the toby into his pocket but kept it there. Flynt waited for it to reappear empty but it did not. Trust only went so far, it seemed, but it had to start somewhere if he was to make any progress.

'Let us begin again,' said Flynt, his voice reasonable but every sinew ready to move the moment he detected a move to pull pistol again. 'Why did you send that message?'

'Who told you I did?'

'That matters little; the fact is I know you did and I would know why. But let me make something clear, and you also have my word on this, should there be any sort of reprisals against anyone regarding this, then I will take it personal in the extreme and there would be repercussions.'

Kelly looked behind Flynt to the open door as if judging whether he could skip past him and evade further questions. 'You'll never make it, Con, believe me. Just tell me that which I wish to know and I will leave you to go about your business.'

'I sent no message.'

'Lies will not work with me. I know you did it and I would have the reason why.'

Kelly breathed deeply through his wasted nose, the sound unusually loud, as if it echoed in the twin caverns. He rumbled around in his throat to scratch up some phlegm and then let fly to the floor. 'I was paid to do it.'

'By whom?'

The smile that greeted the question was rueful, revealing blackened teeth, and Kelly turned away slightly. 'Ah now, if I told you that, I would be little more than a dead man walking, so I would, even more than I am already.'

He turned back and the pistol was back in his hand so swiftly it took Flynt unawares. He would not have suspected the man could move with such speed. 'Sorry, Jonas Flynt, you are a man of your word, but I think the devil and my own mother would tell you – if she were still around, God rest her and keep her – that I am not. Now, if you would be so good as to take perhaps six or seven paces to your left and grant me free passage to the door, I would be most obliged.'

'And if I don't?'

'Then I'll be the man who put a ball into the famous Jonas Flynt. I'll be famous myself, by God, and would drink on that reputation till the end of my days, so I would.'

Flynt made no move to do as he was asked.

'Don't be testing me now, for I am a frightened man and frightened men do desperate things.'

'Of whom are you frightened, Con?'

'The world, Jonas Flynt, and withering under the gaze of the Almighty when I face him, for I have been a powerful sinful fellow, so I have, and one more sin would not look out of place on my book of accounts. So, if you please, step over there and do it quick for I have places to be.'

Flynt's hand began to edge towards the opening of his coat but Kelly saw it and waved his pistol.

'Ah now, I wouldn't be doing that if I were you, for though I believe you most precise in your aim with them barkers I am convinced that at this distance even I couldn't miss. Now, do as I say, otherwise there will be blood spilled here today, as God's my witness.'

The man was rattled enough to be taken at his word on this occasion so Flynt began to move slowly to the side. This behaviour was out of character for the Irishman. Little Nick had said he was no serious villain, and that was true. Constantine Kelly was not a man to wield a weapon. Strike from behind, even stab, but not pull a pistol in a man's face. The way the muzzle trembled in his grip was worrisome.

'I'll come after you, Con, you know that. And when I find you we shall have a conversation considerably more forceful than this one.'

Kelly cautiously eased towards the door, never taking his attention from Flynt. 'He who runs away lives to run away another day. I'll vanish into the streets and do what I can to evade you.'

'Someone scares you more than me, else you would not be doing this.'

Kelly was almost at the door. 'Aye, you're a right terror, so you are, Jonas Flynt, but if there is one truth in this world it is that there is always somebody more terrifying. I have a child, did you know that? A girl, lives with her mother, though we never took the sacrament of marriage, another sin for me to atone for. You would kill me, certainly, but this person would do the same and then kill that child and her mother and anyone who even breathed in their direction. So, you are damned right

I am scared, and right now hopping the twig as far as I can from you and him seems to me to be the best thing I can do. After all, there is nothing here that demands I stay.' Something caught his attention in the corridor and he turned his face away briefly, allowing Jonas to dart his hand to the handle of a pistol. 'So, I apologise, Jonas Flynt, but I don't believe I'll be—'

He didn't get the chance to complete his sentence. An explosion erupted from beyond the door and a pistol ball entered by Kelly's left temple then erupted from the opposite side in a fountain of red. His head snapped to the side and his body tumbled backwards, but Flynt was already in motion before it hit the floor, a pistol free and cocked as he crossed the room in three long strides, wrenching the door open to hear footfalls on the stairs. He followed, aiming his pistol over the railing but caught only the sight of a wide-brimmed hat and a man's broad back as he hit the hallway below, where he stopped and loosed a hasty shot upwards from a second pistol, giving Flynt a fleeting glimpse of a face obscured by a scarf wrapped around his face. Flynt dodged back as the ball splintered the wood at his hand and when he peered over the bannister again the man was gone, but Flynt could hear some sort of commotion followed by the sound of wood cracking and a woman's screams of alarm. He took the stairs two at a time in pursuit, and reached the ground floor, where two elderly men manhandling a large packing case blocked the passageway to the street exit, their faces still bearing surprise at being confronted by an armed and masked man. A door opposite the stairway gaped open, bearing marks of forced entry, and Flynt guessed that the assassin had kicked it open. He followed, his pistol raised, and found a single room, sparsely furnished like Kelly's, and a young mother clutching a child to her skirts. On seeing Flynt she screamed again, shielding the youngster behind her, but he raised his free hand to calm her.

'Have no fear, madame, for I mean no harm. Where did he go?'

She raised one trembling hand towards an open window looking to the back yard that caught nothing of the low winter sun, the waves of mud frozen solid. Kelly's killer was already midway across the yard and vaulting over a low wooden fence to push his way through the pigs nosing around in the filth. Flynt paused to snap off a shot and was gratified to see the man stumble a little, his left hand rising to the right shoulder of his brown greatcoat, but the ball could only have grazed him for he continued his onward passage. Flynt cursed his errant marksmanship as he clambered through the window, dropped to the ground and broke into a run, his boots crunching through the frozen muck. His quarry headed for an open doorway and Flynt knew that if he reached it and made it through the structure, there was every chance he would lose him, for that building led to a maze of alleys and side streets in which a man could easily disappear.

A large pig managed to engineer its way into Flynt's path and squealed a protest as he pushed it out of the way with his knee and shin to reach the rear doorway where he paused. Beyond was blackness in which an assassin could easily skulk. Flynt flattened himself against the wall and withdrew his second pistol, replacing it with his spent first. He held the weapon with muzzle in the air as he concentrated on controlling his breathing, then peered cautiously round the corner of the doorway but could see nothing. He strained to catch any sound from within, the scrape of a boot, the cocking of a pistol, even the taking of a breath, but nothing reached him. What he was about to do was fraught with risk. The man he was pursuing might have been able to reload quickly and was now awaiting sight of him silhouetted against the sunlight, shaded though it was in this back yard. But he had to take the chance. He drew air in through his nose and exhaled from his mouth a few times, slow, easy. He closed his eyes briefly so that they might more easily adjust to the darkness, then slid into the open doorway, low and swift, the pistol in his right hand levelled before him, eyes opening now, ready to react to any movement and hoping that no innocent tenant chose that moment to walk down the passageway.

He met nobody, saw no movement. There were no flashes in the darkness and no pistol balls flying his way. Knowing well that the man he sought had already vanished, he reached the front entrance to the tenement and, having quickly replaced his pistols, scanned the street beyond, where people were about their own business and their own lives.

The entranceway was at the top of a short flight of steps and it gave him a slight vantage point. The street was busy, it being perhaps warmer to be moving in the open air than sitting in one of the hovels, but the brown greatcoat was to his eye of sufficient quality to stand out in this land of the poor. He was rewarded with a flash of such a garment a little way down the thoroughfare, dodging into a side street, so he broke into a run again. This would attract attention but he didn't have time to be covert in this pursuit. He reached the corner and peered around but the narrow lane was empty, although there were discarded packing cases piled near to a doorway, the wood splintered and slats missing, no doubt being used as firewood. The man would without a doubt have reloaded by now and that would make ideal cover for an ambush.

Flynt slid his armed pistol from his belt, eased back the hammer and, after gathering his faculties, threw himself around the corner, his weapon at shoulder height and trained on the wood. His pace was swift but haphazard, and he saw movement through one of the missing slats. Then the man's figure popped briefly into view above the pile to send a shot flying his way, but Flynt's serpentine movement was designed to make him a harder target, so the shot went wide and pinged off the brick wall. Flynt saved his ball until he could make it pay and continued onwards, watchful for the second pistol to come into play but there was no further movement. When Flynt reached the hiding place he aimed his pistol before him but the man had vanished into an open doorway leading into the decaying building behind. Flynt dashed into the dark maw of the corridor, hearing the sound of feet splashing in water ahead. The miasma of human filth clawed at his nostrils from the darkness and he became aware that he was running through an open sewer, the ordure flooding down from above. The footsteps ahead went down some stairs and then there was a bang as a door was kicked open. Light slanted upwards and Flynt saw the familiar brown bodies of rats scuttling away from him, but he ignored them to leap down the steps, the piss and shit flooding down to the open doorway like a noxious waterfall, and launched himself into another back yard, where wooden stairways perched precariously on uneven ground leading to upper apartments. A wooden walkway had been erected across what in warmer weather would be a welter of mud and human filth. The air here was fresher, but only marginally so. His target pounded across the uneven boards and Flynt detected a trace of blood where his earlier bullet had caught him. He stopped, took aim at the man's legs, wishing to bring him down but not kill, for he had questions to put to him, but just as he fired the man veered off to the right towards one of the stairways and the ball puffed up the frozen dirt beyond where his feet had been.

Flynt cursed and put his pistol away, for though he was adept at reloading on the run, he didn't wish to waste any time. The board-walk beneath his feet was poorly constructed and the rotting wood shifted with his weight as he ran, his eyes never leaving the man as he nimbly ascended the wooden staircase and vanished into an opening. Flynt followed, both hands gripping the roughened railings on either side to give him extra purchase as he climbed, cries and imprecations resounding from the interior of the building as his quarry forced his way through.

When he reached the opening, he found his way barred by a burly man brandishing a hefty cudgel.

'Who the fuck is you?' he asked, his accent from across the Irish Sea. 'You with that bastard that knocked my lass on her backside? Damn near killed her...'

His eyes growing accustomed to the gloom, Flynt saw a child crying as she sat against the wall, one arm crooked to her chest, being attended by a stick-thin woman he presumed to be her mother.

'I seek him, friend,' Flynt explained. 'Where did he go?'

'Do you mean him some harm, I hope?'

Flynt felt a smile tickle him. 'I don't intend to befriend him.'

That seemed to satisfy the big Irishman. 'Then he went down the stairs, but be swift, sir, for he moved like winged fucking Pegasus and was no respecter of children, as you can see.'

Flynt nodded his thanks and kept moving, already groaning within, for if the man reached the street he knew there was little chance of him finding him a second time. He took this fresh set of stairs as quickly as he could in the dark and reached the street door.

He paused, again studying the scene, knowing his gut feeling had proved correct. This time there was no glimpse of the brown greatcoat, no way of knowing which way the man had gone, right or left, or which of the many doorways or alleyways he might have ducked into this time.

Flynt leaned against the door frame to catch his breath and swore both loudly and fluently.

16

Flynt made his way back to No Nose's room where a knot of curious tenants had risked leaving the comparative safety of their homes to tie themselves around the still open door. Flynt pushed his way through, his manner and garb setting him as a man apart.

'Are you the constable, mister?' The only person to speak to him was a little girl, her face smeared with what might have been soot. She was perhaps around seven and, unlike Little Nick, had not yet lost the wide-eyed innocence of childhood. He hoped she never would but in reality, even if she survived the double threat of disease and the perils of the streets, his hope was a vain one.

He ruffled her tousled dark hair but did not reply as he stepped into the room. A woman had ventured over the threshold to roam the periphery, no doubt hoping to find something worth stealing, finally seizing upon a basket of logs beside the fire. She froze when she saw him watching her, but when he said nothing scuttled around him with her booty. Others may have already picked the room clean of what little there was, but Kelly had been correct when he said he had nothing worth stealing, although Flynt suspected his pockets would already have been rifled. Kelly lay where he had fallen, blood pooling on the dirty boards around his head where it rested on the right side of his face. His eyes were open and staring towards the door as if still in surprise. The entry hole was round and ragged but the exit wound could not be seen. That was a blessing for those children present, although he wondered if even the little girl who had spoken to him would be in any way affected by the sight. He would lay odds that she had seen violent death before and the presence of blood was not unknown to her. Whether she understood what had occurred was another matter.

He knelt beside the body and stared into the dead eyes. Constantine Kelly was a known snitch, one who would take tales to the thieftakers and the law if there was coin in it. The man would peach on anyone in order to line his own pockets and yet he had refused to part with the name of the one who'd had him send Sam Yates to the bogus tryst at St Paul's. And that someone scared him far more than did Flynt. That was interesting. Flynt well knew his own reputation and so was aware that whoever it was who had terrified Con into silence was a dangerous man indeed.

He gave the corpse one final look, feeling sadness envelop him. He had no love for the man but neither did he hold any rancour towards him. Kelly had suffered in his life and had never done Flynt a personal disservice. There were those of his acquaintance who had ended up in Newgate or Wood Street Compter due to his whispers, but Constantine 'No Nose' Kelly had done what he had to do in life in order to survive. Flynt reached out to gently ease the man's eyelids closed. They had seen all they would ever see and it was time for them to rest. He thought of the mother and child Kelly had mentioned. He had shown concern for them and, rogue though he was, if there was an afterlife, that alone would speak in his favour.

Voices demanding that the people clear the way made him stand and turn to the doorway. The press of bodies parted as instructed and the elegant, if squat, figure of Jonathan Wild entered, his cane ticking on the boards. Behind him was Blueskin Blake and another hefty individual who busied themselves in pushing those who had bled into the room back towards the passageway.

'Jonas Flynt, by God,' said Wild, his words displaying surprise, if not his tone or demeanour, as he flicked his cane towards the body. 'Is this your handiwork?'

'Would I still be here if it were?'

Wild did not reply but a flick of his eyebrow suggested he accepted it. He took a step closer and leaned over the corpse. 'No Nose Kelly finally peached on the wrong rogue, it would seem.'

Flynt had already considered that the murderer might have been one who had suffered due to the man's wagging tongue, but equally it could have been the person of whom he was so scared. He kept his thoughts to himself, though, for that was always best when dealing with the Thieftaker General.

'You were here speedily, Mr Wild,' he said.

Wild's voice was casual as he examined the wound on Kelly's temple. 'My men and I were in the area on official business and heard the cry of foul murder. Naturally, we felt it our duty to investigate, for the parish constable is unwilling to enter the Rookery.'

Flynt saw no reason to query this, for Wild and his thieftakers would often have cause to be in this part of the city, such was its reputation.

Wild straightened and sent a piercing gaze in Flynt's direction. 'And what brought you here, Mr Flynt?'

'I had matters to discuss with this man,' Flynt said, knowing it would do him no good to concoct some subterfuge for his presence. Kelly had spoken his name at the door and there was always someone who would have overheard and might see advantage in passing such intelligence along.

'What sort of matters would they be?'

Again Flynt decided that answering truthfully was best. 'I am invest-igating the death of Sir Geoffrey Dumont.'

Wild allowed that to hang between them for a moment. 'Is that so? On whose behalf?'

'My own behalf. I was acquainted with his lordship and I feel I owe him that much.'

His connection to the judge would not surprise Wild, who had an intelligence network that rivalled that of Colonel Charters, and he would know they had dined together, even though they had not been seen. 'No such investigation is necessary, for the culprit already languishes in Newgate and will hang before the weather turns, I expect.'

'Perhaps, but I must be certain. I'm sure you understand, Mr Wild. Justice is a fickle creature and can so easily be diverted.'

Wild gave him a long stare, one hand on the top of his cane, the other resting on the hilt of his sword. Blueskin had stationed himself beside the door but was listening to their exchange. Wild turned towards him and said, 'Mr Flynt here has doubts that Richard roasted the right man up by St Paul's the other evening. What say you to that, eh?'

Knowing there was some antipathy between his two men, Wild seemed to be on the goad but Blueskin knew better than to rise to it. 'It ain't for me to say, Mr Wild, for as you know it ain't my affair, but it's my understanding that the molly was grabbed a–standing over his honour's deceased corpse. Seems to me there ain't no doubts about his guilt at all and the cove will swing, and there's the right of it.' His attention moved to the body on the floor between them. 'But I would wish to know what Mr Flynt knows of this here milling, for we has been informed that he visited the deceased within this room not long ago. And here he stands over the corpse.'

Damn those wagging tongues, Flynt thought, but kept his manner easy. 'I've already intimated I had business with the fellow, but kudos on your investigative skills, for it is true that I was present when he was murdered.'

Wild gave Flynt a sharp look. 'You did not state this right off, Flynt.'

'I was about to when my friend Blueskin here saved me the trouble.' He saw the man bristle slightly at being named 'friend' which, of course, was Flynt's intention. 'Kelly and I were in discussion when he was shot from behind the door.'

Blueskin sneered. 'And you expects us to believe that?'

'Whether you believe it or no, it is the truth.'

'Did you see the villain who pulled the trigger?' Wild asked.

Flynt shook his head. 'His features were concealed. I gave chase into the back yard and to a building opposite and beyond, but whoever it was escaped into the warren.'

Wild turned to Blueskin. 'Did your informant confirm any of this?'

'He says he heard feet upon the stairway but said nothing of another person.'

'The man I pursued burst into a room on ground level and escaped through a window, the rear door being held fast. The tenant there will confirm what I say. I gave chase through the streets but he eluded me.'

Wild asked, 'Did you speak with this tenant below, Joseph?'

Blueskin seemed reluctant to answer. He was the dog with a bone and intended to worry at it. 'Aye, she said she saw Flynt here chase a cove. But all that he says could be flammery, Mr Wild. He could have being working with this other cove all along and the chase be all show.'

Flynt addressed Wild directly. 'Why would I want to kill Constantine Kelly, Mr Wild? I had no issue with the man.'

Wild breathed deeply and affected the stance of a man employing the wisdom of Solomon. Finally he reached his decision. 'You have no need to worry, for I believe you are innocent, Mr Flynt.' He flicked the tip of his cane towards the unfortunate individual prostrate before them. 'Of this, at least.'

'I am most gratified to hear it.'

'But I remain troubled by the reason for your presence. What connection would a snitch like No Nose Kelly have to the murder of a judge by a molly?'

'That was what I was attempting to ascertain before a pistol ball brought the conversation to a sudden but most permanent conclusion.'

'But what led you to him?'

Flynt watched Wild carefully. It crossed his mind that the thieftaker might be somehow involved and wished to see his reaction. 'It was he who sent the message to have Sam Yates attend at St Paul's.'

Wild's eyebrows raised. 'Did he, be damned! So it was not the judge himself who sent it?'

'No, and had your man Warwick made even the most rudimentary of inquiries he would have unearthed this for himself.'

A brief smirk flashed across Blueskin's mouth as Warwick's name was besmirched.

'That's as may be, Mr Flynt,' Wild said, 'but that doesn't mean that your judge friend did not have this man send the message on his behalf. No Nose was a snitch and it is possible that he would be known to a justice, is it not? And if that justice were of the molly persuasion then such subterfuge might well be necessary, no?'

Flynt had to concede that it was possible. Wild seemed satisfied with his own reasoning, as he was satisfied with most things about himself.

'You must face it, Mr Flynt, the Yates boy is gallows bait. What profit is there in muddying the waters of justice for the sake of one such as he? He and his kind are of no account and have no place in decent society. The Lord God sees them, my friend, and He judges them most severe.'

There was little more untrustworthy than a man who claimed to know intimately what his God would or would not judge, Flynt thought.

'But if you would know more about such men, then I have a suggestion for you,' Wild said. 'There is one who knows of their world with some intimacy. I do not refer you to him lightly, for he and I are not on speaking terms. We were once colleagues, but not friends, for I found his personal tastes perverse and his character loathsome. I think you will have guessed of whom I speak.'

Flynt nodded. 'You speak of Mr Hitchin.'

'Aye,' Wild said, the word coming out on the back of a sigh. 'Speaking personal, I would have *Madame* Hitchin pilloried for what he is, but he is canny and yet retains friends of some influence. But if you must, you have my leave to call upon him and inquire about the nature of the boy Yates, and perhaps even the true nature of your friend the judge.'

Flynt wanted to say that he did not require Jonathan Wild's leave for any action, but he held his tongue to allow the man the comfort of his own pomposity. For now, at least.

–

Charles Hitchin was a tall man who struck a fine figure in his long blue coat and tricorn hat lined with gold braid. His former pupil, now arch rival, Jonathan Wild had pretensions to gentility but could not disguise his street cunning, whereas his former mentor Hitchin, though also of humble beginnings, had developed an air of easy respectability which he carried off with considerable aplomb. However, as Wild had alluded, his sexual life, though often ignored by polite society, was not accepted by it. The man had a wife but that did not stop him from pursuing pleasures with his own gender. Such sexual gratification was more common than people wished to acknowledge, but Hitchin, it was rumoured, had a taste for youth, and that made him distasteful in Flynt's eyes. However, he would have to hide that revulsion, at least until he had gleaned what he wished to know.

Flynt found him in the Cross Keys Tavern in Holborn, sitting at a long table surrounded by a host of children and young men, each with the same hungry, sly look that Flynt knew so well from the streets. Wild had the likes of Blueskin Blake and Richard Warwick heading up crews of felons to do his bidding; Hitchin had these young pickpockets and street ruffians, his 'Mathematicians' he called them, the reason for the nomenclature unknown to Flynt. Hitchin looked decidedly at ease, his coat without blemish, his wig long and curled, his manner oozing charm and bonhomie. One of his hands rested idly on the thigh of the youth to his left while he engaged in conversation with the one on the right, his handsome features creased with humour.

One of the older Mathematicians saw Flynt heading their way and stood to bar his progress. He was a big lad, his blonde hair cropped tight, his blue eyes narrowed with suspicion as they roamed up and down Flynt.

'That'll be close enough, cully,' he said.

'I wish to speak with the Under-Marshal,' said Flynt, purposely giving Hitchin his official title. Unlike Wild, who had adopted the title of Thieftaker General – at least among those within his immediate circle – Hitchin did hold an office of local government. Four years before he had used an inheritance of his wife to purchase the office of Under-Marshal of the city for £700. Flynt understood that the auction price of the office had more than doubled since it was last put up for sale towards the end of the last century, proving how sought-after the position was, for it gave the holder control of the city's watchmen and marshals, albeit shared with the City Marshal above him. The title bestowed upon Hitchin carte blanche to plunder both the perpetrators and the victims of crime, and he duly set about the task with considerable vigour, reasoning that he had paid handsomely for the privilege and would make the most of it. He quickly pulled together his force of Mathematicians and developed the system of taking what they stole and returning the items, for a price. He wrote to the owners, anonymously of course, and suggested that if they wished the return of their property then they should make an appeal to what he termed the greatest proficient in the business of English thieftaking – namely himself – at his address near St Paul's Churchyard. The letters contained a warning that they must ensure that their pockets were well lined, otherwise Mr Hitchin would have nothing to say to them. It was a system that paid him handsomely and one that Mr Jonathan Wild was currently refining to an even greater degree of larceny.

The youth was unimpressed by Flynt's apparent show of respect. 'Has you an appointment?'

'I regret I do not, but I have a matter of utmost importance to discuss with Mr Hitchin.' Flynt sensed the man himself was listening, even though he feigned his attention being elsewhere, so added for effect, 'My name is Jonas Flynt.'

That seemed to do the trick. Hitchin dropped all pretence at being unaware of the conversation and waved the long, tapered fingers of his right hand, his left still caressing the youth at his side. 'Bill, my boy, let the gentleman approach.'

His voice was cultured but Flynt spotted vowels that spoke of Wolverhampton, a birthplace he shared with Wild. The youthful sentinel stepped aside to take the chair he had vacated while Flynt moved closer to stand opposite Hitchin, who studied him carefully.

'Jonas Flynt,' he said, as if savouring the sound of the name. 'I have heard of you.'

'And I you, Mr Hitchin.'

'They say you are a damnable rogue.'

'There is much said in the city, but a great deal of it is mere noise from those who wish to only hear the sound of their own voice.'

'So what I hear are mere lies?'

Flynt permitted himself a thin smile. 'Lies are but alternative truths in the minds of the gullible. And often people see that which is not there but convince themselves that it is.'

Hitchin may have thought he was talking about the rumours he had heard of Flynt's reputation but in reality Flynt's mind echoed with the statements by both the judge and Mother Clap. He was not the man they believed he was, he knew that. In truth, he was perhaps closer to the Jonas Flynt of which Hitchin had heard.

Hitchin smiled. It was a beaming smile that made him appear as if he was a welcoming fellow but Flynt knew that this man, like Wild or any of the other far lesser thieftakers in the city, would have Flynt's liberty taken from him in the blink of an eye if it would profit him, or even on a whim.

'What brings you to seek my ear, Mr Flynt?'

'A matter of the utmost delicacy.'

'And this matter of *utmost delicacy* is what, exactly?'

Flynt looked towards the young faces watching the exchange with interest. 'The kind of delicacy that requires privacy, if you please.'

Hitchin waved his free hand again, those long fingers brushing the air like a wizard casting a spell. 'Speak freely, sir, for these fine young men are my associates in our fight against the scourge of crime in this great city.'

Flynt resisted the temptation to laugh, for though Hitchin and Wild did feel the collars of many a thief, they were themselves two of the greatest criminals the city had ever seen. They received stolen goods, they extorted both victim and criminal alike and they even organised robberies themselves. 'With respect to your fine young men, sir, I would still value a moment of your time for a confidential word. What you share with them after that is your affair.'

Hitchin mulled this over for a moment before he removed his hand from the boy's thigh, his fingers enjoying one final, languid stroke, then pushed his chair back as he waved towards a table beneath a grimy window in the corner. 'Come then, sir, we will repair to yonder table. A few minutes only, however, for I have urgent business at the Session House this day. Upholding the law is a strict master and often my time is simply not my own.'

Good God, Flynt thought as he moved to the table indicated, the man was as pompous as Wild. As Hitchin eased himself from behind the table, the young man named Bill also rose again and followed. Flynt gave Hitchin a questioning look.

'There are many in the streets who would wish me harm,' Hitchin explained, almost apologetically, as he laid a hand on the young man's brawny shoulder. 'Bill here takes care that it does not occur.'

'I wish you no harm,' Flynt said, while thinking that if he had, the man would already be wounded or dead.

'And I believe you, sir, but Bill here,' he squeezed the youth's shoulder, 'he is not as trusting as I, are you, Bill?'

Bill's face was impassive as he held Flynt's gaze steadily. 'You ain't never know for sure and certain what's in a man's heart, Mr Hitchin.'

Hitchin's smile beamed. 'As you see, Mr Flynt, young Bill here is both suspicious of strangers and those he knows, and so is most solicitous of my continuing good health. Fear not, for though in the blossom of youth he is the soul of discretion; but his presence during our discourse is the price for my time and you must take it or leave it.'

Flynt shrugged and continued to the table Hitchin had indicated, picking up one of the chairs and rearranging its position so he could easily see the entire room, especially the gathering of Hitchin's young crew, as well as the front and rear exits. Hitchin's lips twitched as he noted the ritual. 'I see you are a cautious man too, Mr Flynt.'

Bill had positioned himself to Flynt's right, his eyes never moving from him. Flynt pointed his cane briefly towards him before he laid it on the table. 'There are two types of men in our walk of life, sir, those who are cautious and those who are dead. And on that note, I would have Bill here take a few steps to his right, if you please. I grow nervous when someone stands too close.'

There was a pause as Bill looked to his master for guidance. Hitchin thought this over for a moment before he bobbed his head once and Bill duly edged more fully into the periphery of Flynt's vision. Nonetheless he kept his cane at the ready should Bill see an innocent gesture as some form of threat against Hitchin and decide to exercise those muscles of his.

Hitchin laughed as he sat back in his wooden chair. 'Bravo, sir, bravo! Now, your business, if you please.'

'I would seek your assistance regarding a matter in which I have an interest,' Flynt said.

'I am honoured that the notorious Jonas Flynt should seek my aid. And if it is in my power to grant, then you shall have it.'

Hitchin would know that bestowing a favour might prove to be of worth at some point in the future. 'I thank you for that, Mr Hitchin, but I seek information only.'

'In what regard?'

'You will be aware, I am sure, of the recent tragedy regarding Justice Dumont?'

Hitchin's expression grew grave. 'Ah yes, a tragedy to be sure. A fine man, a good man. I would have thought a decent man but the circumstances surrounding his death may suggest otherwise.'

'That is the very subject that I would discuss with you.'

'And what exactly is your interest in this, Mr Flynt?'

'I met Justice Dumont recently. I too thought him a fine man and I would know the truth of the matter.'

'Truth is an elusive thing, is it not? As you said, lies are but alternative truths for some. But what do you think I can tell you? It is my understanding that the perpetrator of this evil crime was caught with his hands still red from his victim's blood.'

'To put it bluntly, Mr Hitchin, do you have any intelligence that his honour was a man who preferred the company of his own sex?'

Hitchin did not answer immediately. He placed his elbows on the arms of his chair and tented his fingers before his face so that only his eyes could be seen, eyes that now regarded Flynt warily. He had seen Jonathan Wild adopt a similar pose and it crossed his mind that this was something he had copied from his former mentor. It was Hitchin who had discovered Wild, recognising his skills as a receiver of stolen goods and manipulator of men, and had taken him under his wing. Hitchin had been suspended from duties at the time, although he had still retained the title of Under-Marshal and had no doubt felt the need to find someone to deal with his under-the-table business while he tackled accusations of corruption. Their shared spawning pool in

Wolverhampton might have helped him in his decision making but that did not prove propitious, for the relationship did not last long.

Hitchin's reply when it came was wary. 'Was he a molly is what you ask, correct?'

'In short, yes.'

Hitchin's eyes narrowed. 'And what makes you think I would know of this?'

The image of Hitchin's hand on the boy's thigh a few minutes before popped into Flynt's mind but an alternative truth was required. 'I know you have long advocated tougher measures be taken against such men and have had your constables raid many an establishment where they congregate. You are also a member of the Society for the Reformation of Manners. I would wish to know if you had heard any such rumours concerning Sir Geoffrey.'

Hitchin tapped his fingertips together as he calculated whether Flynt was making any kind of accusation. Flynt kept his expression open, hoping to convey that his request was entirely based on the man's professional experience with the twilight world of the molly. Publicly, Hitchin denied his sexual nature and was vicious with those who called him upon it, even though it was rumoured that he could often be spotted on Moorfields, known as Sodomites' Walk, with some of his young Mathematicians. There were many men of privilege who preach one thing by day yet do another by night. Such duality had ever been thus and ever would be, for hypocrisy grows with power.

The fingers ceased tapping and threaded together as if the man was in prayer. But his eyes remained ever watchful. 'There are a number of such individuals in high places, as you know, and though I will continue to do God's work where the law is hesitant, I must be careful. I will admit that in my long experience of dealing with these men that the name of Justice Dumont has never been uttered.'

'You never saw him before in the company of other men around St Paul's?'

Hitchin bridled as though Flynt was making an improper suggestion. 'What mean you by that, sir?'

'I mean no insult, or anything inappropriate I assure you. You have a house nearby, do you not?'

'I do.'

'And I wondered if you might have seen the judge walk there, perhaps in conversation with those other men who frequent the area after nightfall?'

Hitchin seemed mollified by Flynt's explanation. 'I cannot say that I ever saw him, but then I am not in the habit of frequenting the grounds of St Paul's by moonlight.'

No, Flynt thought, *you are more likely to be in Moorfield with your young acolytes.* 'And of the young man accused of his murder? Sam Yates?'

Flynt thought he saw something flicker in those ever watchful eyes and perhaps even a slight tightening of the fingers. Did those knuckles seem just a little whiter than before? It was possible that Hitchin was an habitué of Mother Clap's and had, in fact, recognised Sam's name. Or was Flynt himself guilty of seeing something that was not there?

'The name was familiar to me.'

'He led your men to the murderer Arthur Driver, did he not?'

'I believe he did. As foul an individual as ever drew breath.'

'And yet the society of which you are a member contributed to his defence.'

'I am a member, Mr Flynt, but I am not a guiding light. And murder is murder. *Thou Shalt Not Kill*, reads scripture, and my Bible's truth took precedence.'

'And Sir Geoffrey was the one who passed judgement.'

'That is so.'

There seemed nothing further forthcoming so Flynt tried another tack. 'What have you heard of his murder, sir? By playing such a major role in the attempts to keep our streets safer, you have the ear of the legal establishment. Are you aware of any disquiet concerning the young man's guilt?'

'This fellow Yates was arrested by one of Wild's crews and, speaking personal, I am disquieted over any incident in which his rogues are involved. You will no doubt be aware that there is little love between he and I. You know of our personal history, do you not?'

'I know that you found him in Wood Street Compter where he had been imprisoned for debt.'

'That is so. The compters and jails of the city are breeding grounds for young men who are hungry and sly and it is to my eternal shame that I raised him from that pit and gave him some semblance of a reputation. I taught the man all he knows about protecting this city from the depredations of scum and vermin and he repaid me by setting up in opposition and proceeding to pervert the great work on which we were engaged.'

Flynt struggled to keep his eyes from rolling. It was not easy but he did feel the corners of his mouth tug in a smile. Hitchin was so embroiled in his sermon that he did not notice. Bill did, however, for his eyes burned towards Flynt in warning.

'I tell you, sir, that was my greatest error in life,' Hitchin said. 'So, I say again, I am decided uncomfortable with the fact that Wild's men were involved in the apprehension of this young fellow... what was his name?'

Flynt was uncertain if the vagueness over the name was feigned or not. Hitchin had spent his life hiding his true self from those he did not know and was difficult to read. 'Yates, Sam Yates.'

'Quite so.'

'Do you think it possible that he has been falsely accused?'

'I would say anything is possible, Mr Flynt, especially where Wild is concerned. I hear it was Richard Warwick who arrested the fellow.'

'It was. Do you know him?'

'Aye, I know of him. Foul renegade that he is. He wished to become one of my constables but I rejected him, so it was only fitting that he end up working for Wild. If ever there was a man destined to be a Newgate bird, like others of his brood, it is he, but Wild will protect him. For now, at least, for sooner or later his seed will out and he will dangle too, you have my oath on that, Wild or no Wild. Perchance this bogus Thieftaker General will stand alongside him and feel the hemp strangle the lies and treachery from his throat.'

'So you are not aware of any rumours of sexual impropriety on behalf of Justice Dumont? No whispers, secret glances from others in the Session House?'

'It be true that such matters are often known and discussed outside the hearing of the individual themselves, but I have heard no such scandal in relation to his honour.'

Flynt was now convinced that Sir Geoffrey had been lured to St Paul's for the express purpose of murder.

'Would you care for some advice, Mr Flynt?' Hitchin said, as if he were a sovereign handing maundy money to a pauper. 'Look to the man's wife.'

'Lady Dumont?'

'Aye, speak with her regarding her husband, for it is my experience that the wife knows the secrets of a man's heart even though she does not speak of them aloud.'

Flynt considered whether Hitchin spoke from his own experience.

17

Jacob Simmons, Colonel Charters' man, was deeply apologetic. 'Begging your pardon, Colonel, but the cove insisted on gaining entry. I explained that you was not yet to home but he said he would wait so I placed him in your study.'

Charters frowned and glanced across the vestibule towards the closed door Simmons indicated. He was unaccustomed to receiving guests unannounced, which explained his man's flustered expression. Jacob had been with him since his service days, where Charters had found him as a young private standing up to a bullying, drunken serjeant who had been abusing one of his comrades. At the very least such insolence would have resulted in a flogging had Charters not sensed a quality in the young man and recruited him as his servant. They had been together ever since. He had spotted that same quality in Jonas Flynt. Call it what you will – honour, duty, decency – it was something that Charters not only valued but also recognised as a trait that he could use in his work. After Flynt had carried him from that ditch at Malplaquet, his arm shattered, his spirit hovering between this world and the next, it was Jacob who had nursed him through his convalescence.

Charters peeled away his heavy coat and hat and relinquished them into Simmons' waiting arms. 'Perhaps it would be best if you identify the gentleman in question.'

'A Lord Moncrieff, sir, surly bastard if you don't mind me saying so, but ain't that always the way?'

Despite his chagrin at the mention of the name, Charters suppressed a smile. They were master and servant but Jacob was never one to hide his feelings, as that serjeant in Flanders had learned.

He told him not to worry but as he crossed the hallway his annoyance grew, not at his servant, but at Moncrieff, and not simply because he did not like the man. Charters preferred to keep his private life separate from the secret function he performed on behalf of the nation. He had no wife, but he did enjoy a variety of carnal pleasures with a number of women, each chosen and valued for their discretion. Some boasted professional status, others were single and looking for a well set-up gentleman with whom to cleave in matrimony, while the remainder were already well connected by marriage and so had something to lose if their bedroom adventures were ever to be revealed. Not that Nathaniel Charters would breach such a confidence, for though he knew himself to be a rake, he liked to think he was not without a sense of honour, though he did skilfully avoid any long-term liaisons with those ladies whose eyes were set on the altar. His work often meant he had to commit questionable acts in order to protect this still fledgling Kingdom of Great Britain, but in his personal affairs he was as honourable as the next man. As long as the next man was not Lord Moncrieff, who Charters suspected had about as much integrity as a tuppeny whore desperate for her next bottle of gin. Principles in politics were as rare as hen's teeth, Charters had found, but then Moncrieff was no politician in the accepted sense, for he had no constituency to which he must answer. He was an advisor: he who stands behind those who stood in public, often in shade. His father, it was rumoured, had connections to a group known only as the Fellowship, which had exercised Charters' mind of late. They were secretive and Charters abhorred secrets to which he was not privy. He suspected that the younger Moncrieff was also part of the group, whose aims and function were as yet a mystery, but one which Charters was bound and determined to solve in the fullness of time.

Despite his dislike and mistrust of the man, as he entered his study he had to disguise his irritation at his personal space being so invaded, though he did shoot a surreptitious glance towards the mantel timepiece, an elaborate French design set within a bronzed figure entitled Time's Employ. He had British pieces in other rooms of his home but he admired the craftsmanship of Gallic clockmakers, even though he still viewed the country as the enemy. The reason for his glance at the hour was that he had an assignation in a mere thirty minutes, and this particular lady worked to a very tight schedule indeed. Charters did not want her ladyship to arrive only to meet Moncrieff leaving. That would not do.

Moncrieff was seated in Charters' armchair by the fire, which roared in the grate, Jacob being very solicitous of his master's comfort. The annoyance grew when he saw that the man had helped himself to a glass of his favourite port. He was certain that none would have been offered and equally as certain that Moncrieff would not have asked. Inwardly outraged by this flagrant breach of the rules of hospitality, not to mention the display of arrogance, Charters struggled to maintain his outward equanimity.

'I trust you are comfortable, Lord Moncrieff,' he said, hoping that he sounded welcoming but knowing full well there was some bite to the words.

Moncrieff seemed not to notice as he held the glass containing the port against the light from the fire. 'Damn fine drop this, Charters.'

'I like it.' Charters poured himself a glass then held the decanter up in an unspoken query.

Moncrieff nodded, held out his glass for a refill without a word, and Charters obliged, albeit grudgingly.

'To what do I owe the pleasure of this visit?' he said as he returned the decanter to its table.

'I regret the necessity of arriving unannounced,' Moncrieff said after taking a sip of the wine, his tone suggesting that even if his heart was sincerely sorry for the intrusion, which was highly unlikely, it had neglected to inform his voice.

Charters managed to mask his vexation with a welcoming smile and honeyed tones, for he had long since learned that he must never allow men such as Moncrieff to know they had incensed him, for they would see that as a scab at which they could pick. 'How can I help, my Lord Moncrieff?'

Moncrieff took another taste of the port. 'Some disturbing news has reached my ears,' he replied, then added almost as an afterthought, 'and those of Sir Robert.'

'The world is filled with disturbing news, my lord, but which piece in particular is it that sends you to my home on such a cold evening?'

And sampling my port wine without permission, he thought.

Moncrieff studied the colour of the wine once again. 'The affair of Lord Justice Sir Geoffrey Dumont. It has come to our attention that it is that fellow Flynt who has been conducting his own investigation and that you have failed to bring it to a halt.'

Fresh irritation tightened Charter's jaw. He had not spoken to Flynt since the day before but he was due for a report later that evening, after his paramour had returned to the loving arms of her husband. That Flynt had disobeyed his order to leave the matter alone was not the cause of said irritation, more that Moncrieff had heard before him.

'You must order him to cease immediately.' Moncrieff made it sound as easy as sending back an undercooked beefsteak.

Charters took a deep breath, to signify that this was not such an easy task. 'Jonas Flynt is not a man to take orders unless it suits him and I suspect that is one order he would not. He knew the judge and had some affection for him, it seems.'

'Flynt's affections matter little to me, or Sir Robert.' There was that afterthought again, Charters noted. 'He must be stopped from making further inquiries.'

'And this comes directly from Sir Robert?'

Moncrieff's eyes were slightly hooded. 'It does.'

Charters had doubts that were true but he kept them to himself. 'Why does it cause you so much concern? There would seem to be no issues regarding the murder and its perpetrator.'

Moncrieff avoided replying by rising, placing his already half empty glass on the mantel, then picking up the heavy poker from the fireside to thrust it at the wood in the grate. Charters thought this yet another invasion of his privacy. One simply does not enter another man's home and poke his fire. That's like dancing the blanket hornpipe with a fellow's wife in a fellow's own bed.

Once the fire was revitalised, Moncrieff studied the flames as they licked up the chimney before speaking again. 'I would have thought, Colonel Charters, that you would not wish someone to look too closely at the man's death.'

Charters was not slow in catching the accusatory tone. 'I would know what you mean by that, Lord Moncrieff.'

Moncrieff took his time replacing the poker, before straightening and turning back to face him. 'Come, sir, do we still act coy about the matter?'

Although the man's voice was calm, Charters was well aware this was an accusation. 'I assure you I – *we* – had nothing to do with it.'

'It is mere coincidence then that almost as soon as Sir Robert asks you to have the man silenced, he is found gutted in the street?'

'It is.'

Moncrieff's smirk was infuriating. 'As you wish, but now you must bring your dog to heel. We cannot have him nosing around, can we? Who knows what game he might put up.'

'Again, why does this concern you so greatly, my lord?'

Moncrieff drained his glass, set it back down. 'The why of it need not trouble you, Colonel Charters, but I will say this – you will understand that the ship of state often steers its course without your assistance but could founder if certain information came to light.'

'And does this information that seems to threaten the very stability of the state concern Sir Geoffrey Dumont's death?'

Moncrieff did not reply, merely stared back at Charters with those hooded eyes, revealing nothing. Charters pressed the matter.

'And you fear that Flynt might uncover this information?'

Moncrieff maintained his silence as he crossed the room to where his hat, coat and wolf's-head cane sat on a chair. He stared at the coat for a moment, as if expecting Charters to hold it for him. Charters did not move. He was not the man's valet and he would be damned if he would take such a subservient role, to hell with the rules of hospitality. Moncrieff resigned himself to hauling the greatcoat over his shoulders unaided.

Once the coat was wrapped around him, Moncrieff looked to a mirror on the wall to position his hat carefully on his head and began to worm his fingers into his gloves. 'You are a gamester, Charters, are you not?'

'I enjoy turning a card and rolling a die, yes.'

'I will amuse myself only rarely with wagers and when I do it is on a personal basis with gentlemen.'

And such wagers can be damned cruel, Charters thought, as he recalled the money exchanging hands over the still warm body of the tradesman outside White's.

Moncrieff picked up his walking stick, his hand brushing the silver wolf's head lightly. 'I do not like the haphazard nature of the tables. I am a man who likes to leave nothing to chance, for that way I cannot encounter any unpleasant surprises.' He waited for Charters to open the door. This time Charters did play the solicitous host, but only because he wished the man gone from his home. Even so, Moncrieff did not immediately cross the threshold into the vestibule. 'I already have your man Flynt marked down to be dealt with at some point in the future. Put a leash around his neck or I will see to it that something else is placed there. Do you understand me?'

He left the room without finding out whether or not Charters understood. Jacob must have been lurking in the hallway for he heard him say goodnight but Moncrieff, as was his nature, did not respond. It was doubtful he even heard. The front door opened and closed, leaving Charters to dwell on what it was he did not know about the ship of state and, despite Moncrieff's assertion that he did not like to indulge in gaming, why he suddenly felt as if he was being rolled like a pair of dice.

–

It was a most curious sensation walking through the doorway of Mother Grady's house in Covent Garden after being away from it for some months. Prior to that, Flynt had crossed the threshold often, sometimes two or three times a week, in order to see Belle. He had vowed that until he had somehow reconciled his turbulent feelings regarding Cassie he would not return, and yet here he was, taking his hat off as Jerome's smile beamed at him from the open doorway. The fact that he was here on business, rather than in pursuit of pleasure, did help justify his presence, if only to himself.

'Good to see you again, Mr Flynt,' said Jerome as he closed the door behind him to keep out the gnawing cold. 'Been some time since you've come by.'

He held out his hand for his hat but Flynt shook his head. 'I can stay but a moment, Jerome. I need to see Miss Belle; is she free?'

'She's with a gent at moment,' said Jerome, no longer the abashed young man he had been when he first arrived from Yorkshire. He had grown up fast in the keeping of his aunt Mary Grady. 'But if you wish to step into t'parlour, take thee a glass of wine, or there's sherry too if you'd rather, I can let thee know when the lady Belle be free. Shouldn't be too long now.' He lowered his voice. 'T'fellow she be with, he's a got a bit of a loose trigger, if you get my meaning. Tends to go off with t'slightest pressure.'

Flynt smiled. 'Thank you, Jerome.'

Flynt knew his way into the parlour without being directed. The room was usually filled with gentlemen of business and leisure awaiting their turn with one of the ladies, whiling away their time in a game of cards or simply discussing the events of the day over a glass or two, but this night it was empty. Perhaps the continuing cold weather chilled the ardour of the house's many regulars, but also the evening was yet young. The rakes and hellions would still be swilling in the taverns, the married men spending time with their wives, the sad and the lonely who needed succour and a soft touch yet to venture forth.

He poured himself a red wine, for he had never developed a taste for sherry, then warmed himself by the fire. The cold showed little sign of abating, although he did feel that perhaps it was growing a little warmer. The air did not possess the same bite, but the filth in the streets remained frozen.

He heard the door open then close and when he turned he saw Mother Grady staring at him.

'Jonas Flynt,' she said, her Irish accent strong, though sometimes he suspected she exaggerated it for effect. She was a sturdy-looking woman whose features retained traces of the beauty of her youth. Her cheeks sagged slightly, thick powder filling the cracks of her skin like mortar, and her true hair was concealed beneath an elegant wig. She was one of the most successful bawds in the Garden and she kept a clean house. Jerome could handle the bulk of any trouble that occasionally erupted, for alcohol and lust were combustible ingredients when mixed with arrogance and entitlement, but Flynt had seen Mother Grady herself pitch in like a diminutive Amazon with fists, an extensive vocabulary of salty language, and on one occasion wielding a long-handled brass warming pan.

He raised his glass in greeting. 'Madame.'

'I thought I'd seen the last of you.'

'I regret that I have been otherwise engaged and unable to visit.'

'Uh-huh,' she said, moving further into the room and taking a seat on an ornate couch of mahogany and red velvet. She adjusted her skirts in a demure fashion before focusing her sharp eyes upon him. 'You are distracting Belle from her work with this investigation of yours.'

He considered pointing out that it was Belle who had approached him but decided against it. In truth there was every reason to believe that he would have investigated upon his own volition, thanks to Sir Geoffrey's exhortation when last he saw him. 'I am doing what I can to keep her from accompanying me.'

Mother Grady accepted his statement with a single nod. 'She has a mind of her own, that lass. Always has, ever since she came to me. That's one of the things that makes her so good at her profession and that is what will carry her forward.'

The bawd had once told Flynt that Belle had plans for herself and that no man would either aid her – aside from parting with his coin – or prevent her. Flynt knew well that Belle was no helpless damsel. Few of the women he knew were.

Mary Grady seemed to dwell upon her next question for a few moments. 'Think you young Sam is innocent?'

He gave the query some thought before he answered. 'I think he may be, madame.'

This seemed to please her, for her usually severe features softened. 'He's a good lad. I was sorry that he had to leave here but it wasn't the place for a boy like him. He needed to be with his own kind.'

Mrs Grady tightened her face again. 'But always mind that Belle has work to do here and can't go gadding about the streets in search of justice. I give her a certain amount of freedom but I have a business to run and Belle is my best girl.' She gave Flynt a knowing look. 'As well you know... or used to.'

Discomfort pierced at Flynt. Of the three people in this conversation – he and Mary Grady as participants and Belle as subject – only the last was in any way innocent, in spirit and intent if not in the flesh.

'Belle knows right from wrong, Mrs Grady,' he said. 'And she sees what has befallen Sam Yates as a great wrong that she wishes to put right. You should take comfort that somehow you played a part in that, for it was you who educated her.'

'Don't be trying to flatter me now, Mr Jonas Flynt, for I am too old a bird to preen at the words of a handsome younger man. I may have seen to it that she was taught her letters along with the ways of men but this sense of right and wrong of which you speak was something she brought with her to this house. But I remind you that she is also a headstrong and ambitious young woman and she will do what is right for her. It is such spirit that makes her a valuable commodity.'

'Seeing this through is right for her but rest assured she is well aware of her commitment to you as a *commodity*.' Mother Grady's final word had grated with him. 'She will not let you down, Mrs Grady, and that is something I believe you know. So why did you start this conversation?'

She held his eyes for what seemed like a long time before she decided to speak. 'What is fact is that yon judge was murdered, and foully if the stories be true. Belle tells me that the lad was drawn to St Paul's by a message, supposedly from the judge...'

'It may not have originated with him at all, that is what I have come to tell Belle.'

'And that is my point. Someone capable of murder, and then ensuring that an innocent boy is wrongly accused and could well hang because of it, is too dangerous to be put in Belle's way, do you understand?'

There was a fervour in the woman's eyes that showed she actually cared for Belle St Clair, and not simply as the Covent Garden Abbess who owned her papers.

'I will not allow any harm to befall her, Mrs Grady, on that you have my solemn oath.'

'See that you don't,' she said, her gaze losing its intensity and falling away as she realised she had revealed more of herself than she had meant. 'There is coin to be made from that girl and I would not jeopardise my business on some foolhardy crusade.'

Flynt could not hide his smile. Mary Grady had experienced much in life, he could only guess exactly what, for she did not speak of her past. He suspected she had suffered at the hands of men and perhaps that had prompted her to use their lusts and desires and weaknesses in order to make her living. He did not know whether she had chosen that path or it had been forced upon her, although there were rumours of affairs in Ireland and here in London, all of which she declined to confirm or deny. She was hard-headed and ruthless yet she looked after her girls as if they were of her blood, to the point of helping a couple of them set up houses of their own when they became too old, or too weary, to satisfy those men who sought youthful beauty. She had brought Belle across the sea from the Indies for the express purpose of selling her body to those same men, and yet had educated her, taught her the ways of the world. Flynt suspected that Mary Grady saw much of herself in Belle's strong will and sense of worth, and even though the woman before him had the advantage of not being born someone else's property, she had struggled against oppression her whole life. She would take pride in Belle having possession of her own future, much as she had done, and no man would be allowed to claim credit.

She saw his grin and glared at him. 'Don't be thinking I am a weak-willed old woman, Mr Flynt.'

'Nobody would ever take you for being either weak-willed or old, Mrs Grady.'

She let out a short, disdainful bark of a laugh, but a laugh all the same, something Flynt had seldom heard. 'Away with you, I won't be swayed by yon silver tongue of yours. Just you mark my words, if any harm befall that girl I will hold you responsible... personal, do you understand me? You're a fearful vicious man, I've heard tell, but I am a wrathful woman and you do not wish to feel the fire of that wrath.'

Of that he had no doubt and he was about to assure her once again that he would protect Belle at all costs when the subject of their conversation entered the room. As was ever the case, he felt huge pleasure in gazing upon her, but that was tinged with the lingering pain he experienced over how he had used her in the past for his own gratification.

'What news, Jonas?' Belle asked, her eyes glittering with excitement.

He quickly outlined the events of the day, beginning with Little Nick, then No Nose Kelly and finally his interview with Charles Hitchin. Mother Grady's lip curled at mention of his name. 'That creature! He tried to extort money from me very soon after he bought the position of Under-Marshal. He said my house was at risk of fire and for a price he could ensure that it remained safe. I sent him away with a few choice words of the old tongue burning his ears but I had some game lads keep watch for months following. As you can see, the house still stands.'

Lines cut into Belle's brow as she replayed in her mind the inform- ation Flynt had provided. 'So if this man Kelly sent the message on someone else's behalf, who could it have been?'

Flynt caught a glance from Mother Grady designed to remind him of his promise. 'If we discover that, then perhaps we discover the person moving these pieces around the board. It is someone who wishes to remain in shadow, for Sir Geoffrey Dumont walked the streets alone with regularity, though he did travel armed and I do believe he would use the weapon if he had to. So to lure him to St Paul's it would have to be to meet someone he trusted. I would hazard that he received a message supposedly from Sam asking to meet him. He would know of Sam's name thanks to his fingering of Arthur Driver. Thinking he was to see the young man would have set him at his ease and leave him more open to attack from the real murderer.'

'But why? And why implicate Sam?'

'He may simply be a means to an end, someone disposable. As Mother Clap told us, the Society for the Reformation of Manners believe it part of their holy mission to cleanse this city of what they see as sin.'

Mary Grady asked, 'Think you those pious Bible thumpers are somehow involved in this farrago? I wouldn't put it past them to strike at their idea of sin by breaking a commandment or two in the name of God.'

Flynt had to agree. 'There is hypocrisy aplenty within that society, it is true. Both Hitchin and Wild support their cause, at least publicly, while fleecing all and sundry six ways to Sunday. Hitchin has even staged raids on molly houses.'

Mother Grady snorted a laugh. 'Aye, hypocrisy right enough for that is a furrow he ploughs himself right regular. And him a married man too. Although that means nothing, for vows before clergy are often taken to be suggestions rather than solemn promises.'

'That leads me to my next port of call – Lady Dumont.'

Belle's frown deepened. 'Do you think that wise? It will not be an easy conversation, for how do you ask a woman if her husband was a lover of men?'

'I do not think Sir Geoffrey was a molly. I think all this is but a feint, a ruse to prevent further investigation. Justice, they say, is blind but it also tends to be swift...'

Another snort from Mother Grady. 'Justice must be a man, then.'

Despite her focus on the issue at hand, that evoked a smile from Belle.

Flynt continued. 'By presenting a ready-made culprit in the form of young Sam, justice will be satisfied and it will run its course with no further official investigation.'

'Apart from ours.'

'Yes. But Lady Dumont may know something of her husband's work.'

'You would intrude on her grief?' Belle asked.

'I do not wish to but I must, Belle, for time is short.' He paused before he uttered his next words, but felt he had to stress exactly how short their time was in this matter. 'Sam will appear in the Sessions House presently and will without any doubt be found guilty.' He took a breath before continuing again. 'There is another hanging day scheduled in the next week.'

Mother Grady was, as ever, her customary impassive self but her eyes darted towards Belle to see how this news affected her. Belle's face seemed to slacken as the full import of what they faced bore down upon her. She digested this timescale then seemed to tighten her entire body. She stood straighter, her head held high, the Belle that he knew stiffening her own resolve.

'Then I shall accompany you to see her ladyship.'

Another look from Mother Grady but Flynt was ahead of her. 'Belle, I think it best—'

'Jonas, I know what you think and I understand that you mean to protect me, which is why you have continued without me, but in this instance I believe I can be of assistance. A man such as you paying a call on a grieving widow to whom he is stranger might prove something of a drawback, whereas a woman's presence might soften the approach. I will accompany you and will brook no further opposition on the matter.'

Flynt saw Mother Grady give a small shrug, as if to say that Belle knew her own mind. 'You have appointments this night, girl.'

'The hour is too late at any rate,' Flynt said. 'And I have other business that must monopolise my time for the present. We will attend her on the morrow.'

He watched Belle control her impatience before she finally nodded her assent.

18

Charters removed his coat and stood by the fire, watching as Joseph Hines placed a bottle of sherry and two glasses on the table in the upstairs room of the Black Lion. He had entered surreptitiously through the rear and ascended a stairway that was reserved for his use. Hines was the only person within the tavern that knew of his arrival and whom he was due to meet, knowledge of the latter being unavoidable. However, the muscular innkeeper was unlikely to tell anyone as Charters had enough intelligence on him to hang him ten times over. Hines was of use to him, not just to provide a place where he could meet Flynt in secret, but because his tavern was popular with the city's criminal classes. This was a man who knew many and knew much, and so was an ideal recruit to Charters' ranks. It was he who had alerted him to the fact that Jonas Flynt was actively engaged in illicit enterprise, allowing Charters to utilise his undoubted talents in defence of the realm.

'Joseph, are you aware of the incident not far from here the other night which left three ruffians dead?'

Hines turned from the table. 'Of course I am, Colonel, there is not much I don't hear of, otherwise I would be of no use to you, would I?'

'Yes, indeed.' Charters moved from the warmth of the fire to pour himself a sherry, as always marvelling at the precision of Hines' speech. Working in Drury Lane and owning a tavern like the Black Lion and rubbing shoulders with the criminal classes would lead one to expect him to express himself in the vernacular, and he did when dealing with them, but when he spoke to Charters it was as close to the King's English as he could get. 'What can you tell me of it?'

'It was Ben Painter's crew. Ben was known in his younger days as a bit of a milling cove, as they say, always up for a scrap, but of late he's been a freebooter, doing this job or that, but also been rumoured to hush people for coin.'

'A hired killer?'

'That's the word, though you understand I have never had the need to call on such services so really can't say for certain.'

'And his men?'

'They would do his bidding, for he was their upright man.'

Charters fell silent as he tasted the sherry. It was inferior but it would do. 'Is there word as to who might have hired him?'

'Not a peep, Colonel. Whoever hired him, if he was hired, wasn't from around here, for the word is that his services aren't cheap.'

'And the victim, any clue?'

A slight smile played about Hines' lips. 'Whoever it was, he was right handy. With two of them he was in at their beef with a sword, but Ben himself was popped in the chest, his cold iron still in his hand. Ben was expert with a blade, Colonel, but from what I hear it was unbloodied, so he was put down sharpish.' He paused, his lips still twitching. 'Whosoever it was who hushed old Ben was a quick man with both barker and Toledo.'

Charters had the distinct impression that Hines knew who that expert swordsman and marksman was, but he dismissed him without further inquiry. Flynt would be arriving presently and he needed time to think on this.

–

The black coach waited outside the Black Lion, the twin black horses pawing at the frozen ground of Drury Lane, breath pluming from their nostrils. The driver was a hulking brute hunched deep into his greatcoat, the reins resting easily in his gloved hands but his eyes watchful under his low tricorn hat. Another gentleman similarly attired stood by the carriage door as if it were a hackney awaiting a fare. As Flynt passed he heard a soft voice rasp from the dim interior.

'You will be Mr Jonas Flynt, if I be not mistaken.'

Flynt slowed his gait, his hand already twisting the top of his cane to unlock the blade within, prompting the sentinel at the door to throw back the folds of his coat to reveal both sabre and pistol, his hand coming to rest on the butt of the latter as though it were a lover used to his touch.

Flynt strained to see the source of the voice inside the coach. 'And who would be looking for him?'

A low and throaty chuckle greeted his suspicion. 'It has reached my ear that it is you who seeks me, sir, and unless you mean me harm, then I respond to your call in peace.'

Immediately Flynt knew the individual within must be the Admiral. Young Jack had outdone himself this time by putting out the word. He twisted the blade into the lock position and allowed his hand to fall to his side.

'I expected to attend you at the Pool,' he said, taking a single step closer to the carriage, but all he could discern was a darker bulk within the shadow.

'Aye and normally I would have demanded that but in truth, sir, I was curious as to why the famed, or should I say notorious, Jonas Flynt would wish to meet with me.' The man's voice was slightly muffled, his diction halting a touch as if he was taking a breath at every word. 'So I came to you in order to show good faith.'

Flynt gave the guard whose hand had not moved from his pistol a pointed look and heard the Admiral's strange breathless laugh again. 'I said I came in peace and good faith, sir, but it would be folly of me to come without taking precautions. It is a dangerous city, as you well know, and men like you and I each have enemies who would wish us ill.'

Flynt recalled his own words to Charles Hitchin about two kinds of men, those who didn't take precautions, and those who were dead.

The guard gestured to the open door with his free hand, his gaze never leaving Flynt's face. This man was a professional who would detect any thought of malicious intent in Flynt's eyes before it reached his hand. Nonetheless, he stretched out his palm and Flynt knew he was expected to part with his cane, something he made no move to do.

The voice rasped from the blackness of the coach. 'You need have no fear of violence from me, sir, for there is no enmity between you and I. But as you have requested this meeting, then Daniel must be certain that you wish me no harm.'

Flynt had been in such a situation many times but nevertheless was unwilling to enter that coach without the means of defending himself. He studied the man who stood patiently with his hand outstretched. This would Daniel Pickett, the one who had suggested to Ned Turner that remaining within the Pool of London could be detrimental to his commercial health.

'I am not your enemy, sir,' he said, without taking his eyes off Daniel.

'What are enemies but men who, under different circumstances, might have been friends,' the Admiral said. 'So let us remain friends.'

It was clear that he would not be granted congress with the Admiral while he was armed, so grudgingly handed over his sword stick. It was thrust quickly into Daniel's belt then the hand was outstretched again, his chin jutting towards Flynt's coat. Flynt sighed, reached to retrieve Tact and Diplomacy and gave them into the man's keeping. Daniel granted him a satisfied nod before taking a step back.

Another quiet laugh drifted from inside the coach. 'Come, sir, step aboard and I shall know why you had your lad bruit abroad your wish to have discourse.'

Flynt stepped up and settled into the seat across from the owner of the curious voice, who he could still barely see in the dim light. The General's reputation was ferocious and yet few had ever faced him and lived. As far as Flynt knew, his real name was known to no one and when he was spoken of, it was done in whispers, as if to voice his sobriquet too loudly would cause him to manifest like some malevolent spirit. Flynt had heard of him, of how he controlled the Pool of London and indeed much of the Thames coastline as though he were the Royal Navy. He was a big man, Flynt could tell that from the deeper shadow within the darkness of the coach but could not see his face. Pale amber light slanted in from an oil lamp burning outside the tavern to drape itself upon his legs, revealing the wings of a dark overcoat, black breeches and black boots very like Flynt's own. The General's left hand rested upon one knee, the skin puckered and serrated with scar tissue, then was eased away into the dark, as if the man had seen Flynt gaze upon it and was ashamed.

'So, Mr Flynt, how can I be of service?'

Flynt glanced at the still open door.

'Speak freely, sir,' the Admiral wheezed. 'Daniel is my most trusted associate from whom I have no secrets.'

Flynt could not help but think of the similar conversation when speaking with Hitchin and earlier encounters with Wild. These men were situated on opposite sides of the legal divide, though only ostensibly in the case of Wild and Hitchin, and yet they each shared a common bond in that they had enemies who would kill them in a heartbeat. Charters, also, did not move through the city without his own armed escort, discreet though they were. Flynt began to wonder if he should have a bodyguard too, for there were those who wished him harm, as had been proved by the events in the alleyway just a few steps away from where he now sat. That thought made him wonder again who it was that had sent them after him. He had enemies to be sure but could think of none who would hire such rogues to attack him. None alive, anyway.

'It is my understanding that nothing comes in or out of the Pool of London without your knowledge, would that be correct?'

A wheeze seemed to confirm Flynt's assertion.

'With that in mind, would it be possible for you to arrange covert passage on a vessel bound for the Continent?'

'For whom would this passage be booked?'

'That must remain confidential at this juncture, I feel sure you understand. It is a matter most delicate.'

'Illegal?'

'Not in the manner to which both you and I are accustomed.'

There was a silence broken only by the sound of the Admiral's breathing. 'If it were to be done, it would be costly.'

'You would, of course, be amply recompensed for any expenses and rewarded for your services. One other thing. The vessel must not be one that would attract the attention of the port authorities or the excise men. It must be legitimate in its business.'

'The passenger requires to remain sub rosa?'

'Passengers, sir, two, plus three attendants – two maids and a manservant.'

The General moved slightly, his hand coming back into view. 'Two maids and a manservant, eh? They do not travel light-handed. They are of quality?'

Flynt inclined his head in confirmation. 'As soon as they are on board the vessel must make sail almost immediately. It is best that there be no delay.'

'And when would this voyage be required?'

'As soon as possible after the 23rd of this month. I regret the urgency but time is of the essence.'

Another silence, then Flynt saw the man's shape move in the shadows and he leaned forward, his face coming into the light. The entire right side was masked in leather with even the eye covered, but tiny lines of scar tissue snaked out from the edges to cross his forehead and nose, while his mouth appeared somewhat twisted, as if the face cover gripped his lips too tightly. The skin of the cheek visible was smooth and unlined, and the single eye bore into Flynt with sharp intensity. Flynt had no doubt, given the man's voice, that the injuries extended to his throat and chest, and pondered what manner of accident had befallen him to cause such damage.

'Let us speak plain, Mr Flynt,' the Admiral said. 'Your principal, these passengers of which you speak, are traitors to the Crown, are they not?'

Flynt had heard the Admiral was sharp and his assessment of what little he had been told proved it. 'One man's traitor is another man's patriot, General. Does this change matters?'

A brisk chuckle. 'It changes the price, that is all.'

'So you will provide this service?'

'Aye, for a man's politics matter nought to me. But they cannot take ship in the Pool, for the river is yet held fast by ice. Can you convey your people to Redriff, where the tides flow more freely?'

Redriff was an old name for Rotherhithe on the southern bank of the river. Flynt nodded his assent and the Admiral stretched out his left hand, the one that had moved in and out of the light, raising the question that whatever had scarred him so badly had also damaged his right. Flynt grasped the hand.

'We have a bargain then,' said the Admiral.

'You have not yet quoted a figure, sir.'

'I have not yet calculated the true cost. I will send you word when I have it but there must be no haggling. I will quote a fair price and I will not exploit you or your principal, do we have an understanding?'

'We do.'

The General nodded and the solitary eye stared at Flynt for a moment. 'You are a man of honour, I believe.'

'I have my own sense of honour.'

'*Any* sense of honour and justice is a premium in this world, sir. Believe it or not, given my reputation, I too have my scruples. I will not cheat you and I will not betray you. You have my hand on it and that is as much a seal as contract witnessed and notarised.'

Flynt believed him. The handshake was ended and the Admiral merged again into the darkness.

'How will you be in touch?'

'By the same conduit you employed yourself, sir. The lad Sheppard is an efficient messenger, is he not?'

Flynt agreed but was concerned regarding young Jack's welfare. Did the Admiral know of his purpose in the docks? 'He is a good lad who has served me well and it is my wish to make further use of his skills. He is not a native of the docklands and I would hope that he remains safe in this dangerous city of ours.'

He had chosen his words carefully in order to convey his feeling but also to spark a response from the Admiral, who was a man of intelligence and wit. He was not disappointed.

'I know of his purpose in my manor but you need not fear any reprisals. Mr Wild and I have a somewhat curious relationship and he is at present endeavouring to remind me that he believes he has the upper hand. As it turns out, the thieving crew he seeks are also operating without my blessing and it suits me that they be brought to heel. I will throw Wild this bone and he will be satisfied, for the present. Have no concerns, Mr Flynt, your boy Sheppard is but a pawn in our great game, and if he is sacrificed it will not be by me, of that you can be assured. I do not wage war on children, even though they be canny lads sent to spy upon me. Also, I sense that the boy is more important to you than a mere messenger. Mr Wild I can handle, but you, sir, are a different matter entire, and I suspect that should harm befall the boy at my hand then the resulting reprisals would be exceeding unpleasant. I am a man of business, and such an occurrence – war between you and I – would be...' He paused longer than usual in his search for the correct word. 'Inconvenient.'

Flynt could not argue with the Admiral's evaluation of the result of any harm befalling Jack but nevertheless was grateful that he would not move against the boy. He nodded his thanks and turned the door handle.

'You shall hear from me on the morrow, Mr Flynt. I hope this is the beginning of a long and fruitful association.'

Flynt stepped into the street. 'And free from any *inconveniences.*'

That rough laugh reached out again.

Daniel handed Flynt his weapons and then swung up onto the seat beside the driver, who snapped the reins to prompt the horses into motion. Flynt watched the coach proceed down Drury Lane, wondering if he had just shaken hands with the devil.

–

Colonel Charters was warming himself at the fireplace in the upstairs room of the Black Lion, the only illumination in the room apart from two candle lanterns, his foot resting on the hearth, his one arm propped on the tall mantel, a glass of dark wine near his fingers. He stared into the grate, his features pensive, the flames sending his shadow writhing against the shuttered windows.

'You're late,' he said without shifting his gaze from the fire.

Flynt dropped his hat on the table beside the door but did not take off his coat, for it was perishing cold in this room despite the blaze The table was not set so they were not dining, which meant he would not be here long. 'I was detained.'

A grunt from the colonel, who seemed decided out of sorts. Normally he was filled with bonhomie, affected though it may have been, but this night it was obvious his mind was heavy with other issues.

There was silence for a few moments, leaving Flynt free to consider what he would report. He was resolved not to tell Charters of Madame de Fontaine's presence in London nor, more importantly, her mission to free Lord Nithsdale from the Tower. Why he had agreed to aid the plan remained a mystery to him. He could not decide whether it was some latent loyalty to a countryman, even though he be of the nobility, or some desire to assist Christy de Fontaine, whom he could not help but like, or merely because he wanted to cock a snook at the corruption he saw in Whitehall. All he knew was that he wished to shield the plot from Charters' gaze. The colonel thought himself patriot so would feel duty-bound to stymie the escape attempt.

He was pulled from his deliberations as Charters plucked his glass from the mantel above his head and finally turned away from the fire. Flynt steeled himself to field the question of Fairgreave and his suspected lover in Golden Square.

Charters, however, had other matters in mind. 'Tell me, Serjeant, what bad blood exists between you and Lord Moncrieff?'

The query caught Flynt unawares, for his attention had been on the separate issues of the murder of Sir Geoffrey Dumont and the plot to free the Scottish lord. He had thought nothing of Moncrieff since he had seen him for the first time on the ice.

'It is of a personal nature.'

'Personal nature be damned. I had the man at my home this very eve. At my home, Flynt!'

Flynt understood why Charters was so perturbed, for he protected his private life jealously. 'And he inquired after my health, I take it.'

A flicker of a smile perhaps, or merely a shifting shadow on Charters' face from the fire. 'In a manner of speaking. It is my impression he wishes you ill health and I would know why.'

'As I said, it is private.'

'Serjeant Flynt, you have damned little privacy in my eyes. You are mine, body and soul, and though I extend to you a degree of independence of thought and movement, do not forget that I hold your life in my hands. I care not what you do when you are not engaged in my service. I care little where you go or who you see or who you fuck, but when that private life impinges on mine I wish to know why. Now, what have you done to Lord Moncrieff?'

Flynt took a breath. 'I killed his father.'

Charters did not appear taken aback by this news. 'You did not report this. You said the elder Moncrieff died in battle.'

'I stated he died at Sheriffmuir and that was the truth of it. You only needed to know that the man was dead, not the manner of it, nor that it was by my hand.' Flynt took a breath. 'Colonel Charters, you require me to fulfil the missions on which you send me, you do not need to know how I do that and often you do not wish to know. As Machiavelli wrote: the end justifies the means.'

Charters accepted that with a shrug. 'When that end brings a creature such as Moncrieff to my door with dire threats, I will know the means. So what occurred?'

Flynt outlined the manner of the elder Moncrieff's passing in brief, of the chase across a bleak moorland and the final snap shot when the man lunged for a pistol. Charters listened, occasionally sipping his wine. 'So, the new Lord Moncrieff knows of this and would have vengeance?'

'I believe he will suspect it but not be fully certain. If he is of the same stripe as his father then suspicion may well be sufficient. He may also have already tried to have me murdered. The attempt by those men near Drury Lane was no low toby lay but a targeted attack on my person.'

Charters was not taken aback by this either, so Flynt divined he had already reached a similar conclusion. 'So it was you who despatched them after all?'

'It was them or me, Colonel. None of them will trouble the courts.'

Charters sighed heavily. 'In the name of God, Serjeant, I do believe you may be blood kin to the Grim Reaper himself.'

Flynt did not reply. Moncrieff's enmity could merely be vengeance for what occurred at Sheriffmuir but it was also possible that he knew of the sins of his father and wished to silence Flynt for fear word of it would leak, or that somehow he might attempt to claim an inheritance. Men like Moncrieff hid behind the faces they presented to the world. Respectability. Prosperity. Even piety. Any hint of scandal, whether proved or not, could damage all three and Flynt bore sufficient resemblance to the dead Scottish lord to set eyebrows arching and tongues wagging.

'Colonel, why would Moncrieff advertise his intentions to you?'

'It was a mere portion of his message, but the other part also concerns you. You continue to investigate the death of the judge, correct?'

Flynt saw no reason to lie. 'I do.'

'In direct opposition to my order to cease?'

Flynt felt that question required no response, though he could feel the colonel's glare through the gloom.

'This has apparently disturbed Moncrieff and his master, Walpole.'

'Why?'

Charters crossed to where a decanter half filled with wine sat on the table. 'That is what I would like to know.' He refilled his glass. 'What have you gleaned so far?'

'That there seems more to it than it first appears.'

'That, my dear Serjeant, is the way of the world.' He pulled a chair out and sat down at the table, waving his hand in the direction of the decanter. 'Pour yourself a glass, sit yourself down and tell me what you know.'

The air away from the fire remained cool so Flynt gratefully poured a glass of wine in the hope that it might warm his blood, then seated himself opposite the colonel.

'So you will not press me to give up my inquiries?'

'I will not. The day I take instruction from a lickspittle like Moncrieff is the day I hang up my sword and retire to the country to ride the fields with a hound. So tell me, my dear Serjeant, what is it that has Walpole and Moncrieff so exercised?'

'I know not what their interest would be. The only thing of which I am certain is that Sir Geoffrey was lured to St Paul's that night, as was the accused Sam Yates. Someone needed them both in that location for this plot to be successful. Someone wished the judge dead and an unwitting innocent to be blamed.'

Charters digested this. 'So you be sure that Dumont was no molly?'

'As sure as I can be, and Thieftaker Hitchin seemed unaware of any leanings in that direction.'

'Aye, he would be the person to know.'

'Mother Clap was also unaware.'

This seemed to shock Charters. 'You were in her establishment?'

'Aye, Belle and I visited to make inquiry.'

'Belle? Your courtesan? What is her interest in this?'

'She has a personal connection to Yates. It was she who first inveigled me into this quest.'

'And Dumont also knew this fellow Yates?'

'It may be he knew of him rather than actual acquaintance, for the boy steered the law to a man wanted for murder and Sir Geoffrey was judge. Arthur Driver, whom we saw hanged, if you remember. But I feel the judge and Sam were not sexually involved.'

'How certain be you of that?'

'Can any of us be certain what desires lie in a man's heart?'

Something gleamed in Charters' eye and Flynt guessed he was thinking of his own predilections. 'Quite so, quite so, Serjeant. And how came you to be so sure that the judge was lured to St Paul's?'

'He told me he had business that night—'

'Which could have been of a sexual nature.'

'Aye, but that I do not believe, for a fellow named Constantine Kelly was the author of the original message purporting to be from him to Sam Yates. He was enticed into doing so by one whose face I have not yet uncovered.'

'And this Kelly did not, or would not, reveal the individual's identity.'

'He may have, but a pistol ball to the head ended that line of inquiry.'

Charters blinked. 'You shot the man? That was somewhat hasty, do you not think?'

Flynt stifled the slight irritation. 'I do not shoot every person I meet, Colonel.'

'No, 'tis true. Sometimes you run them through.' Charters directed a curt nod to the sword stick now sitting on the tabletop.

'I did not kill Con Kelly.'

'Then who did?'

'I did not see him clear. I gave chase across the Rookery but he escaped.'

'The Rookery! That place is a blight upon the face of this great city.'

It was just one of many such blights. Charters was acquainted with rogues of every type but he lived in comfort, and seldom set foot in the foetid byways of St Giles or Southwark.

Charters asked, 'What will be your next step?'

'I intend to speak with Sir Geoffrey's widow on the morrow.'

'You think she has anything to add?'

'I will not know until I speak with her. Perhaps she will reveal something of why Walpole and Moncrieff would have me cease my inquiry.'

'Justice Dumont was a critic of the current administration and no great admirer of His Majesty either. Methinks he might have harboured fond feelings for the return of the Stuarts. He most certainly thought Walpole to be a scoundrel and was likely to be the source of a series of tips to the gutter press regarding his behaviour.'

'And is Walpole a scoundrel?'

Charters shrugged. 'He is a statesman and there is a hint of the scoundrel in them all.'

'Sometimes more than a hint,' Flynt opined but Charters ignored it. 'Do you think it possible that Walpole ordered Sir Geoffrey's death?'

Charters tensed, the fingers gripping the stem of his glass more tightly. 'I am not sure he would go that far, not with a sitting judge of the Session House. However, Sir Robert is an ambitious man, while

Moncrieff wishes to be swept along in his wake like a gull eating shit from a frigate's head.'

'But is it possible that they ordered someone to perhaps have a few words with the judge in order to have him cease and desist, and that person took it too far?'

Flynt sensed further tension from Charters. 'It is possible, of course.'

From his demeanour, Flynt could tell there was something the colonel was not telling him. 'And if I discover that such is the case, what then?'

Charters drained what remained of the wine in his glass before he responded. 'How fares your Latin, Serjeant?'

'Passable.'

'Are you familiar with the phrase *fiat justitia ruat cælum*?'

Flynt recognised the word for justice but his struggle with the remainder must have been evident for Charters translated for him.

'Let justice be done, though the heavens fall.'

19

Flynt had sent a message ahead to the widow of Sir Geoffrey Dumont regarding his attendance upon her at eleven of the clock that morning and, having received no response, he and Belle duly arrived at the dead man's Hatton Garden home on the appointed hour, to be admitted by a servant in black livery. He displayed no surprise at the colour of Belle's skin, but then his station required a great degree of unflappability. He took Flynt's hat, gloves and coat and Belle's fur-lined cape and hand muff, then led them with some solemnity to the drawing room where Lady Matilda Dumont awaited them, stiff and erect in a high-backed chair by the fire. Her clothes were dark, her black cap bearing a veil which she would wear down when venturing beyond her doors, but within her home she chose to wear it folded back over her head. Even in her current seated position, Flynt could tell she was both slim and tall and he mused she and her late husband would have made a curious couple, he being short and rotund. Her hair, undisguised by wig or powder, was thick and grey, and her face carried the lines of over fifty summers and winters, but Flynt also detected dark shadows and a hint of swelling beneath brown eyes pooled with sorrow. She had been weeping, this tall, striking woman, but she had done so, and would do again, in private. Shock flashed across her face as Belle was announced, swiftly replaced by a neutral expression. Those eyes, however, returned to Flynt's companion throughout the introductions as if curious to know what she would have to do with her husband.

'You may bring tea now, Lester,' she said as she gestured towards a two-seater couch facing the fire. Belle made herself comfortable but Flynt remained standing as the servant bowed slightly and left the room.

'Thank you for seeing us, Lady Dumont,' Flynt said.

'I am in mourning, as you know, but my husband had mentioned you, Mr Flynt. I was curious to meet you but also to offer my thanks for interceding with that lout Fairgreave and his disgusting friends...'

Flynt gave her a slight bow as if to say that it was nothing. He recalled the small pistol the judge had produced and the steely determination in his round face. 'Your husband, may he rest in peace, would have settled that particular matter without my assistance, of that I am certain.'

The woman's eyes rested on Belle. 'Perhaps, perhaps not. But forgive me, my dear, for I was unaware that my dear husband was acquainted with ladies of colour.'

Belle was used to comments being made regarding her race and her smile was one of her most charming. 'I regret I did not have your husband's acquaintance, your ladyship, for I have come to learn that he was a good and decent man.'

'Then why, may I ask, do you attend me? Is it merely because you wish to pay your respects? Do you do this for all grieving widows of my standing?'

Flynt's mind raced to find an explanation that might satisfy, but Belle, being Belle, decided to be as direct as Lady Dumont. 'I am friend to Samuel Yates, the man accused of your husband's murder. I believe him innocent of the crime.'

The judge's widow blinked three times. Flynt thought there was first anger, then consideration, then acceptance in her expression. 'I understand. I recognise that I should be furious at your impudence in coming to my home in this manner, a stranger to me and my husband, but you come accompanied by Mr Flynt and that must mean something.' She faced Flynt again. 'Although your acquaintance was recent and tragically brief, my husband spoke warmly of you. He called you rogue, but said you had more honour than many of his colleagues on the bench or, more importantly, in parliament. My husband was a fine judge of character and his assessment of you is enough for me. Given what this young lady has just intimated, I suspect you are not here simply to pay your respects.'

'We are not, madame,' said Flynt, recognising now that even though she be grieving, she had lost none of her directness, 'but know that I had the utmost respect for Sir Geoffrey, even though our friendship – and friendship I believe it was – was, as you say, brief.'

She bowed her head slightly in thanks before raising her eyes once more towards Belle. 'Thank you both. I must admit it has been… difficult to reach some kind of understanding of what has befallen my husband, and by extension myself.'

She broke off at a discreet knock at the door, which opened to admit Lester carrying a tray with a teapot, delicate porcelain cups and jugs of milk and sugar, while a maid who looked about twelve brought in a steaming kettle. Lester placed the silver tray on a three-legged mahogany table and carried it as though it were royal regalia to his mistress, setting it beside her chair. She laid her hand on the teapot to ensure it had been warmed. The kettle was set upon the floor where she could reach it easily. The girl left immediately but Lester fetched a wooden box with a lock from a shelf in an alcove and placed it beside the tray on the tabletop.

Lady Dumont ran a practised eye over the accoutrements and nodded her approval. 'That will be all, Lester.'

After another stiff bow, Lester slowly progressed to the door while Lady Dumont busied herself with the ritual of making the tea. Not a further word was spoken until the door eventually closed behind the servant.

'It is Bohea,' the widow said after she had unlocked the caddy and begun spooning leaves into the pot. 'So good for the humours and the bloods, I find. My dear husband found it most efficacious when fevered, for it promotes perspiration and encourages natural secretions and evacuations.'

Flynt recognised that the woman was making small talk while she worked mechanically at the process of preparing the tea, though he recalled Sir Geoffrey discussing the benefits of hot chocolate. Obviously the man had an interest in the health values of beverages. He waited patiently, for he knew that she would come back to the reason for their visit in her own time. While the lady's attention was on the caddy, pot and cups, he fired a warning glance at Belle, for he sensed her patience would quickly run thin. Thankfully, she understood and remained silent.

Lady Dumont asked if they required milk and sugar, her eyebrow raised when Flynt requested two heaped spoonfuls, for he had never enjoyed tea, finding it bitter and, despite Lady Dumont's apparent belief that it aided good health, leaving a foul and unpleasant aftertaste. Her ladyship had perhaps considered the cost of two heaped spoonfuls, for the substance was devilish expensive. Not for nothing was it termed white gold. However, hospitality won out over thrift and once the tea was poured, sweetened, lightened to everyone's individual tastes, then the cups handed over, Lady Dumont sat back and regarded Flynt.

'Now, sir,' she said, 'the proprieties have been observed, and you may broach whatever it is you wish.'

The flimsy cup felt awkward in Flynt's hand and he hoped his discomfort in handling something so fine did not show. 'As Miss St Clair has intimated, in addition to paying our respects we have come concerning the recent occurrence concerning his lordship.'

'I thank you for your delicacy but you mean my husband's murder, do you not, Mr Flynt? Please, you must call it what it was. My husband, my loving, loveable man, was murdered.'

Flynt felt a flush rise from his neck to his cheeks. 'He was, your ladyship, and it is our intention to find out who is truly responsible.'

'And you are certain it was not this young man?'

'I am,' said Belle. 'Sam is not capable of such an act. He is a dear, sweet, gentle young man.'

'As my husband would testify, the jails are filled with dear, sweet, gentle young men who commit foul deeds while under the influence of liquor, larceny or lust. And death can occur so very easily, without premeditation. I have lived in this house all my life, it was my father's before it was bequeathed to me, and there was an occurrence not far from here some years ago. Does the name Thomas Dangerfield resonate, Mr Flynt?'

'I must admit it does not.'

'You are not native born – Scotch, are you not?'

'Aye, I am Scottish, madame.'

'Then perhaps you would not know of him and, in any case, you are too young I suppose. And you, my dear, by your appearance and accent are clearly not from these shores and also very young. You are most beautiful too, if I may say so.'

'Thank you, your ladyship, that is most kind.'

Lady Dumont let the compliment lie for a moment. 'But to Tom Dangerfield. He was a thoroughly scurrilous individual. A highway thief, a cheat, a petty rogue, a liar who defamed many and who informed in order to cheat the hangman himself. But the law caught up with him and he was to be duly punished for his crimes. The law does not always see the right of it, I learned that from my father, who was also a judge, and from my husband, but in Tom Dangerfield's case, it was in the right. He was arrested, tried and sentenced to be pilloried and whipped through the streets over two days, first from Aldgate to Newgate and then from Newgate to Tyburn. It was after the first day when he was on his way back, here in Hatton Garden, that a barrister of my acquaintance, a fine man named Robert Francis, felt moved to ask him how he was after his little race with the executioner. I will admit that there was some bite to the remark to which Dangerfield took exception, and he spat upon my friend before calling him a most shocking name which I will not repeat. Incensed by the man's impudence, Robert struck him with his cane, penetrating the eye, and Dangerfield subsequently died. Robert had not planned murder, although it was later claimed that he did, but he had a sword at his side that would have made a better job than a cane.' Lady Dumont took a sip of her tea as she studied the silver stick in Flynt's hand. 'My husband told me you struck a fellow with your cane when interceding on his behalf. Did you know you could so easily have taken a life that night?'

'I hardly struck the fellow at all, madame.'

'Neither did my friend Robert but they executed him for murder all the same.'

Belle exclaimed, 'But it was an accident!'

'There were differing opinions on whether there was premeditation. Some stated that Robert had opined that he would save the hangman the trouble of stretching Dangerfield's neck. I did not then and I do not now believe that. It was scarce manslaughter let alone murder, but the courts did believe it and he was executed like a common thief. So, my dear, can you see how easy it is for someone to kill without meaning to?'

Belle was adamant. 'Sam would never hurt anyone, of that I am certain. And, with respect, this was not a casual blow with a cane, your husband—'

Flynt interrupted before Belle could say something indelicate concerning the manner of Sir Geoffrey's death. Direct she may have been, but there were some things you did not discuss in bright drawing rooms while sipping tea. 'Your ladyship, did you know the judge was attending the vicinity of St Paul's that night?'

The lady set her cup down on the round table. 'You are being tactful with me again, Mr Flynt. I well know the reputation of that walkway and you wish to know if my husband was a sodomite, correct?'

'Madame, I regret that—'

She waved away his apology and his embarrassment. 'I loved my husband very much, Mr Flynt. We shared a life and we shared a bed. There were no secrets between us and I would have known if he was such a man. He was not. I will stake my reputation and my fortune upon it.'

'Then what drew him there?'

'He was summoned. A messenger boy came by earlier in the evening, before he left to meet you for dinner.'

Flynt's guess had proved correct then. 'Did you see this message?'

'I did.'

'And who was it from?'

Lady Dumont looked to Belle. 'From your Mr Yates, it seemed at the time.'

Flynt asked, 'Can you describe the messenger?'

She returned her attention to him. 'It was a lad, common as you can get. Who can tell them apart?'

It could have been Little Nick but Lady Dumont was correct, to the untrained eye all the messenger boys did look alike. He had neglected to ask Kelly, or the lad himself for that matter, but it was possible the same conduit was employed for both missives because it lessened the risk of someone allowing their mouths to flap.

'What did the message say?'

'That this individual Yates possessed information that would interest him.'

'But it did not expand on what that information would be?'

'It did not.'

'Was his lordship surprised by receipt of such a missive?'

'Very little surprised him, Mr Flynt. He was a judge at the busiest court in the land. He had watched high-born and low-life file into the dock and thence to jail or the gallows. He had heard and even witnessed just how despicable people can be.'

'But was he in the habit of making rendezvous in the dark of night to receive such intelligence?'

Lady Dumont paused to brush at the fabric of her dress with one hand before replying. 'My husband received information from many sources.'

'On criminal matters?'

'Sometimes, but more often on political matters. He was a man of principle and a political animal who did not support this Whig government. He had nothing personal against most of the gentlemen in the cabinet, you understand, for he recognised that political differences were views to be debated and discussed in an academic manner. However, he despised Sir Robert Walpole and some of those he gathered around him.'

'Why?'

'He felt they were bringing the government and the country into disrepute by their self-interest. He believed His Majesty did not see them for what they are. My husband was never tempted to personally enter the political fray. He once told me of a gravestone that read "Here lies a politician and an honest man" and spoke of his amazement that they had buried two people in one grave.' Her eyes crinkled at the memory of the jest before she continued. 'But he was a committed Tory. He believed in the mercantile classes and their workers as being the way forward for this nation, not some outmoded idea of landed gentry and aristocrats knowing what is best for the serfs. He believed in justice, Mr Flynt, he believed in the rule of law, and he believed it was the right of every man, and even women, to have access to it. The Whigs do not have such principles. They believe in themselves only and what they can squeeze from the public purse. We have a king who cares little for this nation, and his government's patronage is little more than a whore to be had by whoever has the coin, and that is what drove my husband these recent years. He often said that Walpole's ambition would see him stifle all opposition.'

Flynt could have replied that the previous Tory government, unloved by George of Hanover when he took over the throne upon the death of old Queen Anne, was far from pristine in its dealings but he kept that to himself. They were here for information, not for a debate. 'I have been led to believe that the judge was actively feeding information to a newspaper.'

He watched her for a reaction, expecting her to either deny or decline to answer, but he saw no inclination to either. 'Yes, he thought he was being very discreet, for as a judge he could not publicly say much, or believed he could not. So whenever he found something that revealed the likes of Walpole for the disgraceful men they are, he shared it to that press.'

'And did he believe that Sam was going to provide him with such information?' Belle asked.

'He did, my dear.'

'But what kind of intelligence could my friend possess regarding such men of power?'

Lady Dumont's tone was soft. 'Given your friend's proclivities, he believed it would be something of a sinful nature.'

Flynt asked, 'Did he say as much to you?'

'He did. We had no secrets.'

'Would it surprise you, my lady, if I told you that Sam Yates also received a similar message, saying that your husband wished to speak with him?'

Her eyebrows shot up. 'Yes, Mr Flynt, that would surprise me. And would also go some way in bringing me more fully round to your point of view regarding the young man's innocence.'

Flynt sipped his tea, hiding his mild distaste, for even the addition of white gold did not make it much more palatable. He took a moment to consider his next question but it was Belle who filled the breach.

'Lady Dumont, was there anything of moment that your husband may have heard that could possibly have made his life forfeit in the eyes of those powerful men?'

'My dear, do *you* think it likely that those men would resort to murdering a justice of the realm?'

'Do you think it *not* likely? Have not men such as they committed sins in the name of monarch and country? I have dealings with these individuals in my profession and I know they can be brutish and uncaring. And they talk of their careers and their self-belief. Some believe they are on a mission from God to lead this country and they would do anything to ensure that they complete their work.'

Lady Dumont did not pursue further details on the nature of Belle's profession, though Flynt surmised she had guessed. That it seemed to make not a whit of difference to her attitude towards Belle was laudable. However, something else gleamed in her eye, as if Belle's words had somehow resonated.

'I spoke with the man who sent those messages to your husband and Sam Yates,' he said, hoping to further strengthen their argument. 'He would not tell me on whose behalf he sent them.'

'Why not?'

'Two reasons – one was that he was more fearful of whoever it was than he was of me.'

'And the other reason?'

'He was murdered in my presence.'

'By whom?'

'I did not see the assassin fully, though I did give chase but to no avail.'

'You believe this murderer is the person behind this affair?'

'Or works for him, yes.'

'And this man was killed to prevent him talking with you?'

'Aye. It is my belief that someone was pulling away a loose thread in this tapestry.'

'But this person did not attempt to take your life.'

'He tried, madame. So I would ask you, what did Sir Geoffrey vouchsafe to you that would cause such excessive consternation?'

It was Lady Dumont's turn to pause, licking drops of moisture left by the tea from her lips then carefully replacing her cup on the tray before settling back and studying her hands as she neatly folded them on her lap. Flynt could sense Belle's impatience rising again and he gave her a brisk shake of the head in appeal for silence. The lady must be allowed to make her decision in her own time.

Finally, Lady Dumont breathed in a deep lungful of air and looked up once again to Flynt. 'There may have been something.'

Flynt waited again. Belle seemed to be holding her breath. Like him, she sensed that whatever the woman was about to tell them was important.

'My husband had many informants. People trusted him, I'm sure you understand that, Mr Flynt.'

He bowed to show her that he did, not wishing to speak lest it disturb her flow.

'They told him things, people from both parties, for there are decent men on all sides.' She glanced at Belle. 'Women, too, like you Miss St Clair, for is it not true that men allow their tongues to wag in order to make themselves seem greater than they are? The political world is like a sieve trying to hold water. Information leaks through, despite the best efforts of the government.' She paused again to gather her words.

'A gentleman came to Geoffrey, oh it must have been two weeks since. He met him in this very room, just the two of them, but Geoffrey informed me later of what he had been told. As I said, there were few secrets between us.'

'Who was this gentleman?'

She hesitated, unsure of breaking such a confidence. 'Geoffrey kept his name hidden, even from me. He told me everything he said but he had promised to maintain that level of confidentiality. Suffice to say that it was an individual who holds an administrative position in government, for the great mill of state needs such men armed with quill and paper to keep it grinding. He was an anonymous little man, the sort who could blend into the background with consummate ease, where he could easily overhear things he should not. And he heard something which had disturbed him greatly.'

Belle's impatience would be denied no further. 'Which he brought to your husband's attention?'

'Yes, but not at first. He first took it to another man within government circles, one connected to the security of this nation who he thought would act upon it, but it seemed he did not. Only then did he step outside and bring it to Geoffrey.'

'And what was it he heard?'

Another deep breath. Another pause. 'A plot, Mr Flynt.'

'Against the government? The King?'

She shook her head. 'Against the Tory party. The Whigs have been hungry for power for many years, and now they have it they mean to keep it for as long as they can. In that they are the same as any other party, of course. But it is the intention of certain elements within the Whigs to destroy all opposition, and that means the Tories must be disgraced.'

'How do they intend to do that?'

'There are currently some Jacobite nobles in the Tower and there is a plot active to free one of them.'

Flynt hoped his surprise was not evident but he felt it hit his legs.

'The Whigs are aware of the plot and intend to do nothing to prevent it, then blame certain Tories for their participation. Lord Bolingbroke is already in exile, other Tories have joined him, been arrested or confined to their estates. As you will be aware, there was talk that many were sympathetic to the Stuart cause. If they can make it appear as if just one Tory was involved in assisting convicted Jacobites to escape execution, then that could go some way towards further undermining the party's reputation.'

Flynt processed this. Lady Nithsdale was determined to rescue her husband but he felt it unlikely she would work with the Whigs in order to achieve it. Christy, however, would not be above such intrigue. He knew her to be mercenary in her loyalties but there had never been a suggestion that she had used her particular charms and skills on behalf of the British government, although any effort to further destabilise the political system in London would most certainly be in France's favour. Or had word reached Walpole and the Whigs somehow, and they merely wished to take advantage of it?

'Do you think it possible that the Whigs would murder to keep this scheme concealed?' he asked.

Lady Dumont's smile was thin and grim. 'That, Mr Flynt, is what you must discover...'

20

The hackney lurched through the streets between Hatton Garden and Drury Lane with Belle and Flynt sitting in silence, both considering what Lady Dumont had told them. Flynt's mind remained on Christy and the judge's knowledge of the escape plan. He knew her to be ruthless, if charming, but he did wonder if she would have been quite so merciless as to have Sir Geoffrey silenced. The government official who had heard of the escape plan also piqued his interest, more specifically the person to whom he had communicated his misgivings in the first place. Someone involved in the security of the nation, Lady Dumont had said, and Flynt harboured suspicions of his own as to who that individual may have been and it was on his agenda to speak to him. As soon as he could, he would send a boy with a message to Colonel Charters.

'I have been considering Driver,' said Belle, without turning her head from the window through which she watched London life go by.

'What about him?'

She faced him. 'What know you of him?'

'Little more than you.'

'You have never encountered him?'

He laughed. 'I don't know every rogue in the city, Belle.'

Her expression remained thoughtful. 'I sense there is more we must learn. This connection between Sam and the judge should not be ignored.'

She was correct. He had focused upon mention of the escape and the connection to Christy. 'I'll see what I can uncover.'

She shook her head. 'Leave this with me. There is a cull attending me this eve who should be able to cast some light on Driver's life and crimes.'

'Who is he?'

She smiled now. 'His identity must remain confidential, for we girls have our code of honour much like you, Jonas, but he is a man whose professional duties will, I have little doubt, enable him to expand our knowledge regarding this man Driver. If he cannot, then I feel sure he will be able to find out for me.'

Flynt did not pursue the matter, for he understood that one of the reasons why Mother Grady's house was so popular was because it promised complete discretion. High-born men and those who governed the land could slake their sexual thirsts there without fear of being exposed or preyed upon. This man, from Belle's description, would be someone in the upper echelons of the judiciary, but she would not part with his identity, not even to him.

Before she climbed the steps to Mother Grady's front door, Belle suddenly stretched up and planted a kiss on Flynt's cheek. It was brief and it was chaste and unexpected. He watched her trip nimbly up the steps to enter the house, her smile as she looked back while closing the door warm and even inviting. As he paid the hackney driver, Flynt briefly considered following her, but he had work to do, so he walked to the Black Lion. The air remained brisk but did not burn at his cheeks as much as recent days. Perhaps the weather was on the turn.

Joseph Hines was trimming the wick on some candles when Flynt entered, the tavern busy with midday patrons, many of whom would become the afternoon patrons and on into the evening. Light burst into the room through the open door and did its best to penetrate the grime on the windows. Hines saw Flynt enter and gestured to a pot-boy to complete his task then strode across the room to meet him, wiping tallow from his fingers with a grimy rag.

'I have a message for you, Mr Flynt,' he said, reaching into the pocket of his smock to produce a sealed letter. 'From the Sheppard lad. I didn't know the little rascal had his letters.'

Flynt knew that Jack could form rudimentary shapes on paper, but this would not be from him, he was merely the courier. He did not reply as he opened the seal and scanned the brief lines contained therein. The hand was educated but spidery and he suspected it was writ by the Admiral himself. It told him that all was arranged at Rotherhithe, but sail would not unfurl until the late tide on the 25th, when the packet ship *Vesper* would be ready to accept passengers bound for the Continent. The fee quoted was reasonable and would be collected, the letter said, prior to the ship getting underway.

He folded the note and thrust it into his pocket to be burned later.

'There's another message for you,' Hines said, his heavy eyebrows beetling. 'From Whittington's College. There's someone what wants you to attend him immediately. Do you know of a Newgate bird by the name of Sam Yates, Mr Flynt?'

If Sam had funds to despatch a runner to the Black Lion then hopefully it meant he was being better treated. But why would he be calling upon him and not Belle? And how did the young man know to have the message sent to this particular tavern?

'Aye, I know him. Was there anything further to the message?'

'Nay, just be there quick as you can, at your pleasure, of course. But you must go alone.' He blew out his cheeks. 'I'll say this, rather you than me. I cannot abide that place.'

Flynt did not relish returning to Newgate but he knew he must attend. And whatever it was, the lad had deemed it not suitable for Belle's ears.

-

He paid the garnish to enter the prison and walked across the Press Yard to the main building, fighting his revulsion at entering this foul den once more. It was Josiah Sprigwood who met him, managing a look of haughty disdain even though his swaying demeanour was evidence of a man who had recently made liberal use of spirits.

'Does you come to threaten an officer of this here establishment once more, I asks?'

'Do you need to be threatened to fulfil your office, Sprigwood?'

'I knows my responsibilities better than you does, Mr Jonas Flynt. Aye, I knows your name now, for I have made inquiry and I have learned that you should be enjoying our hospitality, you should, but you be damnable cunning, and so you walks free. But one day, and mark me you should on this point, you will be here and I will have domain over you.'

Flynt did not reply, for in his heart he suspected the man's words may prove prescient. He held out coins and Sprigwood snatched them away. 'I will see Sam Yates again,' Flynt stated, avoiding mentioning that the young man had actually requested his presence. 'And he had best be more comfortable than before or else you and I will be having words.'

Sprigwood sneered and barked out a laugh, his courage buoyed by liquor, further evidence of which floated towards Flynt on the man's breath. 'He is, damn your eyes, but not because you and that jumped-up strumpet made your threats. His funds and garments was uncovered, they were, so he is clothed and better housed than last you sees him, though in here that be marginal.'

Flynt followed the man along a corridor towards a flight of stairs, the scents of the prison swirling around him like foul-smelling wraiths. Somewhere voices lifted in song, a sprightly melody that he failed to identify, but the sound seemed alien in such a dreadful place.

As they ascended the stairs, Flynt said, 'I suspected the funds and clothing might be found eventually. An administrative error, perhaps?'

Sprigwood failed to catch Flynt's sarcasm. 'Aye, such occurrences happen, they do. This here jail is a decided big operation and there be times when little things slip through.'

'Well, friend, I am right heartened to hear that this *little thing* was found.'

Sprigwood unlocked a gateway at the top of the flight and stepped back to allow Flynt to pass. 'I be no friend of yours, and don't be forgetting that, sir. I takes my office most serious and I resent the imputation you made last that I was in some way corrupt. I is a honest man, I is, and am God-fearing. I has the respect of my peers, I does, and your remarks does give hurt.'

It was Flynt's turn to laugh, for the man's pomposity and seeming lack of self-awareness suddenly struck him as amusing. Sprigwood frowned at him as he turned from locking the gate behind them. 'You laugh at me, sir? I am a figure of mockery?'

'Aye, I laugh and I thank you for it. I have laughed not near enough these past few days.'

Sprigwood tutted and led him to a door which he opened to reveal a dark room, the slit of a window shuttered to block out the day, though a sliver of pale winter sunlight cut through a split in the wood to land on the boy himself, lying on a cot. Sprigwood blocked the threshold, his hand held out, his mouth tightened into a thin line. 'I require my garnish to which I am entitled.'

Flynt had been expecting this and dropped further coins into the man's upturned palm. 'Take this, if only for the entertainment value you provide.'

Sprigwood pocketed the coins then stepped away to allow Flynt to pass, feeling the chill in the room even through his coat. It may have grown warmer outside but the thick walls of the prison not only kept people in but any rise in temperature out. As his eyes grew accustomed to the gloom, he saw the remnants of a single candle in a holder on a small table. 'I would have some more light here,' Flynt said but Sprigwood did not move. 'You will not fetch a fresh candle?'

'There be added garnish for luxuries.'

'A candle is luxury in Newgate?'

'Candles cost money.'

'You have been amply paid.'

'His funds is near all used up, they is. No more money for candles unless you wants him to starve.'

'Leave it be, Mr Flynt,' he heard Sam say, his arms moving to clink the chains at his wrists tethering him to the wall. 'I do not wish to see anything further of this foul place than I already have.'

Flynt sighed, his brief good humour evaporating. He perched on the edge of the cot. 'He remains manacled?'

'Orders from the Keeper,' Sprigwood replied. 'The boy's humours is unbalanced, he says, and there is fear he may do himself harm, he may.'

'Your solicitude towards his health is to be complimented.'

'We keeps them healthy so they can face their Maker from the tree,' Sprigwood said, once again failing to catch Flynt's tone. 'And this one here will be dangling there soon enough, he will.'

'He has not yet been tried.'

'Soon enough, says I, and Tyburn-bound is he, for it all be but a matter of procedure now.' Sprigwood's smile remained fast. 'Confessed, he has.'

Flynt shot the boy a startled look. 'Is this true?'

Sam's head slumped a little and all he could deliver was a limp nod. 'That is why I sent for you.'

'Why, Sam?'

The boy shot a glance under his brows towards Sprigwood, who still grinned in the doorway. 'Because I am guilty, Mr Flynt, and I must pay the price for my sin.'

Flynt was momentarily stunned into silence during which he studied the boy lying on the cot. The lad was tense, but given he was admitting murder to one who had been trying to prove his innocence, it was understandable. However, something else troubled him and when Sam directed another glance to the doorway, Flynt guessed that it was Sprigwood. 'Privacy, if you please,' Flynt ordered over his shoulder.

'You has all the privacy you needs, you has,' said the jailer. 'It is my job to be nearby lest you tries to assist in escape.'

'In the name of God, man, the boy is chained to the damned wall, do you expect me to wrench him free with my bare hands?'

'Nevertheless, here I is, and here I stays. Rules is rules. And I will thank you to not blaspheme, for I am a God-fearing man and I do not take kindly to His name being taken in vain.'

Suppressing his growing anger, his earlier amusement now completely gone, Flynt forced his attention onto Sam's face. 'Tell me what happened that night at St Paul's, Sam.'

The boy avoided his gaze. 'You know what happened, Mr Flynt. I met the judge and killed him.'

'Why?'

An uncomfortable shift in position made the chains clank again. 'Does it matter? I did it and let that be an end to it.'

Flynt rose and paced the dim room, sending a glare in the direction of Sprigwood casually leaning against the door frame, that damnable smile still present. 'Who has spoken to the lad since I was here last?'

'Nobody but myself and the Ordinary, who wished to save his soul, though it be damned to everlasting torment. And a Sheriff's man what comes to question him.'

'And to whom did he confess?'

'To the Sheriff's man and me, both humble servants of the law.'

'Under interrogation?'

'It were given freely, to ease the strain on his eternal soul.'

Flynt looked back to Sam. 'Be this true? You confessed freely and there was no duress?'

The slight pause that followed the question spoke volumes. 'It is as Mr Sprigwood says. The weight upon my conscience was great and I had to purge myself.'

'Then tell me precisely what occurred that night at St Paul's. Leaving nothing out.'

Sam sighed, almost impatiently. 'There is nothing left to tell. I had an assignation with Sir Geoffrey. I pleasured him but he refused to pay, and I took my knife and I stabbed him in my rage.'

'I don't believe you.'

'I cannot help what you believe, Mr Flynt, but it be the God's honest. I did it, and I must pay.'

Flynt let that pass. 'Tell me what you saw when you arrived at St Paul's.'

'What I saw?'

'Yes, who else was present?'

Sam seemed puzzled by the query. 'Others like me having tryst, for it is a sodomite walk at that hour.'

'And you pleasured the judge, you say?'

'Aye, he bid me place my hand down his breeches and rub his manhood.'

'And have you performed this service for him before?'

'No, this was the only time.'

The boy spoke as if he was a poorly rehearsed player upon the stage, repeating the words but with no feeling. 'Who raised the alarm?'

'I know not, but I was in a frenzy and unaware of those nearby. But someone did cry beef, for the thieftaker's men arrived.'

'Led by the man Warwick?'

Sam flinched slightly. 'I know not their leader's name, Mr Flynt, God's truth I don't.'

Until that point Sam's voice had been dull but now a desperate tone had crept in. Despite the denial Flynt was certain the man's name had resonated.

'How swiftly did the thieftaker's men arrive?'

'Within minutes. They told me they were in the vicinity on other business and heard the cry of murder.'

Flynt's mouth tightened. They had a habit of being in the vicinity on business. Wild had said the same when No Nose Kelly died, and though it was possible in the Rookery, he felt on that night in St Paul's they were there because they knew ahead of time that murder would be committed. 'And did they take statements from those nearby?'

'There was none around by that time. Everyone had hopped the twig swift-like, them not wishing to be party to murder and to protect themselves, if you get my meaning. These men, those such as I, they need to keep their true selves secret, you understand.'

'And you recognised none of them?'

The boy shook his head. 'It matters little, Mr Flynt, for I did this thing and there is no more to be said.'

'There is a lot more to be said, lad, for I don't believe you. I suspect there has been coercion here.'

Sprigwood spoke up. 'I already said, I did, the boy spoke only to—'

Flynt's head snapped around. 'If I wish to hear from you, sir, I will address you directly. Until that moment I will thank you to remain silent.'

Before the jailer could argue further, Sam spoke again in his lifeless tone. 'It is as Mr Sprigwood said. I had conversation with the Ordinary and he made me see the true extent of my wickedness, how filled with sin my life has been, and that it was time to atone. I killed the judge, sir, and that be all that needs said.' Sam raised his head and the desperate plea returned to his voice as the boy reached out with both hands to clasp Flynt's. 'Please, Mr Flynt, I thank you for all that you have done, and Miss Belle too, but I beg you to leave it be. I am guilty and you must accept that, as I have.'

Flynt felt something clutch at his throat as he stared at the young man now trembling on this filthy cot. Even in the dim light slipping through the slit in the shutters he could see the terror shining in his eyes. That he was lying, Flynt knew in his gut. That someone had applied pressure Flynt also knew. Someone had terrified the boy sufficiently to force him to confess to a murder he did not commit.

And he would find out who.

–

The carriage awaited him at the Whittington Gate and Flynt recognised the men standing alongside as the same who had accompanied Charters to Tyburn. *God's teeth, was that really only a few short days ago?* One opened the door to the carriage as Flynt appeared and he climbed in. Charters regarded him with his customary mocking eye.

'Picking out some decent accommodation, Serjeant?'

Flynt was in no mood for the colonel's badinage. 'I was visiting Sam Yates.'

'There have been developments?'

'He has confessed to the murder.'

Charters pursed his lips. 'Then that will be the end of it and him, I wager.'

'He is innocent, of that I am convinced. Someone has forced him to make confession.'

'How would they do that?'

Flynt looked back to the shadows deepening on the gate. 'I will discover presently.'

'How do you propose to do that?'

'That is something you are best not knowing.'

Charters opened his mouth in silent comprehension. 'And is this why you summoned me here? To tell me this?'

'No, but there are matters associated I wish to raise.'

'And they are?'

Flynt returned his attention to the colonel. 'Why did you have me follow Lord Fairgreave?'

'As I have said before, the why of the matter need not concern you.'

Flynt ignored the rebuff. 'Was it because you believed he was part of a plot to free a Jacobite nobleman from the Tower? A plot known to the Whigs who intend to allow it to proceed in order to shame their political opponents?'

Charters was an old hand at concealing surprise but Flynt saw his eyebrows jerk. 'I suspect denying such knowledge would waste our time, yes?'

There were only a few individuals concerned in national security and Flynt had surmised that the individual to whom the unnamed government official had reported originally was Charters. He was gratified that his intuition had proved correct. 'And you were alerted to this by a fellow named William?'

This time Charters could not fully control his astonishment. 'Good God, Serjeant, you have been busy at the digging.'

Flynt ignored what Charters meant as a compliment. 'Who is he?'

Any intention Charters had of fobbing him off was abandoned. 'William Beardmore was a clerk in government employ, a mousy fellow with a manner so quiet and presence so thin that you would forget he was in the room. That was exactly what occurred. He was present when Walpole and your friend Moncrieff discussed intelligence they had received regarding the plot to free one of the Jacobites.'

'And from where did they receive this intelligence?'

Charters smiled. 'From me, of course, where else did you expect it to come from?'

Charters had eyes and ears throughout the city so it was no surprise to learn this. 'What exactly did you hear?'

'Do you know, Serjeant, I don't much enjoy explaining myself to you but since I suspect you have much to tell me, I will allow it on this occasion only. I heard the merest whisper that there were plans afoot, and they involved that miserable fop Fairgreave.'

'How did word leak out?'

'Fairgreave himself, the chattering fool. He told a friend, a friend told another and it reached me. Frankly, the man is as much use as a pistol without a hammer. I freely admit that I found the entire notion somewhat fantastical but eventually due diligence demanded that I have him shadowed. Did you uncover the secret of the mystery lady in Golden Square, by the way? Was it indeed who you thought?'

'I regret I have been otherwise engaged on your instruction regarding Sir Geoffrey Dumont and so have not pursued that further.' The lie came swiftly to Flynt's lips and he was unsure why. He did not completely trust Colonel Charters, it was true, but he could not fully rationalise keeping the presence of Christy de Fontaine from him, especially now that there was a glimmer of suspicion attached to her name.

Charters studied him for a moment, as if sensing the lie. 'No matter,' he said. 'I suspect there are graver issues here than that lady.'

Flynt silently agreed. 'What instructions did you receive from your masters in Whitehall regarding the plot?'

Charters stiffened slightly at the use of the words 'masters' for he liked to believe he was a law unto himself. Flynt had used the word purposely in order to nettle him. 'They thanked me kindly and said that they were confident the security of the Tower could not be breached without cannon, siege engines and an army of tunnellers.'

'Anywhere can be breached with sufficient planning and intrepidity. Look to Troy and the wooden horse.'

'We understand that, Serjeant, but these men are politicians and their minds are the wheels within the wheels of that horse. Even before I left their company I would hazard they were looking for ways to use this to their advantage.'

'And what further action did you take?'

'Nothing other than setting you upon your mission.'

'Has the security at the Tower been bolstered?'

'No.'

Flynt frowned. 'You have not alerted them?'

'I have not.'

'May I ask why not?'

Charters tilted his head to look out of the carriage's window. 'If my "masters", as you call them, care not if a Jacobite escapes custody, then why should I? There has been enough blood spilled over Mar's ill-advised attempt at rebellion without adding the sanguination of some Scottish nobleman upon Tower Hill. There is little appetite for further judicial vengeance and I have other matters to attend to. If these politicians wish to make capital from a man's flight then so be it.'

'So if the escape attempt proceeds you will not seek to stymie it?'

Charters returned his attention to Flynt but did not reply for a few moments. 'There will be no interference from my office, Serjeant, on that you have my word.'

Flynt could not be certain but he had the feeling that Charters knew far more than he admitted, perhaps even that Flynt had been approached to assist. He had long suspected that Charters had some conduit to Christy de Fontaine, that the erstwhile agent of France had performed some functions for him in the past and not just in the bedchamber. And the knowledge that Walpole and Moncrieff had formed their own plot to profit politically from the escape, whether it succeeded or not, would be salted away in his private collection of such secrets for use at a later date.

'One thing further, Colonel,' Flynt said. 'You stated earlier that it was only eventually that you set me on Fairgreave's trail. Why did you not act immediate?'

'As I said, I found the idea of escape fantastical.'

'So what changed to prompt action on your part?'

Charters exhaled heavily. 'William Beardmore was found murdered in his bed, stabbed through the heart.'

21

Flynt was comfortable in the shadows. He spent much time in them, for in his work it was often advisable to see but not be seen, though it was a failure to do so that had, in a way, set him upon this path. Had he been a little more circumspect that night in Drury Lane then Sir Geoffrey would not have spied him, they would not have become friends and he may not have been so dogged in his investigation. Belle would still have requested his assistance, but had he not known the deceased then he might have been more willing to accept the sexual motivation. Similarly, had he not detested Lord Fairgreave's treatment of the man he might simply have gone through the motions in obeying the orders of Colonel Charters. There was every possibility that he would never have taken the perilous step of breaking into the Golden Square house and there encountering Christy de Fontaine and becoming embroiled in the plan to free Lady Nithsdale's husband. There was Warwick's intervention in the square, of course. That might have prompted what those in Scotland would have termed his thrawn nature to probe further, but perhaps not, for by that time he already had the bit between his teeth. In their own way, all of those elements led to this moment, standing in the darker shadows of a Newgate Street that was already under cover of night, awaiting sight of one man passing through the gates of the jail.

Those gates opened and shut; people came and went, their shoulders hunched against the cold. Link boys began to appear, their torches blazing to light the way for their patrons. The sky darkened, stars twinkled, the air grew crisper, though certainly not as frosty as it had been. Flynt stood alone in an archway leading to the yard of a deserted carpentry workshop, his gloved hands in his pockets, his greatcoat buttoned tight around him, his scarf up over the lower half of his face, his hat low over his eyes. The silver cane was tucked into the crook of his elbow, the comforting weight of Tact and Diplomacy wedged in his belt.

And he waited.

And he watched.

That was another part of his work, the waiting and the watching. Waiting for people to arrive, waiting for people to leave. Fending off and ignoring the elements. As a soldier he had stood in line for hours in pouring rain waiting for the order into battle. As a highwayman he had sat upon his horse in heavy snows as he waited for a coach to come by on Blackheath and other commons. As a thief he had watched for lights to dim or residents to vacate properties so that he could enter by stealth. He had never resorted to the low toby, lurking in alleyways for unsuspecting coves to amble by, even though he was no stranger to dark and narrow side streets. There were times when he made his progress across the city largely through such lanes and byways, avoiding the main thoroughfares and often under cover of night.

Waiting. Watching.

He had idled in his vantage point for over an hour before Sprigwood finally emerged from the gate and, after exchanging a word or two with the gatekeeper, pulled a thick woollen coat around his spare frame, settled a bright-coloured knit cap upon his head then a tall hat of black felt that reminded Flynt of such he had seen worn by an elderly Puritan. The jailer's path took him along Newgate Street, up Giltspur Street to Smithfield and thence past Pye Corner into Cock Lane. Set in the wall of the Magpie tavern was a wooden statue of a naked cherub, marking where the Great Fire of fifty years before had finally been extinguished. There were times that Flynt wished the conflagration had consumed the city entire. Flynt maintained his distance but never took his eyes off Sprigwood's loose-limbed gait, politely rebuffing the businesslike advance made by a solitary but forceful trull offering some solace against the cold with her fleshy delights. Although largely deserted that night, never had a thoroughfare been so aptly named, for it had once been one of the few locations where bawdy houses were legal in the city and was still a hotbed of brothels. The cracksman Old Tom had informed him that the place had been called Cock Lane for centuries, perhaps deriving from the word 'pillicock', a term for the male member, or perhaps because roosters were trained here for the fighting trade.

Eventually Sprigwood, completely unaware of his malevolent shadow, turned sharply into a narrow alleyway between two buildings. Flynt presumed it would lead to the man's lodgings in the tenements beyond, but it was the ideal location for what he needed to do. The wider lane they had just left may have been unusually devoid of pedestrians but it was overlooked by windows, whereas this narrow gap, barely shoulder width, was bounded by two brick walls unbroken by any form of fenestration.

Flynt slid his blade free from its sheath, his tread remaining light as he picked up the pace. Sprigwood only became aware of his presence when it was too late. He began to turn but Flynt already had him clasped by both shoulders and propelled him forward a few paces, then twisted him to slam him against the wall. The jailer began to cry out in protest but Flynt clamped one gloved hand over his mouth while the other held the keen edge of his blade against the man's throat.

'Hush now, friend Sprigwood,' he said, 'for I am decided nervous and any sudden movements might make my hand twitch.'

The man's Adam's apple bobbed and his eyes widened in shock as he recognised at whose mercy he now lay.

'I have some questions,' Flynt said, 'and so I will remove my hand to allow you to reply. But I warn you, if you cry beef or attempt to hop the twig, if I even suspect a gully in any of your responses, then I will open your whistler, do you understand?'

The man's head bobbed with considerable enthusiasm and Flynt eased his hand away.

'Now, let us get straight to the point. Who has been to see Sam Yates?'

'You cannot do this, I am officer of—'

Flynt slapped him with his free hand then raised a finger into his face. 'You will answer me, friend, for I am cold and hungry and I am in a fierce temper. You know of my reputation so you will know that I am not a man who makes idle threats. I could slit you and walk away whistling, for it means no more to me than pissing in the gutter. Now, I ask you again, who has been to see Sam Yates?'

'The Ordinary, the Sheriff's man.'

Flynt's impatience snapped. 'Aye, aye, but who else, out with it.'

'There was nobody else, I tells you, I did.'

Flynt snarled and adjusted the blade to nick the taut skin and draw blood. Sprigwood yelped, his hands attempting to jerk towards his wound but prevented by the weight of Flynt's body against him. They might have been lovers enjoying some rantum scrantum against the wall for all anyone could see from the street.

'That was a warning, Sprigwood,' Flynt said. 'Obfuscate further and the next cut will be deeper. I can deliver many such wounds before you finally expire so make your choice, either blow the gab and cleanse your soul or continue to face it out and be damned.'

Sprigwood's calculation of whether or not Flynt bluffed was evidenced by the darting back and forth of his eyes and the twitching of his lips. Finally he reached the conclusion that his life was forfeit if he did not tell the truth.

'It was one of the thieftaker's men what comes to the lad.'

'Which thieftaker?'

'Wild, it was one of Wild's bullies.'

'Did you get his name?'

A fervent nod. 'Warwick, Richard Warwick.'

Of course it had to be him, Flynt thought, but still asked, 'You are certain of this?'

'Aye, I knows him well, I does, for he has been in the jail many a time.'

Of course he would, for being one of the thieftaker's men would necessitate the transaction of business with felons. 'And Warwick forced Sam to confess?'

Another nod.

'How?'

'The usual way, threats, it was.'

'He threatened Sam with harm?'

Sprigwood's head shook and he even managed a look of disdain, his voice adopting the tone of one addressing a dullard. 'The cove is facing a noose no matter what, so what could Warwick threaten him with that is worse? No, he promised harm would befall those he loved, he did. The keeper of the molly house...'

'Mother Clap?'

'Aye, and that blackamore fancy piece you was with.'

Flynt felt something harden inside him. 'Warwick threatened Belle with harm?'

'Aye, said he'd stitch her up good and proper if the boy don't cough to the killing. Said by the time he was finished with her she'd be lucky to earn a crust as a hedge whore begging for pennies in the street, she would.'

'Why? What is he so afraid of?'

'He says it be his good name at stake. He knows you be looking into it and intent on blackening his reputation with the Thieftaker General and he says he wants the boy to tell the truth to all and sundry, he does, so he brings pressure to make him cough.'

Flynt's mind raced over the permutations. It was possible the man was merely protecting his standing with Wild and beyond, but the fact that he and his crew had arrived almost instantly following the murder remained bothersome. Now he had strong-armed Sam into confessing to the murder. He could be acting upon the orders of the thieftaker, for Wild was ambitious and keen to ingratiate himself with men of power like Walpole and Moncrieff, and had even at least once been in the company of Christy de Fontaine. Or it could be that he was doing it for the politicians, to silence the judge. Or Christy. It may not have been mere chance that it was Warwick who had fronted him in Golden Square.

'And it was the thieftaker's man who told Sam where to send the messenger today to find me?'

'Aye, he said it would always reach you at the Black Lion.'

'What of Wild himself? Has he seen the boy?'

'Mr Wild often visits Newgate but he has not paid no attention to Yates, no he ain't.'

'And there have been no ladies in the company of a large man who never speaks?'

A shake of the head. 'Nobody else, and that's the truth of it, as the Lord is my witness, Mr Flynt. I wouldn't pitch no gammons to you, you has my oath on that.'

Flynt doubted very much if Sprigwood's oath not to lie carried much weight but he did believe him regarding Warwick. He withdrew the blade and stepped away. Sprigwood's hands darted immediately to his wound and dabbed at the blood.

'You has cut me, you has,' he said as he stared with horror at the redness on his fingers.

'A mere scratch and nothing compared to what I will do if I find you gully me.'

Sprigwood took some steps backwards and when he felt he was sufficiently beyond the range of Flynt's sword found his courage. 'You have importuned an officer of the law, that's what I be and make no mistake about it. The gallows await you and you will swing, mark me on that.'

Flynt sighed. 'That's as may be, Sprigwood, but you mark me. If you peach on me I will make it my mission to hunt you down before the law lays a hand upon me and I will slice you up proper. And then I will turn to your family.'

Sprigwood blanched. 'They is innocent, they ain't nothing to do with what is between us as men.'

Flynt had no intention of harming his family but the man had to believe it. 'Original sin, friend Sprigwood. None of us are truly innocent, does scripture not teach us that? And your children are of your tainted blood, your wife infected by it. I would be doing the world a favour in staunching its flow.' He paused to let the threat sink in, swallowing back the bitter bile that had risen in his throat as he gave voice to it, for he knew it made him little better than Warwick.

'Remember that, Sprigwood, if you feel the need to let your tongue flap with my name.'

He sheathed his sword, turned and strode back to Cock Lane, that familiar churning of his gut accompanying him all the way. He knew he should have killed the man but he had been sickened by his own threats. He hoped he did not live to regret his own weakness.

He turned towards Pye Corner in search of a hackney to convey him to the Garden. He felt it his duty to inform Belle of what had occurred and to find out if she had gleaned anything useful from her mysterious, highly placed cull.

—

Charters stared at Sir Robert Walpole across the desk of the politician's private office in Whitehall. He had been granted a few minutes of the man's time and was gratified that his lickspittle Moncrieff was not present for what he had to say.

'There seems to be a misunderstanding concerning what action I took regarding the matter of Sir Geoffrey Dumont.'

To his credit, Walpole seemed somewhat discomfited by the opening salvo. 'I merely wished him to be spoken to, not—'

Charters raised his hand. This man may hold a senior position in the government of the day but time was short. 'As I have already explained to Sir James Moncrieff, I had nothing to do with the man's demise, but I wished you to hear it from me personally, Sir Robert.'

Moncrieff had obviously not passed this information on to his superior, which did not surprise Charters in the slightest, for relief seemed to wash over the politician. Charters had suspected that he was being primed to take the fall for the judge's death, but Walpole's reaction was genuine. 'You admit it was coincidence that the very day I, or rather, Moncrieff and I—'

Charters interrupted once again. 'Indeed it was.'

Walpole took no offence at being cut off abruptly twice. Rather, he seemed more at rest now that his conscience had been salved, though Charters was not about to let him off so easily.

'There does remain the question as to who *was* responsible for the judge's murder.'

Walpole frowned. 'Is there not some fellow now languishing within Newgate awaiting to dance upon the tree? I thought that you had engineered his arrest but now that you tell me—'

Charters cut in once again. 'There is some dubiety over the extent of his guilt.'

'Dubiety?'

'Yes, Sir Robert, dubiety. To put it simply, the lad may be innocent, at least of this crime.'

The lines over Walpole's nose deepened. 'Then if that is the case, and your Company of Rogues had no involvement, who *did* murder Sir Geoffrey?'

'One of my men is working on that conundrum as we speak.'

'Is such an investigation part of your purview?'

'My purview, sir, is whatever I feel threatens the security of this nation and there be suspicion that Sir Geoffrey's murder may be polit-ically motivated.'

Walpole caught up with Charters' gist. 'You suggest conspiracy of some nature?'

'I suggest nothing at this stage, sir, nor do I accuse. As you intimated to me not a few days since, the judge was Tory and had no love for your party, nor you. He was a fierce critic, albeit from the safety of anonymous items in backstreet pamphlets.'

'There are many such critics and if they were all murdered, the streets of London would be awash with their blood. I wished the man silenced, perhaps by some persuasion regarding a hidden sin that you may have uncovered, not slaughtered.'

'I accept that, and I point no finger at you. But it has come to my attention that Sir Geoffrey had some knowledge of a matter we discussed previously regarding the plot to free a Jacobite prisoner.'

Walpole's surprise seemed genuine, but Charters knew the man to be a canny operator who could, like all politicians, spring forth a fountain of tears if he found it propitious to the moment. 'Did he, by God? How on earth did he discover that?'

'People talk, Sir Robert, and others listen. I am such a listener, as was Mr William Beardmore.'

Charters paused to see if the name of the government servant registered. It took a moment but Walpole recalled the name. 'The clerk? The one who died?'

'The one who was also murdered, like Sir Geoffrey.'

'And you say he knew of the plot to free the Jacobite lord? How came he by such intelligence?'

'There be a circular gallery in St Paul's, perhaps you know of it, above the nave, and if you stand at any point your whisper can be heard even if the other person be on the opposite side, many feet away. I know not if Sir Christopher Wren planned it that way or if it be a curiosity of design, but it is a phenomenon. These here corridors of power be much like that. A whisper can be heard as clear as a shout if the right person be standing in the right place at the right time.'

'And Beardmore was that person in the right place at the right time?'

'He was.'

'What exactly did he overhear?'

'You and Sir James discussing the matter that I had brought to you previous, regarding the escape plot. He heard it suggested that the enterprise be allowed to succeed and then used to further discredit the Tories and declare them supporters of the House of Stuart.'

'Damn the fellow! And he brought this to you?'

'He did, but I thought little of it, for the idea of such an escape was a wisp only with no foundation. Until Mr Beardmore was found dead in his bed.'

'I heard it was a case of housebreaking that went wrong.'

'I heard that too, but you must admit that it is damnable curious. And then came the judge's death. Two men who knew of a possible escape plot to be used for political gain both murdered. A coincidence occurs once. A second time suggests pattern.'

Walpole found his bluster. 'Do you make accusation of me, sir? Are you so impertinent?'

Charters remained equable. 'I make no accusation, Sir Robert, I merely state what I believe to be fact. Certainly the two deaths may be unconnected. It may be that the hapless clerk was a victim of some vicious criminal intent on larceny, there was a quantity of silver plate stole to be sure. It may also be that the solution to Sir Geoffrey's death lies not in the political arena but in the legal one. As a judge he would have enemies in the criminal world. But we talk of perception here, sir. Should it even be rumoured that these men were murdered due to them being tied by a common thread, it would look decided suspect, would it not? As I said, a whisper be like a shout in the corridors of power.'

'Then what be your point, Colonel, and make it swift for I have an appointment this eve.'

'It is advice only, Sir Robert. That you allow whatever Scottish lord it is to escape, but you make no political capital from it. You might also consider allowing others their liberty.'

'So you would have the traitors go free?'

'They have already been punished by loss of estate and position. And I do not suggest you liberate all the noble lords. Execute one or two as an example, but show that victors can be merciful rather than vengeful. These men are nobles, Sir Robert, impulsive and ill-advised, yearning for a world that has passed. Allow them to contemplate their folly in exile.'

Walpole sat back in his chair, his fingers twirling a document that lay on his desktop. 'The Tories are a danger to our country, Colonel Charters, I believe that most fervent. I believe my party is the one to make our country grow and prosper. Under our leadership, and that of His Majesty, of course, we can lead the world. Forget the Frenchies and the Spaniards, the Dutch even. They are all spent forces. It is England, sir, that will thrive.'

'Great Britain, Sir Robert.'

Walpole waved a dismissive hand. 'Aye, quite so. Mark me on this, we will one day bring Ireland into this union and then these isles, this kingdom, will truly be united. I believe only the Whigs can achieve this, not the damned Tories. It is Parliament and prudent industry that shall lead the way to the glorious future our race deserves. We shall prevail through our actions, not whispers, eh? Perhaps, however, it is time for some true nobility on our part.' He nodded, as if he had convinced himself. 'Aye, that is the way of my thinking. We shall show mercy, prove that we are the better men.'

Charters suppressed a smile, having achieved his aim of allowing the man to believe that he had reached a conclusion through his own thought processes rather than being steered towards it.

'There is one other matter I would wish to raise, Sir Robert.'

Walpole smiled. 'Then proceed but be brief, I beg of you, for I am already tardy.'

'There is bad blood between your secretary, Sir James, and one of my agents. My most valued agent, if truth be known, and I do not bestow such an accolade lightly.'

'What manner of bad blood?'

'It would appear to be of a personal nature regarding Sir James's father, who came out with Mar last year.'

'Sir James would take issue with such a claim that his father be rebel.'

Charters inclined his head slightly. 'I accept that, but nevertheless he was with Mar's forces and died on the field of battle, but that is not the issue. Lord Moncrieff has developed a severe hatred for my man which I fear may interfere with both our offices. I would request that you pull upon his reins for I would hate to lose my man's services.'

Walpole was twirling the document once again, something Charters now realised he did when pondering an issue. 'Matters of state do take precedence over the personal, I agree. And this fellow of yours, he be vital to your service?'

'He is, Sir Robert. He is a rogue but he possesses skills that have proved most effective in the past in defence of this realm.'

'All your people are rogues, are they not, Colonel?'

'Are we not *all* rogues in some way or another, Sir Robert?'

Walpole's lips twitched and humour sparkled in his eyes. 'Aye, but some of us hide it damned well.' He stopped swirling the paper. 'I will speak with Moncrieff and will pull upon his reins, as you put it, although I will not inform him that you see him as some sort of beast of burden.'

'We all be rogues, Sir Robert, but some of us are also creatures carrying the burden of state.'

Walpole's humour shone again. 'Aye, and sometimes a whip must be cracked, eh? You may leave this with me, Colonel. You have my word upon it.'

Charters thanked him and took his leave, confident that Flynt was safe from Lord Moncrieff, at least for now.

22

Blueskin Blake was alone at a table in the Blue Boar in the Little Old Bailey, a tankard of ale before him, into which he stared as though he sought the secret of existence. He rolled his eyes when he saw Belle and Flynt enter and make directly for him.

'Gawd's sake, you isn't something I needs right this minute, Flynt. I'm enjoying a moment of leisure and would prefer to enjoy it on my lonesome, if you please.'

'It's not you we seek, Blueskin,' Flynt replied, casting his eye around the crowded tavern.

Blake ran a lascivious eye over Belle but she did not flinch. The man had been importunate with her once before and she had bested him, so Flynt was confident she could do so again. As if he had also remembered, Blake dropped his attention back to his tankard. 'Mr Wild ain't here, if it's him you want. He is walking the parish on official business.'

Jonathan Wild had taken to using the tavern as his base of operations and had a small office on the upper floor. Flynt thought the place unusually quiet for this time of the evening, although this was not an establishment he tended to frequent. The presence of the thieftaker's men kept many of the more colourful of London's night-time carousers away, unless they had business with Wild. The owner, Mrs Seagoe, was in conversation with a group of gentlemen who, given their sober clothing, may have been of a religious bent, but the tavern's proximity to the Session House on Old Bailey Street made it more likely they be lawyers. A fiddler sat in the corner, a bottle before him, his instrument resting on an empty chair.

'It's Richard Warwick we wish to see,' Belle said.

Blueskin sneered. 'Then find Mr Wild and you will find him, for they is together. Right cosy they is.'

Flynt understood then why Blake appeared so deflated, for it was usually he who would accompany Wild on his nocturnal peregrinations around the city streets.

'Do you know where they have gone?'

'Down by the river is alls I know, nor care, for that matter.' He raised the tankard to his lips, then stopped. 'Why you wants Warwick? Did you not heed my warning to keep yourself away from him?'

Although they were not invited to do so, Flynt pulled out a chair for Belle before taking a seat opposite Blake. He could use the man's jealousy to his advantage. 'What if I told you that Warwick somehow engineered the arrest of that young lad at St Paul's for the murder of the judge.'

A small smile played on Blueskin's lips, as if he had been waiting for Flynt to catch up with the game. 'Now, why would he wish to do that, I wonders?'

Flynt took a moment to study his face, his lack of astonishment at the suggestion itself astonishing. Blake already knew what Belle had gleaned from her highly placed cull. 'I also learned this very eve that he has coerced the boy to make false confession.'

Blueskin's smile broadened. 'Did he now?'

He pressed on regardless. 'He made threats to harm friends of the boy unless he admitted murder.'

'That don't mean the molly didn't do it.'

'I don't believe that. There is something darker at work here and friend Warwick is involved.'

Blueskin quaffed a deep draught then wiped his mouth with the back of one dirty hand. 'You are convinced of the boy's innocence?'

It was Belle who replied. 'We are. Murder is not in him.'

Blake's sideways glance was not quite dismissive of her but it was damned close. 'Perhaps not, and it be true that Richard Warwick ain't to be trusted, he's a shuffler, a right slippery, sly one too, and a dangerous man and all. If anyone could do such a thing it's him, I would say. The question of it is why, ain't it?'

Flynt spoke carefully. 'I believe you already know the answer to that. My question is why you did not tell anyone.'

Blueskin chortled. 'Why should I? That judge weren't nothing to me and one less molly in the world is no loss, is it?'

Flynt saw Belle bridle at this but he shook his head at her.

'And why should I tells you anything, Jonas Flynt, we ain't friends and I owes you nothing.' Blake paused as a fresh thought struck him. 'We ain't *brothers* neither so I don't need to show you no filial loyalty, does I?'

The emphasis fully convinced Flynt that Blake at least suspected what had occurred. 'No, but you have no affection for Warwick, that much is plain. You owe him nothing either. Tell me where he is. Or is it you fear that your master is also somehow implicated?'

Blueskin leaned forward. 'You suggest Mr Wild has ordered this and I tells you no. Now I shall tells you the why of it. You ain't mutton-headed, Flynt, you be many things – a right bastard being one of them – but you ain't that, so I knows you see me as being somehow diminished in Mr Wild's eyes. And it be true, he is partial to Warwick, but I've seen such happen previous.' He shrugged. 'Mr Wild's patronage ebbs and flows with the tide and at this minute the tide be froze in Warwick's favour but it will not last, Flynt, on that you can make book. Mr Wild knows who is loyal and who is not and he will see Warwick for what he is one day. But something like hushing a judge? Mr Wild wouldn't do no such thing, for he needs such men on his side, but even if he did he wouldn't use no Richard Warwick to get it done.'

'Who would he trust then?'

Blueskin held Flynt's gaze steadily. 'That would be me, as well you knows it, but I ain't had nothing to do with it.'

Flynt knew this to be the truth. 'I know that. I know it was Warwick and I will bring him to justice.'

Blueskin paused for a further mouthful of ale and another wipe of the hand across his moist lips. 'Bring him to justice, you says, like you is some kind of authority, like you is better than me or him or Mr Wild. Yes, Warwick comes from a bad lot. Mother, father, brothers, all flash but nasty with it.' He stopped when he caught something fleet of foot race across Flynt's expression. 'I know, we is all nasty in our way, even you – maybe even you especial, for you hides it behind righteousness...'

Flynt laughed. 'And you do not, thieftaker's man?'

Blueskin had the humour to accept that. 'Aye, you has me there. But I knows what I is and I knows what you is, and I knows what Warwick is. But I don't have no proofs, do I?'

'Then tell us where we can find him and let me put an end to this.'

'Do you have proofs?'

'Let me have a conversation with the man, I'll get it.'

Blueskin sat back, drained his tankard and set it down. He stared at it for a moment, his fingers drumming on the tabletop. Finally he looked up and Flynt knew he had reached a decision. 'I'll tell you, Flynt, but not because I wants to help you or your fancy piece here. I'll do it because I wants to protect Mr Wild, for such doings can reflect bad upon him.'

'I don't care why you do it, as long as you tell me.'

Blueskin asked, 'Does you have a carriage outside?'

–

Blueskin told the hackney driver to take them to the Fleet River near to where it joined the Thames. The waterway had once lived up to its name, in that it flowed swiftly and sweetly, but Londoners, being Londoners, had despoiled it until even the portion that could once have housed shipping was silted and blocked with filth and refuse. There had been an attempt by St Paul's mastermind, Sir Christopher Wren, to clear at least part of it, at considerable cost, but that had failed and once again the water was slow and barely moving, a paradise for vermin and plague.

The buttocking shop in which Wild and Warwick were to be found was at the sign of the Black Cat in Blackfriars. It was a wooden building, sitting in a section of ground of its own which was unusual for this part of the riverside, where the properties clustered cheek by jowl. It was as if no other structure wished to be near this ramshackle edifice for fear it carried some kind of contaminant. Its slats gaped and were in places broken, so the cold air always seemed to find a way inside to defy the heat of the fires burning within. Flynt knew of the place but had never entered, for it provided a place of business for bunters and hedge whores who catered to the needs of those who could afford no better. Wild, Blueskin had confided, used this cut-price school of Venus as an outpost to meet not only with the divers, footpads and bully ruffians who preyed on the honest citizens of the city, but also the mumpers who used all sorts of tricks to shame them out of their coin: the glimmers who claimed to have lost all in a fire, the gaggers who devised elaborate stories of hardship, and the whip jacks who claimed to have been shipwrecked and were now in dire straits.

Flynt instructed the driver to halt a decent distance from the building and to douse the carriage lights so that nobody in the building would see him climbing down. Belle prepared to exit but Flynt urged her to remain where she was. Predictably, she disagreed. 'There is every possibility that this could turn rough,' he said. 'Warwick is not the type to give up without a fight, am I correct, Blueskin?'

Blake shrugged, as if he was only half listening and didn't care what happened. 'If you ask me personal speaking then this bit would feel proper at home in there.'

Belle ignored him. 'I want to see his face when we confront him. I don't care if there is violence.'

'I do care, Belle,' Flynt argued. 'If this turns into a battle royal then I can't be worrying about you getting hurt.'

'I can look after myself,' she said, withdrawing her small pistol from her hand warmer. Blueskin paid attention now, for he would have remembered that same weapon being trained upon his face.

Flynt gently pushed the toby back towards its hiding place. 'Stay here, Belle, I beg you. That establishment is no place for such as you...' He ignored Blueskin's disdainful snort. 'You asked me to do this because of my skills, so let me utilise them.'

Belle seemed prepared to disagree further but then nodded, the little pistol vanishing again inside the fur muff. Flynt opened the door and climbed out, noticing that Blueskin made no move to follow. 'Are you coming?'

'And let Mr Wild know that it was me what guides you here? No chance, Flynt. I told him that I would be along later, and later it will be. Don't worry, I'll be there for the moment of truth.'

That promise didn't make Flynt feel any happier, for he was well aware that Blake would not come to his aid should the battle royal he had mentioned break out.

'I'll stay here and keep Tawny Belle company,' said Blueskin, as though he was bestowing some honour.

'Please,' Belle said, 'do me no favours.'

Flynt walked away, grinning, knowing that Belle was capable of taking care of herself but curious as to what kind of small talk they would engage in with him gone. He slipped the bully at the door a coin to gain entry, taking his hat off before ducking under a low beam and into a dimly lit parlour with four round tables each with four chairs. Vagabonds and mumpers sat around, drinking cheap gin, some slumped in various stages of inebriation, others paying attention to the women who plied their trade among them, enticing them into a back room for fleshly pleasures. There was no joy in this dismal place. It reeked with the burn of cheap tallow, damp wood smoking from fire, and of lives with no meaning. The women he could see doing their best to entice the men at the tables were nowhere near the standard of Mother Grady's girls, nor even those who worked the taverns of Drury Lane and the Garden. These were drab trulls, a covey of bunters whose best days were behind them and were reduced to working here among the cadgers and Bedlam Toms, who feigned madness in order to draw charity. Seeing them, feeling their desperation to make a few pennies in order to buy a bed for the night or even another cup of gin, made him consider Belle. All it would take was one drunken, disaffected cull to disfigure her – or for Warwick to follow through on his threat – and she could be on the road to such an establishment.

Much of the room was in deep shadow and while he acquainted himself with the layout as far as he could, he saw one of the women approach a male customer seated at a table with two other fellows, only to be rebuffed with a cuff across the ear and a foul-mouthed order to keep her diseased hands from him. She stumbled backwards with a cry and tripped over an empty chair to land on the filthy floor. The man rose sharply and reached down to grab her by the bodice, ripping the flimsy material as though it were wet parchment, his other hand raised, fist clenched, ready to deliver a further blow. Flynt was at his side swiftly, his cane jutting out to block the punch, and the man spun towards him, his broad face red with rage.

'Who be you to interfere, cully?'

The man's voice was as furious as his expression but Flynt remained impassive. 'Who I am matters not, what matters is that I will have you leave this poor wretch alone. You have refused her offer of business and have already abused her, let that be enough.'

The man looked Flynt up and down, a sneer lifting one lip, then thrust his face closer. His features were far from pretty but not through a life of hardship, for he had been born with an unfortunate face that simply grew uglier with age. His eyes were narrow, as though a stiletto had been taken to his puffy flesh to slice them open, and his beard was grey and patchy, the skin where visible discoloured, while his teeth were as black as the earl of hell's waistcoat. For once Flynt was grateful for the odour of the candles for they succeeded in shielding the foulness of the man's breath.

The man raised his voice and poked Flynt on the chest. 'I will do as I please with this bunter' – another stab of the forefinger – 'and *you*' – a further finger strike – 'will have nothing to say about it, or I ain't Toby Grimes.'

In the corner Flynt spotted Wild and Warwick, in conversation with some low character, raise their eyes in his direction. Damn it, he thought, he would have preferred to present himself with none of this fanfare. He looked back at the splenetic face of the self-announced Toby Grimes and decided to expend no more words upon him. The first finger poke was insult enough but the two that followed was declaration of war. He lunged forward, his forehead shattering Grimes' nose with a crunch. It was the man's turn to stagger back, both hands darting to his face, blood streaming through his fingers. Flynt did not give him the chance to recover from the shock of that initial blow, for he lashed out with his boot and buried it between the man's legs. He sank to his knees with a stifled squeal, one hand still over his broken nose, the other clasping his squashed manhood. Flynt finished the job with a crack across the skull with his cane and Grimes went down like a tree. His friends seemed rooted to their chairs as though the wright who had made them had left behind some animal glue. Satisfied that they were in no mind to defend their companion's honour, Flynt reached down to help the woman to her feet. She was emaciated, her lifeless breasts exposed through her ripped bodice. Her hair was lank and matted, her face pitted with pockmarks; her age was indeterminate thanks to too much gin, too many men and insufficient hope. She finally grew aware of her indecent appearance and attempted, but failed, to cover herself.

'Thank ye, sir,' she said, her accent Scottish, one arm across her chest to at least hide her nipples, then spat at her recumbent attacker. 'He's a pig, so he is. He has me when he feels like it, abuses me when he don't. He's no so harsh when he's thrusting inside me and whispering love in my ear at the moment of truth.'

Flynt shot a glance towards Wild's table and saw him smile, enjoying the show. He reached into the pocket of his greatcoat and produced a handful of coin, which he handed to the woman. 'Take this, find yourself a bed and also buy yourself a new bodice.' He gestured towards the man now stirring and groaning on the floor. 'He will be of no use to you this night.'

She gratefully accepted the coins, studying them in the tavern's dim light. 'You are a fine, generous man, well seen you are a Scot.' She smiled at him, revealing teeth like tombstones in an ancient graveyard, some upright, some pitched sideways, among them the unmarked lairs of where teeth had once been. 'Would you be wanting some company yourself the night, sir? You'll find I can be most accommodating, so I can...'

Flynt gave her a little bow. 'I thank you kindly, madame, but I have an appointment that cannot keep. But use the coin to get some food and shelter, for the night remains sharp.'

'I will, sir, don't you be worrying about that...'

He left her then, knowing full well that the money would be spent on gin and there was every chance shelter would be the corner of some lane somewhere where she would drink herself into oblivion. If the liquor didn't get her, then the elements, or some cull like the fellow now being helped to his feet by his two comrades, would.

Flynt moved on to Wild's table, unfastening his coat as he did so. Warwick's gaze, as ever, burned with unbridled aggression as he approached, the brown greatcoat he wore against the chill familiar to Flynt's eye. The third man at the table was clearly a mumper who sought sympathy by applying fake sores to his face and hands. Flynt had seen such ruses before. Cleyms, they were called, made of mixing together salt and substances drawn from the crowfoot and spearwort plants, then smearing it on the skin before sticking a rag of linen to it and ripping it off, leaving what looked like an open sore. Powdered arsenic was then applied to make it appear enflamed.

A candle cast an orange glow across the table and the thieftaker regarded him over it with his customary good humour. 'Jonas Flynt, what brings you to this low place, I wonder? Surely not to defend the honour of that bunter, for I know of her and let me tell you, that fight was lost the very day she was born.'

Flynt wasted no time. 'I am here for Mr Warwick here.'

Wild still seemed amused. 'What business do you have with him?'

'With respect, Mr Wild, that is between him and I.'

Wild's eyes were drawn to the door and Flynt risked a glance behind him to see Blueskin coming towards them then returned his attention to the table.

'Richard is my man, therefore if you have business with him then you have business with me,' Wild said, with a nod to Blueskin as he positioned himself at his side. If he suspected any collusion between he and Flynt, the thieftaker did not show it. 'Speak out, sir, for I have matters to transact with this here gentleman.'

Mumpers made money and Wild would have his garnish of any tricks they might pull on the charitable hearts of ordinary people. Flynt was forced to accept that what he had to say would have to be witnessed by all so decided to speak at rather than to Warwick. 'I believe your man is responsible for the murder of Sir Geoffrey Dumont and for bringing false charges against an innocent party.'

Of all the things he might have said, it was clear that was far from what Wild expected. 'By God, man, that is a most solemn charge!'

'It be libel, that's what it be,' Warwick said, his voice low. 'You all hears it, you all bears witness.'

'Mr Warwick may have a case, Mr Flynt. I would ask what your evidence is to make such an allegation? And I warn you, he is my trusted lieutenant and I will take it poorly if your claim proves baseless.'

Blueskin's face remained impassive at his master's show of faith in Warwick but a slight transfer of weight from one foot to the other spoke volumes to Flynt.

'Dick here bore personal animosity towards both the judge and Sam Yates. He loved each man as much as the devil loves holy water.'

Wild addressed Warwick. 'Be this true, Richard?'

Warwick's eyes did not leave Flynt. 'I need not prove nothing, it be up to the libeller to prove truth.'

Wild nodded sagely, as though he were himself judge upon the bench. 'He speaks true, Mr Flynt, what proofs do you have?'

'It is a matter of record. Dick here had a half-brother, by the name of Arthur Driver, convicted and hanged for murder on the sentence set by Sir Geoffrey in the Session House.'

This was what Belle's source had revealed. She had used her considerable skills to make him garrulous and he had told her all he knew about Arthur Driver and his family. Flynt had pressed her to reveal how the man knew so much, but all she would tell him was that though he was part of the legal establishment, he was also a member of the Society for the Reformation of Manners. It was Warwick who had contacted them to engage their assistance in his half-brother's defence.

It was obviously news to Wild, whose gaze swivelled across the table again. 'Was this man your brother, Richard?'

'What of it? That don't mean I had anything to do with snuffing the judge.'

Wild's eyes narrowed as he began to see his man in a different light. He shot a glance at Blueskin, who maintained his emotionless mien but kept his eyes firmly on Warwick.

'He kept his connection with his family secret, for they are notorious, are they not, the Drivers?' Flynt went on. 'He used his mother's name to keep that distance and to inveigle his way into your confidence, Mr Wild. Your knowledge of the city's underworld is wide but you cannot know every Tom, Harry or even Dick. And this one here is a shuffler of note, I understand. He can hide himself and keep his past equally as hid when he has to. But the Drivers were of bad blood, Mr Wild, and the brood entire was vicious, immoral, with loyalty to none but themselves.'

'I have heard of the Drivers,' admitted Wild, 'but thought them all dead after Arthur dangled.'

'All but one,' said Flynt. 'And he sits at your side.'

'But what animosity do you have towards the molly, Richard?' Wild asked. Warwick's gaze raged but he remained silent.

'Sam it was who reported his brother's whereabouts to the law,' Flynt explained. 'There were others who bore witness against Driver and no doubt Dick here would get to them in the fullness of time.'

Wild's mouth worked as he took this in, his hand straying towards the hilt of his sword in front of him. Flynt believed he knew what agitated his mind. Flynt had not proffered actual evidence of guilt but Warwick had kept his family connection from him and that would smart. Wild prided himself on being the canniest man in any room and in this case not only had he been unaware of this man's antecedents, but he had also actually been gulled.

Flynt further pressed the points he and Belle had worked out together. 'I admit to being mystified myself all this time, and believing Sir Geoffrey's murder to be the work of a conspiracy of some sort, but like many such matters it really is remarkable simple. I think you murdered Sir Geoffrey yourself, Dick. You would wish to have your vengeance personally. That was why you were on the scene so speedily to arrest Sam. You killed the judge and you let the lad take the blame.'

'I hears a lot of talk but no proofs,' Warwick snarled, his hands easing below the table. Flynt saw the move, knew to what it would lead.

'You made a mistake, though, in threatening Sam in Newgate,' he went on, his words concealing the brushing open of the folds of his coat with his right hand. 'He would've been found guilty in due course; after all, he is a molly and he was ostensibly caught red-handed. But you panicked when you learned I was on the trail. You thought it would all be a matter of procedure, but someone taking notice was a complication you hadn't considered, so you tried to bring it all to a swift end by extorting false confession. I spoke of suspecting conspiracy but the problem with such is that the more people there are involved, the more opportunity there is for someone to squeak. You involved Sprigwood and he peached on you. Never trust a man who claims to be honest and pious, for he is the least honest of all. The truly honest and pious have no need to proclaim it.'

By the crook of his elbow, Flynt could tell Warwick's hand rested on something in his belt. Wild did not notice for he was listening with rapt attention, without doubt wondering how all this would reflect upon him. Blueskin did, however, and his stance, though still appearing impassive, had tensed.

'It be his word against mine,' Warwick rasped.

'Perhaps, but I am sure if we search hard enough we can find people who will vouch for your antecedents, while your crew, who were waiting near the churchyard, may not be so willing to cover for you if your standing with Mr Wild here is somehow diminished. But that is not the only mistake you made.' He paused to allow Warwick to consider what that mistake was. 'You should never have silenced No Nose Kelly and left me alive, although that was not for want of trying, of course. But it needs a better man than you to take me down, Dick.'

Warwick forced out a laugh. 'You ain't swallowing none of this, eh, Mr Wild? This all be fanciful and not a shred of proofs.'

Wild finally spoke again. 'You make a compelling case, Mr Flynt, but as Richard says, offer damn little by way of evidence.'

Flynt was ready for that. 'You will recall, Mr Wild, when you interviewed me in Kelly's rooms that I informed you that I had fired a shot at the killer as he fled, and believed my pistol ball scraped his shoulder. If you look closely you will see there is a recently mended tear in Dick's greatcoat. A fine job and I commend the seamstress who worked upon it, to be sure, but it can be easy spotted if you know where to look.'

Wild lifted the candle to better scrutinise Warwick's coat. 'I do indeed see a recent repair, and right prettily done too.'

'I would request that you have your man here bare his shoulder, then we shall see how fanciful my case is.'

'What say you, Richard?' Wild's tone already intimated that this was but a formality. Warwick must have caught it too, because he gave the thieftaker a look so cold that it rivalled that of the night outside. Flynt foresaw what would occur next but he had to wait for Warwick to make his move, for when he did it would be further proof of his guilt.

Nothing happened for a moment.

Wild waited for Warwick to respond.

Warwick was motionless.

Blueskin leaned forward slightly.

Flynt waited...

Then Warwick made that move.

He stood so sharply that his chair tipped back and clattered to the floor, his hand raising the pistol he had tugged from his waist towards Flynt, who already had his own pistol aimed across the table. Wild had lunged for his sword but Blueskin gripped him by the shoulder and tugged him away just as Warwick tipped the table over, sending the ornate weapon flying and the bemused beggar to the floor. Flynt had to step aside to avoid being struck by the table and Warwick chose that moment to trigger his pistol, the passage of the ball coming so close to Flynt's cheek that he felt its sharp draught as it flew beyond him. A cacophony of alarm erupted from the brothel's patrons and many rushed for the doorway. Flynt fired at Warwick as he leaped away to a door hidden in the shadows, but the shot merely splintered the wood of the frame.

Blueskin hauled Wild to his feet, who was cursing with some fluency. 'Damn it, Blake, I would have run the bastard through!'

'Begging your pardon, Mr Wild, but your sword was in its scabbard and a pistol ball is damnable quicker than the hand.'

Wild saw the sense of this and snarled, 'Catch him, Flynt, bring that rotting cur back to me, for I will see to it that he faces justice, by God!'

Warwick would indeed face justice, but would not see the inside of the Session House, nor trouble any judge, jury or executioner. It was Flynt's justice that lay ahead, and it would be swift and terrible to behold.

But then he heard a bellow from behind him...

23

Grimes had chosen to use the panic to redress the score. He grabbed Flynt by both shoulders and twisted him round, one meaty fist already swinging. Flynt ducked and neatly stepped free of the man's grip. He didn't have time for this, so he pulled Diplomacy free and levelled it squarely at the big man's face. He didn't wish to waste his second shot on this imbecile but Grimes didn't know that. All he could see was the deliberate set to Flynt's jaw and the warning in his eye. Grimes backed away, hands raised in surrender, and Flynt whirled away towards the door.

Outside, Flynt scanned the dark waste ground around the building but Grimes' intervention had given Warwick precious moments to melt into the darkness. He thrust his spent pistol and his cane into his belt as he loped the length of the building towards the front, where the sluggish Fleet joined the frozen Thames. The customers who had spilled out to escape the violence within clustered in a group under the yellow light of the brothel's exterior lamps, chattering excitedly among themselves, the Scottish woman he had assisted among them. When she saw Flynt round the corner, she moved away from the group.

'D'ye seek yon bastard Warwick? For he ran in yonder direction like his arse was on fire.'

Flynt nodded his thanks and picked up the pace in the direction she pointed, his boots pounding on the hard-packed earth, the carriage looming out of the night ahead and Belle standing beside it.

'Did he come this way?' he shouted, then realised she had never seen Warwick before.

Belle understood immediately. 'That way,' she pointed.

He flew past her. 'Stay here,' he threw over his shoulder, knowing she would follow but also that her garb and footwear were not conducive to hot pursuit.

He ran past storehouses and warehouses, all dark, for few goods were landing as the vessels carrying them in or taking them out could not get past the ice field. Finally, he detected Warwick's footfalls up ahead although he couldn't see him, but did hear a man's voice cry out in warning and the barking of a little dog. He picked up his speed, eyes scanning the darkness around him, broken only by pinpoints of light on land and vessels stranded upon the ice. Further downriver the lanterns of the buildings crammed upon London Bridge and of the traders upon the ice twinkled in the frost. It was a spectacular sight but he had no time to enjoy the view, and followed the sound of the warning calls, finally seeing an old man, by his garb a former seafarer, standing upon the bank looking out to the river. A small terrier stood near the edge of the ice, his front paws lifting as he barked into the darkness.

The man heard Flynt approach and gestured with a hand holding a pipe. 'Some mutton-headed young ninny has taken himself onto the ice,' he said. 'I tried to warn him of the peril. The night may still be right brisk but there be a thaw in the air, I can feels it, but he calls me for a windy old fool, aims a kick at old Bouncer there, setting him to a-barking, and off he goes.'

The dog had padded back to his master and stood looking up at Flynt as if expecting some kind of reward for his service. As the man talked, Flynt squinted out towards the surface of the river, head cocked to catch further sounds of Warwick's feet on the ice.

'That ice will crack soon,' the old sailor continued, his pipe back in his mouth, and the pungent aroma of cheap tobacco caught on the soft breeze drifted towards Flynt, reminding him fleetingly of his father back in Edinburgh. 'Seen it before, I has, on this here river. Happens right sharpish when it happens, ice begins to melt and then of a sudden it begins to break up. I tried to tell that cove but he was having none of it.'

Flynt thanked the man and stepped towards the river, but was halted by a gnarled hand on his arm.

'You wouldn't be proposing to do similar, would you now, mate? Yonder ice field be treacherous.'

'I thank you, sir, but I must take the risk.'

Flynt eased his arm from the man's grip and continued to the edge of the frozen surface. It was colder here but the man's words echoed in his mind, so he stepped gingerly upon the ice. Away from the man's voice, the slight wind lighter here, he could now make out the crunch of Warwick's footfalls ahead, but the Thames was wide and he would easily lose him. He continued further for many minutes, the barking of the dog receding as the bank vanished in the dark. Every nerve was tensed for any attack and each tread was taken carefully for he imagined he felt the ice give under his weight. The sensation underfoot was similar to walking upon the ageing boards on the walkway in that Rookery back yard. It felt in turns both brittle and springy and he was certain he could hear ice begin to crack with each step. He dared not run across this treacherous waste, he knew that, so resolved to appeal to the man's pride.

'Richard Warwick!'

He paused to let his voice carry.

'Think about what you are doing. You may escape me this night but you know I will hunt you down. There is business between us that must be settled. Do you wish to be one who looks over his shoulder from now until the end of your days?'

He waited for a response but heard nothing. However, he could no longer hear the sound of Warwick's running, so perhaps he had come to a halt and was listening. He checked behind him, saw torches moving to and fro like fiery insects on the bank, and considered whether the man had somehow worked his way back. No, he would have heard him, of that he was certain.

'Let us finish this here and now,' Flynt shouted, moving further into the darkness, each step cautious, realising that Warwick could be reloading his pistol and waiting for him to come into range. 'Show yourself, Richard; let us face each other like men.'

He stopped to listen again. The breeze swirled the frost particles on the surface and somewhere he could hear the ice shifting. Perhaps the old sailor was correct. The weather remained cold but Flynt had no idea how cold it had to be for the water to maintain its solid state. He stepped forward again – warily, gently – visions leaping unbidden and unwelcome into his mind of the river suddenly opening up and swallowing him.

'That be close enough, Flynt.'

Warwick's voice came out of the darkness ahead. Flynt halted, peered into it but could not see him, though he thought he saw a shape blot out a series of lights on the opposite bank.

'Do you intend to hand me to Wild and the law?'

He had moved again, for his voice now came from a few feet to Flynt's right. Flynt reasoned that if he could not see him then conversely Warwick could not see him either. All the same, he turned sideways to present as slim a target as possible and raised his pistol in the direction of the sound.

'Only one of us will leave this ice field alive.'

A short, sharp laugh. 'You has become justice made flesh, has you?'

'In your case, aye.'

'Why?'

'A promise I made to the man you murdered.'

'And you keeps your promises, do you?'

'I try to.'

Silence then as Warwick processed this. 'Think you better than me, eh? That it?'

'No, Richard,' he said truthfully. 'But I made a pledge that I must keep. The man you murdered was my friend. The woman you threatened when forcing Sam Yates to confess is my friend. I have few friends, and when such as you takes them from me, or menaces the same, then I act.'

A moment or two of silence was filled with the soft murmur of the breeze, the rustle of the hard ice flecks at Flynt's feet and the occasional, but still disconcerting, crackle of the ice. He swore he felt something give beneath him and glanced down, fearful of seeing fissures threading outwards from his boots, but the glistening surface seemed intact. A stirring in the darkness made him raise his eyes once more and Warwick emerged into his vision, his pistol level. Flynt hadn't fully expected him to show himself but perhaps something in what Flynt had said about friendship resonated, for the man had done what he did in the name of kin. He walked with confidence, the ice groaning beneath his feet, coming to a halt within pistol range.

'So,' Warwick said eventually, circling to his right, 'what does we do now? Stand here and look at each other like this until one of us freezes?'

Flynt kept pace by moving to his left, grateful for the motion as he believed the blood in his feet was beginning to solidify but forcing himself to ignore what he was convinced was occurring below. 'You could surrender yourself to your fate,' he suggested.

Warwick tilted his head, feigning consideration of the suggestion. 'You know what, Flynt? I really doesn't see me doing that.'

Flynt really didn't see him doing that either but he was right, they could stand like this, each with the other under his gun, for hours. 'A duel, then, like the gentlemen do.'

Warwick's laugh was sharp and cut through the air between them like a pistol shot. 'We ain't neither of us gentlemen, Flynt, even though you adopts the airs of one.'

'It seems as good a way as any to resolve this, no?'

Warwick's shoulders twitched in agreement. 'So what does we do? Forgive me if I ain't acquainted with the ways of gentlefolk.'

'We each raise our pistols to the heavens and on the count of five we aim and fire simultaneous. How does that sound?'

Warwick smiled once again. Once again, it was devoid of any warmth. 'Very civilised.'

'One of us will die this night, Warwick, by the other's hand. You have been responsible for murder, I suspect not merely Sir Geoffrey and No Nose Kelly.'

'And you, Flynt, is your hands clean? How many lives has you taken over the years, eh? How much blood stains your conscience?'

Too much, Flynt thought, far too much. But he could not allow that conscience to trouble him at this moment, for there was more blood to be spilled by his hand. 'Shall we begin?'

Warwick remained amused by the entire concept but he shrugged once more. 'Why not? One way or another I'll get off this blasted ice.'

Flynt was the first to put up his weapon, the muzzle in the air, knowing he risked leaving himself open to Warwick not adhering to their agreement and for a brief moment it seemed he had misjudged, for Warwick's pistol remained steadfastly aimed in his direction. A brief memory of a similar bargain with Kelly sprang to his mind. The Irishman had reneged and he had little doubt the same would occur here, but then Warwick smiled and slowly bent his elbow upwards. Perhaps there was something of honour alive within him after all.

Flynt began the count.

'One…'

They continued to circle each other, pistols cocked and muzzles held upright lest the charge tumble from the barrel, neither man allowing his gaze to move from the other. The distance between them remained steady, the circumference of the circle they created constant, each step rasping on the ice.

'Two…'

Flynt's body was taut as he moved, keeping sideways towards Warwick, once again presenting as small a target as possible. Warwick did the same.

'Three…'

The darkness between them was too intense for him to see the man's eyes, where the command to move would flare first. He knew in his heart that Warwick would not allow the count to reach its zenith and had to be ready to move at the first sign of action.

'Four…'

Round and round, their steps slow and careful, neither of them breaking their gaze or hitching their step, the wind swirling with them, the ice creaking and shifting in the darkness. If Warwick was to make his move it would be now. Flynt opened his mouth to complete the count.

He sensed the change in Warwick's stance and threw himself to the side just as he jerked his hand downwards to discharge his pistol. But he wasn't swift enough and agony seared his shoulder as the ball from Warwick's weapon buried itself, the shock of it numbing the nerves of his arm and forcing him to let his pistol drop. He spun away, knowing it was useless to reach for his second pistol as he had not reloaded it after firing in the brothel. He fumbled with his left hand for his cane, drew it, but by then Warwick was upon him with a roar, barrelling into him to send him sprawling, the cane bouncing off into the darkness. They slid for a few feet with the force of the charge, Warwick on top, the surface of the ice moaning with the sudden pressure of their bodies, as if in warning. He bucked the man off and rolled away, agony pulsing through him from the bullet wound, his right arm dangling as if the life had drained from it. Warwick shot to his feet with considerable agility, pulling from a sheath under his coat a long-bladed knife.

'So much for being civilised,' Flynt said, as he slowly pushed himself upright with his left hand.

Warwick's voice was as low as his crouch, the knife waving before him, blade against his wrist, 'We is all beasts of the wild, Flynt, fighting to survive, and this life be nothing but survival, is all.'

And then he moved again, leaping forward, then back, then to the side, the blade slicing the air before him with uncanny speed, every movement designed to disorientate. Flynt risked a glance at the ice, saw the surface give a little with each step, then forced himself to keep track of where the knife was, hoping to catch the wrist wielding it with his good hand, but the man moved too quickly and the pain from his wound had slowed his faculties. He felt the slash across his chest before he knew the lunge had connected and then Warwick danced away again, his laughter carving through the air. Flynt felt further pain numb him and he looked down to see that the keen steel had cut through both greatcoat and garments below to rip flesh. He staggered back, cursing himself for not simply silencing Warwick when he'd had the chance.

Warwick hopped from one foot to the other as though he were keeping himself warm, the smile he wore infuriating in its confidence, oblivious to the effect his sharp movements had on the surface. 'Not so cocky now, eh, Flynt? Thought you had bested me, but you ain't.'

He watched as Flynt lurched to the side, right arm swinging of its own volition, left hand clutching at the chest wound, blood streaming through his fingers. Then he darted forward again. Flynt tried to get out of his way but one quick whip of the blade sent another jolt of agony coursing through his body, this time from his upper left arm. Warwick hopped backwards again, still laughing.

'The famous Jonas Flynt. There be folk what talk about you as though you is some form of legendary creature, but look at you now. You ain't nothing, is you? Nothing at all.'

On the final word he attacked again, his knife low and sweeping across Flynt's thigh just above the lip of his boot. Flynt cried out and dropped to one knee, the heat of the wound searing his skin.

'I'm no legend,' Flynt managed to say, though his words sounded as if they struggled to leave his throat.

'That you ain't,' Warwick said, his tone conversational, as though they were having polite discourse over hot chocolate. 'You is just a lot of talk, a lot of chaff, all mouth but nothing else, ain't that the way? All your talk of honour and friendship and promises, what's it worth now, eh? What's it worth, Mr high-and-bloody-mighty?'

Flynt did not answer, but hauled himself to his feet again and staggered almost aimlessly, ignoring the contempt that coated Warwick's gaze and words. Warwick watched him, still hopping in place, a move designed to keep Flynt guessing as to when the next lunge would come.

'Look at your claret, spilling all over the ice, and look at me, not a scratch on me.' He laughed again, performed his little jig again. 'You would leave me here for dead, would you? Not bloody likely, I say.'

Flynt slumped to his knees, his left hand supporting him. Blood dripped from his shoulder, his chest, his arm, his leg, and he looked at it thickening on the ice for a second, then drew in a deep breath. Warwick was expert with his steel, for the wounds he had inflicted were sufficient to cause pain but not to kill. He could keep this up for hours without despatching him. The irony that he had made a similar threat to Sprigwood was not lost upon him, even in his beleaguered situation.

'You must have…' – another breath, the words vibrating with pain – 'loved him very much. Your brother.' Another breath. 'Arthur Driver.'

Warwick's laugh was mocking. 'He was a bastard, literal and otherwise. He abused me and he caused me pain when we was chits.'

Flynt's head slumped a little and he moved the hand holding him steady a little. 'Then why…?'

'Why did I kill the judge and that creature Yates?'

Flynt could not find the strength to speak so merely nodded.

'Because he was still my brother, a bastard's bastard though he was. His blood was my blood and he should not have had his neck stretched for the murder of a damned molly. Ask me, he did the world a favour in hushing that unholy creature. Yates was a molly too, and he had the damnable cheek to turn Artie over to the law. These people, they ain't got no right to do nothing like that, for they is scum, they is. The Bible tells us so. *You shall not lie with a male as you would with a woman, it is an abomination.* You know your scripture, Flynt? Leviticus, that is. And then there's Romans: *Men committed shameful acts with other men, and received in themselves the due penalty for their error.* Abominations, Flynt, shameful acts. The judge said the killing was an affront to decency. Imagine that! Hushing a damned molly is an affront to decency. And he smiled when Artie was turned off, Dumont did. He smiled, took pleasure in it. For that alone he deserved what he got.'

Flynt believed Warwick knew little of decency but he did not have the strength to debate it. 'I suspect… that your biblical knowledge was limited before you took up the Society for the Reformation of Manners…'

Warwick sneered. 'I needed access to the law and they provided it. Didn't do much good in the end, thanks to your judge.'

Flynt needed a little more time. He took a deep breath. 'So they were not involved in the murders?'

'Gawd, no. They is a bunch of holier-than-thou saints but they weren't no party to it. I used them is all and they didn't suspect nothing.' He performed his little jig again, pleased with himself. 'They is all book-learned and comfortable but not a one of them realised that I despised them. A bow, a scrape, a few mealy-mouthed scriptural words and they thought I was one of them. But a means to an end is all they was for me.'

Flynt watched the ice beneath the man's feet. It was now or never. 'You know what, Warwick?'

'What?'

Flynt caught his breath again, as if the effort to speak had drained him. 'You know the problem with men like you?'

'No, but I suppose you intend telling me, eh?'

Flynt's head dangled a little as he adjusted his position once more, but the effort to speak seemed too much for him and he tumbled onto his side. Warwick grinned and continued to caper around him.

'What's up, Flynt, cat got your tongue, eh?'

Flynt breathed deeply, summoning his strength. 'Not done yet, Warwick. I'll tell you.' He settled himself more easily on his back, his wounded arm remaining immobile and outstretched above his head. 'The problem with men like you is this...'

And then he bolted upright, the pistol that had flown from his grip now back in his right hand but without the strength to raise it too high. 'You all talk too damned much.'

Warwick's eyes widened at first with surprise and fear and he instinctively crouched as if he could spring away, but then he relaxed and his confidence returned when he realised that the pistol was not aimed directly at him. 'You can't even hold it straight, you won't hit me at that angle.'

'I don't need to,' Flynt said and fired.

Warwick laughed as the bullet buried itself into the ice beneath his feet, but his mirth froze as almost immediately the already weakened surface began to fracture, the impact of the gunshot causing tiny cracks to radiate around him. He looked down, saw the gaps widen, and tried to jump away but the fissures were too fast for him. They spread outwards and around him, causing the ice to buck slightly, sending him sprawling, the crash of his body serving only to shatter the brittle surface further. He cried out as a massive section tipped upwards and he slid into the water below, his hand grasping at the uneven plane for support. He hung there for a moment, only his shoulder and head visible, his eyes meeting Flynt's, the panic within them dissolving as the knowledge of his predicament became clear, to be replaced by open defiance.

'Fuck you, Jonas Flynt,' Warwick said and let go. He vanished immediately into the darkness of the Thames water.

Flynt exhaled heavily and slumped onto his back again, pain stabbing at him from his wounds. He had used the last ounce of his strength to grab the pistol but now he was spent. He stared up at the night sky, at the stars glittering above, each breath sending new shards of agony through his body. He would lie here, he thought, gather his strength and then make his way back to the shore. Yes, he needed some rest. Just for a moment.

He had made a serious error, though. He should have dragged himself away. And there was a price to pay for his lethargy.

He felt the crack opening beneath his spine and then smaller rifts forming like tributaries and he tried to roll away but, like Warwick, he wasn't swift enough. The ice opened like the mouth of a sea creature and swallowed him whole, the water so cold it hit him like a punch, forcing the air from his lungs. He swirled around, his good arm reaching up to grasp the lip of the opening and haul his head above the surface, gasping for breath. His body had numbed almost immediately and he knew he had to get himself out of this freezing grip, but his clothes, his coat, his boots, weighed him down and he had not the strength to clamber free. He tried to cry out but his voice was hoarse and weak, the sound hanging just beyond his lips and dying in the night air. He began to shiver, his flesh seemingly becoming one with the ice to which he clung. He looked towards the bank, thought he saw those flame-like creatures moving somewhere close but away from him. He had to alert them to his position. He had to find his voice. He took a deep breath and forced a cry, much louder this time, and was rewarded by one in return and the torches diverting to come his way. He smiled, his trembling increasing. He could hang on here long enough, he thought. He would be found and he would be saved.

And then hands grasped his ankles and began to drag at him as they moved up his legs, to his waist, pulling, hauling, climbing.

Warwick.

How he had survived that long Flynt could not tell but he had and here he was, using Flynt as a ladder to safety but in so doing dragging him down. Or perhaps that was his intention. Perhaps he knew there was no hope of survival and in his hatred wished to ensure that he took Flynt with him.

He gripped Flynt's shoulders now and hauled him downwards, back under the water. They flailed there together, causing the leaden water to swirl around them, and Flynt twisted to face Warwick, saw teeth gritted, eyes filled with rage and loathing and determination as he pushed Flynt further into the deep while thrusting himself upwards.

Flynt tried to summon the strength to battle back but could not find it. The cold was gone now, replaced by something that seemed almost like peace. Why not let it go, he thought. Why not leave the cares, the guilt, the heartbreak of life behind and just float away here and now. After all, would his passing matter? Belle would mourn, Jack probably. But nobody else. Charters would find a new weapon to wield. Wild might be relieved. Cassie...

Something in his mind broke when he thought of Cassie, for she would never know he was gone. For a long time she had thought him dead, then learned he lived and would think he lived still. And her son – their son – would never be the wiser.

No, Flynt thought. *Not by your hand, Richard Warwick.*

He gathered what reserves he had and kicked his legs to propel himself upwards, gripping Warwick by the lapels of his coat and pulling him back. The man struggled, lashed out, but the water slowed his movements. The intense cold freezing his pain, Flynt wrapped the fingers of one hand around Warwick's face and thrust him deeper into the water. Warwick tried to free himself but Flynt was determined.

Not you, Richard Warwick, never you.

His lungs crying out, he dragged the man further from the opening above, forcing him down, down, down, then let him go with a final shove and drove himself upwards, thrusting his head into the opening and gulping in lungfuls of night air, river water spluttering from his lips and nostrils, his hands again clinging to the ice for support. He took a deep breath then ducked his face quickly back down and saw Warwick had drifted for a brief moment but was kicking himself back.

Time to end it.

Flynt lashed out at his face with one booted foot. In the open air it would have been vicious but muffled by the water, the blow only served to slow him down. His movements sluggish, his body desperate again for air, Flynt kicked him again and was rewarded by the sight of a tendril of blood streaming from his nose. He jerked his head upwards again, drew in some more air, then returned it under the surface. Warwick's movements were slowing considerably but he was still determined. He came back again, but Flynt merely placed one foot on his chest to keep him in place. The manic gleam that Flynt had seen in his eyes earlier was gone and there was only terror now, as he tried to remove the boot holding him down but found himself too weak, and wounded though he was, Flynt had the advantage of being closer to the surface and able to draw breath. Warwick's movements grew more sluggish, his attempts to pluck the foot away more ineffectual, until finally he stopped moving at all, his arms drifted out to his side and he began to sink away, his lifeless eyes staring upwards at eternity, until he vanished in the murk.

Flynt clung to the ice, weak coughs expelling a little water, his breath growing shallow, not feeling the cold now, pain no longer an issue. He couldn't pull himself out. He couldn't stay in the water. He didn't know how long he could survive like this and didn't care. He had refused to allow Warwick to be the one who took his life but now he was happy to drift away himself.

Voices.

Hands.

Strong hands.

Pulling at him. Freeing him from the frigid grip of the water. Dragging him across the ice.

He looked up, saw the broad face of Blueskin Blake looking down at him, heard his laboured breathing as he was hauled away from the opening. The strain was evident on the man's face but he noticed Flynt's eyes were open and he glared at him.

'This don't mean nothing, Flynt. We still ain't friends… but you does owe me for this.'

Flynt tried to conjure something of wit in retort, but his mind was as frozen as his body. He saw the old sailor hove into view, his dog in his arms. The ice was firmer as they neared the bank, even Flynt could discern that, and he felt more hands on him, assisting Blueskin. He saw Wild leaning over him, one word on his lips.

'Warwick?'

Flynt could not reply but he raised one trembling finger to point to the centre of the river and then shook his head. Wild understood and disappeared from view. He heard someone say something about building a fire. The old sailor, he thought, saying they needed to get him out of the wet clothes instantly. Then he heard him say, 'I told you it would work. Keep flat on the ice, I said, spread the weight. I told you, did I not?'

Flynt heard Blueskin agree and then mutter a brusque thanks, then the shadows closed in and Flynt was prepared to give himself up to them.

Then another face. A beautiful face. A face filled with concern.

'Cassie,' he said.

But as he allowed the darkness to take him he knew it was not her face.

24

The gaunt bulk of the Tower of London loomed in the moonlight as Flynt waited beside the carriage. Gregor sat in the driver's seat, staring at the gates, his big face as usual betraying no emotion. It had been an hour since Christy de Fontaine and Lady Nithsdale had entered the fortress. They had been accompanied by a woman with whom Lady Nithsdale lodged, introduced to Flynt as Mrs Mills. She was tall and broad and struck him as being very formidable indeed, which, given the company she kept that night, was quite a considerable feat.

Christy had not apprised him of the actual means of escape so he did not know what to expect, or whether he would be forced to decamp with haste himself. When he saw her earlier she had seemed considerably fleshier than normal, her trim frame suddenly well padded, and had appeared both surprised and pleased to see him. His sole function had been to arrange the onward passage but recent events had prevented him informing her of the details before now. He had also felt duty-bound to be present, given he had wrongly suspected that she might have been behind the death of Sir Geoffrey. On this occasion, at least, he had misjudged her, not that she was aware of it. When she saw his right arm was pinioned to his side to prevent movement, she had touched it gently, her expression one of solicitude.

'You have been in the wars again, darling,' she had said, her words glib but her eyes genuinely troubled.

'I'll survive,' he had replied.

She did not ask what had occurred but he felt her concern for his welfare was heartfelt. Not that it would prevent her sometime in the future placing that same welfare in jeopardy if it suited her purpose. He felt guilt over having suspected her but he was not blind to her character.

Now, awaiting her return with her friends, Flynt wandered over to stand by the horses and glanced up at Gregor, hoping to see some form of expression flicker on his face but, as usual, there was nothing. The wound Flynt had inflicted during his flight from the Golden Square house did not trouble him, so either it was not deep or Gregor had the ability to ignore pain. They had lingered here together in silence and, even though there was little love lost between them, he felt he should attempt to make some sort of discussion.

'It grows perceptibly warmer,' he said. The weather as a conversation starter was hackneyed but tried and true. In this case it availed him nought for the big Russian continued to sit as though transfixed by the gate, the reins held in his hands ready to propel the twin black horses forward when the time came.

Flynt was not to be deterred. 'It has been remarkable cold here, but I would hazard that such extremes are commonplace in Russia.'

His words provoked no response. Flynt sighed. 'Tell me, Gregor, do you speak or is it that you do not understand English?'

That made the man's eyes lower from the gate to stare at Flynt. That was something at least. At least he understood English. 'So you are mute? Or is it simply that you do not wish to converse with me?'

Gregor seemed to lose interest and returned to his scrutiny of the Tower. Flynt smiled to himself and patted the neck of the horse closest to him with his good arm. It reminded him of his own animal, which he still had not named, referring to her merely as Horse. He had once been told by a stable boy in Edinburgh that every beast deserved a name, especially one as fine as his. And yet his mount remained, figuratively, unbaptised. He wondered if this handsome pair had names.

He looked back at Gregor. Perhaps the man really could not speak. He had never heard him utter a single word, although he thought he'd heard him groan once – Flynt's thumbs had been buried in his eyes at the time.

Flynt moved around the carriage, stamping his feet, and stared out to the Thames, its swollen waters grey and turbulent, punctuated by blocks of ice bobbing downstream. The old sailor had been correct, the chilly stranglehold the elements held on the city had eased with incredible swiftness. Some of the vessels trapped by the freeze remained fast but a few others were able to float free. The watermen would soon be able once more to ply their trade up, down and across the Thames. The Frost Fair traders had managed to pack up their tents and accoutrements before the thaw, and gossip now circulated regarding a party of fellows who had decided to go a-walking on the surface to see how far they could get and who had not been seen since. The gossip – and a number of wagers in the coffee houses – concerned how soon their bodies would be discovered.

Of Warwick there had been no sign. The sea creature into whose mouth Flynt had felt he had fallen when the ice erupted had swallowed the man whole and had not let go. Belle – it was she he had seen before he allowed unconsciousness to flow over him – had overseen his clothes, stiff with ice, being stripped from him and his body warmed by a blazing fire on the bank, before having him transported to Mother Grady's house. There she tended to his knife wounds, which though profuse in their sanguination, were not too deep. However, the pistol shot to the shoulder required the services of a physician. Though his body was scarred, blade wounds mostly, he had never before been shot. It was an experience he was not keen to repeat. He was thankful the thickness of his clothes had prevented the bullet from progressing too far into his flesh but the surgeon's blade gouging the metal from his body was agonising. Again, fortune smiled upon him for the metal ball had not shattered upon entry and had missed all bones and major blood courses. A hot iron then seared the wound shut and he was ashamed to say that this last torture proved too much for his weak frame and he succumbed to a faint. He remained weak and he felt a shiver come upon him as he gazed upon the floating ice and the dark water.

Wild had visited him the day before. He had not thanked Flynt for his service in unmasking the killer hiding behind what he no doubt believed was his respectable profession, but there was some appreciation shown, and he pledged to do everything in his power to have Sam freed from Newgate. Once this duty at the Tower was seen through, Flynt was to collect Belle from Mother Grady's and meet the thieftaker at the prison. Wild, meanwhile, would be spinning a tale to explain how he had not been gulled by Warwick's lies.

The sound of the gates opening drew him back around the carriage to see four figures hastening towards them, all in female garb. It wasn't until they came closer that he saw that one was a most peculiar woman indeed.

'Lord Nithsdale, I presume,' he said as he opened the door.

The man stopped to study him and Flynt did the same. He was dressed in women's garb, his face, including his heavy beard, concealed under rouge and paint, his eyebrows powdered white. 'You are Mr Flynt, I understand.' The nobleman held out a hand. 'I thank you for your assistance, sir. You have been of service to my lady wife, I understand.'

Flynt held out his left hand. 'In a small way.'

His lordship was taken aback by which hand was proffered until he noticed his wounded right. 'Was your injury received in carrying out this service?'

'It was caused in pursuit of another matter.'

One powdered eyebrow raised. 'Of honour?'

'You could say that.'

His lordship seemed inclined to know more but Lady Nithsdale gave her husband a gentle push towards the carriage. 'William, we must make haste, for your absence will soon be discovered.'

The nobleman gave Flynt a grateful nod. Flynt gave him a small bow. He was not one to defer to nobility but his life had been saved by others endangering theirs and so he must have had something of merit in his nature. In that moment, Flynt fully understood what had remained elusive for days, the *why* of his involvement. He had thought it perhaps a vestige of the youthful rebelliousness that had taken him off to war all those years before, or his fascination with Christy de Fontaine, or simply that he found the notion of public execution distasteful. Now he realised that it was a means of atonement, that by saving this one life – even that of a stranger and a member of the landed gentry to boot – he was in some small way making up for the other lives he had taken. Some of them deserved to die – and he thought of Warwick here – but there were others who did not and it was they who weighed upon his conscience.

The horses whinnied a little and shifted their hooves as Lord Niths-dale climbed aboard, his wife following, also giving Flynt a look of appreciation, then Mrs Mills who, Flynt saw, was wearing a different cloak from the one she had before entering the Tower. Finally Christy stood before him, her figure back to her customary slim self. He now began to understand how the escape had been engineered. If correct, it was a most daring enterprise and Christy had been right when she said that a man being present might have complicated matters, for even though the plot was known to the government no warning had been given to the Tower's guards, and there was no legislating for an eager turnkey rumbling the entire affair. The women would have been in considerable peril if their plan had fallen apart in any way and, as Flynt pieced together the sequence of events that had transpired inside those walls, he understood how brave they had been.

'Thank you, Jonas darling,' she said softly.

'I did very little, Christy. You ladies did all the difficult work.'

'I mean for trusting me,' she said and stood on her toes to kiss him lightly on the cheek. It was a sweet, chaste gesture and, Flynt knew, quite out of character. 'It could not have been an easy matter.'

'I didn't, not really.'

She reached up and brushed the cheek she had kissed with her fingertips, her touch cool but at the same time energising. She smiled, something sad and tender playing in her eyes. 'I suppose you never will.'

She climbed aboard and closed the door behind her, then opened the window to lean out. 'Swiftly now, Gregor darling, we must be away from this place.'

Gregor cracked the whip above the horses' heads and they imme-diately pulled away, taking the fugitives first to the Venetian consul's house, for Fairgreave had succeeded in his task. Christy blew Flynt a kiss. 'Until next time, my sweet.'

'And whose side will you be on then, Christy?'

She laughed. 'Any side you wish, darling. Once sated I can sleep anywhere!'

She pulled her head back in and the carriage trundled over the still hard-packed ground, leaving Flynt smiling in its wake.

–

Finding Sir James Moncrieff in his study was becoming a habit that Colonel Charters was keen to break. Jacob was once more apologetic as he explained how the man had demanded entry and to be allowed to wait upon the colonel's return, and Charters once more assured him there was no need. He found Moncrieff again in his own favourite chair, having helped himself – again – to a glass of his port wine. This time, however, his features were dark and he snapped at Charters as soon as he entered the room.

'Who gave you the right to discuss my personal business with Sir Robert, Charters?'

Charters smiled, glad that he had discommoded the man sufficiently to provoke this rage. 'My position gave me the right, Sir James. My love for my country gave me the right. My desire to see this country strong gave me the right. You would do well to consider these things yourself.'

'What lies between your man and I has nothing to do with the country or its security, therefore it has nothing whatsoever to do with you.'

Charters poured himself a glass of wine but this time did not offer the man another. 'And yet you chose to inform me of your enmity towards him.'

'That was a courtesy.'

Charters turned. 'Let me make something clear, Sir James, when it comes to my work I do not recognise courtesy. I have a task, given me under the seal of His Majesty, and it is often onerous, but I will perform that task with the passion of a zealot, without fear or favour.'

'It was none of your business,' Moncrieff insisted, unimpressed by Charters' wave of the flag, 'and you had no right taking it to Sir Robert.'

'I had every right, sir, for Jonas Flynt is, as you say, my man.'

'He is murdering scum.'

'Quite so, but he is *my* murdering scum and this nation has need of his services.'

Moncrieff sneered. 'If this nation has need of such creatures then we are in a most perilous state.'

Charters was unruffled. 'It takes many hands to run that ship of state you once mentioned. Some of them are slick with blood but they do their duty. They do it not for king nor flag but solely because it is what they do and I use that for the greater good.' He sipped his port. 'But there are those whose hands are soft and perfumed. They profess patriotism but in reality they do what they do solely for themselves.'

Moncrieff rose, his face stiff with fury. 'What do you mean by that?'

Charters adopted an innocent expression. 'I mean nothing by it.'

Moncrieff advanced upon him, his demeanour threatening. 'I would know what you imply, sir.'

Charters stood his ground. 'I imply nothing.'

'I do not believe you.'

Charters smiled. 'Do you call me liar?'

'Do you call *me* corrupt?'

Charters didn't flinch, for it was time, he believed, to put this popinjay in his place. 'Allow me to be frank, sir. I said I inferred nothing and I did not, I state as a bald fact. I would put my faith in Jonas Flynt, and indeed I have done so many times, before I would put an ounce of trust in such as you. I believe you and your kind to be a danger to this country, far greater even than the French, for you are the enemy within.'

'So you call me traitor?'

'Not in the accepted sense. You do not work with our foes but neither do you work for the good of this country, rather for your own profit. You are not alone in this or any government but currently it seems to be a canker that has spread far. It will adjust, it always does, but in the meantime it will be people like me – and Flynt – who will call you to account when we can.'

Moncrieff was nearing apoplexy in his rage. 'If you should repeat this in public I would have you out upon the field, be damned if I wouldn't.'

'And should I ever feel the need to make these charges public then I will be honoured to give you such satisfaction, for I am confident that I am the better man with one arm than you are with two. So take my fair warning, my Lord Moncrieff. Tread lightly. Be circumspect in your dealings, for my eye is upon you and any of your friends who hold similar views.' He purposely did not mention the Fellowship, for he did not wish to tip his hand regarding his knowledge of their existence, but he was convinced that Moncrieff was of their number. 'And it be not only my eye, but also that of Jonas Flynt and, believe me, I am protecting you as much as him. He is not a man you wish to cross, as those men I believe you sent a few nights ago learned to their cost.'

Moncrieff was a politician used to obfuscation and venality but he could not completely disguise the flickering expression that confirmed Charters' surmise. That it was he who had hired Ben Painter had been merely a sword thrust in the dark but it had hit home. It was possible that the same man had also been despatched to silence William Beardmore, but that would never be proved. Moncrieff quickly affected a look of disdain. 'Really? I heard he almost died upon the river not two nights since.'

'Do not believe everything you hear. Jonas Flynt is a hard man to kill.'

25

Flynt hired a hackney to convey him and Belle to Newgate in order to collect Sam and take him home to Mother Clap's. Belle had spoken with Mother Grady about a room in her house but the madame's belief remained firm that the boy was better among his own kind.

'*His own kind,*' Belle raged as the carriage clattered towards the prison. '*We* are his own kind. We are *all* one kind, are we not? Different skin colour, different religions, different tastes but underneath are we not all one kind?'

Flynt rested his head against the back of the coach, his eyes closed. 'She meant it charitably.'

The pain of his wounds still cut deeply and the trip to the Tower and then this to Newgate had proved wearying. He wished to take to his own bed in the Golden Cross and sleep but he would see this through. Jonathan Wild had already obtained the necessary permissions from the court but had pledged to attend the prison with them in order to smooth the way, for bureaucracy had a way of making a simple task more complex. Flynt warned him there would be no further garnish issuing from either his purse or Belle's, for the keeper and his men had already had more than their share.

Belle still fumed. 'Does she believe I have a kind, and that it is not the ladies with whom I have lived and worked and laughed for these many years? Is that what she believes?'

He did not respond, for he knew that there was nothing he could say that would blunt her fury and excuse Mother Grady's thoughtless words. Such casual prejudice against Sam, and by extension herself, had nettled her.

'You look pale, Jonas,' she said, the sharp edge to her voice suddenly gone. He opened his eyes to find her peering at him, her expression now soft. 'You remain weak.'

'I am well enough,' he said, managing a brave smile.

'You nearly died,' she said.

He did not reply but merely closed his eyes again.

'One day this life of yours *will* kill you, Jonas.'

'Life will kill us all in the end,' he said.

'Do not be glib, Jonas, not with me. I cleaned away the blood, I dressed your wounds, I held your hand while the physician pulled that ball from your shoulder.' He felt her hand on his arm and he opened his eyes once more to see her beautiful face etched with genuine disquiet. 'I would not have you hurt again. You are most tender to my heart, do you not realise that?'

He laid his own hand on hers and threaded his fingers through hers, swallowing back the emotion that threatened to clog his throat. 'And you are most tender to me, Belle. Death has a habit of taking those I love and I could not countenance that happening to you. Death does not want *me* but uses me instead as a conduit to take better souls than mine before their time.'

'And also to take blacker souls than yours.'

He sighed, his eyes closing once more. 'Sometimes I am unsure if there *are* souls blacker than mine.'

It had been a matter that had played upon his mind for some time. He found himself in myriad situations where death seemed imminent and yet he never feared it. When he and his friend Charlie Temple had fled the field in Flanders, it was not because he thought that if he had remained he would die, but because he had grown weary of the cavalcade of mortality that he had witnessed. He had grown tired of the blood, the mud and the agony of those around him and he had to escape it. Even on the ice with Warwick, when his own blood flowed and it appeared the man had the upper hand and he had considered allowing death to take him, he had never felt completely that he was facing his own end.

Belle did not pursue the matter further but he could feel her questioning eyes upon him. When the carriage jolted to a halt he was grateful, for her attention would be taken up by the reunion with Sam. This was confirmed when he stole a casual glance at her face and saw the anticipation glow in her eyes. He was glad he had played a role in creating that beam. He knew her life to be hard, albeit comfortable, but she bore it well. If he could save her from it, he would, but short of spiriting her away as his father had done with his second wife and her daughter, there was nothing he could do. And that made him feel helpless.

Wild awaited them under a lantern by the gate and even in its dull illumination he could see his features were grave. Belle, attuned to the moods of men, sensed something was amiss.

'What is wrong, sir?' she asked.

Wild knew of Belle but had never met her before so was taken aback by her directness. His eye flicked over her before he replied, 'There has been a tragedy within.'

Flynt guessed what had occurred. 'Sam?'

Wild nodded and looked to the ground. 'I regret to say...'

Belle reached the same conclusion as Flynt and a low moan escaped her throat. 'No...'

Wild's words were businesslike but he could not meet her eye. 'He took his own life, just this morning. His manacles were loosed to allow him to eat and he opened his wrists with a knife.'

Flynt felt shock ripple through him. 'I was told he was manacled for his own safety for they feared he would do this.'

'Aye, but the keeper ordered that they be removed.'

'Why?'

'Because he had been told the lad would soon be declared innocent and freed. Regrettably, nobody informed the lad himself and in his despair...'

'The jailers did not tell him?'

'There be two who work that ward and each thought the other had done so.'

Belle was weeping softly and he reached out to take her in his arms, ignoring the dull pain from his wounds. As her face buried in his shoulder, feeling his own tears burning his eyes and a pain growing in his chest over his friend's anguish, he thought of his words to her earlier regarding his relationship with death, for here was another soul with which he had contact that was taken before his time – and Flynt himself may have been the cause.

A name came to his mind.

Sprigwood.

It was possible he had somehow manipulated Sam to take his own life as a means of punishing the boy and, through his death, Flynt and Belle.

He felt his heart harden. If only he had killed the jailer when he had the chance. If he ever became certain that the man had been instrumental in driving Sam to his doom then that day may yet come.

—

Belle immediately took to her room. Flynt sensed that his presence was not desired so he remained below to explain to Mother Grady what had occurred, and request that Belle be allowed a night free of male company. She agreed but Flynt could not tell whether it was out of concern for Belle's well-being or because he dropped a hefty purse into her hand as compensation for lost business. He thought perhaps he saw something flash in her eyes and a very slight movement of her hand to return the coin but, if he did, it was a brief moment of morality before the purse was consigned to the folds of her dress.

He should have returned to his lodgings in search of some much-needed sleep, for his body continued to ache, but instead he repaired to the Shakespear's Head. It was where he had first seen Sir Geoffrey and where they had enjoyed their first conversation over a convivial glass. He found a table in a corner and signalled to Melody, the serving girl, to attend him. He studied her face as he ordered brandy, telling her to bring the best bottle in the house.

'Do you remember me, girl?' he asked. 'I was with Sir Geoffrey Dumont a few nights ago.'

She nodded then curtsied. 'I remember, sir.'

'Do you know he is dead?'

She looked genuinely saddened. 'I do, sir. He was a fine gentleman. A nice gentleman.' She lowered her voice and leaned closer. 'And there ain't many of that sort in here. Begging your pardon, sir, and hoping I don't offend you.'

He gave her a smile, which felt strange upon his face this night. 'I am not offended, Melody, think nothing of that. He was a good man, a decent man. He gave you a reward that night, I recall.'

She straightened away from him again. 'He did.'

'And he told you to ensure that your employer did not take it away from you, did he not?'

The serving girl's gaze flicked instinctively towards the bar to see if the rat-faced proprietor was watching her but he was nowhere to be seen. 'He did, sir.'

'But he took it, did he not? And gave you that?' He indicated the black eye she sported and her hand jerked to cover it. 'Tell me true, Melody.'

Another glance towards the bar confirmed what he already suspected. He felt his teeth grit a little and he drained the glass of brandy he had poured from the bottle. It was the good stuff, right enough, so he laid a handful of coins on her tray. 'Take this, and keep this here bottle special for anyone who comes perhaps needing some kind of uplift.' He poured himself another then set the bottle down beside the money. 'I care not who it be, whether bully ruffian, honest gent or Covent Garden Nun. If you judge them to be melancholy, then give them a tightener from this bottle and tell them it's with the compliments of Judge Dumont and Sam Yates.'

'Who be Sam Yates?'

Flynt paused. 'Just a lad who believed that, in the end, dying was easier than living.'

She blinked a few times as though she were battling tears. 'I will try, sir, but my employer will not countenance it. He will take your bunce and then continue to sell the contents of that bottle to all who will pay.'

'Leave him to me. Now, you go back to your duties, and if you ever have need of me then you ask around for Jonas Flynt and I will come.'

The girl's face rippled with conflicting emotions, surprise giving way to recognition, then confusion and finally suspicion. 'What do you want of me, sir?'

'I want nothing, girl. Sir Geoffrey had a soft space in his heart for you and I will honour his memory. There are times when people need help, when they have nowhere to turn. Now you have someone to call upon.'

'Why?'

He thought about this, for he was unsure himself. 'Because I couldn't help Sam Yates.'

He suspected she was still unsure of what was expected of her and he waved her away. She stammered thanks and he watched her head to the bar, occasionally shooting a glance back towards him. He downed the brandy in one gulp, closing his eyes for a moment, allowing himself to enjoy its warmth. He was exhausted now, every muscle, every nerve, every sinew, every bone weary. His wounds ached. His temples thrummed. But he had one more task to complete this night.

He pushed himself to his feet, placed his hat upon his head, picked up his silver cane from where it rested on the table, and set out to find the tavern's owner.

Historical note

On 23 February 1716, William Maxwell, the 5th Earl of Nithsdale, was broken out of the Tower of London ahead of his execution, by his wife, the Countess Winifred, along with Mrs Mills and a Mrs Morgan, who I have perhaps unfairly replaced in my story with Madame de Fontaine. The slim Mrs Morgan carried a spare set of clothing concealed within her own and, with one visitor only allowed in the cell at a time, gave them to Lord Nithsdale. Mrs Mills followed, feigning much weeping and wailing, with her face concealed behind a handkerchief. She changed into the spare set of clothing, while Lord Nithsdale changed into hers, make-up covering his full growth of beard.

Lady Nithsdale made sure that there was a great deal of back and forth between the ladies, thus confusing the guards as to who was in and who was out. When her husband emerged, feigning tears and with his face covered – as Mrs Mills's had been – with a kerchief, Lady Nithsdale made sure she walked in his wake to hide what was deemed a masculine stride. The guards were so discombobulated by the traffic that they didn't notice that four women left the prison when only three had entered. The countess even returned in order to have a conversation with her husband in his cell, herself playing both parts.

It was a daring plan, pulled off by three women who saw what had to be done and did it expertly.

The words used by Lady Nithsdale when telling Flynt of her appeal to the King were her own, adapted from a contemporary letter to a friend.

Of the eight nobles held in the Tower, only two were executed. The following day, James, Earl of Derwentwater, and Viscount Kenmure were beheaded on Tower Hill. The former spotted a rough patch on the block and asked the headsman for it to be removed lest it hurt his neck. His head fell with a single blow. It took two to detach Kenmure's.

In 1717, all rebels were pardoned, unless you happened to be one of the much reviled Clan Gregor, who had already been proscribed by the Stuarts, and the Hanoverians continued that tradition because, as one contemporary noted, 'Plunder and booty is their business.' The pardon, however, would not bring back the 'common' men who had already been executed, nor was it of much comfort to those transported to the colonies.

The River Thames did freeze during January of 1716, although I have extended it into February. A Frost Fair was established on the frozen surface and a group of men did indeed go walking on it to see how far they could go. They were never seen again. The description of the stalls and activities was gleaned from a woodcut of the period.

The treatment of homosexuals was relatively laissez-faire at this time, although as Mother Clap predicted, it would not last. Such sexual acts were illegal but the law was not strenuously applied. Dan Cruikshank, in his masterful *The Secret History of Georgian London* (Windmill, 2010), notes that in the years between 1699 and 1721, there was a trial for homosexual 'offences' approximately every three years but no convictions. Thanks to campaigners, including the pious individuals who formed the Society for the Reformation of Manners, this attitude changed and prompted ten trials in two years from 1726, with most of those accused found guilty and four put to death. Margaret Clap, who did exist although perhaps not in business at the time of my story – my account of her early life is fabricated – was also arrested for keeping a disorderly house and was punished at the pillory. The public, Mr Cruikshank reported, was not as keen on punishment as the judiciary and she seems to have been relatively unharmed.

I have used the terms 'molly' and 'sodomite' because they were in usage at the time. 'Homosexual' was not coined until the following century, and 'gay' took on its meaning in the twentieth century. The other slang terms used are also of the period and reflect the attitudes of the day in some people. No offence is intended.

On a general note, the underworld slang terms are all based on actual terms used in Hanoverian London during the 18th century.

The Pye Statue at Cock Lane may not have been in place in 1716, but I liked the idea of it being there, so have included it. It is now golden but originally the fat little cherub was wooden.

Sir Robert Walpole, Charles Hitchin, Jonathan Wild, Jack Sheppard, Edgeworth Bess and Blueskin Blake were all real people, although not necessarily as I have painted them. The feud between Wild and Hitchin did take place, and the latter was indeed gay with a liking for younger conquests. The charges of corruption referred to by Colonel Charters were actually preferred against Walpole and he was known to have a wish to stifle any opposition.

The taverns and inns mentioned all existed. Even the tale Lady Dumont tells of Thomas Dangerfield and the case of Half-hanged Smith that Flynt recalls are drawn from history. The wagers described by Charters – of the race between raindrops on the window and whether the man who dropped in the street was dead – are also based on actual bets placed in White's, although in reality of a slightly later vintage.

The mention of the reverend who led a band of smugglers on the Romney Marshes is a nod to the 'Doctor Syn' books by Russell Thorndike, a series I loved as a child and which were, along with *Treasure Island* and *Kidnapped* by Robert Louis Stevenson, my introduction to historical adventure.

However, the Fellowship, a group of powerful men who manipulate governments and events in order to garner power and profit, is entirely of my invention.

Or is it...?

Acknowledgements

No book is the work of one person. Yes, the author sits alone and pounds out the words but there is an army of people who come together to transform those pages of typescript into the volume you are holding now.

I'd like to thank Kit Nevile, and all at Canelo, for their continuing faith in Jonas Flynt, and for his helpful notes on how to improve the original draft. Also Kate Berens, the copyeditor, for her vigilance in catching errors.

Thanks are due to my agent Jo Bell for championing the work, and to fellow author Denzil Meyrick for his continual support – and for the almost constant insults.

My circle of crime writers who are always on hand to offer advice also should be mentioned – Caro Ramsay, Theresa Talbot, Michael J. Malone, Gordon Brown, Neil Broadfoot.

Of course, thanks are always due to the reviewers, bloggers, booksellers and librarians without whom we could not get the titles before the all-important reader!